AGAINST
THE LAW

Also by David Gordon

AGAINST THE LAW

A JOE THE BOUNCER NOVEL

DAVID GORDON

A Mysterious Press
book for Head of Zeus

First published in the US in 2021 by Mysterious Press,
an imprint of Grove/Atlantic, New York
First published in the UK in 2021 by Head of Zeus Ltd

9 7 5 3 1 2 4 6 8

A catalogue record for this book is available from
the British Library.

ISBN (HB): 9781801104777
ISBN (XTPB): 9781801104784
ISBN (E): 9781801104807

Interior design by Maria Fernandez

Printed and bound in Great Britain by
CPI Group (UK) Ltd, Croydon CR0 4YY

Head of Zeus Ltd
First Floor East
5–8 Hardwick Street
London EC1R 4RG

WWW.HEADOFZEUS.COM

For Matilde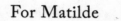

PART I

PART 1

1

JOE WAS IN HELL. Or close enough. The suburbs of hell. And he was stuck there with a kid who was bugging the shit out of him.

"I'm hungry," Hamid said, sprawled face down in the dust, in the middle of nowhere, staring at nothing.

"Have one of those protein bars," Joe told him. Joe was lying beside him, holding the gun.

"Those shits taste like sawdust. Or actually, they taste like dirt. The same dirt that we're lying in, and that I already got in my mouth and nose and eyes and ass crack. I don't need any more. I want a chicken parm sub from Defonte's. And a hot shower. And a bed with clean sheets."

"Sounds good," Joe said. "You can buy me one too, with your share of the money. Meanwhile protein bars and bottled water are free. Pretend like you're working at Google."

Hamid snorted derisively but started chewing a protein bar, which shut him up for a minute at least. Joe wasn't used to chatter on this kind of mission. But he couldn't really blame Hamid either. He wasn't exactly thrilled himself. This was the last place he'd ever choose to be, though he found that he visited often enough, in his nightmares. It was a place whose memory he tried to erase, first with alcohol and later with opium and heroin. It was a place that had nearly killed him, and left him wounded, physically and mentally, wounds that had finally begun to heal. And now he was back. By choice. In hell.

3

Joe was prone, on a low ridge, in camouflage clothing, holding a rifle, and staring through a sniper's scope at a patch of desert road. All around him, poppy fields spread, their brilliant red and pink and purple petals open like eager mouths, smiling at the orange sun, which blazed and bled into the hills as it sank and dusk gathered between them. This was the province of Helmand in Afghanistan. He was waiting for a heroin deal to go down, and for a bandit to come out of hiding and steal it. No one Joe knew had ever met or even seen this bandit unmasked, but his name was Zahir al Zilli, Zahir the Shadow, and Joe was here to kill him. That was what brought him back to this place he never wanted to see again. That and a half million dollars.

❖

There was a time when Joe did this sort of thing for a living, full-time—as a Special Forces operative dispatched on top secret missions around the world. Then he retired, or the government retired him, erasing his records and sending him home with a bad case of PTSD and some substance abuse issues. Now assassinating drug lords with terrorist ties was more like a hobby, something he did part-time when he wasn't busy with his regular gig, as a bouncer at a strip club in Queens, not too far from the airport. However, this strip club (which was techni-cally owned by an eighty-something widow) belonged to Gio Caprisi, a Mafia boss and Joe's childhood friend, and when the heads of New York's underworld—Russian, Dominican, Black, and Chinese gang leaders among others—decided they had to organize and fight any terrorist cells in the city, to protect their domains and keep the government off their backs, Gio had tapped Joe, and the bosses made him their sheriff, empowered to pursue his quarry throughout their territories. He was 911 for people who don't call the cops.

His last job for them had involved blocking a heroin shipment that was being used to fund terror overseas. Joe had stopped it and, with the help of his crew, had also stopped the smugglers, permanently.

But the mastermind behind it, a mysterious figure named Zahir, was still at work, hijacking heroin shipments bound for established US and European dealers and funneling the money to terror cells. Zahir's New York pipeline was still operational but no one knew how the heroin got in. And everyone back in this corner of the world, the source of the highly-sought-after "Persian" dope, was terrified of Zahir, though no one knew his last name, or what he looked like. Or those who did know were dead.

So Little Maria, a major player in the New York dope trade despite being less than five feet tall, had put a bounty on Zahir's head and implored Joe to find that head and cut it off. Generally speaking, not even a half million dollars would tempt Joe to pop over to Kandahar for a weekend of sunbathing and souvenir shopping but, despite grave misgivings, he felt a certain nagging obligation to close out this business once and for all. Not to mention, friends like Gio Caprisi and Little Maria are hard people to deny when they come asking a favor. And enemies like Zahir and his New York connections, whoever they were, are dangerous enemies to leave alive.

Joe's last caper had left some loose ends. For one thing, Maria had really wanted to get her hands on that Persian heroin, which had ended up literally in the wind, four million dollars' worth tossed out of the car window by Joe's colleague Yelena, who didn't approve of dope. And speaking of Yelena: an ace thief and deadly fighter, she and Joe were a good team at home and on the field, but her own past had caught up to her. A child of the Russian prison system and a natural-born criminal, the Russian secret service, the SVR, had set her free on the condition that she spy on the Russian mob in New York. Now, thanks largely to helping Joe, her life was in danger from both Moscow and Brighton Beach and she had vanished, most likely, Joe figured, never to be seen again. Then there was Donna Zamora. Donna was an FBI agent with whom Joe had repeatedly crossed paths, and while their relationship had been strictly professional—she was law, he was crime—she had ended up shooting a terrorist, Heather Kaan, to save Joe, under circumstances the FBI might not understand. Joe had returned the favor by getting rid of the body. And so on . . .

Let's just say Joe's life, the simple life of a strip club bouncer who lived with his grandmother in Jackson Heights and liked to read and watch *Jeopardy*, had suddenly gotten very complicated, and the idea of settling it all with one quick trip to Afghanistan, and one well-placed bullet in the brain, had seemed to make sense. The money didn't hurt either. A half million dollars in cash could finance his very simple life for a very long time.

❖

"Look," Hamid said, interrupting Joe's thoughts. "Here they come."

At the end of the last job, Joe had taken a cell phone off the corpse of a dope smuggler, Felix Habibi, and though it hadn't contained much data, Juno had managed to trace a few calls and emails to a nondescript office building in Kandahar. However, all Joe discovered was a bland import/export office owned by Wildwater Corporation, US military contractors. That didn't mean much. Maybe someone who worked there was involved. Maybe just someone who used their Wi-Fi. Maybe nothing at all.

Then Maria got a tip from her local sources. There was a big exchange going down; a large shipment of heroin processed from these opium fields would be sold to traffickers, who would smuggle it to Albania, then on to Italy and the rest of Europe. It was just the sort of target Zahir chose, so Joe and Hamid had driven out in their Range Rover Defender and set up here, Hamid with a pair of high-powered binoculars and Joe with the rifle. Joe was white and lean, in his thirties, in worn desert camo pants and jacket, an old black T-shirt and brand-new sunglasses, his last pair having gotten smashed in a fight at the club. His hair was a bit ragged and he had a few day's scruff on his chin. Hamid, short and boxy, with a heavily muscled upper body, was in jeans, Nikes, and a black hoodie, his hair and goatee freshly trimmed.

Hamid was his translator. He was a fluent speaker of Farsi, known locally as Dari, but he wasn't local. He was from Brooklyn, and a tough, somewhat troubled kid, though not by Kandahar standards. He'd dropped out of school, gotten into some minor scrapes with the law, mostly just fighting and dealing weed or molly, but enough to make him the black sheep of his high-achieving family. This was his chance to make them proud, as proud as they were of his older sister the doctor or his brother the social worker. Joe was well-liked in the Muslim community, where he was known, or at least rumored, to have stopped a large-scale terror attack, sparing New York thousands of deaths, and sparing New York's Muslims the inevitable reprisals they'd suffer, despite the fact that many of them, like Hamid's own Persian parents, had come to New York fleeing religious extremism and violence. When Joe took on this new mission, his young friend Juno, a tech genius and delinquent from Bed-Stuy who often worked with Joe, had recruited Hamid, whom he knew from the clubs. Juno told him he'd make enough to open his own club, and get to roll with a kick-ass secret-agent type. Instead he was bored to death, lying in the dirt or staring at buildings all day and night, or watching Joe read from the paperback that was poking from his back pocket now: *Selected Poems*, the cover said; selected, Hamid guessed, by some guy named Rilke. What kind of person reads poems for fun?

But now, sure enough, a small caravan of two SUVs, one open and one closed, was making its way over the tracks that led through the hills. The open one held armed men in *khet*—the long, tunic-like top—and *partug*—the loose-fitting pleated trousers, folded at the waist. Some wore vests or military jackets and all had *kufi* or turbans on their heads. The second vehicle would have the dope, plastic-wrapped kilos packed into boxes or sewn into sacks.

Adjusting his scope, Joe scanned the landscape, and spotted a rising dust trail coming the other way, from the nearest small village. There was a closed Jeep and behind that a surplus military truck. The buyer. This would be the dope trader Maria knew about, an established supplier who would repack the goods and, through bribes or deceit, send them on to their next stop, the price doubling each time they changed hands. Depending on the quality, the bricks in those trucks might be selling for three to six thousand dollars each, less for a large purchase of course. By the time they hit New York, they'd be worth fifty to eighty thousand a piece. Opium production dwarfed all other sectors of the Afghani economy and war had been good for business. Lack of government control had led to a surging crop, which would lead to a flooded market, which meant lower prices, higher quality, and eventually, dead junkies.

But Joe wasn't here about any of that. The way you survived in this world was to mind your own business and watch your own ass. His job was to kill Zahir, if he showed. What difference did it make if one or two more trucks full of dope got through or not?

The dust trails converged and, as dusk crept over the raw landscape, the earth shifted between shades of brown and tan, rust and red. Below him was the road, then another lower ridge, and beyond that, the poppy fields, a sea of flowers, the fat petals like soft, sleepy heads, drooping atop their stalks, like an army of angels descended to earth. He'd seen men die in these fields. He'd seen US soldiers patrolling between the flowers, and children tending the crops. He'd seen civilians blown up accidentally by American ordnance and his fellow soldiers tortured by insurgents. He knew that 42% of the world's opium came from this one province, more than all of Burma, the number two supplier after Afghanistan. He knew that opium fed the worldwide drug epidemic and financed the Taliban who made life hell for so many of those who lived here. But it was still a beautiful sight. That was the thing about hell; it could look a lot like heaven.

Then, as the two parties met and halted, Joe caught a glimpse of something else, a small dark shape moving on the horizon. It was just a flicker, with the sun behind it, and then it was gone, but Joe knew; someone else was there.

"Don't move," he told Hamid, who was fidgeting. "This is it."

The exchange happened fast. Two men stepped from the lead vehicles, and Joe watched through the scope as the money changed hands, a leather grip that the seller unzipped, checked and then re-shut. He yelled a command and his men began quickly unloading, handing off the packages to the buyer's men, who quickly loaded it onto the truck. Other men stood guard, standing in a loose perimeter, weapons drawn. In a few minutes it was done. They climbed back into the trucks and, in a cloud of dust, turned around and raced off the way they'd come.

"Shit . . ." Hamid muttered. "That's it, I guess."

"Shhh . . ." Joe silenced him. "Just wait."

He remained still, moving only enough to refocus the scope, because the black speck he'd seen before, or almost seen, was on the move. Really that was all he saw, movement, a gray shape moving in the gray air, now that the sun had disappeared behind the horizon. But something was moving fast now, and he heard a faint buzz as well, like a mosquito. The mosquito darted along the far ridge, then down a winding path to the road in the direction the seller had gone. Joe focused: it was a figure on a motorbike, dark clothes and scarf billowing, rifle strapped to its back.

"Let's go," Joe said and rolled back, then got to his feet. Hamid followed, shouting questions, but Joe didn't answer as he scrambled down the steep hill to where the Defender was parked out of sight. They got in and Joe pulled out, wrestling the wheel as they plunged down the rutted path, then hitting the gas as they reached the road. He sped until he heard the whine of the motorcycle and then eased back. Now they were following the biker, who was in turn, it seemed, following the money.

"Is that Zahir?" Hamid asked, catching his breath between guzzles of water.

"Maybe," Joe said. He opened a water and drank. The MO was all wrong. Zahir stole the dope not the dough. There might be a hundred or hundred and fifty thousand dollars of whatever currency in that bag. Not a bad score, but nothing compared to what that product was worth on the streets of New York. And what was the point of having a network like Zahir's if you weren't going to use it? Plus, Zahir wrote his name in blood and terror. Take the dope and the money, leave a pile of corpses and burning trucks. That was the way to get people's attention in this neighborhood. One armed man on a bike wasn't especially impressive. Though, Joe supposed, it depended on the man.

Night fell as they reached the village, just a few buildings around a market square, with homes and small shops staggered along the dirt streets from there. There was no one in sight. He moved slowly, cruising around the square at walking speed. Just then a man came running, sprinting right past the truck without a glance. Joe nosed the truck into the lane he'd come from. Two more young men ran by.

"Zahir!" one yelled. *"Zahir darad meeyayad!"*

Now Joe saw a café, lit from within. The bike was parked out front, beside the dust-covered Jeep the seller had been driving. Men rushed through the door and scattered.

"Zahir!" one screamed as if warning the town about a fire.

"Al Zilli! Al Zilli!" another yelled as he bolted past. The shadow. Joe parked.

"Wait here," he told Hamid.

"Don't you need me to translate?"

"Zahir!" an old man yelled as he quickly hobbled by on a cane. A younger, wider man raced past him, tripped and fell flat, then jumped up and fled.

"I think I get the gist," Joe told him. "The keys are in it. If I'm not back in ten minutes, drive back to the hotel. If I'm not back there by tomorrow, go home."

"What if you don't come back at all?" Hamid asked, suddenly quieter.

Joe smiled and patted his arm, reassuringly. "Then at least you got those free protein bars." Leaving the sniper's rifle, he took his Beretta M9 pistol and jumped from the truck. "See you soon, kid."

Then he crossed the road to the café. He removed the safety on his gun and positioned it in front of him, proceeding carefully, though the men who ran by him, all heading the other way, barely gave him a glance. He approached the door, just a curtain hung in the archway, and went in low, thrusting the curtain aside. The café was deserted. Glasses of tea and hookahs sat abandoned. Stools were overturned. A cat wandered by, unconcerned. A sudden whistle made him swing left, pistol aimed. It was just a kettle boiling. More tea. Joe quickly checked behind the bar, turned the heat off under the kettle, and then made his way to the back door. He suspected there was another room where opium was smoked, a scene with which he was all too familiar. He eased the door open slowly with his free hand, then stepped into the dimness. Immediately he smelled it, that odd but distinctive scent, somewhere between gooey brownies and rotting fish. The perfume that the poppy only releases in smoke. The scent of dreams and slow, happy death. A few men lay on their backs, sprawled on thin mats, their heads propped on pillows, eyes closed or seeing nothing in the gloom. They hadn't run when Zahir came through. They were beyond care. That was what you paid for here: to not give a shit for an hour or a night. Joe crossed the room, leaving the lotus-eaters undisturbed, and crept through the exit, which led to an alley in the rear.

There was Zahir. A figure all in black, black tunic, loose black trousers, a black turban, and over his face, a cotton ski mask. He wore gloves and held a rifle pointed at the seller, a bearded man in his forties, who kneeled now, hands clasped together, as if earnestly praying and offering up the gift of the zippered bag, which was on the ground before him. Just as Joe entered, Zahir reacted, leaping like a cat, and somersaulting out of his line of fire. But Joe didn't fire. There were windows behind Zahir, and he was afraid of his bullets entering the neighboring building. Instead he moved too, ducking right, trying to take cover against the wall while training his pistol on Zahir, whose gun pointed back at him. The kneeling man trembled between them, with both guns leveled right at his skull. They were in a standoff. If either moved, even to take a shot, they'd be exposed to the other. Joe stayed perfectly still.

That's when Zahir, while keeping his gun on Joe, began to slowly lift his left hand, palm out, as though holding traffic. "Don't shoot me, Joe," the figure said in a familiar voice, peeling away the mask and turban. Blond hair tumbled out.

Smiling, Joe lowered his gun.

"Hi Yelena."

2

DONNA WAS IN HELL. But at least she had her pal Andy there with her. He was the one who, as they walked into the training center that morning, had quoted Dorothy Parker, and whispered in her ear, "What fresh hell is this?"

Hell, at least for today, was FBI Terror Response Training. Important of course, and extremely serious business, but they'd been getting sent to new sessions every time the alert level bumped up to orange, which was rather often lately. And while it was supposed to be mandatory for all agents, those on active field assignments could postpone it indefinitely, which only reconfirmed how inactive her own career was, if she was back down here again, stuck in school while her teammates were out playing, catching, and scoring in the field.

Special Agent Donna Zamora worked the tip line in the basement of the FBI's New York office, sorting through the avalanche of information that poured in every day and sifting for gold. Special Agent Andrew Newton was her best friend in the office, and as a gay Black agent and a Latina they felt the need to support each other in what often felt like the Fraternity of Boy Investigators. Even worse, Donna's ex-husband, a devious CIA agent, had deliberately undermined her, planting doubts about her integrity, suspicions that she might be in league with mobster Gio Caprisi and sleeping with Gio's known associate, Joe Brody. None of which was true. But what even Andy didn't know was that Gio had, in his cockeyed scheme to protect New York from terror and keep it safe for crime, handed her key information in two investigations, and that she was, against her better judgment, entangled with Joe—emotionally, if not physically or legally. Even her mom had become pals with Joe's grandmother. Their last interaction had led to several dead terrorists and a destroyed heroin shipment, all evidence of which Joe had conveniently made disappear. So she was clean—in her record and conscience. But still, confirming that you are *not* working for the Mafia is hardly the ticket to promotion. Which is how she ended up back at Terror Response Training. Again. Today's topic? Neutralizing Explosive Devices.

Wearing safety goggles and gloves, with a small tool kit beside her, Donna was seated at a long table with her fellow trainees, each preparing to defuse a make-believe bomb. Hers was a cluster of wires, pipes, and electronics packed into a Hello Kitty rolling suitcase. Donna peered suspiciously at the clean-cut men around the table, earnestly bent over their suitcases, wondering if they'd deliberately given her the pink one.

"One minute . . ." the instructor clicked his stopwatch. "Go!"

As it happened, even if they did stick her with the girly-bomb, they'd done her a favor: she recognized this device as almost identical to one she'd worked on in her last course. She quickly unscrewed the cover from the timing mechanism, a cheap digital clock set for thirty seconds, and rewired it to keep it from knowing how much time had really elapsed, then located the main wire set to trigger the ignition. Her stomach grumbled. She'd been too busy feeding her daughter Larissa that morning to eat herself.

"Was that a bomb I heard?" Andy asked in a whisper.

"Shhh . . ." Donna answered.

"Ten seconds . . ." the instructor said. "Counting down to . . ."

"Lunch," Andy whispered beside her, and this time she couldn't help giggling.

"Something funny, Zamora?" the instructor barked.

"No, sir!"

"Okay then, two seconds . . ."

Suddenly flustered, Donna snipped the wire. Her bomb buzzed loudly.

"Trip wire, Zamora," the instructor said. "You killed us all. At least you died laughing."

"Sorry, sir."

"And Newton . . ."

"Yes, sir?"

"At least you were right about one thing today. It is time for lunch."

❖

"I'm sorry, Donna, lunch is on me," Andy told her as they walked to the choose-your-own-salad place.

"I'm getting salmon. Serves you right. Now I've got to retake that class next month."

"I know, I know. Ari hates it too, always asking how come I have to be such a wiseass."

"Exactly, listen to your husband. The secret to a happy marriage is less wisdom. More ass."

Andy chuckled as they entered the powerfully air-conditioned deli. It was still hot enough outside to raise a little sweat walking here, at least in his suit, despite the hint of autumn in the early September air.

"Speaking of which," he said as they got on line. "Ari has someone he wants to set you up with. A journalist."

"Are you crazy? I'd be better off working for the mob than sleeping with a reporter."

"Not a real reporter. He's like a culture critic. You know, analyzes TV shows or whatever. Anyway, he showed me a picture. Handsome. And . . ." Andy touched her shoulder as if making his key point, ". . . he told Ari he likes strong women."

"So? What am I, a wrestler now?"

"He means strong in character, dummy." They were at the counter now and the cook was waiting. "Go ahead, order your salmon."

❖

Back in the office after lunch, sipping a plain black double espresso—Donna usually had Sameer, the coffee cart guy, make her a latte with two sugars, but all that talk about asses and possible dates got to her—Donna settled into work, scanning the logs she kept of calls and emails received and turning over something she'd been thinking about for the past few weeks. Finally, she stood, downed the last of her coffee, and marched into her boss's office.

"Excuse me, sir, can I ask you something?"

"Shoot," Agent-in-Charge Tom Foster answered without lifting his eyes from the report on his desk.

"What do we know about White Angel?"

He looked up, frowned, and removed his reading glasses. "That a trick question? I get enough riddles from my kids. What's next, knock-knock jokes? They love those."

"I'd call it more of a rhetorical question," Donna said, sitting across from him. "The answer is nothing. But we should. It's a brand of dope. Apparently very powerful, very pure, and whoever's behind it is taking over a lot of territory, muscling in on the usual crews."

"So?"

"I'd say we have a major new player in town. And the rumor on the street is that junkies are calling this dope Persian."

"What do junkies know?"

"About junk? A lot. And that case we just closed? The heroin smuggling? Also Persian."

"As I recall, all we recovered was a couple grams of stuff, right?"

"Yes, sir."

"And the ring are all dead or missing?"

"Right."

"That sounds like a closed case to me. Congratulations."

"I'm just saying, it feels like there could be a connection. Maybe I should arrange an undercover buy, get a sample, and compare it."

Tom stood up, sighing dramatically. "Donna. What is today's date?"

"Sir?"

"The date. Today's date."

"September second?"

"Good." He swept his hand over the window that looked out onto the crowded, bustling square. "And what major event is about to turn this whole area into a giant pain in my ass in exactly nine days?"

"September eleventh, sir."

"Right again. And just like every year, every federal, state and local agency from the NSA, CIA, and Homeland Security down to the MTA, sanitation, and parks department are squeezing my balls about one thing—terror threats. Is this a terror threat?"

"Not yet," Donna admitted.

"Not at all," he corrected. "It's a drug case. And not even a federal one, as far as I can see." He looked out the window, peering bitterly at the people walking, talking, eating snacks, sitting on benches, and taking photos of each other, as if he were angry at them for providing such nice soft targets. "If they start selling that Blue Angel or whatever to tourists in Ground Zero, let me know. Otherwise, refer it to local PD." He glanced back. "Anything else?"

Donna shrugged. "Knock, knock."

He frowned. "What?"

"Knock, knock."

He sat down with another sigh. "Who the hell is there?"

"To."

"To who?"

Donna pointed a stern finger at him. "To whom!"

He blinked a couple times then grinned widely. "Hey that's pretty good."

Donna saluted and left.

3

DETECTIVE GERALD PARKS WAS in hell. Or close enough. He was stuck in a filthy unmarked car, baking in the sun, with a partner who not only had BO but insisted on smoking, which was clearly against regs, explaining that being on stakeout constituted exigent circumstances, since he couldn't take a cigarette break. Not only that, but after ordering a double beef burrito for lunch, which stank the car up even more (Parks was vegan and competed for the department in long-distance races), he had clearly farted, despite ardent denials. Then he claimed that the smoke from his cigarette would help cover the smell.

"Isn't that what they say?" Detective Fusco, his senior partner, asked. "To light up after you rip one?"

"That's a match. And you just denied farting anyway. If this was an interrogation you'd be caught contradicting yourself."

"Match, cigarette, it's the same idea—you actually need smoke. And if this was an interrogation, my lawyer would argue the first law of evidence: he who smelt it dealt it."

"Whatever," Parks said, rolling his eyes. He was trapped in hell with a gross fat infant. "You want to talk about dealing it. Tell me why we're here." He nodded at the scene unfolding down the street, which Fusco and he had been discretely observing from afar. It was a corner in Sunset Park. A couple of teenagers in drooping, pegged jeans and hoodies were standing on the corner. Most folks walked right by. But a steady string of more scraggly characters approached the youths, who directed them into a nearby alley. A minute later the same person would emerge and quickly rush away.

"Because," Fusco said, unbuckling his belt. "My gut tells me something isn't right here."

"Yeah it tells me that too. I'd say it's the burrito and coffee for starters."

"Out there, genius." Fusco nodded at the usual hustle playing out. Parks shrugged.

"Looks like a pretty standard cop spot and some friendly neighborhood dope fiends to me."

"Yeah but who are the guys working it?"

"I don't know. Nobodies. Kids."

"Chinese kids."

"So?" Parks braced himself for some racial shit. Not that he was Chinese. He was African-American, from Fort Greene. His father was a retired high school principal, his mother a nurse and community activist. A lot of his friends wondered how he could be a cop, considering all the conflicts it raised for a politically-conscious Black man, but Gerald had always wanted to be a detective. It sounded simple, but seeing his sharply dressed father head out to work each morning, tie and pocket square and polished shoes, and come home drained and exhausted gave him a simple goal: he wanted to wear nice suits to work, but he didn't want to sit in an office. He liked being out in the fresh air, in the street. Though not in a car inhaling some fat-ass's farts. He also had a gift for solving puzzles, for analytical thinking. And he was brave. So he excelled on the force, rose quickly, and landed this assignment, as junior partner with Fusco in Major Case as a prize. Because despite everything—the bad jokes, the bad breath, the farts and cigarettes, and even the suspicious phone calls from what sounded like angry bookies—Fusco was a top investigator and a legendary detective. He was the real deal and Parks was determined to learn from him, if there was anything left in him but gas.

"Chinese neighborhood, Chinese drug dealers. Standard," he told Fusco.

"And the last spot I took you too? In East New York? Who was selling there?"

Parks gritted his teeth. "Black kids."

"Right," Fusco said. "Black neighborhood, Black kids. Also standard. Selling what though?"

"Dope, man. Heroin. What is this?"

"What brand?"

"The touts were yelling White Angel. It's the bomb, apparently."

"Right." Fusco checked his gun and took the keys from the car. "Come on, let's take a walk. Get some fresh air. That cologne you wear is driving me nuts."

Chuckling, Fusco lumbered from the car and started walking down the street, while Parks followed, trying to control his temper and, yes, taking some deep, cleansing breaths. Maybe this was Fusco's brand of ball-busting. And okay, he was new on the squad. But he was no rookie, and he didn't plan to sit still for any hazing. He'd knock him right on his ass.

But Parks's attention shifted quickly, and he jumped into high alert when he realized where his new partner was leading him—right into the bustling little operation they'd been observing.

"Five-O, Five-O."

"Cops yo!"

"Police coming!"

The lookouts and touts—immediately recognizing that a heavy white guy in a rumpled, blue suit, food-stained white shirt, and creased red tie walking with a well-built, six-two Black man in a glen plaid with a subtle dark green woven in the gray, with a crimson tie and matching pocket square, could be nothing but cops—vanished, as did the customers, scurrying off like roaches in the light.

"What the fuck?" Parks asked as Fusco walked into the alley. It was empty. "You really think they were going to hang around, answer your questions?"

"Don't need them to," Fusco said. Eyes on the ground, he walked to the end of the alley and downstairs into a stairwell. He drew a utility combo knife from his pocket then bent over, grunting a little, and came up smiling. "Here," he said, holding a small, torn glassine envelope by the corner with the knife's tiny tweezers. "Got a small evidence bag?"

Parks took one out and held it open. Fusco dropped in the envelope, then held it up. It was stamped with a small, poorly reproduced image: an angel, wings spread.

Fusco grinned. "A Chinese crew in Sunset Park and a Black crew in East New York, both selling the same brand of dope? That, my tofu-eating, nonsmoking, perfume-wearing young friend, is not standard. Is it?"

"No," Parks said, examining it more closely. "It definitely is not."

"Interested now?" Fusco asked, lighting a cigarette as they headed back to the car, a chorus of whistles alerting the block to their progress.

"Very interested," he said, and grinned.

❖

Unfortunately, their boss, Captain Maureen O'Toole, didn't share their interest.

"Who cares?" she asked, looking at the small collection of used baggies they'd laid on her desk.

"Captain," Fusco said, "this White Angel crew is all over. Not just Brooklyn. They're in Harlem. On the West Side. Maybe the Bronx too. They're organized. And the product is strong. Junkies are dropping right and left."

"He's right," Parks added. "I checked around, and everyone on the street is saying White Angel is the bomb." It was a bleak truth of the dope business—killing off some of your customers was the best advertising there was. Junkies heard about ODs and knew that meant the brand was legit.

"I repeat, who cares?" O'Toole repeated. "I'm asking. Literally. I know I don't. Junkies OD'd? In other news, drunks threw up and pigeons shit on a statue."

"But you have to admit," Parks added, "for a gang to be crossing ethnic lines like this, taking on different groups in different neighborhoods. It's highly unusual."

"But this isn't the highly unusual case squad, is it? This is the Major Case squad. And what they meant by Major Case is a case where anyone with a rank of major or up is going to catch shit from the press or the politicians."

Fusco glared. "So you're saying come back when some rich white kid or celebrity dies."

The captain pointed at him. "Now that is inappropriate and discriminatory, right detective?" She winked at Parks. "Teach your new partner some manners." She pushed the baggies toward them. "And file this crap under NHI."

As they walked back to their adjacent desks in sullen silence, Parks muttered to Fusco. "What's NHI again? I don't remember it in the manual."

Fusco snorted. "It's not in the fucking manual. Dealers killing junkies? NHI means No Humans Involved."

4

GIO WAS IN HELL. As boss of a Mafia crime family, one of the youngest in memory, he was used to having people fear him. And since he was the one who had organized the city's other organized crime bosses in a joint effort to stop terrorists, much of the credit for thwarting a recent attack and for blocking a dope shipment that would fund a terror network had gone to him, at least in his world. Not to mention that in the process, two rats who'd been talking behind his back were eliminated, one a powerful Irish boss named Pat White who'd now been replaced by the Madigan Brothers, his allies. Gio's power and glory had never burned so bright.

So why had he woken up with a groan, full of dread at opening his eyes today? Why was his stomach in knots? The truth was he was heartbroken. And he was scared.

He was heartbroken because the other rat, the second government snitch talking about his business behind his back, had been his accountant and his secret lover, Paul. Since his early teens, Gio had nursed and smothered a hidden desire, a need to take a break from being a man and, as a woman, to be dominated, abused really, by a handsome young man, ideally blond and blue-eyed, like Paul. With him, he'd fulfilled that desire and more, he'd found intimacy and love. Until his love betrayed him and had to die. But Gio hadn't killed him. His wife had.

Carol, Gio's college sweetheart, his partner and the mother of his children, was his other true love and the other half of his broken heart.

Discovering the truth of their affair as well as the fact that Paul had been pressured into feeding the government information on Gio's crimes and hidden fortune, his wife, a harmless civilian afraid of guns, a child therapist for Christ's sake, had shot Paul, and Gio had disposed of the body. Since then things had been a little weird around the house. Finally, after a few failed attempts to talk it all over, Carol had come up with this plan—the worst idea Gio had ever heard—but Carol reminded him he'd said he'd do *anything*, which is why he was sitting here now, scared shitless. Gio Caprisi, feared mob boss and deadly criminal, was heading into couple's counseling.

The waiting room was nice enough—patterned carpet, fabric couch, lots of pillows, flowers in a vase and more flowers in the paintings on the walls and the embroidery on the back of the wooden armchair—like the granny's cottage in a kid's cartoon. But the cozy, soft vibe vanished when the door to the inner office opened and another couple came out, a big guy in a tracksuit and a thin woman in white slacks and loose silk top. The guy looked crushed. The woman looked furious.

Gio squirmed. Carol squeezed his hand and whispered in his ear. "Just be honest and it will be fine."

Gio nodded, squeezing her hand back as a tiny woman in her seventies stood in the door. She wore denim overalls over a T-shirt, sandals, big glasses, and had a thick head of gray curls. Earrings and necklaces dangled. She smiled warmly and held out a bangled hand.

"Mr. and Mrs. Caprisi?"

Nodding, Gio stood formally and buttoned his jacket over his tie, as if in court. Carol popped up and shook hands.

"I'm Carol and this is Gio."

The old lady beamed, taking Carol's hand in both of hers. "So nice to meet you. I'm Dr. Meg Stein. Please come in."

She ushered them in, Carol leading the way, and shut the door behind them. Five minutes later they were rushing back out, Carol in the lead again, and Gio mumbling apologies. Neither spoke till they were in the car, her car, the Volvo wagon. She put the key in but didn't crank it.

Instead they sat, both with their belts on, and stared. Finally, Gio spoke in a low tone.

"Not so easy being honest is it?"

Carol stiffened, and gave him some sharp side-eye, but said nothing.

In fact, Gio had been honest, more or less: When Stein, or Dr. Meg, as she preferred, had asked what the main problem that had brought them to therapy was, Carol had said, "infidelity," and when Dr. Meg asked whose, he'd raised his hand. Avoiding specifics, like gender and flogging, he nevertheless explained that he'd been seeing someone, that it was a purely sexual arrangement (which wasn't entirely true), and that, for him, it was completely separate from his marriage, a need he simply had to fulfill. And when the shrink asked why he assumed his wife couldn't fulfill it, he cleared his throat and said, "Well, it's a kink thing I guess."

"Oh . . ." she said, still smiling blandly. "And Carol, that's not in your wheelhouse? Sometimes we can incorporate these desires into the marital sex life, find ways to fulfill each other's fantasies."

Carol squirmed and Gio spoke: "More specifically . . . a kink thing with a man."

"Oh . . ." the shrink shrunk a little. "I see. And where is this man now?"

Silence. Gio shrugged. "It's over. He's gone. For good."

"And Carol," Dr. Stein asked, turning to her, "how does that make you feel, hearing Gio say he's gone for good? Does that make you feel better? Do you believe it? Do you believe he's really gone forever?"

That's when Carol stood up. "I'm sorry," she said. "I can't talk about this." And she ran.

And now, in the car, she finally spoke, turning to Gio and saying, "I guess I'm like you now, full of secrets and lies and crimes I can never speak of. But I'm new at this, so sorry if I have a hard time swallowing my guilt. Not that you ever feel any."

"How do you know that?" Gio asked, anger flaring for a moment, then looked at her. "Is that honestly what you feel? You feel guilt? You wish you hadn't killed Paul?"

Carol shook her head. "No . . . actually. I don't."

"I didn't think so," Gio said. "And neither did I. Until now. I feel guilty about putting you in that position." He touched her shoulder. She stiffened, staring straight ahead, but didn't pull away. "But I don't blame you either."

"The honest truth? I'd do it again. And that's why I feel guilt."

He squeezed her tighter. "You just did what you had to do."

Now she glanced at him. "So did you."

Gio's phone beeped. He shifted but didn't reach for it. Carol nodded. "Go ahead. Check it."

"It's work," Gio said and checked it. A text: *Diner When? F.* "It can wait," he said.

Carol shook her head. "You might as well go. I have to get back to the office anyway."

"Okay," Gio told her. "Drop me outside the Parkview Diner on your way. I can call Nero or someone for a ride later."

As she started the engine and pulled out, Carol smiled ruefully. "Do you know how jealous I would have been before, worried about who you were meeting?"

"You wouldn't be if you knew, believe me," Gio said, picturing the sweaty face breathing stale smoker's breath on him. "But then again, you don't really want to know."

❖

Carol dropped Gio in front of the diner and he went in, stopping by the men's room to splash water in his face, then got a take-out coffee at the counter before leaving again by the back door. Fusco was in the rear of the parking lot, by the dumpsters, smoking, with his city-issued black Chevy Impala nearby. Knowing how Gio felt about smoking, he stomped on the butt as he approached. He'd lost heavily on last week's games and needed Gio's goodwill, his protection when the bookies started to call.

"So?" Gio asked, stepping out of view, into the space between the dumpsters. He sipped his coffee. "You look into this dope thing for me? This White Angel?"

Fusco shrugged. "I tried, Gio. I staked out the spots. I even got baggies. But my captain doesn't give a shit. She won't approve an investigation."

"She doesn't give a shit about a new heroin operation taking over New York? That's a sad commentary on the state of law enforcement today." In fact, Gio wouldn't normally give a shit either. His own involvement in the drug world was minimal—some weed and coke along the routes his family's Italian Ice and Soft Serve trucks worked on the Long Island beaches in season, and a general oversight over the trade in speed, molly, and so forth in his territories. A dispute among heroin dealers uptown and in Brooklyn was not his problem. But a big new operator with a superior product and organized enough to take over territory could upset the whole ecosystem. That worried him.

"I'm sorry, Gio," Fusco was saying. "What about that other friend of yours? You know, the guy they call sheriff. Put him on it."

"He's not a real sheriff, Fusco. He can't arrest people. That's what I have you for."

"I didn't mean . . ."

"Anyway he's out of town on business. What would get this captain of yours interested?"

Fusco shrugged. "She's interested in whatever the bosses tell her to be. Like if the mayor's office starts bitching. Or the feds."

Gio snapped his fingers. "Good idea. Make that call."

Fusco wasn't aware he'd had an idea. "The mayor won't take my call, Gio. He doesn't even know who I am, thank God."

"Not to the fucking mayor, you big mook. The FBI."

"I need more evidence that it's a federal case. Can you tell me more?"

"I can tell you that there's no opium fields in Brooklyn. Or Queens. Or even Staten Island last time I checked. So that means the shit comes in from somewhere out of state. Probably someplace far away where they wear turbans. And that's federal, right?"

"Sure, Gio . . ."

"So, you're a detective, get out your magnifying glass and go find some clues and shit, Sherlock." Gio finished his coffee and tossed the cup into the dumpster. "Or else pay what you owe."

"Right," Fusco said. "I understand. I'm on it."

"Good. I have every confidence in your abilities." As he turned to go, walking back to the diner, pulling out his phone to dial Nero, he shouted back: "You have a week."

5

AGENT MIKE POWELL WAS in heaven. Or maybe that was a
stretch, he admitted: no one, even those born there, could quite describe
the Helmand region of Afghanistan as heaven these days. A rugged environment, it had its own harsh beauty and a graceful, ancient culture, but
had been riven by constant warfare since 2001, under Taliban control for
years, and torn by conflicts over the opium crop for who knows how long
back into history. It was considered to be the most dangerous province in
Afghanistan—which is saying something. But for Powell it was a chance
at redemption and maybe a shot at much more.

He'd been a rising young CIA agent, a smart analyst and a tough,
effective operative, but his marriage, to an FBI agent, Donna Zamora,
derailed him—or maybe even deranged him. He was intensely jealous
and controlling, an impulse that was itself, ironically, beyond his control. He couldn't help it. He found himself spying on her and eventually even using agency resources to try and snoop, all of which bit him
right in the ass when they divorced. He lost custody of his daughter,
Larissa, and came close to losing his job. But the agency decided it was
less embarrassing—to itself—to just bury him, so he was parked in a
secure New York office, running interference with the locals and feeding
information to his luckier colleagues overseas. Then Joe Brody entered
the picture. Convinced that something was up between him and Donna,
both romantically and criminally, and forgetting at times that even if

28

she was seeing Joe (which he had no evidence of) that wasn't exactly "cheating" now that they were divorced, Powell tried to implicate them both in a recent case involving a diamond heist and heroin being brought into New York by terrorists. Instead, when the case broke, he was the one who ended up on the losing end: two of his informants vanished or dead, the FBI and NYPD recovering the stones, and, he suspected, Joe Brody eliminating the terrorists. Powell was screwed and expecting to really be fired this time when his phone rang, and his life changed.

The voice on the phone had identified itself as Zahir, a somewhat mythic figure in intelligence circles, known as the Shadow. Zahir offered to help Powell, to act as an asset more or less, in exchange for unspecified favors. Why did Powell believe him? He didn't. After ten years in the CIA he didn't believe anything. Not only did everyone, and he meant *everyone*, lie, even when someone told the truth, it was for a reason, and that reason was often secret, a lie of the heart hiding behind the facts. But Zahir made him curious. For one thing, he'd called on Powell's secure office line, which wasn't supposed to be possible. Then, as soon as he'd told him he was at least interested in talking, Powell found himself transferred. Not, as he'd feared, to sit and stare at the Bering Straits in some ice tower for the next year, watching Russians scratch their frozen balls, but to Athens, an active station overseas. Did his superiors wonder why the fuck-up of the month was suddenly operational instead of getting punished? Probably, but they didn't question it. After all, they too believed nothing except that everyone lies—it's an occupational hazard. So who knows? Maybe the higher-ups had a use for Powell. Maybe this *was* a punishment in some inscrutable way. Or maybe the whole catastrophe had been part of some bigger, better lie and so not really a failure at all.

In any case, when he arrived in Athens, Powell was handed a fake passport and a plane ticket to Kabul and told to rendezvous in Kandahar with one Rick Toomey, formerly a black ops commando for the army, presently a military contractor. Powell's new assignment? To offer assistance and expertise to the people Toomey worked for, the Wildwater Corporation, a company that did business with the US military and intelligence forces in the Middle East. In other words, after a season on the bench, he was back in the game.

But the real joy didn't kick in until later. He had gotten to the hotel, taken a shower, and changed when there was a knock on his door. Toomey. He was, Powell had to admit right off, a good-looking man: blue eyes, close-cut blond hair, easy smile. He was also, he quickly learned, excellent company. Asking if Powell had eaten, he immediately dismissed the idea of dining in the hotel and took him to a small, comfortable, homey place where they sat in a lovely courtyard and, as soon as he stepped in and smelled the roasting lamb, he knew the food would be excellent. It was. And over dinner, coffee, and the drinks he surreptitiously supplied from a bottle of scotch he poured under the table, Toomey kept up an easy, funny patter, regaling Powell with stories about the time he came under fire while in the latrine and had to take cover in the waste tank, the time he had to crawl in silence under the legs of some tied-up camels and remain still while one pissed on his head, and the time he broke into the wrong villa in a South Asian city, thank God he was only there for recon, and had to flee after accidentally catching a US diplomat in bed with a Chinese diplomat.

"What a relief to be talking to someone with top security clearance," he said, as Powell laughed. "Normally I have to redact my best material." He poured them both more scotch under the table and handed Powell his. "But what I'm going to tell you now is outside the parameters completely. It has no level of classification because it doesn't even exist."

"You're going to tell me who Zahir is," Powell said. He sipped his drink; really he just touched it with his lips. He was on high alert and wanted to stay that way.

"If you still want to know. Only a half dozen people in the world do, and if you become one of them, there's no going back. Now's your chance to walk away."

Powell shook his head. "I came too far to leave without answers."

"Good," Toomey said, and smiled that craggy, movie-star smile. "I'm glad to hear you say that. But first, a couple of questions. Then some answers." He pulled a folder from his satchel. "Since you've been tapped to join us, a few new faces have shown up around here. I wonder if you can identify any of them."

He slid the folder across and Powell looked: surveillance shots of varying quality, taken from odd angles with a long distance lens. The first few were of someone he didn't recognize, a young guy, Middle-Eastern looking but in a Supreme hoodie and jeans so probably American or Western European. "Him I don't know." The next were of a blond woman in her mid to late twenties. He couldn't name her, but it was easy to picture her with a gun on a dark Brooklyn street. "Her I've seen. But I don't know much."

"That's okay," Toomey said. "We do. Another associate of ours has known her since she was a little Russian brat stealing candy." He tapped the third set of photos. "What about contestant number three?"

Now Powell smiled, as he flipped through the photos of the lean, hard-looking man in the sunglasses and the black T-shirt. "Oh, him I know very well. That's Joe Brody, aka the bouncer, aka the sheriff, aka a big pain in everybody's ass back home."

"A pal of yours?"

"Hardly."

"Good," Toomey said, closing the file. "Because he's just expanded into ass pain over here as well. And they cure that with a bullet in Afghanistan."

"Suits me," Powell said, and that was the moment when he realized this new job was going to be more like a vacation.

Toomey finished his drink and stood, holding out his hand. "Then let me be the first to say welcome aboard, Mike."

Mike stood and shook. "Thanks, Rick."

Toomey shouldered his satchel and threw some cash down on the table. "Now let's go upstairs and meet Zahir."

6

YELENA FOLLOWED JOE AND Hamid on the highway back to Kandahar, Joe mostly deflecting Hamid's eager questions about Yelena—yes, he knew her and they had worked together before, yes, she was the badass Russian chick Juno had told him about—though Joe didn't answer when Hamid asked if Juno had really dusted her butt for handprints (he had, but he should have shut up about it)—and wondering about questions of his own, like how the hell did she get from Queens, where he last saw her, fleeing a room strewn with corpses, to a dope deal in deep Afghanistan?

Back at the hotel where Joe and Hamid were staying, all three went to the restaurant, found a quiet corner, ordered, and, while Hamid gorged, Yelena talked and Joe listened.

"I knew when I left New York that I couldn't go anyplace where I am known for a while. First I tried France, the Riviera. The beach was nice. But I got bored. And I needed money."

"Bored?" Joe asked. "It was only a few weeks. Why didn't you just rob the fancy hotel safes? Take it easy for a while?"

Hamid snorted as he scooped humus into a pita. "Wow you think robbing hotel safes is easy?"

Joe smiled at Yelena. "For her it is."

She shrugged. "Stealing old lady's jewelry is more something for when I retire maybe."

Hamid laughed. "That's awesome. You're like the pink panther."

Yelena frowned. "Pink? Because I am a girl?"

Joe waved it off. "It's a movie. Believe me she's more of a black cat. So then what?"

"I got recognized. Some Russian oligarch's mistress knew me so I had to go before word got to my enemies in Moscow. I heard about the bounty on Zahir. I decided, why not come here and kill him?"

Hamid laughed again, his mouth full, waving a shish kebab skewer. "Just like that? That's cool as shit."

She narrowed her eyes at him. "Shit?"

Joe explained. "It's a compliment. He's impressed. He's okay; Juno knows him."

She nodded at that. She liked Juno.

"You're totally awesome," Hamid told her. "Cat burglarizing. Killing overlords. Like a Marvel hero."

Yelena looked doubtful. "Thank you," she said politely.

Joe handed him a napkin. "Stop drooling and eat with your mouth closed." Then to Yelena: "So what happened? No luck finding Zahir?"

Yelena laughed. "There is no Zahir. How do you say, the myth you use to scare children so they behave?"

"The boogeyman?"

"Yes. Zahir is the bourgeois man that scares smugglers, so they give up their loads." She shrugged. "No one has seen him. No one even knows anyone who has seen him. Finally I decide, it's easier to just be the shadow than to find him."

Hamid laughed again. "Sorry," he said, hands up. "I'll be quiet. It's just . . ." He leaned toward Yelena, "Hanging with this guy's been pretty dull. Juno said he was a badass, but all he does is read poems and, like, silently brood, lurking in the dust. You know?"

Now Yelena laughed. "See?" she told Joe. "He thinks I am cooler than you. And a badder ass."

Joe nodded. "I'm not arguing. You win. Especially in the ass department."

"Yo, let's a get a hookah," Hamid suggested. "It's called a chillum here I think."

"Maybe later," Joe said. "I want to check out this first." He pulled a folded page from his pocket: the printout of a map and a photo of a nondescript five-story building. "Juno couldn't get much off of Felix's cellphone," he told Yelena as he handed her the papers, "but some of his messages are from an IP address that connects back to here."

"We already drove by yesterday," Hamid complained. "It's just a regular office building."

"He's right," Joe admitted. "Nothing to do with politics or fundamentalists. Just shipping and receiving for a company called Wildwater. Some kind of contractors. But . . ." He grinned at Yelena. "As long as you're in the neighborhood, I bet they have a safe."

She laughed. "This is Joe's idea of a date," she told Hamid.

"Oh man, I'd love to see you work," he gushed.

"Easy," Joe said. "You need to stay in the room, get in touch with Juno, and be ready to relay whatever we find."

"Don't worry," Yelena told him. "I know a good hookah place in Kabul. And also one back in Astoria."

❖

The Wildwater office in Kandahar was in a nondescript five-story office building close to what the local paper optimistically called "the famous" Shaheedan Square. Joe and Yelena took her motorbike, with her driving, still in black but minus the mask and turban, and Joe behind her, one arm snaked around her ribcage, his chest against her, a bag with their weapons and her tools on his back. It was late, and there was not much in the way of nightlife. A few cars and bikes rolled through the traffic circle in the center of the square. Taxis and motorized, open-backed carts cruised for passengers or loitered by the cafés. They parked in the alley behind the building, walked into the loading bay where, during the day, trucks came and went, and while Joe kept watch, Yelena got in the door in less time than most people took with keys.

The building was drab, concrete and steel, dusty and filled with import/export firms and companies supplying the military. Finding their way upstairs with flashlights they'd covered with tape, leaving just a small beam, they headed swiftly and silently to the top floor, where the lock on the office door was even less serious than downstairs.

And at first glance, there wasn't much to protect. It was an office much like any other, a little less modern than the New York equivalent—desks, chairs, filing cabinets, old desktop computers, a watercooler. In a back room, with a bigger desk, a bigger chair, and a much-napped-on leather couch, Yelena spotted an old freestanding safe.

"You work on this," Joe whispered, handing her the bag. "I'll deal with the stuff in the office."

Joe went to a desk with an old computer, just a step or two above floppy disks, and turned it on. While it slowly booted up he got out the iPhone Juno had given him—his own phone was a basic flip—and called the only number on it, Hamid's.

"Hey," Hamid said immediately.

"It's me," Joe said.

"I know."

"Do you have Juno patched in?" Joe asked.

"Hey, bro," Juno shouted into Joe's ear. "I'm right here, back home in the studio. How's Afghanistan? You hit the beaches yet? I hear you met an old friend too."

"Afghanistan is landlocked, Juno. And let's be cool on the phone, right?"

"Sorry. You're right. You ready to transmit?"

"In a minute," Joe said. He set the phone on the desk and pulled a cord from his pocket. The screen now asked for a password, but Joe ignored that and plugged his cord directly into a port on the rear of the machine. He plugged the other end into the phone. "Okay," he told Juno and Hamid, "you're hooked up."

"I'm on it," Juno said. "Hamid, just chill and monitor the signal."

"Right," Hamid said. "I'm chilling."

The computer screen flickered with a stream of numbers as Juno hacked in remotely, and Joe began inspecting the papers on the desks, using his flashlight and, with a small camera, snapping photos of anything that seemed remotely interesting. There wasn't much: purchase, shipping, and customs documents, packing lists and invoices for shoelaces, water bottles, sunglasses, tires, and blankets—all the mundane crap that it took to run a war, most of it harmless except as trash in a landfill, and as a waste of tax money. No extremist tracts or receipts for heroin. Hopefully, Yelena would have better luck. Meanwhile he snapped away without much enthusiasm, pausing only when he saw, from the documents flashing by on the screen, that Juno was in and downloading the contents of the hard drive. He picked up the phone, which was still connected to the computer.

"Hey guys. How's it going?"

"It's going," Juno said. "But I don't know where. Looks like a bunch of bookkeeping crap to me."

"Yeah same here . . ." Joe began, but then dropped the phone, as Yelena came running out of the office, bag in her hand.

"Go!" she yelled as she slammed the office door behind her, but she didn't need to say anything. Joe knew from the look on her face. They bolted across the room, throwing the hall door shut behind them, and were just turning a corner of the hallway when an explosion ripped through the building, obliterating the office they were just in and rattling the entire place. They dove to the floor, instinctively clutching each other. The sound was deafening. Plaster dust poured down. The whole structure groaned like an old ship, but it held. After breathing in the dark for a second, and registering that he was alive and, except for the ringing in his ears, unharmed, Joe found his flashlight and clicked it on.

"You okay?" he asked Yelena, still whispering, though it hardly mattered. The whole neighborhood was awake.

"Yes," she said. "Just my pride is hurt."

36

"We can bandage that later," Joe said. "Let's go."

They began to make their way downstairs, a bit slower than before, stepping carefully over fallen signs and toppled trash cans, though for the most part, the rest of the building seemed intact.

"Booby trap?" Joe asked as they hurried down.

"A very good one too," she told him. "Better than the shit safe."

She explained that the old safe had been wired with a high-tech explosive device, set to destroy the contents of the safe if it was opened, along with anyone nearby.

"Guess working here isn't as boring as it looks," Joe said.

"But we won't know why," Yelena said as they reached the street level and went back out the alley door. "Sorry, Joe."

"Don't worry about it," Joe told her. "At least we got out clean."

But he spoke too soon, because shortly after they got back on the bike, and Yelena started to drive, a Humvee with floodlights and a machine gun mounted on the roof came straight down the alley at them.

7

TOOMEY LED POWELL UP a dark staircase and knocked on the door. A moment later, it drew back and he entered a large private dining room, opulently furnished with cushions and drapes, dim lights and filigreed, openwork panels filtering the night air. No one was dining, however. The table held an ornate tea service—from the scent he knew it was chai green tea brewed with ginger and walnuts—as well as a bowl of fruit and dishes of sweets. A ruddy-faced, heavyset old man in a pink dress shirt and khakis sat at the head, ignoring the tea and treats and holding a glass of rosewater and lemonade over ice. He wore a wedding band, a Rolex, and an excellent toupee, and the blazer draped over the back of his chair had an American flag lapel pin. He looked familiar. He could have been a senator, except that then Powell would have recognized him.

To his left sat a tougher, harder-looking man with close-cropped salt-and-pepper hair and a seamed, tanned face. He wore an expensive white silk shirt and expensive navy silk trousers and a gold Russian cross around his neck. Russian then. There was an unlit Cuban cigar and a gold lighter on the table before him, next to his tea. Across from him, on the American's right, sat a younger, heavily muscled man, his hair grown out but still neat, in a camouflage T-shirt and jeans, with a USMC tattoo and an open laptop on the table. An ex-Marine, working no doubt for the senatorial American.

The fourth person in the room was a mystery. For one thing she was female. Also younger than the others, probably in her twenties, though she could have passed for a teenager, still with a layer of baby fat, her chubby cheeks dotted with pimples. She had a striking look, reddish auburn hair expensively chopped into a decidedly unmilitary, artful mess, very fair skin that could not have seen much Afghan sun, and striking green eyes. She wore a thin vintage Grateful Dead T-shirt cut high to reveal a few inches of soft belly, torn jeans, and a black biker jacket. Was she the Russian's mistress? No. Not flashy enough—she wore a black leather choker and an Apple watch but no gold or makeup, expensive high-top designer sneakers but no heels, and why would he have her here anyway? She was young enough to be the American's daughter, but first of all, Powell didn't sense she was American, at least not all-American like the older man, and she was languidly sprawled on some cushions smoking a chillum, tobacco mixed with hash, and sipping Sharbat-E-Rayhan, a cold drink made with basil seeds, staring at them all with a look of total impudence and indifference, as if they had mildly disturbed her private party—hardly the type for take-your-daughter-to-work-day. Plus she was armed; from the way she sat, and the way her jacket draped, it was clear to Powell that there was a handgun strapped beneath it. But all that was beside the point: the sharp, cold look in her eyes made it clear she was not here on anyone else's arm. She was no pet. She was a predator.

The other mystery was who was not here. No Afghanis. No Arabs or Middle Easterners of any sort. No one who could plausibly be Zahir.

"Gentlemen," Toomey said to the table, pointedly ignoring the woman, who blew steamed smoke into the air. "Let me introduce you to Mike Powell, CIA."

All three men turned to him. The older American stood. "Mike, I'm Bob Richards, CEO of Wildwater. Thanks for coming out." He reached across the table and gave Powell a CEO-quality handshake. Of course: Bob Richards was ex-NSA, from before Powell's time, and now headed up a company of military contractors, operating worldwide, handling everything from logistics, supplies, and construction, to training and security, to, some said, mercenary warfare and covert ops with which official agencies didn't want to be connected. "This is Jensen, my assistant," he added.

"It's an honor, sir," Powell said, then turned to Jensen who rose, shook, and sat back down, hands on the keyboard.

"And this is Nick," Richards said, settling back in his chair.

The Russian smiled but did not stir or shake. "I prefer Nikolai. But first names only for now, I'm afraid," he said in fluent but accented English. "You understand."

Powell smiled back. "SVR?" he asked, guessing he was with the Russian Intelligence Service, the successor to the KGB.

"I am here unofficially like you. To advise and observe." He shrugged. "So not even really here at all."

"Have a seat, Mike," Toomey said, pulling a chair out and taking one himself. "Let's talk." He turned to the others. "Mike has already been pretty helpful, confirming the ID on Brody."

Now Jensen spoke, looking up from his screen. "You say he was ex-Special Forces, but I can't find a record. Not even high security."

Powell nodded, realizing now that of course they'd been listening to him and Toomey downstairs. "There is none. His records have been erased. Make of that what you will."

"Black ops," Jensen said.

"Pitch black. That's all I know."

"And now he's gone rogue, you say? Doing hits and pulling jobs for a Mafia family?"

Powell shrugged. What did rogue even mean, in his present company? "He grew up with Gio Caprisi. But maybe, before I say more, you should tell me why I'm here."

"You're here because there's a war going on, Mike. Same as us," Toomey said, but Richards waved him down.

"What Rick means is, some of our likeminded colleagues in the company thought you were our kind of people, and that you'd fit in."

40

"Fit in with what?"

"War is expensive, Mike. You know that. Everyone does. But what the public doesn't realize is that it doesn't just cost money and lives, it takes time. And it takes will. Iron will. Politicians haven't got the stomach for that; they're too worried about reelection. They're cowards by nature. And the public doesn't have the patience. They want, as they said back in Vietnam, to declare victory and go home. Have a parade and be done with it. Go back to sleep." He shrugged. "So a group of us, people in the military and intelligence communities, professionals like yourself, along with some members of the present administration, decided to step in and sort of . . . guide things along. Make sure the will didn't weaken, as we see this thing through to victory."

"Whatever that takes," Toomey added.

"You mean Al-Qaeda? ISIS? The war on terror?"

"We mean the war for the future of the world," Toomey told him.

Richards spoke again, leaning back in his chair. "Like Rick said, we are, as you know, embroiled in a conflict. The war on terror, of course, but that's just part of it. It's a clash of civilizations, of value systems, east versus west, freedom versus slavery."

"Christian versus Islam," the Russian, Nikolai, said. "For us too. We even fought right here, in this same place."

"It's been going on since 9/11," Richards said. "Longer really."

Toomey laughed. "Try a thousand years."

"And it won't be settled in my lifetime either," Richards said, with a wave of his hand.

"And Zahir?" Powell asked, taking this all in.

"A useful fiction," Richards said. "A way to stir the pot. Or stoke the fire, you could say. When will falters, and interest flags, we use Zahir to keep the voters—or should I say viewers—focused back home, which keeps the politicians on point, which keeps the right parties on the ground here off balance or in need of our help."

Powell nodded. "And all of which keeps the arms and money flowing."

Richards smiled. "Like I said, war is expensive. And victory takes men who aren't afraid to get their hands dirty, and to apply pressure when necessary. Men like us. And you."

Toomey leaned over and squeezed Powell's arm. "Men with a will of iron."

All eyes were on Powell, gauging his reaction, but Jensen broke in, addressing Richards.

"Sorry sir, but we've had a break-in at the Kandahar office." He turned to Powell. "It looks like your pal Brody and the Russian girl are sticking their noses in. Almost got them blown off too."

Toomey stood to see the screen and, for the first time, Nikolai seemed concerned. Richards explained to Powell while Jensen spoke into his earpiece. "We have the office booby-trapped. They won't find anything." He turned to Toomey: "But what about the latest shipment?"

"It's already en route," he said. "I handled it personally. Nothing can stop it now."

"Good," Richards nodded. "Then all they've done is destroy our evidence for us."

Jensen reported: "Our security team is on the way to intercept them now. And I scrambled the chopper."

"Let's go," Toomey said. Nikolai stood too and prepared to move.

"Care to observe from the air?" Richards said. "Might be your last look at Joe Brody."

"I'll pass sir," Powell said. He'd been given a lot to think about, and although he knew he was already involved, even by listening, he was hesitant to commit to action. And, happy as he would be to see Joe's head on a stick, he also knew that operations involving Joe Brody tended to get out of hand. "It's been a long day, and I'm just getting my bearings."

"We'll talk later then," Richards said and left in a hurry, flanked by the other men. Suddenly Powell found himself alone with the young woman who was now staring right him with an odd smile and blowing fragrant smoke like a Cheshire cat.

8

Yelena turned the bike around when she saw the Humvee coming, and sped back the opposite way, just as the gunner opened fire. Bullets whistled invisibly past Joe's ears and flattened themselves into the concrete. Then another truck, carrying more men, came around the corner of the alley, blinding them with roof lights and sealing that exit as well. It did, however, have the immediate benefit of halting the gunfire, since the gunners on both vehicles knew they were likely to hit each other. Cursing under her breath, Yelena stopped and spun the bike around again, touching her boot to the ground for balance. She drove them back into the loading bay of the building.

"So?" She looked back over her shoulder at Joe, who was pulling a machine pistol from his pack. "Fight here or go back upstairs?"

"Keep going," Joe told her, and as the first truck turned into the bay behind them, he was ready. Aiming carefully from the rear of the bike, he shot at the gunner, who dropped down into the interior of the Humvee, then sprayed the front, shattering the windshield and the lights. In the momentary dark, as the men inside took cover and began to scramble out, Yelena drove the bike through the doorway and, revving the engine, began to take them up the stairs, nosing the front tire slowly over the steps while Joe hung on. They rode up, taking the turns slowly and then pushing it on the flights, bouncing up, moving at about the pace of a quick jog. Looking down into the stairwell, Joe could see flashlights playing

43

over the stairs, and make out the sound of men yelling or squawking over the radios. They weren't far behind. Then, at the top landing, Yelena jerked to a stop.

"Hey, what's up?" Joe asked, putting his feet down for balance and standing as the bike bucked, braking hard, but before she could answer he saw: the blast had taken out the supports for the stairs and a big chunk of the landing, leaving bits of twisted rebar and broken concrete. In essence, it had cracked the top floor of the building in two. One side, where the office had been, was wrecked, with collapsed interior walls and a sagging ceiling. The other, which had the roof access, was messy but intact. And between them was a jagged gap several feet across.

"Now what?" Yelena asked. "I don't have enough room to jump it. I can't get the speed."

Joe looked around. "I have an idea. Take this."

He gave her the bag and slung his gun over his shoulder, then went to the bombed-out office. The metal door had been blown clean off its hinges, but was otherwise undamaged. He squatted down and began to drag it over to the open gap. Meanwhile, Yelena removed an automatic assault rifle from the pack and focused on the stairs. The top of a head appeared and she fired, dinging the helmet like a bell. The man fell back with a yelp.

"They're coming," she called to Joe.

"Give me a minute," he grunted as he hoisted the door to a standing position against a wall then walked it a foot or so further. Yelena fired a burst, keeping the attackers downstairs. Now Joe had the door standing at the lip of the open gap, and he let it fall, landing with a thud on the other side, and forming a small, precarious bridge. Immediately gunfire erupted from below, as the men in the stairwell saw and heard Joe moving above. Joe jumped back as the bullets shot up, while others ricocheted off the door, causing panic among the shooters below.

"Okay," he told Yelena. "Take it across. Carefully."

She handed him her rifle and he took up a stance, watching for movement and firing the occasional burst down the stairs or through the open gap into the dark stairwell, more to hold them back than because he expected to hit anyone. At the same time, as Yelena edged the bike over the door, shots came up from below her, hitting the ceiling above, which showered dust, or ringing against the metal under her wheels. Once she was across, Joe took a deep breath and darted after her. He could see that all the gunfire had weakened the damaged ceiling even more, plaster and bits of ceiling tile were dropping away, so while she drove slowly out the exit onto the roof, he fired up at the ceiling while pushing the edge of the door with his foot. A beam fell, raining metal and concrete into the stairwell, and Joe could hear men shouting as the door clattered into the gap, falling on them. Firing across the now-reopened moat, he backed out onto the roof exit and shut that door behind him.

It was actually a lovely night out. Not that Joe had time to savor it, but the sudden quiet and the cool, dry air, the sleepy town around him and the thick swirl of stars out over the impenetrable dark of the desert made him wish, momentarily, that he was out on a blanket under the sky. Or better yet, home in noisy, stinky, never dark, and practically starless Queens.

Now they were on the roof, and safe for the moment, but where did they go next? Staying on the more stable, undamaged side of the building, Yelena cruised the bike slowly around and Joe ran to the edges. The front and one side faced a street corner, where he saw another truck full of men unloading, and ducked back as one took a quick shot at his head. The rear was the alley they had just fled. The remaining side overlooked a narrow airspace, and then another building, two stories shorter. Beyond that, Joe could see a single-story structure that housed a row of shops during the day.

"Do you think you can make the jump?" he asked Yelena.

She was about to ask him if she had a choice but noticed something and pointed instead. It was a helicopter, cruising above the city and headed for them. "Guess we will find out."

Joe took his belt off, passing it through the front loops of his pants and then got on the bike behind Yelena and buckled it around her waist.

Now they were strapped together. The chopper approached, the sound and wind growing as it lowered itself like a black beetle from the night sky. He adjusted the scope on the rifle. "Let's go," he said.

Yelena circled slowly back toward the wrecked part of the building, taking it to the furthest point she could safely bring the bike, giving her the longest runway for takeoff. She cranked the throttle, revving the engine as high as she could while holding the brake. As the helicopter arrived over the roof, it hit them with a spotlight. Yelena released the brake and the bike shot forward.

As they raced toward the edge and the alley below, Joe raised the rifle, bracing the stock against his body and turning up toward the chopper, which blinded him with its glare. He opened fire, blasting into the light, trying to stay centered while the bike carried them across the roof. Now the chopper opened fire too, bullets hitting the roof around them as the gunner in the air found his range. As the chopper shifted, trying to get a better angle of fire, the glare shifted momentarily too, and Joe was able to see the origin of the beam of light, spilling from a lamp attached to the bottom. He fired again. With a pop, the light went out. They were plunged back into the darkness. The gunner kept firing, but he was aiming blindly now, staring into shadow and with the thunderous roar of the chopper hiding any sound from the bike.

Joe grabbed Yelena with his free arm, holding on tightly as they reached the flat edge of the roof and went over, soaring across the alley. Joe held his breath as, for a moment, they were airborne, floating through space. He could feel Yelena's heart pound under his hand. Then they landed with a thud on the lower roof next door. The bike wobbled, swerving crazily as Yelena fought for control, and Joe put his feet down a couple times to help balance it. More shots rang out as the helicopter came from behind.

"Keep going," he shouted into her ear. The roar was deafening. As the tires bit, gaining traction on the roof, she cranked the throttle and they took off, crossing the building in seconds and flying over the far edge while bullets shot over their heads.

Now they were on top of the shops. A long gallery with shop fronts facing a square, this roof was more uneven, comprised of plaster and wood, and with covered seating areas, barrels of water, laundry hanging on lines. Ducking low to avoid getting clotheslined, they plowed through some sheets and took cover under a patched-together sheet metal roof that ran along one side of the building. While Yelena idled, Joe unbuckled himself and reloaded the rifle.

"We're never going to outrun that chopper on open ground," he told Yelena.

"So we make a stand here," she said.

He handed her the machine-pistol from his pack. "Here, fire off some rounds to get their attention."

She nodded and began cruising slowly, staying under the cover of the roof. When she heard the chopper approaching, coming around from the side, she took a few shots in its general direction. Gunfire fell like hail on the metal roof, some bullets zinging away while others punched through weak spots and hit the surface around her as she sped out of range.

Joe ran back to where the roof began, climbed onto a table and slowly peeked over the edge. In the moonlight, he saw the chopper lowering itself like a spider, trying to find a position that would let the gunman, who sat beside the pilot at an open panel, aim under the metal roof and sweep the area with gunfire. Yelena fired another burst from a spot further down and the chopper shifted a bit more to try and reach her. Bullet holes appeared in the roof around her as she zoomed up and down.

Joe, who knew they were facing away from him, trying to see under the shelter, stood and propped himself on the metal sheeting, aiming carefully at the chopper, waiting for his shot, while the pilot adjusted his position.

"No hurry Joe," Yelena yelled out. "Just relax and take your time." Moonlight poured in around her as the machine gunner turned her shield into a colander.

Now Joe could see them, the pilot and the gunner, with a few more figures in the seats behind them, all yelling over their headsets as they tried to home in on Yelena. But still he waited, totally still, breathing carefully, eye on his scope.

"Come on," he whispered to himself. "Just a little more."

"I'm running out of roof here Joe," Yelena called out. She fired again, one lucky bullet clanging off the rotors, then quickly sped back down the gallery toward him.

The pilot turned too, trying to find the source of Yelena's fire, and exposed the open panel to Joe. He pulled the trigger.

In a flash, the gunner crumpled, killed instantly as gunfire entered the interior of the chopper. Joe kept firing, sending a stream of lead into the chopper, which swerved away like a fly from a swatter. At this low altitude, just four or five meters off the ground, the chopper quickly lost stability. It spun wildly over the square, stirring up a small storm of dust and paper, scattering the few souls present—mostly taxi drivers, late night café goers, cats and dogs—and then landing with a thud, banging headfirst into a wall. The rotors hit the concrete with a terrible wrenching sound and broken machine parts shot off like shrapnel as the aircraft came to rest.

With a grin, Joe ran over and got on the back of the bike, where he could see Yelena smiling too. "Good shot," she told him.

"Thanks," he said, slinging the gun onto his back and grabbing hold of her. "But I think I only killed the gunner. We better go."

"Next stop, ground floor," she said, revving up. "Everybody off."

She hit it and they sped along the roof, picking up speed and, as the edge approached, she yanked the handlebars up, popping the bike into a wheelie that took them over the side. Letting the bike go as they fell, they dropped into the back of a cart that sat parked in a row with others, waiting for a late-night fare. The bike, with greater momentum, overshot the cart, hit the ground hard, and crashed.

For a couple of seconds, Joe, Yelena, and the driver were all completely disoriented, as the fabric awning over the rear of the cart collapsed and they tumbled into the bed of his truck, which contained only two empty side-benches for passengers. Yelena was the first to recover her balance, leaping up with her usual agility and pointing a gun at the stunned driver. Joe freed himself from the fabric and stood, pulling a US hundred-dollar bill from his pocket and showing that to the driver too, as he began to yell at Joe in Dari.

"The gun or the money," Joe told him, pointing at each. Finally the driver nodded, and reached for the bill. Yelena lowered her gun. "Good. Thank you," Joe said, repeating it in Dari. *"Kheili khoob. Moteshakeram!"*

The cart took off, speeding down a side street and into the dark town, while Joe tried to remember the name of his hotel.

9

Toomey liked this guy Joe. Or he would have, under other circumstances, where they didn't need to kill him. Like if they'd just been in a bar somewhere, trading stories over a beer. At first, he hadn't thought much about him. The only reason they even went up in the chopper was to observe: Richards because he liked to play general, sit there and watch his money at work; Nikolai because he had to report back to Moscow; and Toomey because he needed to be sure that everything went off like it should. His mission was too important to leave to amateurs. It was only when he saw them riding that bike across the roof, the girl jumping it expertly, and then Brody taking out the searchlight, doing what he himself would have done, that he began to think he was finally dealing with some pros. Then they pulled some shit that really impressed him.

First they took cover under a metal shed that shielded them from the bullets that their gunner, Tony, a kid who'd done a tour shooting insurgents before he signed on with Wildwater as a merc, was raining down on them indiscriminately. Then, as he deduced later, the Russian woman drew their fire, tricking the pilot, Trey, into exposing their flank, the open panel by Tony. A skilled sniper, Brody must have been lying in wait. He took that kid out like he was winning a teddy bear in an amusement park. Outstanding shot.

His next shot stunned Trey, bouncing off his helmet and ricocheting into the fuselage. Another hit the bulletproof plexi, which was great when Brody had been shooting at them before, but now the bullet struck the plexi from inside and bounced back, grazing old Richards himself in the leg and ruining those nice pants. Richards yowled, Trey took evasive action and rapidly ditched, Nikolai cursed in Russian, and Toomey grinned, bracing himself for the crash.

They went down in a corner of the square. The chopper was totaled of course, but strapped in and helmeted, they were all fine, just a little battered and whiplashed. Except for Richards, moaning and carrying on, never having been shot before. It was nothing, a scratch, but the blood was spreading through his khakis. Toomey used Nikolai's handkerchief to bind the wound. Trey took off his helmet and let down that ponytail that he insisted on, a trademark gesture that he thought let the world know he was a free man, but that really just showed he was at least a decade out of fashion. Actually, both were true: he was one of Toomey's best men, a brave and ruthless fighter who, much like Toomey, was more at home in a warzone than in any of the places—Florida, where he grew up, the Marines, where he'd learned his skills, or Colorado, where his one-time fiancée now lived—that might have passed for "home." As for family, it was his team that mattered. And now, head still ringing, he was cursing and swearing vengeance on Brody for taking out Tony, his pal. Nikolai just shook his head at the mess and lit a cigar. Toomey called for help to come fetch them, patted Trey on the shoulder, and silently congratulated Brody in his head. He'd look forward to crossing paths with him again some time, and to buying him a beer. Or killing him. Or both.

10

JOE AND YELENA RODE back to the hotel in the motor-cart, lounging on the wadded fabric that had once been the roof, watching the night sky flow over them like a river of stars between the buildings.

"Sorry, Joe. All I did tonight was get you in trouble."

"And get me back out," he told her. "Anyway, I think I learned something important."

"Watch out for booby-traps."

"That there was something there worth booby-trapping. And sending a small army of mercenaries with a chopper to protect. I think you were right all along. Zahir is just a front. And now we know it's a front for a US corporation. Wildwater."

"So what will you do?"

"Catch a plane. Why chase the shadow around here? Especially now that they're onto us. Let's go back home. Start looking at Wildwater and see what we find."

She turned to face him. "You say we and let's. But New York is not my home."

"And Kandahar is? If you want to retire, fine. Go to Tulum or someplace. If you want to get into trouble and help earn this half million, come back with me."

She smiled. "Trouble and money are always tempting. But don't forget, I already made some money today. Not half of a half million, but enough for a nice slow trip around the world."

The cart came to a stop by the hotel. "Sorry. *Mote'as-sefam*." Joe told the driver again as they climbed down. The driver shrugged. A hundred US dollars for a short ride more than covered some repairs. For him at least, it had been a good night. The small hotel was silent and dark. Joe used the key he'd been given, and they went quietly upstairs to where Joe and Hamid had adjoining rooms. A light shone from under Hamid's door.

"I will think about it tonight," Yelena whispered. "Meanwhile, we should take turns on watch until we leave for the airport. Tell Hamid to rest first." She squeezed his hand in the dark. "And we will try not to wake him up."

Smiling, Joe found the right key and was already saying, "Hamid, you missed a real party," when he swung the door open and found him, sprawled across the bed, dead eyes staring up at them, blood from his slit throat staining the white sheets red.

❖

Joe and Yelena moved immediately and in silence, automatic responses taking over, drawing their weapons and checking the other room and the bathrooms, which were all empty. There was, sadly, no reason to check Hamid; even a glance at his body, marked with slashes and burns, twisted with breaks and bruises, revealed that he'd been tortured before he was killed. The rooms had been ransacked, but all that was missing seemed to be Hamid's phone and laptop, as well as the satchel containing Yelena's money from the earlier exchange. They packed fast, pausing only for a moment over Hamid.

"I can't just leave him," Joe said. "I'm the one who brought him here. I owe his family more than that."

"You know you can't bring him," Yelena said. "The people here are very religious. They will know what to do. They'll treat him properly, and say the prayers."

Joe nodded. "That's more than I can do." He reached out and closed his eyes. Then they shut off the light and left.

❖

Powell felt like he was in hell. He felt damned. He'd met the devil and he, or in this case, she had just sucked out his soul. And the devil's name, which we know is Legion, was, surprisingly, Vicky. He didn't know her last name and didn't want to. He already knew too much, more than he could ever forget.

After the others rushed out to investigate the break-in and explosion at the local Wildwater office, the only person remaining in the private lounge besides himself was the striking but feral young woman in the torn black jeans and black leather jacket. Powell's intention had been to say goodnight and retreat to his hotel room, but she had other plans. She stood, set down her hookah, and grabbed her small leather backpack.

"Come along, company man," she said in a posh British accent, as she led the way out. "I've another errand to run for the boys. You can observe and advise me."

At first, Powell was frankly excited. The revelation of the Zahir group's true makeup and purpose had troubled him, but he was prepared to accept a certain amount of troubling; he was, after all, in the CIA. They had a long history of making murky alliances with sordid parties in the hope of achieving sometimes dubious goals, always, of course with the country's best interests in mind. That same history begged the question of how well this strategy usually turned out—in Cambodia for instance, or Iran or Cuba—but that, to Powell, was academic. Doing nothing while the world rushed into chaos and horror wasn't an option. And maintaining some sort of James Bond–like, or even better, Superman-esque moral purity and detachment was, literally, a fairy tale. The only thing to do was play the dirty game as best as you could, and the very fact that they'd sent him here demonstrated that he, and they, had some of his superiors' tacit approval. The CIA had been mixed up in the heroin trade at least since

Vietnam. They'd armed and funded warlords and opium traders in these very same valleys back when the Soviets were their common enemy. If intervening in the dope trade now saved some American lives later, so be it. It was all part of the usual game.

But this woman was not usual. Powell followed her downstairs to where a young, dark-skinned man, fine-featured and exquisitely muscled, in jeans and a white T-shirt, was standing beside a black Range Rover. He jumped to open the rear door, shut it after them, and drove.

"I'm Mike Powell, by the way," Powell said, as they moved through the evening traffic, extending a semi-ironic hand. "I wonder if you'd like to tell me where we're going?"

"Victoria," she'd said, her eyes facing out the window, his hand ignored. "Though I prefer Vick or Vicky. We are en route to ask someone a question or two."

Powell smiled to himself. Here he was, riding in an expensive car through an exotic city, accompanying a strange woman to a mysterious rendezvous. This really was like a scene from a movie and he had to admit, to himself if never to anyone else, he was delighted. For the first time in a long time, he was excited to be a spy.

❖

They pulled up in front of a small, nondescript hotel, with a tiny, threadbare foyer rather than a proper lobby. The driver approached the old man behind the counter, speaking rapidly and drawing a wallet from his pocket. He waved some sort of credential, and then, after the cringing old man handed over a key, began to count out money, while Vicky, without further ado, took the key and proceeded quickly upstairs. Powell followed, starting to have more questions, but before he could formulate them, she stopped in front of a door, turned to him with a finger over her lips for silence, and handed him the key. Then she drew her gun.

Powell had no gun. And this wasn't the sort of meeting he'd been expecting. But there was no way to call a time-out now, so he carefully slid the key into the simple lock set in the doorknob, turned it, and stepped aside as he pushed it open. Victoria went in first.

There was only one man in the room. A dark-skinned kid in western clothes, a hoodie, jeans, and sneakers, with closely buzzed hair and a neat goatee. Powell realized he'd been in the photos Toomey had shown him. Now he was wearing headphones and staring so intently into a laptop that he only noticed them when it was too late, eyes going wide in terror, and hands rising, as Victoria put her gun in his face.

❖

Powell had seen people tortured before. He'd even participated in beatings or waterboardings. He'd put people in hoods where they couldn't see or hear, or kept them awake with blinding light or noise. He'd worked with creepy CIA interrogators and ruthless Mossad experts. He'd even seen plain old cops smack suspects around. But he'd never seen anything like Vicky, he'd never seen a true sadist go to work on a victim and take the kind of pleasure in pain that he saw that night. By the time she was done, the poor kid was praying for death, and when—after extracting all the information she could about his mission in Afghanistan, about Joe Brody and the Russian woman he knew only as Yelena and the bounty that New York gangsters had offered for the head of Zahir—she finally took his life, she did it with an expression he could only describe as joyful, smiling, eyes aglitter, as she brushed his head soothingly with one hand, telling him he was a good boy, and then releasing him from his broken body and from a world of pain by expertly slicing open his throat.

Then she turned to Powell, as thrilled as if she'd just been on a funhouse ride: her pupils were dilated, her breathing rapid. Her fair skin was flushed and the pulse beat in her own throat. She ran her tongue over her parted lips. She was, he realized, aroused, sexually, and to his horror, he realized, so was he. He was also disgusted.

"You didn't have to do that," he said. "He would have talked. He's just a kid. You didn't have to kill him."

She smiled. "Don't worry. One more dead boy doesn't add up to much in Afghanistan. There's a war going on, remember?"

"But he's not Afghani, is he?" Powell argued. "He's American. He's from Brooklyn, for God's sake."

"Well then," Vicky said with a shrug, "he should have stayed home, shouldn't he, where it's safe? Now then . . ." She casually reached between his legs, feeling where, without his own consent or control, he responded to her touch. "Are you going to continue to bore me? Because if so, you can find a cab, and I'll ask my handsome driver to escort me safely home."

That was when Powell understood that, like some character in an old folktale, he had met the devil and without even knowing it, had traded away his soul.

❖

Joe and Yelena were on the highway. When they came down from the hotel, they'd found their driver still out front, taking a smoke break after bundling up the torn fabric from his truck's awning. "Kabul?" Joe asked him, gesturing to Yelena and himself. He pulled out another hundred. "The airport in Kabul? *Beh fooroodgah?*"

The driver hesitated. It was more than four hundred fifty kilometers; it would take all night. And he already knew these foreigners were armed and in some kind of trouble. Then again, trouble was not unusual in Kandahar, nor were armed foreigners, and this one was holding out another hundred-dollar bill. He added yet another, two hundreds, making three for the night. The driver shrugged and pocketed them, then got his engine going while his passengers settled in the back, using the fabric to improvise cushions.

And so, Joe and Yelena got to take in the view after all, riding through the desert at night, watching the ancient landscape pass, the moon rise and fall, staring up from their makeshift bed at the infinite stars, which had outshone all the names they'd been given and the countless prayers they'd heard, until, alive for one more day, both finally drifted into sleep, holding each other under the silence of heaven.

PART II

PART II

11

PARKS WAS AMBIVALENT: DISGUSTED by what it must be like to live in Fusco's body, but intrigued by his mind. Here he was, on his own time, spending the night in a van he cashed in a favor to unofficially borrow, working an off-the-books stakeout on a Brooklyn cop-spot, while Parks, admittedly, was home eating veggie burgers with his wife and kids. He might have been less impressed if he knew that Fusco was twice-divorced, that his kids didn't speak to him, and that if he hadn't been here, surrounded by soda bottles, candy wrappers, McDonald's bags, and, good Lord, were those Funyuns, his night off would have been spent losing at blackjack, but still . . . he'd put in the work, followed his hunch, and now he'd called in his partner to show him what he'd found: an honest-to-God clue. Classic detective work that Parks had to respect. This was why, as he discreetly shut the van door, and crept into the spare seat, he was feeling proud to be partnered with Francis "Fartso" Fusco. Then he kicked over the piss bottle.

"Oh Jesus fuck!" Parks called out as his foot, shod in an expensive soft leather boot that he was wearing with clean, new jeans and a button down shirt on his night off, kicked over a one-liter soda bottle that he realized, with horror, was full of urine and not very well sealed. Liquid gurgled out.

"What's wrong?"

"You disgusting pig!" Parks jumped up, pointing.

"Oh shit . . ." Fusco reached down and grabbed the bottle, moving it to a more stable spot. "Watch where you step."

"Watch where I step?" Parks was furious. "Watch where you empty your diseased bladder you gross animal."

"It's a stakeout," Fusco wheedled, in the same tone Parks's kids used when they wanted to skip flossing on a camping trip.

"Look, why the hell am I even here to witness this horror?" Parks asked, keeping well away.

Fusco checked his watch. "Because the show's about to start. Sit down and quit bitching." He patted at the chair and Parks gingerly sat so that he could see out the rear windows, filled with one-way glass. "And if you're thirsty," Fusco added, "help yourself to some soda."

"Fuck you, Fartso."

Fusco chuckled, then reached for his camera as he saw something. "Okay, here it is. Look."

They were in a dusty, graffiti-covered old van, parked up the block from the projects, with a good view out the back of an entrance between two brick towers. Young lookouts steered customers around the corner and into one of the buildings while civilians came and went, minding their own business. A car approached, slowing as it reached the spot.

"Black Mercedes?"

"Exactly. It's the re-up. But never mind the dope, watch the guys." He put the camera to his face and began shooting. Parks watched as the Mercedes, black metal gleaming and chrome glaring in the streetlights, rolled to a stop at the corner. The driver, with slicked-back hair, a thick gold chain, and a lot of ink showing under his white sleeveless T-shirt, peered out his window, watching for cops. The front passenger, a big man dressed in a tracksuit, with a shaved head and also a lot of black, prison-style tattoos, stepped out as a young kid rushed up from the closest doorway. The big man grabbed a paper grocery bag and handed it to the kid, who immediately scurried back over the sidewalk and vanished into the projects. The big guy jumped back in and they rolled.

"So kid, tell me what you see," Fusco said, still snapping away, getting the plates, till the car turned the corner.

"Nothing. A typical re-up. But we already know they're selling dope here. Maybe if you followed them."

"Not in this. They'd spot us in five minutes. We need a real team to do that. But what else did your keen detective mind notice?" He showed him the screen of the digital camera and scrolled through pictures he'd just shot. "Or are you one of those jerk-off liberals who claims not to see skin color?"

Now Parks grinned. "They're white."

Fusco grinned back. "Exactly."

"White gangsters dropping off the stash at a Black cop spot, in the projects."

"Not something you see every day is it?"

"Not something you see ever."

"So the plot thickens."

"No doubt, we got ourselves a bona fide mystery here."

"See," Fusco said, patting his shoulder. "I knew you had a detective's mind behind that pretty face."

"And I always knew you had some wisdom buried in all that fat and bad breath," Parks answered, happily. "But now what? I mean, you had me at heroin. You really think this is going to make the boss fall in love with this case?"

"Nope. I'm playing the long game here. But the next move is yours. That's why I called you in."

"Oh yeah?"

Fusco peered into the interior of the projects. "I need you to go in there and cop us a bag of this bomb dope everyone is talking about."

"Why me? Cause I'm Black?" Parks asked, incredulous.

"Exactly," Fusco said. "Look at me. I'm an old fat white guy who looks like a cop, as you never get tired of pointing out."

"And I'm dressed better than you, motherfucker. You think I look like a junkie?"

Fusco shrugged. "You look like a pansy. But pansies get high too sometimes. I'm not prejudiced."

Parks shook his head. Then he noticed something. "Here we go. Give me that camera." He took the camera and started shooting, as an emaciated white boy with stringy hair, dressed in rags, came loping along. "Now that's what a junkie looks like."

The junkie passed the van and went up to the lookout, a Black teenager, who nodded him in, then waved and whistled to his cohorts.

"Yeah okay, so what?" Fusco asked.

"So you wanted dope, I'm getting you dope," Parks said. "For free." The junkie disappeared around a corner and emerged seconds later, a new spring in his step. "Let's give him a block or two before we roust him."

Two blocks later, as the junkie turned a corner, Fusco pulled up sharply, and Parks jumped out, grabbing him up. They cuffed him, patted him down, took his dope and dragged him back to the station, where to his great relief, they told him they would turn him loose in exchange for surrendering his drugs and signing a statement about when and where he'd obtained them. He eagerly agreed. The dope was in a small wax paper envelope, taped shut and stamped with a crude design: an angel, wings outstretched as though in blessing or mid-flight.

"Now what?" Parks asked as they finished the paperwork and added this newest piece of evidence to the growing file on the case they were definitely not supposed to be working.

"Now," Fusco said, with a belch as he guzzled a Diet Coke (*I mean, really*, Parks thought, *Diet? Why bother?*), "I call a guy I know at the FBI and ask a favor."

12

DONNA WAS THINKING THAT maybe she kind of liked this guy. Sort of. Gary was handsome—dark wavy hair and deep brown eyes and more built up than most guys she dated, with the big shoulders and arms of a gym rat. Smart too. According to Ari, he made big bucks in finance but had grad degrees in math and computer technology rather than the usual MBA. The dinner was lovely. Donna couldn't recall the last time she had such delicious wine, or drank so much of it, or laughed so much and felt so free, of work, stress, everything. He neither bragged about himself and his career nor made her feel weird about her own: why would a nice girl like her be wearing a gun and chasing villains? Did she have some kind of issue? Some unresolved, repressed anger she wasn't in touch with? *Not at all*, she always wanted to say, *my anger's getting in touch right now. And it has a message for you: Fuck off.*

But Gary was different. He seemed genuinely interested, impressed, even fascinated by what she did, listening raptly as she talked about her training and experience. By the time they got to dessert, she even found herself revealing how she'd been the best shot in her class at Quantico and kept up at the range weekly, about her martial arts training, and about the course in disarming bombs she'd just done—though she fudged the part about failing it. Before she knew it, the panna cotta was gone and she'd been blabbing for twenty minutes. She felt embarrassed suddenly, rambling on like this, even bragging, but when she stopped herself she realized that Gary was not bored or staring in shock, he was smiling warmly and his narrowed eyes were gleaming, the pupils enlarged. He was totally engaged, even, she ventured, aroused. Interesting. The check appeared and he reached for it and she let him. She smiled at him, her sexy smile, the one with the parted lips and melting chocolate eyes, took a last sip of wine, and, as he put his card in the binder, reached out to give his wrist a quick squeeze.

"Thank you," she said, keeping eye contact, "for a wonderful evening."

"The first of many I hope," he said; then, "It's so nice out tonight. Shall we walk?"

❖

It was just as they were having their first kiss that the fight started.

Gary had been right. It was indeed a nice night. The restaurant he'd chosen was in Tribeca, so they ended up walking by the river. They wandered along, side by side, first chatting, then in comfortable silence, as other folks drifted by on foot or wheels. The trees and grass seemed to filter and diffuse the city light and noise into something softer—the glare into moonlight, the yelling and honking into soft laughter and warm conversation. The traffic on the West Side Highway became another river, whispering behind them as they leaned on the railing, shoulders touching, hers bare and smooth, and stared across the Hudson toward New Jersey. The river was never really still of course (she was an Uptown girl, from Washington Heights, and the river was in the background of all her memories, its smell wafting over the rooftops in the summer, the biting winds chapping her hands and face in the winter), but tonight it looked polished, gleaming, a black lacquered surface held taut over the currents that stirred beneath it, like a sleeping body under a black silk sheet. That was when she felt Gary cover her hand with his, and squeeze it, and she squeezed back, like a little message passing back and forth. She felt him move, turning to her profile and she turned to face him and there they were, eye to eye, holding hands, and they leaned together, as her eyes shut, and their mouths softly met. A perfect first kiss.

"Fucking bitch!"

Lips still touching, her eyes opened, and she saw Gary's also open wide. The voice was coming from behind them.

"Where the fuck do you think you're going?"

Some big loudmouth white guy, or red guy really—he had the telltale blush and sweat of an angry drunk—in a half-unbuttoned shirt and khakis, was yelling at a woman, also white and blonde. She was dressed to go out in a red dress and heels, but her hair was falling out of its ponytail and her makeup was streaked with tears.

"I said, where the fuck do you think you're going?" The guy was close to her now, no doubt breathing booze in her face. She turned away.

"Home," she said and started walking. The drunk reached out and grabbed her hand.

"Do not," he screamed now, "do not fucking walk away while I'm talking to you!"

While this drama played out, Donna had silently flipped a mental switch and was back in work mode. She checked discreetly for her gun (ankle holster), badge (purse), and phone (back pocket), and got ready to intervene if necessary, already assessing how she would take down this big bag of guts. But her training also made her hesitate, be sure a crime was actually happening before she took action—since just being a loud drunken slob was technically still legal in New York State, unfortunately. A lot of the local economy depended on it. And that's when she realized that Gary, the civilian she'd just been kissing, was already getting involved.

"Hey," he called out, stepping away from her and toward the blowhard, blocking her view, which was bad. "Excuse me."

The drunk turned on him. "What the fuck do you want? Directions?"

"If the lady wants to go, let her go," Gary said, stepping closer, his wide back to Donna now.

"Mind your own goddamn business," the drunk said and turned after the woman again. She was walking away fast, trying to just exit the whole scene. The drunk reached for her, she pulled away, and the strap of her dress tore. She screamed. Gary grabbed the guy by the arm, yanking him back, which was no problem, because he was pretty strong and relatively sober, but also left his body wide open and with his weight all on one foot, off balance, which became a problem when, with the sudden focus and viciousness mean drunks are prone to, the guy whirled around, breaking free of Gary's grip and pulling a switchblade from his back pocket. Gary now jumped back, stumbling, and fell to the ground as the drunk came at him, blade first.

That's when Donna moved. Gary, by exacerbating the situation and also placing his body between herself and the drunk, had left her with only two real options. The first was to draw her weapon and order the suspect to freeze. The problem with that was he was really close to carving Gary open and so, if he didn't freeze, like instantly, she would most probably have to shoot him. Having a random encounter escalate from yelling and a torn dress to lethal force in ten seconds was not something she looked forward to explaining.

So she went with option two: she jumped over Gary, kicking the knife from the assailant's hand, then swiveled, her other foot coming up to catch him hard in the belly and knock the wind out of him. As he bent forward, gasping, she stepped to the side, tripping him by kicking his ankle and then using all her weight to force him down, so that he flopped onto his face, right beside Gary, who was just getting his bearings. She ground a knee into his back to keep him in place, bent his arm back to keep him in pain and under her power, and then drew her weapon, pressing the barrel against his neck so he could feel it in his alcohol-and-rage-sodden brain.

"FBI," she yelled, standing up now, gun in two hands. "Do not move, or I will shoot and kill you."

"Okay, okay," the guy yelled into the concrete against which his face was being smushed by her foot.

"You okay miss?" she asked the woman, who was watching all this in a daze, one hand holding up her dress. She nodded.

Then she turned to Gary, who was now on his knees, unharmed but stunned. "Gary, can you do me favor?" she asked. He looked up at her, his expression one of amazement. "Can you get your phone and call 911?"

❖

Actually one of the passersby who had witnessed the fight had already called 911 and some cops, who'd been patrolling the park nearby, appeared almost immediately. Donna identified herself and showed them her ID, then explained what had gone down. The older, male partner cuffed the suspect and led him off. His younger, female partner dealt with the victim, or victims if you counted Gary. But once she took down all their info, and the woman was safely in the back of a patrol car that had arrived meantime, Donna pulled her aside. She was an Asian woman in her mid-twenties with bobbed hair.

"Listen," she asked her in a low voice. "I know you have a ton of paper-work to do, but I was kind of on a date here. You mind if I come by and finish all this tomorrow?"

The officer shrugged. "I don't see why not. He's so drunk, by the time we book him and dump him in a cell he's going to be passed out anyway. You enjoy the rest of your evening." She glanced at Gary and smiled. "He is pretty cute."

"Isn't he?" Donna agreed, regarding Gary, who was back on his feet and looking fine, if still a little dazed. "Thank you so much."

"It's a pleasure," the cop said. "And Agent Zamora?" She extended her hand. "Nice work."

"Thank you, officer," she answered and shook. "I appreciate that."

Then she went over to Gary.

"Hey how you feeling? Are you okay?" she asked, her voice low and soothing, though she herself actually felt pretty great. She gave him a hug and he squeezed her back with real feeling.

"Wow," he said, "that was something. I'm a little nauseous. You were amazing back there."

She hid her grin. "I'm just glad no one got hurt. Especially you. And nausea is normal. It's the adrenaline and the shock. It will pass. But you're okay otherwise? Feeling fit?"

"Sure," he said. "Thanks to you."

"Great," Donna said, taking his hand, and leading him away from the crime scene. "Because when you were giving your statement, I couldn't help overhearing that your address is very close by."

13

"YOU ARE A NO good, lying, cheating, adulterous bastard!"

"I know . . . I'm sorry . . ."

"You betrayed me, our family, everything . . ."

"I know . . . you're right . . . I deserve to be punished . . ."

"You deserve to be beaten, whipped . . ."

"Yes! Please! Punish me . . ."

In a rage, Carol swung the belt up high and then brought it down, hard, across her husband's back. The buckle knocked hard on the side of his head.

"Ow! Damn it, Carol . . ." He grabbed his head and rubbed the spot where no doubt a small contusion would rise.

"What happened? What happened?" Carol bent over him, suddenly frantic.

"Don't use the buckle end, Jesus . . ." Gio said, pissed.

"Oh my God, I'm so sorry, I didn't even think about it."

"Obviously not."

"I'm really sorry. Do you want me to get you some ice for it?"

"No, no, it's okay. Maybe after. Just hold it the other way and try again. Double it up. Gives you better control."

"Okay. That's a good idea."

"And whip my ass, not my head for Chrissakes."

"Yes, Gio. Sorry. I'll try."

Carol tried. She doubled up the thick leather of Gio's belt, the casual one he wore with jeans, gripped it tightly in her fist, and tried to focus, but she felt like maybe the moment had passed. It had, she admitted, been all her idea. After their attempt at couple's therapy failed spectacularly, she was depressed, but one point the therapist made stuck with her: she'd asked why Gio's special needs couldn't just be incorporated into their marriage. At first, she'd been defensive—he was the betrayer, the violator, the weirdo. Why should she adapt? But then she began to think that maybe this would promote deeper understanding and communication and eventually healing. It could be a breakthrough.

So she brought it up, and though he seemed irritated and embarrassed by the idea at first, totally dismissive, she told him they had to do something, so tonight, with their son out at a movie and their daughter eating dinner at a friend's, they decided to try. It was super awkward at first, and sexually it did nothing for her, but once she got into it, Carol had to admit it was a release. Just as, according to Gio, being dominated like this was a chance to give up control, to be free of the tension and responsibility he carried all the time, so for her, it was kind of liberating to let out all the anger and outrage she'd been holding in (well, not exactly holding it all in, she did shoot that man) but which she had not been able to voice directly to Gio in this way, and with him in a posture of supplication and surrender, accepting it.

It was amazing, she thought, her mind drifting for a second, how much we therapists could learn from our supposedly "sick" patients, how people instinctively found their own solutions, their own strategies for psychic survival. Maybe this could be theirs.

She lifted the belt again, high up, and was bringing it back down with all her might, when her hand, a bit sweaty, slipped, and the end of the doubled belt snapped out of her grip, catching her in the eye. She squealed in pain and Gio jumped up from the floor, standing over her solicitously.

"What's wrong, baby? Are you all right?"

"My eye . . ."

"Let me see." He took her face gently in his hands. She blinked up at him, tears flowing from that one eye. "Looks okay," he told her.

"Guess I'm a pretty crappy dominatrix," she said.

"The worst," he told her with a smile.

"Sorry . . ."

He started laughing.

"What?"

"Stop apologizing! I mean it's hard enough to just keep a straight face . . ."

"Oh right, sorry!" And with that, hearing herself, she burst into laughter too. Then she caught her own image in the mirror: there she was in her best stockings, garters, and a bustier she hadn't worn in ages, holding a belt and laughing. And there was Gio, her husband, squeezed absurdly into her largest pair of cotton panties, which were still basically choking him. It made her laugh harder. "You can't keep a straight face?" she yelled, pointing in the mirror. "Look at you!"

He saw himself and started to howl, clutching his stomach as he laughed. He lay down on the bed and she flopped beside him. It felt so good to be laughing together like this. It had been forever. She felt all of her tension and anger, all of her grief and bottled up fear exploding out of her. She was purging, they both were, as they rocked back and forth laughing, and suddenly, as one emotion after another passed uncontrollably through her body, she felt an overwhelming lust, an animal horniness that seemed to erupt out of the wild, primitive laughter that contorted their bodies. She rolled on top of Gio, straddling him, and furiously, they began to make love.

"Mom! Dad! Anybody home?"

It was Nora, their daughter, stomping up the stairs and yelling. Both Gio and Carol froze. "Did you lock the door?" he asked.

No. In a panic she jumped up and ran for her robe. But where was it? She'd flung it somewhere when first revealing her role-play outfit.

"Hey, you guys . . ." Nora's voice rang out from the hall. Realizing he had no time, Gio just put a pillow over his groin, hiding the flowered panties and the erection that distorted them, and then clutched at the blankets as the door opened. Carol simply turned to face her daughter in a fake casual pose, hands absurdly on her hips.

"Oh my God," Nora blurted as she stormed in.

"Haven't you heard of knocking?"

"It's like 7:30," Nora replied, somewhat off topic. "Who's in bed or undressed at 7:30?" Her eyes widened. "You guys weren't doing it were you?" Her face was a mask of horror.

"Don't be silly," Carol said.

"We were just talking," Gio added, having now got most of his body under cover.

"In your underwear?" Nora asked.

"Why not?" Carol asked, sitting on the bed and crossing her legs casually. "We're comfortable with our bodies."

"Gross," Nora decided.

"Anyway," Carol said, "Why are you home at 7:30?"

Nora shrugged and sat on the bed beside her. "I don't know. Mr. and Mrs. Turner are nice but sooo boring. And they're vegan, which is totally cool and like commendable, but the food had no taste, so . . ." She shrugged. Carol rubbed her back.

"Want me to heat up some sausage and peppers?"

"Nah . . ."

"I've got an idea," Gio said, glancing at his watch. "I've got to pick your brother up at the movies. What do you say we go by the warehouse after?"

"Yes! Can we?" Nora jumped around on the bed and Gio made sure to hold his covers down.

"Sure. It's a hot night. Just let me get dressed and we'll go. We can catch the last run before it goes out."

❖

And so, Gio and Carol threw on some clothes, decidedly nonfetish, though he did grab the belt and loop it through his jeans, picked up Jason, and headed to the warehouse where his family's fleet of Italian Ice and Soft Serve Frozen Custard trucks were headquartered. In a tradition that had begun when his kids were small and that, he realized suddenly, they would soon be too old for, he requisitioned one of the trucks, giving the driver a paid night off, and drove the route himself, with his kids handling sales, scooping ices, dispensing ice cream into cones, and squirting whipped cream and syrup onto sundaes, under Carol's supervision.

The truth is, that ice cream truck song can turn you into a psycho after a while, but otherwise it was pretty perfect, steering the old truck along the road, pulling in at beach parking lots and boardwalks, in the square white box with Caprisi's painted on the side in red cursive. He'd done this with his grandfather, who liked to personally take a truck out now and then and give out free ices to the neighborhood kids, who ran to line up when they saw his kindly face behind the wheel. Good memories. He'd kept up the tradition with his own kids as a lesson in hard work and in the family's working-class immigrant roots. Though he'd decided to spare them the lesson he'd learned another time when, on a different run late at night, with his father and grandpa, he'd had to dig in the freezer under the cartons of ice cream bars and retrieve the plastic bag which contained two hands, both rights, which they'd saved when disposing of a couple of rivals months before and used to plant misleading prints at a crime scene. The experience almost turned him off toasted almond bars, his favorite.

His family were complicated people. No wonder he had issues. But for now, for tonight, those issues seemed far away, and he felt calm, happy, and grateful, feeling the ocean breeze touch his skin, the sultry night air mingling with the frozen drafts from the ices, hearing his children laugh and the happy shouts of the customers ordering, and beyond that the sound of the ocean, crashing softly on the sand. He parked facing the beach, so he could hear the kids while watching the water, a dark wave under a dark sky, lit here and there by the moonlight, ceaselessly appearing and disappearing on the shore. While she talked to their kids, Carol reached over and stroked his head affectionately from behind, playing absently with his hair. Unknowingly, she kept touching the place where she'd hit him, which was now bruised and tender. But he didn't say anything or let himself flinch: the perfect joy he felt was more than worth the pain.

14

THAT NIGHT, WHEN HIS brother died and returned from the dead, Liam was more grateful than ever to have Josh there with him.

They'd first met working for Joe, on his last caper: Liam as the youngest of the Madigan brothers, up-and-coming Irish hoodlums, Josh, freshly arrived from Israel, as a new member of Rebbe Stone's crew. When Josh was shot, Liam had transported him to safety, and the unspoken attraction between them had bloomed. They'd been a couple ever since.

This day had started early, with a hijacking: a load of digital cameras, Chinese-made cellphones and fancy vacuum cleaners, the kind you strapped to your back. A guy Liam's middle brother, Sean, drank with had tipped him off to it. He worked in the port of Newark and for a fee would let Sean know when the truck was leaving. The tricky part was how to take it: though more than one gangster had vanished into the surrounding swamplands, there was no way to guarantee that the truck would be heading down an empty road at a conveniently quiet hour. In fact, as it turned out, it was early morning, when the whole area was bustling.

Luckily, Liam had come up with a clever scheme and Josh, with his army training, had been able to implement it quite easily. Brandishing a fake manifest for a missing shipment, they walked onto the shipping company's yard before the truck ever even left to pick up the container. They found the right vehicle and, while Liam stood lookout, Josh had crept under a wheel well and attached a small explosive device with a tiny radio transmitter.

Next, they got back in their own truck, a tow they had borrowed from their pal Cash, a highly successful car thief from the Chinese section of Flushing, who used a large junkyard called Reliable Scrap as his cover to strip and move stolen cars. They'd painted over the Reliable logo and switched the plates. Then, while the semi they had rigged was inside the port being loaded, they waited, drinking coffee and watching day break over the reed-filled wetlands, looking at the sun glint on the silver towers of chemical plants and burn through the wavering fumes while planes from Newark Liberty Airport passed, leaving jet trails overhead, listening to the songs of whatever strange birds could thrive in this wasteland and still find something to sing about.

"There it is." Josh pointed.

"I've got it," Liam said. "Let's give him a little more rope."

He put the tow truck in gear and slowly rolled out, while Josh got ready with the radio control. They let the truck get about fifty yards ahead on the road that led to the interstate, and then, as it cruised along between fenced-in waste ground, Josh pressed the button and the truck's front right tire blew. The whole rig shimmied, as the driver fought to steady it. Air brakes huffing, he slowly pulled over. That's when Liam drove up, honking, and stopped alongside.

"Hey," he yelled to the driver. "I just saw that blowout. You need some help?"

"Good timing!" the driver called back.

"Let's pull off over here," Liam told him, and guided him slowly onto a broken asphalt side road that ran into the high weeds, screened from the traffic.

"Now then," he said in his bright Irish accent, as he and Josh got out and met the driver as he climbed down from the cab. "Let's see if we can be of some assistance."

❖

A few hours later, Liam and Josh drove the truck into a South Williamsburg warehouse owned by Menachem "Rebbe" Stone. It looked like any of the other Hasidic-owned warehouses that stretched along the street: a brick hulk with a fenced-in yard, weeds sprouting in the cracked concrete. A pimply young man in a wide-brimmed black hat, white shirt, and long coat, with a sparse reddish beard, pulled the gate back, and they backed in, parking with the rear of the truck at the loading dock. Another thickset fellow looked down from the roof and nodded at Josh as he climbed from the cab. He too was in black, and heavily black-bearded, as were most of the men here. A few younger men had short, trimmed beards like Josh and were in regular clothes—jeans and polo shirts or button-downs—but still with yarmulkes and tzitzit, the knotted threads, dangling from their undershirts. They opened the truck and quickly began unloading, passing cartons to a forklift that was likewise operated by a skullcap-wearing bearded man in a white shirt and black trousers—his missing jacket the only accommodation made to the oppressive heat inside the dusty warehouse. Josh sat on the truck fender and lit a cigarette and Liam sat beside him and watched: for a lad from Belfast this was exotic indeed. Then a stout, older man with a stringy gray beard that hung like a tie over his shirt passed by, muttering something that Liam couldn't understand but that included the words "goyim" and "fagalah," at least one of which he could guess at. He let it pass, figuring it wasn't his place to intrude, but Josh felt different. As the mutterer passed, Josh reached out and grabbed his beard, hard, yanking him down so that he was bent nearly double and groaning. "What did you say?"

"Nothing, nothing . . ." the mutterer mumbled now, struggling but too scared to raise a hand.

Josh began singeing off strands of his beard with his lit cigarette. The man squealed and squirmed. Liam smelled burnt hair.

"You know what I did in the army don't you? Do you know how many ways they taught me to hurt you just with this cigarette? Do you?" He yanked harder.

"No . . ." the man shook his head, still straining as the beard pulled at his flesh.

"I'm not sure either. Let's count and see . . ."

"Yoshua!" a voice with an old-world lilt to it reached them from inside. Josh looked up. It was Rebbe, who had emerged from an inner office. "Stop fooling around and come here."

Josh let go immediately and the man gasped, stumbling back as if released from a tether, and then scurried off. Josh handed his cigarette to Liam, who took a drag then stomped it out, grinning.

Rebbe put his arm around Josh and led him off to a corner. "*Luzzem,*" he said. "Don't bother with that *meskite*. He's a nobody. A nudnik. Not worth your time."

"Yes sir," Josh said.

"Your family back home, they're okay?"

"Yes, everyone is fine, thank you."

"And the job, no troubles?"

"No. Smooth."

"Good work, boychick." He squeezed his cheek, hard enough to leave an impression, then called to another tough-looking man in a long black beard and black suit. "Shlomo, get a couple cameras and one of those vacuums and put them in my trunk."

❖

In no time the goods were unpacked and distributed to camera and electronics stores run by Orthodox Jews as well as other dealers further down the pipeline: Black-owned appliance stores in Bed-Stuy, an Italian hardware shop in South Slope, even a discount place along Atlantic run by two Palestinian brothers. This was New York. Meanwhile, Liam and Josh disposed of the truck, leaving it under the BQE, had dinner at a Mexican place, and then circled back to pick up their share of the proceeds. It was a nice score, not at all bad for a day's work, and Liam knew Sean would be pleased with how things turned out. He'd been complaining about money and had called a couple times to ask about the dough, so Liam was surprised when he finally called to say he had it and Sean didn't even pick up. But then again, that was Sean. Jack, the eldest, was the grown-up, steady brother. He was married already with a second kid on the way, and the kind of tough guy who had no trouble using a gun but would rather try his fists first. The scar tissue on his knuckles testified how often that was sufficient.

Sean was the wild middle brother. The one who got into scrapes as a kid, dropped out of school, who got drunk and fought now, and who, Liam suspected, might have developed a taste for other substances as well. And Liam? He was the baby, the spoiled one, pretty and clever, who got top grades at school but still preferred the life of crime to the life of the mind, and found, when the time came, that violence, when necessary, caused him no bother at all. They'd been brought over from Ireland by Pat White, a distant relative and then the boss of what was left of the Westies, the Irish mob who once ran Hell's Kitchen and still ran a share of bookmaking, extortion, robbery, political influence, and murder. But Pat had sold them out, and the Madigan brothers, with an assist from Gio, were in charge now.

"Mind if we swing by me brother's?" Liam asked Josh now. "I know that eejit too well. Even if he's dead drunk, he'll wake up yowling for his money like a babe for a tit."

"Of course not," Josh said, squeezing his hand. "It's a nice night for a drive."

So they cruised up the West Side to the rent-controlled walk-up that Sean had taken over when the former occupant, a one-time bank robber turned FBI snitch named Harry Harrigan, had been disposed of. Now the Madigans controlled the building, along with most of Pat's other assets, like the parking lot where they left Josh's Volvo convertible.

They buzzed. No answer. Was he drinking at a local bar? If so, he would have answered his phone. A neighbor came out, opening the street door, and they climbed the stairs and rang. Still nothing, but he could hear the TV.

"Come on, wake up, you moron!" Liam yelled, banging the door. It swung open. At this both men froze. Liam reached down and pulled the revolver he had in his ankle holster. He glanced at Josh, who nodded, and carefully stepped in. The lights were on. The TV was playing. Sean was alone, spread on the couch. His face was white. His lips were blue. His eyes were staring up at nothing. Drool curled from his slack mouth. And a needle dangled from his arm.

❖

It was Josh who knew what to do. He'd had medic training and it kicked into action. He immediately checked Sean's pulse and breathing and then got him on the floor where he performed CPR. Liam watched, frozen in horror.

"Liam! You need to focus," Josh yelled at him, as he pumped Sean's chest. He tossed him his keys. "There's a bag in the trunk of my car."

Snapping out of it, Liam caught the keys and sprinted frantically down to the lot, running right past the attendant to fetch the small first aid kit, and came back, breathing hard. By then Liam had him breathing shallowly, alive, if just barely. He tore the kit open, found the Naloxone, and injected Sean. Instantly, he was back, rejoining the living with a scream that made it seem more like a nightmare than a joy, perhaps similar to the scream he'd uttered at birth.

Later, after they'd made sure Sean was all right, and he'd cried and apologized, and Liam had cried and cursed him out and then forgiven him, and they'd gotten Sean to bed (though not before he remembered to ask for his money), they shut the bedroom door, and Liam put his arms around Josh, his eyes still shined with tears. "You saved his life. I don't know what to say. I was useless. Thank God for you, Josh."

Josh smiled back. "You saved mine too, remember? And risked your own for me."

Liam shook his head. "That's shite. We were partners on a job and you were just wounded. This is different. He was dead. Dead."

They gripped each other then, tight, and Liam, as if sharing a secret, whispered to him: "I love you."

Josh whispered back, "I love you too."

Before they left, Liam picked up the syringe and broke it with an expression of disgust. He threw it in the trash with the tarnished spoon Sean had used to cook the shot that had nearly killed him. That *had* killed him, Liam corrected himself, since his brother had died before Josh brought him back. And there on the coffee table beside it was a torn little envelope, coated with a trace of bitter powder, and stamped with the image of an angel, wings up, as though still poised to fly off with your soul.

15

USING ALL HER TRAINING and stealth, Special Agent Donna Zamora carefully turned the doorknob and entered the premises at 7:15 A.M. Taking care not to alert the occupants, she crept into the living room, silently shutting the door behind her.

"Morning, hon. Have a fun date?"

Donna froze in shock, regarding her accoster with horror. She did not, however, draw her weapon, as much as she might have liked to. Watching her from the kitchen doorway, with a cup of coffee in her hand (it was Donna's favorite mug, the one her daughter Larissa had painted for her with rainbows and suns), was Gladys Brody, Joe Brody's grandmother and, to Donna's extreme discomfort, her own mother's new best friend.

"Gladys! Why are you here?"

"I'm waiting for your mom. We're going to AC."

"Oh right. I forgot. Did you hurt yourself?" Gladys had a therapeutic cuff Velcroed around her lower arm.

"It's for the slots hon."

Her mom came in, from Donna's bedroom, where she slept when staying with Larissa overnight, already dressed and carrying a bag. She broke into a warm smile and came to kiss Donna. "Good morning, *mija*. You had a fun night I guess?"

Mortified, Donna glared at her. "If stakeouts are fun. I told you I was working."

Her mom shrugged.

"Gladys . . ." Donna changed the subject. "How's Joe these days?"

"He's working a lot too, like you. Out of town business trip."

"Really? I didn't know bouncers went on business trips. Did he have to go throw a drunk out of a strip club in another state?"

Now her daughter came out rubbing her eyes, looking heartrendingly adorable as she did every morning, in her pink Disney nightgown, her long hair floating like a cloud around her. "Mommy!"

She ran over for a hug. "I dreamed about pancakes."

"You did?"

She nodded. "Daddy came to take me and brought a bear."

"Sorry sweetheart. Daddy's at work, I told you. He had to go away. But I'm sure he will bring you something when he gets home. Now come on, let's make you some pancakes."

As she led her daughter toward the kitchen, she wondered if what she'd just told her was true. Her ex, Mike Powell, was CIA and, as far Donna knew, had suddenly been reassigned to a top-secret mission overseas. Abusive and controlling during their brief marriage, he had become obsessive, almost a stalker, during their divorce. But he had always been a loving and dutiful father, visiting Larissa often, attending school events, paying his share. Recently, however, he had revealed himself to be a real creep, the kind of creep who thought that undermining her career might somehow paradoxically win her back or teach her a lesson. The kind of creep who thought that rejecting him was something she needed to be punished for. This made dealing with him and arrangements for their daughter go from tense and awkward to full-on toxic, so when he suddenly announced that he was leaving and that where and why and how long were all classified, she was, frankly, relieved. But she couldn't explain that to Larissa. So she kept saying that Daddy was away, and would be back soon, though she fervently hoped that was not true.

She poured orange juice and handed it to Larissa, then poured coffee for herself.

"Donna!" her mom called out. "The van is here. We're going." Larissa ran over. "Come kiss Grandma goodbye. And give Aunty Gladys a hug."

Aunt Gladys? Donna sighed. She had to admit that she was fond of Gladys herself, and her friendship did seem to be brightening her Mom's life up a bit, though when she referred to Gladys as her "partner in crime," did she get that Gladys was an actual criminal with a rap sheet longer than most of the suspects Donna investigated at the FBI? It was one more complication in her already too mixed-up life. Speaking of which, there was Gary to think about now as well. She'd crept out while he slept, having told him in advance she needed to get home and relieve her mom from babysitting duty.

As if on cue, Donna's phone buzzed. It was a text from Andy. *So???*

Frowning, she texted back: *It was fun. Nice guy.*

Just fun? She felt Andy jumping down her throat from over the phone. *When Gary never called Ari for the post game briefing we thought—score!*

Um . . . she considered, then typed. *It got a little complicated. I will tell you later.*

I'm meeting Blaze for a beer later. Come and tell me all about it!

Blaze was Deputy Federal Marshal Blaze Logan. She and Donna had worked together, ending up in a couple of tight spots, and had become pals. Then, as an openly gay federal agent, Blaze had found she had a lot to talk to Andy about as well.

Great, she texted with one hand as Larissa, having distributed her kisses and hugs, took the other, chirping "Mommy! Pancakes!" *Just pick someplace quiet where we can actually talk please.*

Done, he answered, though Donna didn't believe it. She went in to start the batter, and while her daughter loudly requested bananas, and her mom and "Aunt Gladys" left to party in Atlantic City with their van full of old biddies, she found herself wondering, where in hell did Joe really go on his supposed business trip, and why?

❖

Joe woke up from a nightmare as they landed. Or rather, Yelena woke him.

"Joe," she said, "Joe," shaking his shoulder lightly and speaking softly into his ears.

"Huh?" His eyes popped opened. "What?"

"You're scaring these people."

He sat up and looked around. A flight attendant was crouching over them and, across the aisle, a woman a sweat suit with a blanket wrapped around her was staring in alarm. The heads of two small children, a boy and girl, peeked over the seats in front of him, their mustachioed hipster father hovering with a look of stern disapproval from behind his cool glasses.

"Sir . . ." The flight attendant leaned in, scolding him. "You can't yell and use foul language. You're disturbing the other passengers."

"Sorry," Joe said, nodding and rubbing his eyes. He'd thrown his own blanket on the floor and his Rilke paperback lay twisted on his lap, as though he'd tried to strangle it.

"Now please return your seat to the upright position," the flight attendant said. "We will be landing soon."

She moved on. The lady across the aisle kept glaring. "Disgusting," she muttered to no one.

"Sit down," the dad told his kids, then told Joe, "Chill out, all right, dude? You're scaring my kids." They didn't look scared, as it happened. They were grinning.

"You sit down and put your belt on," Yelena told him, flatly. She looked him the eye. "Imagine how upset they'll be if you get injured. Badly."

His eyes widened at her. Then he sniffed and sat back down.

"What was I saying?" Joe asked Yelena.

"Nothing. Just yelling fuck and shit like usual."

"Oh . . . sorry . . ." He saw the kids still peeking at him, now with their eyes pressed to the cracks between the seats. He winked at them. They giggled. Then he turned to look past Yelena and out the window. They were descending rapidly. The engines roared. Moisture streaked the glass like tears as they tore through the atmosphere. Mist clung to the plane's wing in shreds. New York City was emerging from the clouds. He was home.

❖

Toomey heard the ruckus coming from where Joe and Yelena were sitting. He happened to be up, stretching his legs, before returning to his seat in business class. Those two, of course, were back in coach. That figured. Like Joe, he was sure, Toomey had flown many times in military planes, choppers, and private CIA jets, but on commercial flights, which soldiers took more than most civilians realized, coming or going from leave, reporting to new posts, they were strictly consigned to the cheap seats. He'd never sat up-front with the rich folk until he became a consultant. That was one of the things he'd point out to Joe if he were trying to recruit him. Which he would be happy to do if destiny hadn't set them on different paths, paths that were now converging.

That's how Rick Toomey thought of himself: a man of destiny, a warrior, like a samurai or a knight. He fought for a cause and lived by a code, and he would, he fully expected, die by it one day as well. But not today, so why not fly business class, put his feet up, sip champagne and flirt with the flight attendants? He'd earned it. That was the problem with society today, no code, no purpose and it was as bad, or worse, among the rich up here than among the poor. The poor had an excuse. The rich had an obligation. But now only poor boys fought wars, those who couldn't buy a way out, or those who saw the military as their one way out. Like Joe, who, he knew from his research, had been offered a choice of jail or army: either way he'd serve. Say what you like about the aristocrats in the olden days, however much wealth and luxury they had, they still sent their sons to die for king and country. It was what they were bred to do. Now that was over. The military too had its own aristocracy, and that was where Toomey was bred. His father had been a colonel in the Marines and then an instructor at West Point. Choosing to go into the Special Forces meant Toomey himself would never rise to top brass, be a general, and sit around the Pentagon drinking coffee, but that was okay, the old man understood. Like Joe they were born to serve.

That's why Toomey was on this flight to New York. With Felix and Heather, their New York people, out of action, Toomey decided to shepherd this shipment himself, and be there to meet it when it came through. It was too important. Especially this one. It was carrying his destiny. And though he worked with Richards and his cronies at Wildwater (worked *for* them they would say, since they were paying for this plane ride and the steak he had consumed) he didn't respect them or trust them; they shared his values but not his code. They were rich but not aristocratic warriors, not samurai or knights.

That was why when Toomey saw Joe and Yelena in action, he smiled, and when they took down the chopper he was in, he laughed: it was a laugh of recognition. He had known immediately what Joe was: a warrior like him. And it seemed especially fitting when he learned that it was Joe Brody and his Russian cohort Yelena Noylaskya who had taken out Felix and Heather. He had found a worthy adversary, someone it would be a pleasure, an honor, to fight with, whether as comrade or foe. And if it had to be foe, so be it. That's why, when he heard Joe yelling and realized what was up, he grinned. Now he knew his opponent's weakness as well as his strengths. He was wounded. It was just in a place no one could see.

Yelena too was a warrior, and Nikolai had spotted her right away; he knew her, apparently from back when. All he would say was that she was well-known in the underworld in both Moscow and the Russian parts of New York, that she had worked for them but now seemed to be working for herself, and that she could be handled.

"Handled by who?" Richards had barked at Nikolai, still smarting, his ass and ego both bruised by that bumpy ride in the chopper. "You?"

"Why not?" Nikolai had smiled slyly, in that spook way—CIA or SVR, they were all the same. "I was her handler after all. I trained her."

But now, it seemed she'd gone feral again, snapped her leash, and Nikolai was spreading the word to his people. She was on the endangered list with Joe. Toomey chuckled at the thought, that while they snoozed uncomfortably in their cramped, hot, stinky seats, they were in fact in the cattle car that would take them to slaughter. The flight attendant, who was helping return his seat to its upright position, thought the grin was for her. She smiled back, bright white teeth, bright blue eyes, and glistening blonde hair.

"You seem happy to be in New York. Business or pleasure?"

"Both, I hope," he said, giving her his dimple. "What about you?"

He was just her type, he knew: clean-cut, handsome, strong-jawed, with a military bearing even in his navy blazer and khakis. Plus sitting in the expensive seats. A catch. She made a pout and let her Southern drawl ooze out, sweet as syrup. "I love New York but gosh it's so big. I never know what to do or where to go for fun."

"Sounds like you had the wrong tour guide."

She giggled. "Maybe so. Can you recommend one?"

He chuckled. "As it happens, I might be available. But I'm all out of brochures."

Now she gave him a real laugh and a real smile. "Then why don't I just give you my number?"

❖

The problem with Toomey, Victoria thought to herself as she watched him from afar, is that he takes all the fun out of being a sociopath. Just look at him, towing his luggage from customs into the chaos of JFK airport, frowning at the common rabble everywhere, hunting for the driver with his name on a sign. So uptight. So stiff and constipated. Always droning on about duty and destiny and all that boring bullshit.

When she found herself, as a kid, in a therapist's office, hearing herself described as "an extreme antisocial personality with poor impulse control, aggressive and narcissistic tendencies, and no capacity for empathy, guilt or remorse," she thought, *Hooray! Sounds like a right party for me! I can do anything I want!* And that was what she did, anything she wanted, or anything they paid her enough to do.

Victoria Dahlia Amalia St. Smythe was the last rotten fruit to drop from an exhausted, shriveling branch of a once proud and aristocratic family tree. She never met her father but was told he'd gotten married to get his hands on his trust fund, despite being exclusively interested in men and drugs. He had duly died of his pleasures. Her mother had been the schizophrenic descendent of an ancient, inbred, and now totally broke family, married off to get a piece of that same trust fund, and, for most of Victoria's life, had been locked up in a very posh loony bin. The cost was about that of a luxury spa, and the fund having been rather diminished by Daddy's bad habits, there wasn't much left for little Vicky. At first, old family friends arranged for her to get a scholarship to the public school her forebears attended, but paying for Cambridge was out of the question. Plus there was that girl whose eye she'd put out in a badminton dispute, whose family were still, unlike hers, quite rich. So Vicky was cut loose, and for a couple of years she floated from the squats, where she hung with the punks, to the high-end clubs, where she seduced the sons (and daughters) of her family's former friends, who were terrified she might carry on the family trade and trick one of them into marrying her. Finally, a black car picked her up and whisked her off to a fancy office, where she was asked if she might not like to serve her Queen and country.

"Whatever do you mean? Run for parliament?" she had asked. Not quite. They had something more off the books in mind. Like a spy.

A spy? She considered it. At first it seemed even crazier than running for parliament, all that code-talking and stuffing microfilm up her bottom, but then she thought, *Actually, when you think about it, James Bond is really a sociopath, isn't he?*

But that wasn't quite what they meant either. MI-6 was definitely not looking for her type. They meant really off the books. So she was sent to a school that suited her much better than Cambridge would have, and learned martial arts, weaponry, shooting. She was even sent abroad for courses in torture. Then she was sent to take care of a prostitute who was blackmailing a very wealthy and powerful man. Next an Irish nationalist, once a big man in the IRA, who was considered to be a threat to the new order of things. Since she was strictly freelance, with employers who didn't want to know or see her between jobs, she quickly found there were other people eager to pay very well for her services. Soon she was one of the world's most highly paid assassins. That was how she met Richards, as a referral through some of the powerful parties who were backing him, and he had more or less put her on retainer. Which was why she was here, in New York, keeping an eye on things, and ready to solve the problems these more gung ho, know-it-all macho types were prone to create. Essentially, that was what she did: rich, powerful people, mostly men, made disastrous mistakes and she cleaned up the mess. And she loved it.

That's why, unlike Toomey, she'd put a bit of effort in, and met this flight in a long black wig, trendy oversized glasses, a Yankees cap, a tight sports bra–like top with a padded bra under it, tight jeans, and sparkly high-top sneakers, looking, she thought, just like some trashy American here to meet her dumb boyfriend or pathetic little relatives. She even had her nails done in multiple colors and a little glass jewel in her belly button. While Toomey found his driver, barked at him for not holding the sign that said "Toomie" high enough, and marched off, still wheeling his own bag, she was enjoying herself. And that's why, when she saw Joe and Yelena come by next, carrying only a backpack and a small gym bag, less luggage than Vicky used for makeup and wigs, Yelena with a cigarette in her mouth ready to go, and Joe, unshaven with his hair sticking up and talking on a flip phone, Victoria actually stepped up and in her best New Yorkese (her sponsors had sent her to acting classes too, and she could do a number of accents) asked: "Excuse me, Miss. Can I get a cigarette?"

Yelena turned to her quickly, as though startled, then gave her a stare so piercing that Vicky somehow expected her to see through her disguise to the truth. Thoughtfully, she plucked the cigarette from her lips and handed it over.

"Thanks babe," Vicky said, winking as she placed it in her mouth.

"The cabs are this way," Joe said, striding off, and Yelena turned and followed.

Now, Vicky thought to herself, those two look like fun.

16

WHEN HE GOT HOME from the airport, Joe was relieved to find his grandmother out. He had Yelena with him, and while the old time grifter in Gladys recognized and appreciated a fellow pro, and Yelena had even brought vodka and caviar to their first meeting, the grandma side of her nature suspected that this girl wasn't a healthy long-term romantic choice for her Joey. So he was happy to find the note she left—*gone to AC*—on top of the fresh laundry she left on his bed. He also dipped into the stash of money she kept squirreled away from Joe's previous earnings, which he mostly passed on to her. They showered, changed—Joe took a clean black T-shirt and jeans to replace the ones he'd been wearing—and stopped in at his favorite Thai place for a big lunch before getting on the train to Bed-Stuy to break the news about Hamid to Juno.

❖

Juno took it hard.

"What the fuck did I do?" he asked Joe, distraught, as they sat on the couch in the studio/bedroom/high-tech lab he ran from his Mom's basement. His eyes were full of tears. "I knew that kid for years, man. Now I got him killed."

"You didn't get him killed, Juno," Joe told him now. "This is on me. I was supposed to take care of him."

Yelena shook her head at them both. "Are you two finished?"

"Sorry?" Juno asked, in shock.

"You are both wrong. Neither one of you is responsible."

"So who then?" Juno asked her.

"I don't know. And I didn't really know Hamid, like you did. But we worked together and I liked him. So I am going to find out who did this, and I am going to make them pay. If you are done wallowing in guilt and self-pity, then you can help me."

Joe frowned at her. She had a point, but she could have used a lighter touch with Juno, whom he still thought of as a kid. But Juno burst into a laugh.

"Damn I missed you, Yelena. I've never seen such an ice-cold bitch with so much heart."

She smiled. "Thank you, Juno. I missed you too."

Juno sniffed. "Okay, then, let's do this. What's the play? Get strapped and go hunting? I'm ready to get heavy on this one."

A tech wizard, Juno was definitely on the brains side of the business, and Joe wanted to keep him there. He didn't need another Hamid on his conscience. "For now I want you to start going through all the data we managed to send back before the bomb in the safe blew." He handed him the camera as well. "I know we lost the phone and the laptop, but maybe there's something in what we do have. Some clue."

"Clue to what?" Juno reached for his own laptop and pulled up the files. "Yeah Hamid sent me a ton of stuff, thousands of pages. All of it total bullshit: shipping records, boring ass emails about defective canteens, bills of lading, invoices. I never though being a terrorist dope smuggler could be so lame."

"But they are smuggling it in, somehow. That's the point. And you're the only one I can think of who can figure it out."

"Aye aye, captain," Juno said, saluting. "I'm on it."

"Thanks," Joe said, clapping his shoulder as he stood. He pulled out a thick roll of cash. "You need any dough right now?"

"Nah this is for Hamid."

Joe peeled off some bills for Yelena. "Get whatever you need. And maybe look around for a safe place to stay."

"What's the matter Joe?" she asked as she folded the bills and tucked them into her pocket. "Grandma won't let you have a girl sleep over?"

Juno snickered, then waved at Joe. "Hey I understand. My ma's strict too. She's at church right now. Baptist."

Joe smiled. "She's kidding. My grandmother's in Atlantic City right now. Blackjack."

❖

Joe went to the YMCA to meet Frank. He was midway through his own Sunday ritual, working out and then taking a steam. Frank Jones was a painter of some repute, a Black man in his seventies, who had been a Marine in Vietnam. He'd met Joe at the VA hospital, when Joe had just kicked dope and was feeling crazy, and Frank had invited him up to the studio to talk. He too had managed his nightmares and flashbacks with alcohol, drugs, and denial, and then found a more workable long-term solution: he painted them. Frank hadn't known Joe very long, but he gathered he wasn't the type to phone up just to say hi. So when Joe had called from the airport, asking if he could come by later, Frank told him where he'd be.

"So where you been?" Frank asked as the men sweated, side by side, wrapped in towels, Frank sprawled comfortably with his back against the wall, Joe sitting up, hands on his knees. Around them the room filled with hissing steam. Droplets ran down the walls. A few old men sat across from them, vague sweating lumps in the thick clouds, and a big guy, with a towel over his head, was bent forward as though concentrated intently on sweating as hard as he could.

"Afghanistan," Joe told him.

"Shit, man, what were you doing there?" He waved it off. "Never mind. I don't want to know."

The big man got up, poured a bucket of water over his naked flesh and left.

Joe waited for the door to shut. "I lost someone. A team member. I guess I feel responsible. Anyway, since then the nightmares are back."

"Yeah well what did you expect? You see me hopping over to Da Nang for a weekend?" He laughed. "Who am I kidding, I haven't even been to Brooklyn in years. Speaking of war zones, I hear Bed-Stuy is full of white hipsters now. Is that true?"

"Pretty much."

"Damn." He shook his head, then sat up and faced Joe. "Look, you woke up your devils right? I checked in a dictionary once, when I couldn't sleep. Nightmare comes from Old English. Mare was an evil goblin, like a demonic bitch that attacks in your sleep. Now you stirred her up. That's all. Let it pass."

Joe glanced at him. "Did yours?"

He shrugged. "Well I ain't going to lie to you. It's like this old scar . . ." He fingered a small knobby patch on his thigh that Joe could see was once a bullet wound. "Used to be so noticeable I was embarrassed to wear shorts. And of course it hurt like a motherfucker when it was healing. Now I forget it's there. Sometimes in the cold I feel it. And heat helps. The steam. That's one good thing about getting old, all your scars fade. Course by then, a bunch of new shit has gone wrong. But then the VA pays for it. So you're all set."

"You're not really reassuring me here."

"My point is . . ." Frank pointed to a couple of Joe's own scars, a white line that ran along his calf, a small patch of discolored skin above his elbow. "These looked worse, I'm sure, back when you got them. Twenty years from now they'll be hard to find. Same with the inner scars. The ones on your soul. Are you the same as before? No. But it fades." His eyes narrowed as he located the star-shaped brand on Joe's chest, up above the ribs on the left, off to the side of his heart: "Not that though. That's fresh."

"Yeah," Joe said, touching it reflexively, then sitting up so it was less noticeable.

"And it's not a scar is it?"

"No," Joe admitted. "Not exactly."

"Yeah well, it's like they told you when you were a kid. Nightmares aren't real, man. They can't hurt you." He nodded at the star again, or in its direction. "It's reality that will kill your ass."

An old man got up, naked, and began doing a series of squatting exercises in the steam. "Talk about nightmares." Frank muttered as he stood, tightening his towel around his waist. "I'm going to grab a cold shower and a hot steak. You coming?"

❖

Yelena went back to Brighton Beach with mixed feelings. She was definitely looking forward to the food. And where else was a Russian girl supposed to fade into the background? On the other hand, it was where her enemies were strongest. So her plan was to get what she needed, weapons, ID, and delicacies, and then go back to Queens to stay with Joe and Gladys, at least for the night. First stop was the Grandmaster Chess Shop, run by an old-timer everyone called Grandmaster, though no one had ever seen him play chess. He sold weapons from the basement, and she immediately felt better as she strapped a 9 mm Beretta to her ankle and stashed another, smaller .22 in a clip-on holster in the small of her back. Finally, she slid a knife in a sheath into her boot.

Then she went to see Vova. Vova was another old man, who didn't even speak English but who made a good living preparing expert false IDs in a cluttered apartment overlooking the boardwalk, every inch stuffed with books, Cyrillic newspapers, and huge antique pieces of furniture, armoires, leather armchairs, and heavy, padded couches. The first time Joe and Yelena worked together and found themselves on the run, they had hidden at Vova's and he'd given them IDs and credit cards on credit. This time Yelena had cash. But it didn't matter, Vova always greeted her the same way: he removed the ever-present cigarette from the corner of his mouth to give her a hug and kisses on each cheek, followed by a toast with vodka.

"Where's your boyfriend?" he asked her in Russian. "You know, the American from last time, who said he didn't drink." Vova chuckled at the memory of what he assumed was an absurd joke.

"Joe? He's not my boyfriend." She told him what she needed—a complete set: passport, cards, the works—and he took some digital photos of her against a white wall. Then she went shopping while he worked. She went to Gourmanoff's and spent the rest of Joe's cash on caviar, blinis, duck, blintzes, and a host of other treats, then returned to Vova's and laid the spread out after clearing the heaps of newspaper, books, and overflowing ashtrays from his table. He provided vodka, tea, and—by the time she was done with desert—her documents, which he brought out to the terrace, where she'd gone to escape the smoke, which even by her standards was getting to be too much.

"*Krasivaya!*" she'd declared, thanking him with a kiss on each cheek. He blushed happily and lit another smoke. He was proud of his work. He had used a real blank Russian passport, obtained God knows where, forged a few entry stamps for authenticity, and threw in an international driver's license and a couple of credit cards as well.

She tucked them away in a pocket and turned to gaze out at the beach. It was a warm night and the boardwalk was buzzing. Everywhere below them Russians talked, ate, laughed, smoked, drank, and ate more. They filled the cafés and bars, the restaurants and the benches. Kids ran back and forth over the planks of the boardwalk and, in the moonlight, you could see teenagers clustered together on blankets on the beach. Off to the right, the lights of Coney Island pulsated as the rides spun and the roller coaster snaked back and forth. Snatches of conversation reached them with bits of random music. And behind it all, the ocean came and went, a constant whisper, forever arriving on the beach and forever falling away, back to the edge of the horizon, where the world ended and infinite darkness began.

"You understand, Vova, they are looking for me?"

"Who?"

"Bratva."

He smiled, showing his hodgepodge of metal Russian and gold American dental work, with some fake white teeth and a few real ones, stained the color of smoke and tea. "Let them look. One trouble they have with us old-timers from the Soviet days? We've already been tortured by the best. I learned how to lie in Siberia." Then he pulled out a key. "You need a place to stay too, Lenushka?"

She smiled sweetly. "Thank you but not tonight. I'm going to Joe's."

"Ha! The one who's not your boyfriend?"

Yelena shrugged. "He's a friend. Anyway, his grandmother is there too."

"All together in one apartment? Like back in Moscow! What kind of Russian girl are you? Can't you find a rich American with a good job?"

"He has a job," Yelena told him.

"What job?"

She grinned. "He throws drunks out of a strip club."

"What?" Vova shouted. "And he doesn't even drink!" He laughed so hard the cigarette fell out of his mouth and dropped like a falling star to the beach.

❖

Donna ordered a round. By the time her mom got home from AC, ahead by thirty bucks after eight hours of work but happy so whatever, and they got Larissa to go back to bed, and then Donna got downtown to the, of course, roaring gay bar, Andy and Blaze had had a few. Donna fetched them refills and a beer for herself.

"Okay, so spill it," Andy said.

"Let her at least taste her beer first," Blaze put in, calming Andy with a steady hand and leaning back in her chair. "Then spill it."

"What is this," Donna asked, "good cop, drunk cop?"

Blaze shrugged. "You left for your dinner date at seven P.M. and came home, according to witnesses, at seven A.M. The evidence speaks for itself."

"Fine. I got laid," Donna said, toasting them and then taking a long drink. "About time too."

"Hallelujah," Andy said. "My husband is a genius. He's definitely getting laid tonight too."

"How was it?" Blaze asked, clinking bottles with her.

"Nice."

"Uh-oh," Blaze said. "Nice isn't good."

"Nice sucks," Andy said.

"No. Nice is fine," Donna said. "It's nice."

"What was wrong?" Andy asked. "Too fast? He was probably overeager."

"No . . . no . . . I mean he was eager all right . . ."

"Too small, right?" Blaze asked with a knowing nod.

"Now why would you say that?" Andy asked her. "You don't even like dick."

"No but if I did I'd sure want a lot of it."

"Well I can't argue there," Andy said and they toasted again.

Donna laughed and shook her head. "I'm glad you two agree. Just leave me out of it."

"Okay, let's rewind. How was dinner?"

So Donna told them the story, the lovely dinner, the warm vibes, the after-dessert walk, the perfect first kiss, and then the drunken asshole and the fight, followed swiftly by Agent Zamora's intervention and arrest.

"Well that explains it," Andy said. "You threw his game off. Civilians aren't used to seeing that shit."

"You emasculated him," Blaze said. "You practically cut his balls off."

"I had no choice," Donna said. "That drunk was about to cut something off for real. And for the record his balls were very much intact. Actually . . ." She shrugged. "The whole thing turned him on."

Andy nodded. "I've seen you kicking guys' asses and it is pretty hot."

"Works for me," Blaze agreed. "She's great in a bar brawl."

"So you went back to his place . . ." he prompted.

"And everything was fine. More than fine. Terrific."

"He like tore your clothes off and . . ." Blaze suggested.

"What? No. Jesus. He, you know . . ."

"What?" Blaze asked, clearly a little buzzed now.

"He went downtown, right?" Andy said. Donna nodded and he frowned at Blaze. "What kind of dyke are you anyway?"

Blaze shrugged. "So okay, he's a man who knows his place. So far so good."

Donna sighed. "Fine. So yeah that was great. And then when we were, you know . . ."

"Fucking?" Andy suggested.

"Right, thank you Andy, when we were fucking, that was great too, but he kept talking about seeing me take down that dude, how powerful it was and all that."

"Uh-oh," Blaze said.

"And then after," Donna said, plunging ahead, relieved now that she was getting it all out there, "he asked if I'd like, reenact that with him, like role-play arresting him, and even asked me to take out my gun, you know, without the clip, and . . ."

"Fuck him with it?" Blaze suggested.

"Make him suck it."

"I knew it." Blaze slapped the table. "The guy's a bottom."

"Total bottom," Andy said, shaking his head. "I should have known. Typical Ari. When he said the guy liked strong women I thought that meant he liked Meryl Streep movies. Not shrimping."

"What's shrimping?" Donna asked.

"Ask him and see," Blaze said. "But finish the story first. What did you do?"

"I said I was tired and we went to sleep. Then as soon as it was light I snuck out."

"Typical top." Blaze shrugged. "So what's the problem? Sounds like a pretty good date."

"I didn't say problem," Donna phumphered. "I just. I mean, no judgment. It's just not my thing."

"You're not looking for a bottom bitch," Andy said.

Donna wrinkled her nose. "Not specifically, no."

Andy nodded. "Okay, fine, you want a top. That figures."

"Sure," Blaze agreed. "Someone who makes *you* kneel and suck the gun."

"No." Donna set her beer down with a thud, like a gavel. "I mean, are those the only choices?"

"Then what do you want?" Andy waved beseechingly.

"I want an equal! I want passion and love! And great sex! With a partner!"

Andy and Blaze looked at each other. Andy shrugged.

"Straight girls . . ." he said.

"Don't get me started," Blaze told him.

It took a couple more beers and an order each of calamari and fried mozzarella sticks before, having finally exhausted the topic of Donna's sex life, Andy remembered the call.

"Oh right, I almost forgot," he said, when the subject of Monday being the next morning came up, "I got a call from the NYPD. Fusco. He's Major Case Squad."

"I know the name, sort of," Donna said. "He was on that last thing, the smugglers."

"Exactly. He still is, sort of. He has some evidence, a sample of this new heroin going around and he wants our lab to test it. He's hypothesizing that it's from the same supplier as your Zahir."

"What?" Donna sat up and focused. "Really? What did you say?"

"I said send it over. I asked the lab to compare it to the dope you so bravely obtained last time. And Janet said she'll run it tomorrow."

"And you waited till now to tell me this? This is major news. This is a case breaking wide open. Possibly. Maybe."

Andy smiled. "Honey, cases possibly maybe break open all the time. Now you getting laid, that is major news."

❖

When Joe got back to the apartment, his grandmother was in her chair, counting her winnings.

"Joey!" she beamed at him. "I knew this was going to be a lucky day."

He kissed her and sat on the couch. "How'd you do in AC?"

"How do you think?" She fanned out her money. "How about you?"

"Crapped out," he said. "Let's not talk about it."

"Fine."

"But I did want to tell you. You remember Yelena?"

"The Russian."

"She needs a place to stay."

"When?"

"Tonight. She will be here any minute. Sorry."

"What sorry? I've always encouraged you to bring home friends."

"I get the feeling you maybe don't like this friend so much."

"I didn't like that hyper one from third grade, what was his name?"

"Danny."

"Who broke the lamp. Melinda is very nice."

"Yelena."

"I'm just not sure I like how you end up when you play with her."

Joe smiled. "Fair enough. Though I remember you drank your share of that vodka. But she's not coming over to play. That's what I have to tell you. She's on the run."

"Law?"

"Maybe. And Russian mafia. She's out getting guns and a new passport now. But it could get dangerous."

Gladys frowned at her grandson. She folded the money and tucked it into her bra. "Then what are we talking about? Of course she can stay."

17

"IT'S A MATCH."

Donna and Andy were in the lab, which was down the corridor from her cramped little tip-line office, getting the results on the heroin sample from Janet, the forensic scientist.

"It's the same supplier?" Donna asked, feeling the tingle of excitement pass up her spine: her hunch was becoming a legit case. "It's Zahir?"

"Give me a break," Janet said. "I'm good but I'm not that good. I can't tell you the name of who bagged it up. It's from the same region. SWA."

"Southwest Asia."

"Right. The chemical composition is completely different from samples that come from, say, Mexico or South America. I can even say it probably came from the same country. Afghanistan. One big difference, though. That original sample, from the crime scene? That was like ninety-nine point nine percent pure. This is street ready." She peered through her glasses at the report on her table. "Contains lactose and cornstarch." She shrugged. "But it's still really good. Just about fifty percent pure. If good is the word I want." She pulled her vape pen from a pocket of her lab coat and peeked down the hall before taking a hit and blowing it at the air vent.

"Good dope means a lot of junkies dying out there," Donna said.

"Dying happy," Andy added.

"Cynic," Donna told him, then to Janet: "You, however, are better than good. You're the best. Lunch is on me."

"K-town?" she asked. "Turntable Chicken Jazz?" Janet was Korean-American and while she usually ate every day in the choose-your-own-salad place, she'd been craving spicy fried chicken. She was also a serious jazz nerd.

"I was thinking of the choose-your-own-salad place, to be honest," Donna told her.

"That chicken is really good," Andy noted. "And I have the car."

"Come on, vinyl and spicy chicken, it's like two of my biggest fetishes in one," Janet said.

"Fine," Donna said. "Now I'm craving it too. Okay, here's the plan. I pay. You order," she told Janet. "You drive," she told Andy. "And if we run late, we use the siren."

But they never made it out to lunch at all that day because when Donna stopped by her office to grab her bag, there was a message from Zahir.

❖

If you're looking for a nice spot to grab lunch and catch up with an old friend, not many would choose a strip club, but it suited Gio and Joe: it was quiet (they didn't open till six when the after-work crowd started drifting in), private (it was Gio's place), and oddly cozy without the noise and sweat and lust in the air; a cool, dark place for two old pals to split two heroes—one sausage and broccoli rabe, one prosciutto and mozzarella—washed down with Manhattan Special Coffee Soda. Gio had picked the order up on the way.

"So you think this Wildwater corporation is behind it? Why?"

Joe shrugged. "Why not? Soldiers smuggled dope back from Vietnam. So in our new corporate age, it's the contractors. Even the crime is outsourced."

"Sure. My dad knew some of those soldiers. From Frank Lucas's crew. But you're saying the top people in the corporation are in on it."

"I'm not saying anything yet. But someone in that office was connected to Zahir. Someone who also just happened to have a combat-ready squad and an attack chopper to send after us. That's no grunt with a balloon full of dope up his ass."

"Okay, but we still don't know how they get the shit into the country," Gio said. "Or who is moving it for them here. Or why a bunch of American businessmen, corrupt or not, would be financing terrorists. What I do know is what's up our own ass. Our heads."

"You're right," Joe said. "Sorry, Gio. If you want someone else to handle it . . ."

"Who the fuck else is there?" Gio waved it off. Then he sat back in the booth and took a breath. "No. I'm sorry. I wasn't mad at you. It's just . . . let's just say, I'm pretty comfortable outside the law. Sex, drugs, gambling, corruption, even violence when necessary . . . that's my . . . what's the word?"

"Career?"

"Métier is the word I was looking for but okay, fine. My meat. I admit it. But this other shit: religion, politics, nationalism, or whatever. People blowing up each other's children. That I have no fucking idea what to do with." He smiled sheepishly. "Except send you. Which isn't fair. So I'm sorry."

Joe nodded once and drank his soda. Gio took a breath and went on: "Also." He shrugged. "I guess things have been a little tense at home too. You know, since Paul left us."

"A little?"

"A lot."

"I can imagine."

"I mean, we're working on it, Carol and me. Trying . . . things. But it's like . . ." He held up two sandwich halves, one sausage, one prosciutto. "My life had these two sides, dark and light. And now they're getting mixed up."

Joe grinned at the sandwiches. "But they're both still pork."

Gio laughed. "Well I don't have a vegan side, I admit."

"Actually," Joe said. "I do know what you mean. That trip kicked my dark shit up too. It ain't easy pushing it back down."

"I guess that's also my fault. And I'm sorry about the kid Hamid. But at least you're back, safe, in the light." He waved his sandwich at the gloomy bar where topless women would soon be laboring for horny stiffs. "Then again, there are those who would say our light side is pretty dark too."

"I guess it's relative. Different cuts of pork," Joe said and went back to his lunch. Gio's phone rang. He set his food down and wiped his mouth and hands with a napkin.

"It's my cop," he said, and answered. "Yeah? Interesting. Thanks." He shut the phone. "So . . . that new brand of dope on the scene? The one undercutting Maria and the rest?"

"Yeah?" Joe asked.

Gio reached for his sandwich. "Fusco had the FBI test a sample and it matches the shit you took off of that smuggler you whacked. So, Zahir or Wildwater or whoever the fuck they are, one thing we do know?" He took a big bite of sausage and bitter greens and chewed. "They're here."

18

Wɪʟᴅᴡᴀᴛᴇʀ's ᴄᴏʀᴘᴏʀᴀᴛᴇ ʜᴇᴀᴅǫᴜᴀʀᴛᴇʀs ᴡᴇʀᴇ in Midtown, in a glass and steel tower that was somehow both grandiose and anonymous, like a red carpet full of supposed celebrities you've never heard of. Robert Richards, the founder and CEO, was holding a press conference that day, and since it was open to the public, Joe decided this was as good a place as any to begin. Dressed like a tourist, in cargo shorts, Yankees cap, sunglasses, and a T-shirt that said "NYC Fuhgeddaboutit," and with a camera slung around his neck, he passed through a metal detector, then entered the building's giant atrium, where chairs and a small stage had been set up. The floor was of the same textured stone as the walls, which soared above them. Beyond a row of desks, elevators and escalators rose. There were cameras, lights, and a fair-sized crowd comprising bored reporters, enthusiastic employees, and a mix of people interested in politics and business and those just looking for an air-conditioned place to sit and eat lunch. Joe took a seat in back.

On his chair, on every chair, was a brochure with a picture of Bob Richards climbing aboard a helicopter much like the one Joe had shot down. He was giving the camera a thumbs-up, his coiffure suspiciously blond and still in the wind. It also contained a bio—Harvard business school, investment banks and hedge funds, then NSA for fifteen years—before he branched out into the war-biz to build an empire of his own. The following pages showed Wildwater's vast operations around the world, though the office in Kandahar was overlooked. Then music played over the loudspeakers, a screen lowered over the back of the stage, and they ran a short movie that showed everything Joe had just read in the brochure. Next the host was introduced, a shill who would ply Richards with planned questions, and Joe didn't bother to catch his name. He introduced Richards, giving a more personal, warm version of the same bio yet again. By the time the great man stepped on stage, Joe was ready to nod off from boredom. It was about five minutes into the "conversation" that his ears finally perked up.

"Look, government has its function but that is being redefined in our time. You want a package to get there quick? Do you mail it? No way. You send it via FedEx or UPS. Funny things is, in their own way, these are paramilitary-style operations, with their attitude toward logistics and chain-of-command. They learned from the military. If you want technological innovation, do you go to the government or to Apple? If you want to buy something and get it on time at the best price? Amazon. Again and again, in every sector, we've proven that professionals are the way to go. Medicine. Communications. Even space exploration. Everything except the most important thing. Security."

"Well that's an interesting point, Bob," the interviewer opined, lamely trying to come off as if he hadn't heard it yet. "But can you explain just what you mean?"

"It's simple, Jim. Today we have a vast, bloated, inefficient military, with politicians at the top, who are amateurs after all, career bureaucrats in the middle management, and volunteer soldiers on the front lines. Now, no one honors those troops more than I do."

"Of course, Bob. One hundred percent."

"But do we really want our sons—and increasingly our daughters—out there? Let me ask you a question, Jim. Would you send your kids off to catch a burglar or put out a fire in the neighborhood?"

"No way, Bob. That's crazy. I'd call the police. Or the fire department."

"Exactly, Jim. That makes good common sense. Call the professionals. Well all I'm saying is, it's time for us to leave war to the professionals. By outsourcing operations to an organization like Wildwater, our nation will be safer, while also saving lives and money long-term."

"Sounds great to me, Bob? What do you folks think?"

The front half of the audience, full of employees who'd been shepherded down from the offices upstairs, cheered on cue. The rest clapped half-heartedly. A few continued eating sandwiches and looking at their phones. As reporters started calling out questions, the less-invested audience members began to disperse, and Joe stood as well. He wandered the lobby, taking photos: there was no reason to hide it here, though he was more interested in the security cameras and elevator banks than most tourists.

The press conference ended and there was applause, though less than at the opening, as people were eager to make their way out, and Joe joined the flow, chewing gum and following the line to the revolving doors. That's when he found Yelena.

She too was in disguise, and, considering how hard it had been for him to spot her ponytail among the others, she'd done an excellent job of camouflage. She wore an oversized pink sweatshirt that said PINK on it (which he thought was just naming the color until she explained it was a brand), black running shorts, pink running shoes, gigantic dark sunglasses, and a black wig under a Mets cap. They'd arrived separately, and had agreed to rendezvous in the park, so he just walked by without a second glance. Then he got her text: *Saw someone. Following. Tell you later.*

❖

Upstairs, in the executive conference room, Mike Powell sat staring at a row of screens.

As a career government employee, he wasn't sure how he felt about Richards's speech as it played on one, but he was certainly impressed with the technology deployed on the others, particularly the facial recognition software.

"Freeze four," he told the tech, who hit a key. "Close in on that guy, the one in the ball cap. No, the other one in the other ball cap. There . . ." he turned to Jensen, Richards's right hand, who was overseeing operations from here while the boss was on stage. "That's Joe Brody."

"Track him," Jensen told the tech, and the camera zoomed in tight, following Brody as he took photos of the building. Jensen turned to Powell. "I take it he's not an architecture buff."

"Nope. He's casing the joint." He watched as Brody, smiling innocuously, flowed with the crowd, through the revolving door, out of the building and off camera.

The door opened and Richards came in, without his sidekick and media handlers, but still with makeup on his face. Jensen jumped up.

"Terrific job, sir."

"Thanks. Damn those hot lights." He grabbed a water from the table and sat in the biggest, best seat at the table. "I think it went well. Crowd could have been bigger but Fox and CNN both said they'd cover it. The *Times* asked a question. What did you think?" he asked Powell.

"About the *Times*, I have no opinion. But I am interested in why Brody was there." He pointed at the frozen image of Joe on the screen. "This means he's connected Zahir to Wildwater."

"Because of the office? There was no evidence there for him to find. It's a dead end. The question is what led him there in the first place."

"And what he is looking for here," Powell told him. "Money? Dope?"

Richards laughed. "Not in this building. We piss test the janitors for Chrissakes." He finished his water. "Zahir's business is conducted completely outside of Wildwater. By very capable professionals."

"Toomey," Powell said.

"And as we speak he is moving to make that operation more secure, and more profitable, than it has ever been. As for unwanted guests like your friend Brody . . ." He shrugged. "We have a professional to handle that too."

Vicky, Powell thought, but did not say the name, as if it were a curse word. He just nodded.

"I will retest all our security, sir, but I don't see us as vulnerable to intrusion," Jensen said.

"Don't worry," Richards said, wiping his forehead with a hankie and taking off a swatch of orange. "We run a tight ship here, Powell. And a clean one."

"I hope so," Powell said, still dwelling on Brody in his getup. "Just remember, Joe Brody is a thief first and foremost. So ask yourself, what did he come to steal?"

❖

"Zahir is coming, America. You have been warned." Donna paused, letting the ominous email sink in. She was in the office of her boss, Tom, reading him a printout while Andy and Janet listened.

"That it?" Tom asked, taking a big bite of his sandwich. It was ham and Swiss on rye, with mustard and a pickle, as Andy and Janet both noted. They were hungry.

"The dots connect," Donna said.

"What dots?" he asked, mouth full.

"Thanks to Janet's tests and the info we have from NYPD, we now know that Zahir has moved from smuggling heroin to distribution at the street level. We also know that the funds are flowing back to terror operations overseas. And now we have a threat, their first operation on US soil."

"Goddamn it, I got mustard on my tie," Tom said. He grabbed a napkin and wiped while he talked. "You're right, Donna. It could be terrorists slinging dope in Brooklyn. It could also just be a crew of normal, patriotic All-American heroin dealers who scored some Afghani dope. And that money could be going to terror . . . according to a CIA snitch who promptly disappeared and an old Irish mobster who ended up in a Jersey swamp. You think Zahir did him too?"

"No, sir."

"Me neither. And as for this threat." He crumpled his napkin up and tossed it toward the trash. "Add it to my pile. You know how many we get a day?"

"Yes, sir. I read them all. We get a lot."

"Exactly. Plus there's what Homeland gets. And the CIA." He lifted his pickle. "Here's what I think. So far this still smells local to me. So give it to the locals. Andy, who's the detective who sent the sample?"

"Fusco."

"Give it to Fusco. Let him chase the shadow if he wants. Now then, can I finish my lunch?"

On the way out, Andy checked his watch. "So much for chicken and jazz," he told Donna. "You owe us."

19

THAT NIGHT, THEY HIT Alonzo first. Along a quiet street, in a sleepy part of Flatbush, a van pulled up to a plain two-bedroom house on a block of plain houses. Perhaps a sharp-eyed neighbor had noticed the security cameras or that the weedy lawn was a bit overgrown. Or maybe the mailman had realized that, aside from junk addressed to Our Neighbor and the electric bill, there was no mail. Black SUVs slid in and out of the automatic garage, lights burned dimly behind the always-drawn shades, but there was no trouble, and no noise, aside from faint music, if anyone had bothered to listen. Though he had never set foot in it, and his name appeared nowhere on any paperwork, this house belonged to Alonzo.

Alonzo controlled a big piece of the organized crime in the African-American neighborhoods of Brooklyn, a managerial feat that involved overseeing and disciplining his own unruly troops and protecting his territory and assets from others while also building his legitimate business profile, which included restaurants, clubs, car services, janitorial and landscaping companies, as well as a music label and a boxing gym.

This house was special though: it was the main stash. This was the central warehouse for Alonzo's dope and coke operation, though it had been years since he himself was in the same room with the drugs, or any mind-altering substance, beyond a cigar or a cognac. Or the edibles and vapes that his younger brother, Reggie, insisted were the future but that sounded like some silly bougie shit to Alonzo.

The dope came from Little Maria, a Dominican drug overlord—or was it overlady?—who had maintained and expanded her late husband's empire, mainly in Spanish Harlem and the Bronx. His coke came from Colombians and Mexicans in Queens. The product was brought to this stash house, where it was cut, bagged up, and then sent out to the network of lieutenants who in turn ran the crews that sold the drugs from corners and alleys, storefronts, project courtyards, and tenement buildings all over Brooklyn. Of course there were always other players, independent crews who set up shop on an unclaimed corner or vacant lot, smalltime dealers who peddled drugs from their apartments via word of mouth or in the back rooms at clubs (not his clubs of course), and even established figures who held their own small patch of territory; but none of that really bothered Alonzo. As long as he had the best real estate and the best product, he sold all the shit he could possibly get his hands on and made more money than he could count. And it was his supply connections as well as his relationships with Anton the Russian, Rebbe, Gio, Uncle Chen from Flushing, and others, that allowed day-to-day business to proceed smoothly and with minimal friction. Until now.

Now a dirty gray van was cruising up to his stash house and parking in front of the house next door, under a tree, out of range of the cameras. Inside the van were four men, all in black fatigues and wool caps that pulled down to ski-masks. Silently, in the darkness, two slipped out and crept, crouched low, across the neighbor's lawn and through a missing board in their fence to take cover against the aluminum-siding-covered wall of the house. Lights glowed in the windows and hip-hop played within the walls. One man quickly jimmied the dark basement window while the other kept watch, then slid in. Except for some crap left by the previous tenant, it was empty. He waved his partner in.

They put on their night vision goggles and drew their AR-15 rifles. Then they proceeded carefully up the stairs. The basement door was only locked with the doorknob mechanism, which the first man easily popped with the jimmy. They could hear the music and voices inside. The second man whispered into his headset.

"Set."

The answer from the van came: "Stand by."

Another man got out of the van, also armed but carrying a small hatchet as well. He jogged across the lawn, keeping low in the shadows, but less worried about the cameras now, because as soon as he reached the main power cable that ran up the wall of the house, he swung the hatchet hard, twice, and the cameras died, along with the lights and music. He then dropped the hatchet, which was tied to his belt, and raised his own rifle while moving to guard the door. The van now rolled forward, to stop right in front of the house and block the view.

"Go," the voice said over the earpiece. "Proceed right about three meters to the kitchen. Three persons."

The two men in the basement went through the door, into the main house.

"What the fuck? This a blackout?" they heard a rough male voice bark, though the gunmen saw a hallway in the underwater green of their goggles.

"You got any candles?" another voice asked.

"Why would I have candles, motherfucker? You got a birthday cake?"

The gunmen entered the kitchen, where they saw three men sitting around the kitchen table, weighing dope on a digital scale and bagging it up for sale. They opened fire.

"Two more in the room to your right," the voice from the van said. The driver was watching the feed from an infrared camera, mounted on top of the van, that registered the body heat in the house. Two other men had been on the couch, watching TV. Both drew their own weapons when they heard the gunfire, but in the darkness, one ran right into the gunmen coming from the kitchen and was shot dead. The other, a local kid named Reverb, ran for the door. He opened it to find a black-clad man in a black mask pointing a rifle at him.

"Oh shit," he said, raising his hands.

The man pushed him in as the two other gunmen joined him, having cleared the house. They lowered their goggles and flicked on their headlamps as the third man shut the door.

"Don't shoot, officer," Reverb said, dropping his pistol. "I'm unarmed."

"I am not officer, not anymore," the gunman told him, speaking in some kind of accent, German or Russian or French or something.

"You ain't? I thought you all were SWAT or some shit. With those outfits." He nodded toward the kitchen. "Well then the stash is in there. Take it."

"We don't want your crap shit," the guy said in his awkward English. He waved his gun at Reverb and the flashlights bounced off his face. "Your phone. Quick."

"Y'all want my phone?" Reverb shrugged. It was a new iPhone, but he'd bought it stolen anyway. He held it out. "Here."

"Call your boss. Tell him what happened here."

Now Reverb was really confused. "You want me to call *my* boss and tell him you just boosted his stash, is that right?"

They nodded, headlamps bobbing. Reverb shrugged. "All right, it's your funeral."

He called. "Hey it's Reverb," he told whomever answered. "I need to get word to the big man. We just been hit . . . just now, motherfucker! They still here, like chilling in the living room . . ." He was about to go on, but his call was cut short, with a bullet through the chest. He fell dead. The gunman stepped on the phone, crushing it under his boot, then set a small incendiary device while the other two moved quickly through the house, dousing the sparse furnishings with accelerant. They left the dope on the table.

"Ready," the gunman said over his mic to the van driver, who responded: "Clear. Come on out." He slid the door of the van open and put it in drive, watching the still-quiet street.

They left, shutting the door behind them and hurrying to the van. The fire started immediately but they were long gone before the neighbors noticed that the house was engulfed in flames.

❖

Alonzo was watching a western. It was *Tombstone*, one of his favorites, and he was in his recliner, sharing a bowl of gourmet salted caramel popcorn with Barry, his bodyguard and go-to man, since his kids preferred *Star Wars* movies and what they now called the Marvel Universe—it was just regular superhero comics in his day—and his wife didn't like movies with violence. So they were all upstairs. He was in his family room, in his house, in a leafy, calm, prosperous, and very safe suburban New Jersey town. He had a dentist for his left-side neighbor, and a tax attorney across the street, though with his corner lot on high ground, his house was nicer than either. They were just getting to the best part of the movie, the famous shoot out at the OK Corral, when the phone rang. The work cell.

"Fuck. Hit pause, will you?" Alonzo asked Barry, who had a handful of popcorn. Frowning, he stuffed it in his mouth and chewed while he searched for the remote among the cushions on the couch. "Yeah?" Alonzo said into the phone, and then barked at Barry, "Pause, I said! We're missing it."

"Immooking . . ." Barry mumbled with his mouth full, checking on the floor.

Then, as the voice on the phone spoke, Alonzo held a hand up for silence. "You fucking with me? Really? All right you better get down there and see. I'm rolling now."

He closed the phone and turned to Barry. It was his brother, Reggie, on the phone. The guy who ran their dope operation had called to say that a kid named Reverb had called him and said the main stash got hit.

"Who would rob you LZ?" Barry asked, finally swallowing. "What are they, crazy or stupid?"

"I don't know," Alonzo said, standing up. He was in track pants, T-shirt, and slippers. "I plan to ask them that just before I kill them." He found his car keys on the coffee table and tossed them to Barry. "Get the car out. I gotta tell my wife I'm leaving and find my shoes."

So Barry wiped his hands, pulled on his sneakers, and headed out to the driveway, where Alonzo's BMW was sleeping, absently picking popcorn from his teeth. Alonzo ran upstairs, rapped on the bedroom door, and called to his wife, who was reading in bed. She nodded, used to this, the way a doctor's wife is. He kicked off his slippers and stepped into sandals, then came back downstairs. No one paid any more attention to the gunfight that was now raging on screen. He was out the door and halfway down the drive when Barry started the engine and the bomb went off.

❖

Next they hit Little Maria's stop and cop spot. She was the Queen of Washington Heights and this operation was the jewel in her crown, a smooth-running operation catering to the commuters and the suburban trade who rolled back and forth across the George Washington Bridge, as well as cars coming down from the Bronx or up the West Side Highway. Basically it was like a drive-thru. You cruised slow down the block and a kid ran out to your car window, checking you out and asking what you wanted. You told him and he took your money and signaled to his boss. Then another kid ran up with your product and dashed off. You drove away happy. Meantime the runner was at the next car in line. It ran like this, 24/7, with a major rush before and after work, at lunchtime, and all night long on the weekends, except for when the cops came by. Every so often, they'd set up a checkpoint and start pulling over cars, especially those with Jersey plates. This scared the customers but they always flocked back soon enough—like pigeons that had been scattered from the roof. Other times, the cops tried to seal off the street, pulling up and blocking the corners, then sweeping up everyone in between. But the only ones holding drugs or money on the street were a few juveniles with a few bags each—the runners, who knew nothing useful anyway, except that if they just kept their mouths shut they'd be sprung in no time. The crew bosses, who sent them back and forth, were clean and the guards who watched over everything would ditch their pieces in the sewer drain and bolt. The stash and the cash were held in one of the buildings and moved periodically—a basement, a hallway, an apartment where they paid the tenant for use of a window—but the cops never made it that far before all valuables were removed. The small amount Maria lost to the law was just a cost of business, like spillage.

That's what the lookouts were for. Stationed on key corners, stoops, and rooftops, they watched for cops, at which point they'd call out *"Llegada!"* (Coming!) and the whole operation would simply fold, disappearing into the woodwork. So, for anyone who wanted to do more than collect a few minor arrests and fill a quota, the first thing to do was take them down. The gray van pulled up, and two men got out. Both wore tracksuits, the camo of this neighborhood, and as they passed the lookout on the corner, one said, "Hey kid," and distracted him, while the other hit him with a taser. He fell and they dragged him between two parked cars to sleep it off. Then they broke into the basement door of the building and ran up the four flights. The lookout on the roof never saw a thing; he was too busy looking out, down the street, for police. The first man through the roof exit shot him, a silencer on his pistol, then took off his pack and set up in his spot. His partner got on his earpiece mic.

"Ready."

The van driver pulled out now and came down the block, stopping in the center, as though he were a customer looking to cop. The runner came up to his window. "What you need? C and D, man. Gran Diablo is on the money . . ."

"What I need, bro," the driver, a muscled-up white man with a blond ponytail, "is for you to tell your boss to close up shop. We're taking over this block. White Angel is moving in."

"Huh?" The white dude had an accent, sounded like a surfer or something, but that wasn't the problem; he was just talking nonsense. But he'd parked so that he blocked the whole street so, after a couple of tries, the runner ran back and told Miguel, who was overseeing the crew from the doorway of a nearby building. Miguel sighed, cursing in Spanish, and grabbed his piece from where it was hidden in a disused planter, stuffing it into his jeans, then went down to see what this joker wanted.

"Sup?" he asked the white guy in the van.

"You the boss here?"

"Why?" Miguel asked. "You ask to see the manager or some shit?" He lifted his oversized Yankees jersey and showed the gun. "You want to talk to the complaint department?"

The white guy smiled. "No complaint, bro. Just letting you know, White Angel moves in here tomorrow. Giving you the chance to pack up and go in peace."

"Right," Miguel said. "Thanks for sharing. Now why don't you peace the fuck out man, before I lose my sense of humor." He half drew the pistol, finger on the trigger.

The white guy raised a hand. "No problem. Take care." He pulled away. Miguel spat in the gutter, shaking his head, totally unaware of the sniper's scope trained on his forehead. One shot took the top of his head right off.

Panic erupted, but there was no time to hide. In thirty seconds the key members of Maria's top crew lay dead or wounded on the ground. And the shooters were on their way out. They got back in the van and headed for another building nearby. Maria's own.

❖

Maria's apartment, on the top floor of a building with a river view, was almost impregnable. She had another, fancier house in the Bronx, but this was home, where she had lived her whole life, and everyone in this building knew her. The kids sitting on the stoop worked for her and kept an eye on the whole block. The super's wife, who kept her ground-floor apartment door ajar, noted whoever got on the elevator. Even the guy who sold flavored ices on the corner would have alerted someone if a van full of armed men had pulled up. So they went in the one way she didn't think to worry about: from above.

First the van stopped one street over, on the other side of the block from her building. Four men slipped out, and unobtrusively broke into a basement door of a building. They took the elevator from the basement to the top floor and left via the roof exit. No one bothered to notice. They crossed over to the roof of Maria's building and, with a crowbar, busted open the door to her roof. Then they came down the stairs. Using a battering ram like the cops did, they rushed down the hall, broke her door open, and entered.

Their attack was flawless, and should have succeeded without a hitch, except for two things: First, Maria happened to be in her bedroom with her boyfriend, Paco. If she had been in the living room, watching TV with her Tia, she would have been killed instantly. As it was, they shot Tia, an old woman and the one truly harmless person on the premises. Her eyesight was too poor to shoot anyone, and the strongest substance she handled was hot sauce. But the commotion drew the attention of Maria, Paco, and Duque, who was the second problem.

Duque was Maria's dog, a ferocious pit bull. As soon as the action started in the living room, before Maria and Paco could even get out of bed, Duque was up and running. He tore into the living room, leapt onto the man who had just shot Tia, and sank his fangs into his groin. The man howled in pain, dropping his gun and struggling with the dog, who locked his jaw and ground in deep, chewing his way through fabric and skin. The gunman beside him was distracted, trying to get a clear shot at the damn dog, and the other two had gone to check the kitchen and the office. This gave Maria and Paco a chance. Paco was twenty-two and pretty, with a neat goatee, dark, deep eyes, a lean muscled chest and gold cross, wearing only his boxers. He was a good lover and a fine companion for Maria, who was at least twenty years his senior, but he was not the smartest guy in town. He grabbed his Tech 9 from under the bed and rushed out. Seeing the dog ripping into the man's groin, and distracted by the screaming, he yelled "Duque!" and shot the guy Duque was attacking, just as the second gunman shot him and the dog both.

This, however, gave Maria time to think. Dressed in her red bra and panties, she pulled her Uzi from where it was always strapped under her bed, peeked carefully through the doorway, and opened fire, killing the man who'd killed her dog and boyfriend. By now the two other gunmen were coming back into the room and she shot the one pushing through the kitchen door first, blowing him back into the kitchen and sending the door swinging after him. But the one coming from the office got her.

He had dropped to the carpet when he saw Maria shooting, so when she swung back to pick him off, she missed, riddling the wall with bullets. From his prone position, he fired back at Maria under the dining table, shattering her shinbone. She stumbled back, firing wildly just to keep him pinned down, then threw her door shut and hit the button on the wall. By the time the gunman got up and across the apartment, he was too late. She was in her panic room and the metal door had bolted, essentially sealing her in a vault. The gunman tried to gain entry with the crowbar, but by now the whole building was in an uproar, so he fled the way he came. The last thing Maria had the presence of mind to do before she went into shock was text the super's wife the code to her panic room door. That way the EMTs were able to gain entry.

❖

Joe was watching *Jeopardy* with Gladys when Yelena came home. She knew the routine—no talking during Alex Trebek—so she went to the kitchen and got her vodka from the freezer, then sat on the couch and waited for a break, while Gladys called out the answers, getting an impressive number right. "What is phosphorous? Who was Bertolt Brecht? Where is the Suez Canal?"

At the commercial, Yelena followed Joe into the kitchen while he got himself a seltzer from the fridge.

"So," he asked quietly. "Who'd you see?"

"Someone I hoped never to see again. Unless my gun was in his mouth. Nikolai Kozlov, the SVR agent who threatened me with life in prison if I didn't work for them."

"Your Russian handler? What was he doing at the Wildwater building? Watching the show?"

She shrugged. "I saw him getting off the elevator. So I followed but he got in a car and left."

"It's a big building," Joe pointed out. "He could have been visiting some other office."

"Yes, if you believe in coincidence," Yelena said.

"I don't," Joe admitted. "So with Wildwater involved and now this Russian, this is starting to smell like spooks."

Yelena wrinkled her nose and poured herself another drink. "Smells like bad shit to me."

Joe nodded. "That's the CIA scent I remember, all right. As soon as the spies get involved, everything turns to shit."

"A lot of our oligarchs come out of the old KGB. Your Richards, the Wildwater CEO. He is like one of these too." She sneered. "They're just greedy pigs who don't have the courage to be real outlaws."

Joe grinned. "I didn't realize you were so politically engaged. You're an anarchist."

She laughed. "No. I met some of those anarchists. They talk too much. I'm just an honest thief, like you."

Joe clicked his soda bottle against her vodka bottle as Gladys called in from the living room. "Bring me a Fresca, will you? It's Final Jeopardy." So they went in and joined her, and then ordered Indian food, and Joe was pleasantly surprised to see how well his grandmother played host, matching Yelena drink for drink, regaling her with tales from her grifting days, and swapping shoplifting tricks. Then his phone rang. It was Gio. Someone had just tried to kill him.

❖

Gio had been busy all evening, taking care of one of his most boring chores, counting money. Like many businessmen with varied and far-flung enterprises, he spent a fair bit of his time simply making the rounds.

The difference was that while more conventional business owners hoped to be picking up earnings at these stops, Gio was dropping them off. He was laundering money, with Nero driving beside him and Big Eddie in back with a duffel bag full of cash, tribute that had been passed up the line from the many rackets Gio owned or allowed to proceed with his blessing.

His first stop was Laundry Town, and he braced himself for the same stale jokes. Like clockwork, Big Eddie held up the duffle.

"Hey boss I got your laundry right here. Drop if off dirty, pick it up clean. Fluff and fold, am I right?"

Nero chuckled obligingly, but Gio couldn't take it anymore.

"Let me ask you Eddie, how many years we been coming here?"

"I don't know boss, five, ten?"

"And every week you make the same fucking joke. I just can't stand it anymore."

"Sorry boss."

He turned to Nero. "And you laugh. How can you still think it's funny?"

"Sorry, Gio."

"Okay new rule. From now on, no jokes about laundry or dirty money or anything unless you just thought of it brand new and you are absolutely fucking sure it's funny. Got it?"

"Yes, boss."

"Sure, Gio."

"Great, thank you." Gio sighed. Still, as a way to clean illegal proceeds, he had to admit it was one of his brightest schemes. They showed up during a weekday night, a slow time, and immediately headed through the door marked employees only. Neither the senior citizen behind the counter nor the two West African women folding drop-off customers' clothes, nor the few bored civilians watching their underwear spin, took any notice at all. In the back office, Gio sat at the desk, opened the old fashioned safe, and began to fill it with money while Nero did the paperwork.

Laundry Town, which was now a small chain of six laundries that Gio had built up using the old Italian couple who owned the first one as fronts, was a cash-only business. People dropped off clothes or dry cleaning at the counter, or they slid bills into a machine that put credits on a card to use the machines. Either way it was easy to simply add more receipts and more income to the books. The only real supplies were detergent, cleaning fluid, and water, so there was little to worry about in the way of inventory. The managers, that is to say Gio's fronts, got to run the business and pocket the legit proceeds. Gio ran his own cash through, had the business show it as corporate profits, and then took it back as earnings from his stake in Laundry Town, Inc.

Next stop was Paradise Nail Salon. Same deal here. A Korean mother of three had been left to run the place alone when her husband died. Gio had stepped in to offer support and protection, and one of his corporate shells had bought the storefront where she worked. Now she managed three shops—two of them former video stores, another great cash business for Gio, and one of the few he enjoyed visiting, until the bottom dropped out of it—and Gio had the same arrangement with her.

The biggest hassle was Jocko's, a bar and music venue out on the island, simply because it was the loudest and most crowded and because of the added attention that anyplace with a liquor license got. Gio made it work for him though: he had the manager order more booze to offset the extra cash he pumped in, then took it as a write-off and used it to supply drinks for the illegal gambling parlors he controlled. That was Gio, smart, careful, and on top of every angle. So the last thing he expected, when he finally arrived, tired and bored, at his last stop, was to be stepping into a trap.

Especially not at Café Primo. This place had been in the family forever. It was in Carroll Gardens, which had been a deeply Italian neighborhood in south Brooklyn for decades, with the scent of semolina bread baking on the corners, bathtub Madonnas on the front lawns, and even a mural in salute to John Gotti. The space had once been a social club, one of those storefronts with painted-over windows where wiseguys used to hang out, scattered all over New York. This one had become a Caprisi joint when Gio's father won the building shooting craps. It sat there, a neighborhood fixture, hosting card games and the occasional load of stolen merchandise, until the area began to change. Rents rose, new, wealthier people moved in, the bakeries became *boulangeries*. Pretty soon the little storefront was simply too valuable for three old guys to sit out front on folding chairs in shorts and black dress socks all summer. It already had a marble counter and a fine, old-fashioned espresso/cappuccino machine, the kind with the eagle on top, and all the character, tin roof and tiled floor, that a chic designer would charge you a fortune to copy. Gio got a new sign painted—Café Primo—and put his cousin's kid, who had "trained" as a barista, whatever that meant, in charge. The place did great business, though it was always a little sad to come by here. You know times have really changed when not even the Mafia can afford the rent. Still, he saved it for his last stop, so that along with dropping off the money, he could relax a little with a well-deserved espresso and a single pignoli cookie—his pants were getting tight.

So when Big Eddie came out with three coffees on a tray and set them down at the outside table that Gio's cousin had reserved for them, Gio had asked, "What about the cookies?"

"Sorry boss, I forgot," Eddie had said, turning back. Gio sighed and was blowing on his coffee when Eddie came rushing over, without any cookies, yelling "Boss!"

"What?" Gio had barked, impatiently, but before he could register anything else, Eddie had flung himself through the air, knocking Gio to the ground, toppling the chairs and tables and taking two bullets in his broad back.

Gio heard the shots and felt glass raining down, but from under Eddie's bulk he couldn't see what had happened. It was a drive-by. A car had pulled up, and a man had hung out the passenger window, raising a machine pistol. He'd opened fire at Gio, hitting Eddie instead and shattering the shop window behind them. Nero had dropped to the ground behind the upended table and drew his pistol, returning fire. Gio was unarmed, but as he rolled Eddie off, he drew the gun from Eddie's shoulder holster and likewise shot at the car, which was now speeding away.

"Eddie!" Gio said, using all his strength to roll him over. "Eddie!" He was dead, with both rounds still inside him. It was only then that Gio realized some of the blood on him was his own. Splinters of falling window glass had sprayed his back like buckshot, shredding his white dress shirt, and now blood was soaking through.

The first call Gio made from the ambulance was to his family, to check on them and let Carol know he was okay while Nero dispatched soldiers to his house and his mother's house and raised the general alarm. The second was to Eddie's family. And the third call was to Joe.

PART III

PART VII

20

WHEN JOE CAME DOWNSTAIRS the next day, Nero was waiting, standing at the curb with his car double-parked. They hugged and Joe told him, "Sorry about Eddie."

"Thanks." Nero nodded. "He was a stand-up guy to the end."

"No doubt."

Nero opened the rear door for Joe, and he slid in next to Gio, who shook his hand.

"Sorry," Gio said. "I can't hug with this fucking back."

"Right," Joe told him. "Sorry to hear about Eddie."

Joe could see his friend was distraught, so he waited while Nero got in and they started moving. Then Gio spoke, looking out the window at the tumult of Jackson Heights, silenced now behind glass.

"You know he took those bullets for me," Gio said.

Joe nodded, even though Gio couldn't see him, and waited for him to continue. "And the last thing I ever said to him was yell at him for forgetting my cookie."

He turned back with a bitter look on his face. Joe squeezed his hand. "I'm sure it rolled right off him. He was like that. Big shoulders."

"Yeah. You're right. He was all heart." Gio smiled. "And no brains."

"Better than the opposite."

"Ain't that the truth," Gio said, then yelled: "Fuck!" He punched the seat in front of him and Nero flinched. "I'm going to miss his dumb fucking jokes about the laundry."

❖

Nero took the Brooklyn–Queens Expressway into Brooklyn, then the streets. As they moved deeper into South Williamsburg, they seemed to be traveling not just through space but time. Soon they saw only men in black—black coats, black hats, black beards—and women in headscarves or caps and long skirts, pushing strollers or leading flocks of kids dressed like miniature versions of themselves. More and more of the writing on the storefronts was in Hebrew or Yiddish and Joe was struck, as he always was, by how many of the windows, whole sides of tall apartment buildings, were barred, elaborately so, with rectangular, cage-like structures. Were they to keep people from getting in, he wondered, or getting out?

This was the land of the Hasidim, the ultra-Orthodox Jews who formed a highly insular community of their own, an Old World town within the secular modern city, with their own institutions, schools, businesses, even their own neighborhood security patrols, and rabbis who ruled by their own religious laws. Of course, they also had their own outlaws. That's where Rebbe came in, as the oldest and most respected Orthodox gangster, a king among his tribe. And now they were in his land.

As they stopped for a light, Joe saw a man who was loitering on the sunny corner nod at Nero, who nodded back. He was a tall guy in a wide brim black hat with a pointed black beard, and a long black coat over his black pants, like wearing a solar energy panel, Joe imagined. His eyes prowled the street watchfully, and he had his right hand in his coat. He was armed.

Now Joe noticed other men stationed around, on corners and on stairs, watching from windows, even on the rooftops, black forms silhouetted against the sky like scarecrows. They turned into a small, dead-end street and found it blocked by what looked like a bakery delivery van—Hebrew writing and a painting of matzoh. Nero stopped. A young guy approached the car. At first glance he looked more modern, in jeans and with a hipster vibe to his beard—but he wore a knit skullcap and had the telltale knotted strings, the tzitzit, dangling from under his Kurt Cobain shirt. Nero lowered the window.

"Caprisi," he said, and the guy peeked in back at Joe and Gio. He nodded, signaling as he stepped away. The truck rolled back.

"Tight security," Joe said as Nero pulled forward.

"After last night, we decided only Rebbe could guarantee safety for this meeting. All of us targets in one place."

Most of the block was taken up by a huge old warehouse. Nero turned into the driveway and a large, metal gate was rolled back by a bearded guy with a skullcap and a rifle slung over his shoulder. Another, who could have been his brother, stood watch, rifle in hand. Joe clocked two more on the roof as they rolled into the warehouse. The walls were as thick as a castle and light filtered in from high, barred windows. There was probably still coal dust on the pebbled glass. Inside, a row of delivery trucks stood against one wall, by the other, a row of expensive, late-model luxury cars and SUVs. The guests. And by itself in a corner was a private ambulance, with two EMTs sitting on the back bumper. Nero parked and they got out. The other drivers were gathered in a group, chatting and smoking. Cash waved at Joe from where he was leaning on his hood—no doubt he was driving his boss, Uncle Chen. Liam Madigan, who was there with his eldest brother, ambled over.

"Gio, I'm terribly sorry to hear of your loss. I always liked Eddie." He shook both their hands. "Anything I can do," he said. "Just ask."

"I'll be in touch," Joe told him.

"And I'll be ready."

Beside the trucks were towering pallets, stacked twenty feet high, with plastic-wrapped blocks formed of boxes of matzoh, each one emblazoned with a bright yellow Moische's logo. It was like a fortress wall towering above them, with no way through or around it. Beside it stood Josh, with a headset mic and an Uzi on a strap over his shoulder.

"Joe," he said, with a grin, "good to see you," and then to Gio: "Just a second, sir."

Gio nodded and Joe winked as Josh spoke into his mic. They heard an electric motor and suddenly a large chunk of the wall lifted up and began to ease back, opening a doorway wide enough for both men to walk through. A forklift, manned by an old graybeard, dressed in black of course, had pulled back with the load. He waited for them, then rotated the forklift and backed out through the passage he'd made, sliding the brick back into the wall behind them. They were sealed in with matzoh on all four sides now—the warehouse was stacked to the ceiling, leaving a large open space in the center.

Several folding tables had been placed end to end, then covered with a long white tablecloth to form a single surface. Another nearby table held tea and coffee urns, pitchers of ice water, rows of cups and glasses, sugar, and milk. On folding chairs around the table were Uncle Chen, true to his name, a bald, round, avuncular-looking old man who was the ruthless boss of Flushing; Anton, from Brighton Beach, representing the Russian Mafia, furiously smoking acrid Russian cigarettes; Reggie, Alonzo's brother, younger and thinner than Alonzo, with a high fade where Alonzo had his head shaved, was dressed like a grad student in a button-down and jeans, and looked a bit out of his element; and in a navy blue suit and red tie, Jack Madigan. At one end of the table sat their host, Menachem "Rebbe" Stone. And at the other, still with red lipstick, polished nails, and diamond rings despite being in a wheelchair and with an IV dripping into her arm, was Little Maria.

"Gio," Rebbe called to them. "Yosef!"

He came around, arms open wide, and hugged Gio tightly. Gio flinched in pain, but took it, along with a ticklish kiss on the cheek. Rebbe had come up in the world with Gio's father and he'd known Gio his whole life. He shook hands warmly with Joe. "Thank you for coming. You want something? Tea? Coffee?" He shrugged at the stacks around them. "Matzoh maybe? No? I don't blame you. Then sit, sit, please."

They took the empty chairs that were left and Rebbe stood at the end of the table. "Welcome friends and thank you all for coming. I'm flattered that you'd ask me to host this meeting, and I hope you can see that we are safe here, from our enemies and from listening ears. If you don't think matzoh can stop a bullet you haven't tried to use the can after Passover week at my house. Oy." He patted his belly as chuckles echoed in the cavernous space. "But no more jokes. I apologize. It's a sin in a time of mourning. And let me say, I know I speak for us all when I offer my deepest regrets to those of you who lost people last night—Gio, Maria. *Olav ha-shalom*, may they rest in peace." The others nodded. Anton and Jack crossed themselves. "And Reggie, your brother is in our prayers." Reggie nodded shyly and fidgeted in his chair. "Uncle Chen," Rebbe said, turning to the old friend and rival beside him, "I hear you were hit last night as well."

Chen nodded. "A Sunset Park operation. They took out one of my best dealers. A kid I've known since he was in the fifth grade."

"What a waste of a young life," Rebbe said. "So then, we know why we are here. Let's begin. First off, I know Maria wants to say something, and she can only stay a short time. Maria?" He nodded to her and took his seat.

"Thanks, Menachem." Her voice was raspy. "As you can see, I am still not good. All night I was in the hospital and they didn't want to let me out. But I told them I had to be here, even if I crawled, so here I am. So forgive me if I sound a little loopy, they gave me something for the pain." She shrugged. "Is pretty good shit, I should find out their supplier." This got a laugh. She grinned, then grew serious and raised a painted claw. "But this is what I came to say." She spat her words out. "*Rapa tu mai*, these *mama guevos*, who violated my home. I put my curse on them. They killed the ones I love most. My aunt, who never done nothing to nobody, except cook and pray for us all. And they took my precious boy, the love of my life, Duque."

"Was that her boyfriend?" Gio whispered to Joe.

"Not quite," Joe answered under his breath.

"And also," Maria went on, "while he was defending me, those bastards, *hijo de la gran puta*, they kill my boyfriend Paco too." She winced in pain, then took a breath, and continued. "So you know how me and my associates, in the import business, we offered five hundred thousand for this Zahir. I'm here to say that we talked today and now we are going to double this. One million dollars, for the head of the piece of shit who did this to me, and to us."

A murmur went around the room. Reggie raised a hand, like in a classroom. "I want to say I'm kicking in another hundred grand, on behalf of my family, for what they did to my brother."

Gio nodded. "Me too. In the name of Big Eddie."

Rebbe looked at Chen, who nodded at him, and then at Jack and Anton. They all nodded back. He spoke: "I know we all want to help with this. So let's make it two million. The price for justice against the enemies who attacked us here in our own hometown." He turned to Joe. "So. That's what we asked you here for. What do you say, sheriff?" He showed his crooked teeth through his snow-white beard. "Two million dead or alive."

While the others waited, Gio leaned in to Joe's ear. "Let's just make that dead."

Joe nodded at him, then smiled at the waiting bosses. "Let me see what I can do."

21

DONNA STOPPED AT THE coffee cart where Sameer, a cheerful young Yemeni man, stood in a plexiglass box steaming milk and buttering bagels.

"Make it a double today, Sameer," she told him.

"Coming right up." He poured her a latte with an extra shot of espresso. "Here you go. Now go catch those bad guys," he said, as he did every day.

"I'll try," Donna said, clipping her ID to her jacket as she headed toward the entrance to the Federal Building. She too said that every morning, though she rarely thought she'd have the chance to actually chase one. But that morning, before she even got to her office door, a passing colleague told her Tom was looking for her, so she knocked on his door instead.

"Yeah!" he yelled, turning from the window as she entered. Once again the endless parade of civilians was passing across the square, constantly threatening to ruin his day by getting killed. "Sit," he said. Donna felt like he was talking to a dog but she sat, swallowing her annoyance with a long sip of coffee.

"Well you're in luck," he told her.

"Really?" She asked, skeptically hopeful. He didn't sound happy about it.

"Yeah. As of last night we have a citywide drug war."

"Oh . . . great?"

"Anyway enough noise got made that the police department is assigning their Major Case Unit. And since our lab made the connection with that last case, they've asked us for help. But I've already got every agent on full alert for 9/11 with all days off cancelled and overtime coming out my ass, so all the help they're getting from me is you. Have fun," he added, and turned back to the window.

❖

Thanks to all his pushing, Fusco was now running the White Angel investigation, but the truth was, he wasn't even sure what he was investigating. He'd begun nosing around White Angel because Gio told him to. Then his own cop instincts, which were much more reliable than his terrible gambler's hunches, told him something was up, except no one but maybe his partner believed him. Now, with the FBI lab results and the half dozen bodies that had dropped all over town in one night, all of sudden everyone was sure there was a case, and that it was major as hell, but still no one, not even Fusco himself, knew what the fuck kind of case it was.

The FBI chick, Zamora her name was, came by just as he was pondering these heavy thoughts over a breakfast burrito with extra cheese. Parks was sipping some kind of tea that smelled like medicine.

"Detective Fusco?" she asked. A looker. The classy type, in one of those black power suits the feds favored.

"Yes, you found me, come on in." He moved his burrito to his left hand, wiped his right on his pants and shook. She held her smile. "This is Parks," he added.

"Nice to meet you," she said and shook Parks's hand too, transferring some of Fusco's burrito grease.

"Welcome," Parks said, grabbing a couple of deli napkins and handing her one. "Please sit down."

"Yeah, have a seat," Fusco said, taking another big bite. "We were just discussing the, uh, nature of this case. Maybe you'd like to give us the FBI's read on it."

"Well . . ." Donna looked down at the one empty seat and saw the greasy burrito wrapper. She leaned against a table. "We," and by *we* she meant herself, "think that Zahir, up till now, has been smuggling dope into New York and using it to fund terror overseas. Now it looks like maybe he's moved in. He's distributing here directly, and we received a threat about a possible terror strike as well."

"A threat?" Fusco asked. That was news to him.

"That's classified."

"Credible?"

She hesitated. "Semi."

"And you do terror or drugs for the FBI?" he asked.

"A little of everything," she said. "I handle information that comes in."

"Comes in how? You mean CIs? Do you have one on this case?"

"Mostly via phone or email actually. Some tweets."

"So like a receptionist?" Fusco asked, and Parks, like someone who sees another, metaphorical bottle of piss about to spill across the room, leapt in.

"Agent Zamora," he said. "Do you have any evidence to link the drug activity, or last night's violence, to Zahir? Or to terror at all? We've been watching this White Angel crew for a bit, and they just look like regular homegrown gangbangers to me."

Fusco waved his burrito at Parks and a spray of juice dotted the files on his desk. "He's got a point. No reports of guys in turbans and bathrobes slinging dope in the projects, yet."

"So what do you make it as?" Donna asked.

Parks shrugged. "Turf war. White Angel has the best package in town, maybe because of your Persian connection, sure. They use that leverage to poach more territory until, last night, war finally breaks out. Bound to happen sooner or later." He sat back and crossed his legs, revealing argyle socks and lovely brown wing tips. "And that's if these incidents are even all connected. New York City is known to have more than one shooting in a night."

"As you can see, Zamora," Fusco said, "Parks has a brain, rare in the NYPD, which makes up, somewhat, for the hassle of trying to eat lunch with a vegan. You're not vegan are you?"

"No, I'm not."

"Of course not. What was I thinking? Your people love pork way too much, like mine. Sorry."

Donna frowned, unsure of whether to be offended, or accept this apology, or what. Fusco marched on, running a thick, greasy finger over the pages spread on his desk. "But he is missing one curious aspect of last night's parties. Crime scene reports suggest that the shootings by the bridge last night were done with a high-powered rifle from a rooftop. That means a sniper, with some skills rarely seen among uptown corner boys. The device in the Brooklyn stash-house, as well as what I've got on the car bomb in Jersey—they're being very cooperative because it's a small town department hoping like hell this is our mess—both are high-tech gear of the sort used by commandos and shit."

"You're thinking what, military?" Donna asked, as Parks leaned over the desk to read the reports.

Finished with his breakfast, Fusco belched into his fist, then reached for his coffee. He dumped in a sugar and stirred with a finger. "I'm thinking, whatever kind of war this is, for dope or for Allah, it's being fought by soldiers." He took a sip and sat back, resting the cup on his burrito-filled belly. "I just hope we don't need an army to take them down."

❖

Joe called in the troops. But before he could take out the target, he needed to locate it, and the one spot where he knew they'd be was at work, selling dope. Or more precisely supplying it, since there was little chance the kids peddling bags of White Angel knew any more about their bosses than the kids who sold for Alonzo or Maria. It was like asking a gas station attendant the address of the CEO of Exxon's house. So what he really wanted to catch was the re-up, the moment when the invisible power had to show its hand, even if it was just dropping off a package.

From what he'd learned at the meeting, White Angel's busiest spot was in East New York, a largely ungentrified piece of Brooklyn where, in parts, a certain degree of lawlessness still prevailed: hookers walked streets, boozers huddled on corners, and junkies lined up for junk, especially when word was out that the quality was this high. Reggie and his driver, who knew the area well and drove with a Glock on the console, picked up Juno and Joe. Juno got in back with Reggie. Joe rode up front with the driver, and asked him to cruise past the spot, rolling slow so that Juno could take pictures from behind the tinted glass.

The block was derelict and abandoned at night: the back side of lots where bus and delivery companies parked their vehicles, a vacant space full of monster weeds reaching over the toppled fence, a boarded-up auto repair shop and an abandoned, crumbling tenement. At the corners there were bustling tenements, where regular people tried to live their lives, a bodega, and a bus stop, but the middle of the block was a no-man's-land and that's where White Angel was sold.

Joe clocked the lookouts on the corner, teenagers slouching against a wall or a car, who'd send up a signal if the cops rolled by, then the touts, who steered you toward the product while singing its praises. Then a ragged row of junkies, lined up against a fence, trying to look casual while shuffling impatiently, like passengers on a really crap airline waiting for a flight to oblivion. One by one, they'd be sent in the vestibule of the abandoned building, then emerge a second later, now hurrying away as the lookouts admonished them to walk not run. The setup was secure, if simple. If anybody suspicious came along, they just closed up shop and locked the front door. No one standing outside would have anything more incriminating than a bad attitude—except for a few unlucky dope fiends with their hands in their pockets. Even if the cops charged in, Joe knew from circling the block that this building had a rear entrance that led to the vacant lot behind, then to the neighboring yards or the street. Any stash would be tossed along the way. Whether in the deserts or at the borders or on the corners, trying to stop the flow of drugs was like grabbing a fistful of water from a rushing river: it ran right through your hand. Maybe you caught a minnow.

Reggie waved at the scene, dismissively. "I've been telling my brother for a couple years now, all this is the past, man. I got us a chain of vape shops and joints selling CBD. That shit moves like crazy and it's legal. Sell it right out in the open, and no fear of drive-bys neither. I wanted to name it for Alonzo, like ALZ CBD or something, cash in on his profile but you know him, all secretive and shit, so I went with Doctor Vape and like a hip-hop vibe with graffiti for the packaging. And now, for the hipsters, we got the Brooklyn Sweet Oil Society." Excited, he leaned up between the seats and tapped Joe's shoulder. "Check it out, Joe, I got a factory making custom Doctor Vape Pens and I'm even designing my own vape juices. You should try some, like Mellow Fellow or Royal Crown Cream. Or I bet you'd dig my Professor Smooth Berry. I'll send you some sample cartridges."

"I don't smoke," Joe said, trying to be polite. He didn't want to say that those things looked ridiculous to him and they stunk. Every time he saw someone hit one, he had an urge to slap it out of his mouth.

"It ain't smoke," Reggie explained. "It's flavored steam with nicotine in it. And now CBD. And soon THC. All legal. That CBD stuff? We sell it in chocolate, oil, body lotion. White folks buy it for their fucking dogs! Soon it will be in their kids' milk. And when they legalize weed, like any minute now, we are poised to dominate that shit. That's what I told Alonzo, let them have the dope, dude. Let somebody else get shot up or blown up over this raggedy ass strip of dirt."

"You've got a point," Joe conceded. "Times change. There will probably be a Starbucks in that building soon. But addiction is addiction. There will always be dope."

"King Heroin. You sound like my brother." Reggie lowered his voice in imitation of Alonzo: "Change the names but the game remains . . ." He shook his head. "Yeah, he's old school like you. But now he's in a coma." He lapsed into silence as they turned a corner. They passed another bodega, a flat tire repair place, and a corner restaurant whose sign read Chinese-Burger-Chicken-Donuts. Reggie went on. "I say be more like your man, Gio. Now that's a cat I'd like to just study for a minute."

"I'll recommend you for an internship," Joe said.

"I worked for the man," Juno piped in, taking his face from the camera.

"Word?" Reggie regarded his skinny young seatmate with new interest.

"Yeah." He chose his words carefully, glancing at Joe up front. "I mean he's cool and he pays right but, all due respect, he ain't exactly some softy running a start-up, like riding a scooter around the conference room and shit. New suit and an MBA but you can't hide those cold-as-fuck shark eyes. Give me the willies."

Reggie sighed. "Guess that's why him and my bro are friends. Even stone killers get lonesome sometimes, need someone to talk to."

Juno cleared his throat, and when Reggie glanced over, he nodded his head toward the back of Joe's head. Reggie hastily added: "Not that being a stone killer is automatically a bad thing." But Joe's mind was elsewhere.

"You get what you need Juno?" he asked.

"Yes sir."

He pulled out his phone. "Okay, then let's get going. I need you, Cash, Liam, and Josh all together to explain what we're going to do. I'll call Yelena. And stop if you see a Salvation Army on the way. I need some clothes."

❖

They met in the back room at Club Rendezvous. It was convenient, safe, and—crowded and loud as it was—a random assortment of criminals wandering in one at a time drew no special notice. They just walked by past Sunny, the enormous African bouncer who was on duty when Joe was off, and who got that name because of the wide, gold-capped grin he gave the world—and also past the discreet extra muscle Gio had added since the attacks, a silent white guy in a suit, with a gun under the table—then crossed the busy room full of patrons, around the stage where the dancers played, and down the rear hall toward the restrooms, the dressing rooms, and the manager's office door. The manager, a pot-bellied, white-bearded dude they called Santa politely pointed them all to the couch and chairs, then got up from his desk and left, shutting the door behind him. Liam and Josh were next to each other on the couch, self-consciously keeping a few inches apart, which no one else noticed. Juno was at the end of the couch, arranging the street photos he'd printed on the coffee table. Cash sat backward on a kitchen chair, leaning it forward on two legs to see the pictures. Yelena curled in the armchair. Joe rolled the manager's desk chair out and sat.

"Thanks for getting here so quick," Joe told them. "I don't have to explain why."

"Take out these bastards before they get us," Liam said.

"That's the goal, yeah," Joe said. "But the first step is identifying them. So tonight we follow the dope, see where it takes us, and learn as much as we can."

"Recon," Josh said, "like the army."

"Or like cops," Cash added.

"Funny you should mention that," Joe said. "We're going to need two cars. One I don't care, as long as it's clean enough not to get you pulled over. The other one, we need a Chevy Impala, like an unmarked cop car."

"Done," Cash said, nodding.

"And you two clean-cut, handsome young fellows," Joe said to Josh and Liam, "try to look like cops look when they're trying not to look like cops."

Liam laughed. "You're just saying that because I'm Irish."

"Well white anyway," Juno pointed out.

"You mean I have to shave?" Josh asked. Since leaving the military he had made a point to grow out his hair and beard.

Joe shrugged. "Well the mustache is good. Just trim it and tuck your hair up under a cap or something. Think Serpico."

Josh frowned. "You mean the sign?"

"That's Scorpio," Cash told him. "*Serpico* is an old movie with Al Pacino playing a cop. Pretty good though."

"Don't worry, Joe. We get it," Liam told him.

"Juno, you know what I need from you. The cars will be parked here and here." He pointed to the spots on the photos, then stood and went to the manager's desk. "And does this printer do color copies?"

"Shitty ones," Juno told him.

"Good," he said, pulling out a twenty-dollar bill. "Make me four shitty copies of this, both sides."

"And what about me?" Yelena asked, after listening to all this in silence.

"You are going to be my guardian angel, perched right here." He leaned over and tapped a photo. "But first I need your help with makeup and costume. And I need a clean syringe."

❖

A couple hours later, Juno and Cash were sitting in the Chinese-Burger-Chicken-Donut place, with a selection of those items on the table between them.

"The problem with this kind of place," Juno was saying as he fiddled with his phone. "The donuts taste like chicken. The chicken tastes like an old burger. The burgers taste like stale donuts."

"And the Chinese food just tastes like shit," Cash agreed. "It's cause they use the same oil for everything."

"That's what comes from trying to give people everything they want. You end up not wanting any of it."

Cash sat up, his head tilting slightly toward the window. "Check the Benz."

Juno turned casually, still holding his phone. Sure enough, a black Benz had stopped up the block, in front of the vacant lot that backed onto the White Angel cop spot. A kid slipped like a rat from a crack in the corrugated metal fence. He ran to the car and a hand came out, passing him a black plastic bag. He scurried back and disappeared. The car rolled.

"Get it?" Cash asked.

"Got it," Juno said. The high-quality lens he'd used to replace the one on his phone's camera had captured the car and its license. "Let's dip." They stood, leaving their plates untouched. "All this talk about food is making me hungry."

❖

Meanwhile, Yelena was in Joe's room, doing his makeup. First she skillfully used blush, powder, and pencil to do the opposite of what they were sold to do: make him look worse—paler and with dark circles under his eyes. She even used some of the stage makeup she'd bought to add a sore to the corner of his mouth.

"Perfect," she said, showing him in her hand mirror. "Now I won't worry about the other girls kissing you."

He laughed, trying to get used to the odd feeling of it. "Now what other girl would do my makeup and then hit me when I asked her?"

"Hit you?" Yelena gave him a searching look. "For real?"

"Yeah, here . . ." He held out his arm and pointed to the crook of his elbow.

"How hard?"

"Hard enough to bruise."

She shrugged. "If you say so . . ." and gave him a walloping slap.

"Good," he said. "Again. A bit harder."

She laughed and gave him a couple more.

"Ow, good, that stung . . ." he said, wrapping a belt around his bicep as he watched the redness swell on his skin. "Though you could pretend to enjoy it less. Now hand me the needle."

At that she frowned, watching as Joe broke the seal on the fresh syringe (Cash had obtained it from a diabetic neighbor). He found a vein and expertly eased it in, then pulled back, drawing a little blood, then booting it back in. He pulled it out, then repeated the process a couple times.

"You're very good at that. Too good," Yelena told him.

148

"Some things you don't forget," he said with a grin, but she was no longer in the mood to laugh. In fact, he was pretty creeped out himself. He had butterflies in his stomach, an edgy, empty feeling that had nothing to do with missing lunch. A little blood remained around the punctures and he let it dry.

22

JUNO AND CASH WERE in a car Cash had provided, stolen but with legit plates, feasting on jerk chicken from a takeout place Juno knew. They were parked around the block from the cop spot, with a receiver on the dash. Liam and Josh were in a black Impala, likewise borrowed, parked over a block the other way. Yelena was on the roof of the warehouse, overlooking the dope operation, with a sniper's rifle. It was dusk.

"Clear here," she said into the little mic attached to her earpiece.

"All quiet," Juno said. "Last time the re-up took a few hours, but they've been hopping since it started to get dark. Expect we'll see them soon now."

Liam checked in too. "Couple of hookers gave us the stink eye," he said. "So I guess we look like real cops. Otherwise quiet here too." His stomach grumbled. "Quiet and hungry. Wish we had some of that chicken."

"I know you do," Juno answered. "That's where all the cops in the neighborhood go."

❖

Forty minutes later, the black Benz pulled up at a traffic light down the street. Juno got on the line: "Showtime."

"Standing by," Liam said as Josh started the engine.

"I'm ready," Yelena said, pressing her eye to the scope.

Joe came shuffling into view. He was wearing clothes he'd bought at the Salvation Army, then had Cash drive over a few times: a polyester print shirt from the '80s with missing buttons and a tear at the elbow, worn pants from an ancient suit, his oldest pair of Converse. He had a ball cap pulled down low, one of Gladys's cigarettes behind his ear and dirty nails. He joined the line, standing behind a bent, bald man who looked seventy-five but might have been forty in dope years. The touts moved up and down, calling to the other passersby.

"Yo White Angel here! On the money!"

"Boy and girl! Boy and girl!"

A dark-skinned guy in his late teens, with a sleeveless undershirt, baggy jeans, and a heavy gold chain was working the door. The bent man went inside and then came back out, shuffling quickly off the other way. The door guy looked Joe over.

"You new around here?"

Joe nodded, avoiding eye contact, and shuffled his feet. "I heard your stuff was on the money."

The guy looked him over suspiciously. "Got tracks?" he asked.

Joe nodded again and, darting a glance up and down, rolled his left sleeve up then quickly down. The guy saw his marks, and also noted with distaste the blood-stained syringe poking out from his trouser pocket.

"Okay, make it quick," he said, tapping the door three times. "Cop and go."

"Thanks," Joe muttered, stepping by him as the door unlocked and opened from within. Another even younger guy stood in the vestibule, wearing a Nets jersey and jeans cut so low you could see the red briefs encasing most of his ass.

"What you need?"

"Dope. A bundle."

"Where's your money?"

Joe held out his folded bills and flipped the corners quickly. Five twenties. With a nod, the dealer opened one of the apartment mailboxes set in the wall behind him and pulled out a small bundle of ten sealed baggies, bound with a rubber band. He handed them to Joe and took the money. Then, just as Joe was turning to leave, he put out a hand to hold him.

"Hey, this money's no good!"

Joe grabbed the dealer's hand and bent it behind his back until he howled, banging on the door. "Help! This dope fiend's ripping us off." As the door opened, Joe pushed him toward it while grabbing the waist of the dealer's low-riding jeans. With a quick jerk he pulled them down around the ankles.

"What the fuck?" the dealer yelped, and as the door guy came in, he shouted "His money's fake," stumbling over his pants and falling on the floor. The door guy reached over him and grabbed Joe's wrist. Joe pulled out his syringe and jabbed it deep into the meat of the door guy's arm.

"Ah! Shit! My God!" the door guy yelled in horror as he realized what it was. Joe left it poking out and ran, sprinting down the hall toward the rear of the building.

"Re-up's there," Juno said now, over the earpieces. "One guard by the back door and the runner."

Joe came tearing out the back door, surprising the guard, another teen, who was standing there, gun out, watching the other way, as the runner, a twelve-year-old kid, darted through weeds that were taller than him, toward the hole in the fence. Joe grabbed the guard's gun by the barrel, twisting it away while he tripped the teenager and dumped him on the ground. Pointing the gun, he ran toward the runner, who stared at him in shock.

"Out of the way," he yelled.

The kid promptly stepped aside, still watching in amazement as the guard and both of the door guys came out after Joe. As he ran, Joe popped the clip from the gun and then tossed the separate pieces into the deep weeds.

"Get that junkie! Get him!"

Joe felt them gaining as he reached the hole in the fence and slipped through, tearing the ass of his pants.

At first, Donna had been thrilled to be invited on the stakeout. Detailed to the NYPD Major Case Unit as FBI liaison, she felt like she was on a field trip, or away at camp. After their preliminary peek into the heroin operation known as White Angel, they'd decided that the East New York location was the busiest, most-longstanding, and most likely to yield usable information, so they'd rigged up a realistically-crappy-looking delivery van with their high-tech equipment and parked it on the corner while the dope dealers grinded up the block. But the excitement wore off after the first six hours of total boredom, and when Fusco, who'd promised to bring food, surprised her and Parks with a load of inedible junk from the Chinese-Burger-Chicken-Donut place, which immediately stunk up the van, she began to wish she were back in her nice, clean, air-conditioned office.

She supposed that was why, lulled into a stupor, she took a minute to recognize Joe. She was actually in the middle of a yawn, or trying to yawn without breathing in too deep, as yet another scuzzy junkie crept up to the tenement door where they sold the dope. But something about his profile caught her eye, and she looked closer. And there he was: Joe Brody, always popping up in her life at the worst moments, like fate. Her first thought was that he was using, strung out, and to her surprise she felt . . . compassion. A desire to help rushed up in her, to save him from himself. He was a veteran after all, and even as a criminal, he had done more to serve and protect his fellow citizens than most of the cops and Federal agents Donna knew. Not to mention saving her career as well. But there was more to it, she knew. She had feelings about Joe, though she wasn't entirely sure what those feelings were; fear and distrust were as present as fascination or admiration, and moral horror mingled with physical attraction as she watched him on the screen. But then she took in his odd clothing; even his walk was different. Was he in costume or something? Was he a junkie or was he *playing* a junkie?

"Hey try to zoom in on that guy. The white customer."

"Why?" Parks asked. "You know him?"

"Maybe. He looks familiar." In fact, Donna, knew very well she couldn't say how she knew him, since he'd disposed of the body of terrorist Heather Kaan after Donna put a bullet in her. Fusco leaned in and took a look too.

"Just another junkie. Probably seen his mug shot or something." He finished a donut that smelled like a cheeseburger and wiped his hands on his pants. "He ain't going to lead us to the kingpin. That's for sure."

Donna couldn't argue with that, so she sat tight and just watched as Joe went in the door to cop. Then something weird happened—they heard yelling and banging from inside. The outside man, the door guy, ran into the building, and a beat later, the lookouts came rushing over too.

"Shit," Donna said. "Something's happening. We've got to move in."

"Move in on what with what?" Fusco asked. "This is just a low-key stakeout. It's not like we've got a SWAT team standing by."

"We don't even know what's happening," Parks added. "Or if it pertains to our case."

Donna nodded. She knew they were right—or rather they would have been right, if it were anybody but Joe. She had no idea what he was up to, but her complex feelings were suddenly a lot simpler: fury. He was up to something and she was pissed. Seconds passed by. "What's behind this building?" she asked.

Fusco shrugged. "A vacant lot full of dog shit, cat shit, and probably human shit too, if you're lucky."

"I'm going to check it out," she said as she made for the door. "Keep rolling!"

But as soon as he had recognized Joe, right after Donna had, Fusco had surreptitiously kicked the cable out of its socket and disconnected the camera's live feed from the recorder.

❖

When Joe came through the hole in the fence, the black Benz was there. As he emerged, a broad, white guy in a tracksuit was getting out of the back seat, holding a black plastic bag. He stared at Joe in wonder. Alarmed, he yelled, "Sergey!" Another guy, shorter, heavily-tatted in jeans, white sneakers, and a white V-neck T-shirt, opened the front passenger side. Joe went into a slide, and as his other pursuers came through the fence, he rolled under the car.

Breathing hard, but safe for the moment, Joe pulled the device Juno had made for him from his pants. It was a small tracker, coated on one side with a powerful epoxy. Joe switched it on and peeled off the backing, then stuck it to the underside of the car. It held. Meanwhile he saw feet surrounding him and heard the voices they belonged to.

"Grab that dumbass!"

"How? He's hiding under there like a bug."

Joe identified the white sneakers, who he figured to be in charge, and grabbed his ankles, pulling hard. As the guy fell, Joe rolled out, boxing his ear, leaving him dizzy and ringing. Joe scrambled to his feet, and the bagman and the guard both jumped him. He elbowed one in the nose, breaking it, and kicked the other in the shin, trying to disable them without seeming too professional about it, keeping his arms tucked close and taking some hits on the back and shoulders without exposing anything too vital. Then he broke free and ran with the whole crew pounding after him. That's when the cops showed up.

As Joe neared the corner, with the two door guys right behind him, the guard limping slightly after, and the rest trailing curiously, a black Impala came swerving across his path, with a red light spinning on the dash.

"Hold it," a loud voice that Joe knew was Liam's fake New York accent boomed over a speaker. "Police!"

Everyone scattered. But as Joe turned to run, Josh leapt from the car and grabbed him, throwing him onto the hood of the car. Liam jumped out too and held him.

DAVID GORDON

"Where do you think you're going?" he asked. "What's the big rush?" He quickly frisked Joe and pulled the stolen bundle of dope from his pocket. "What's this?"

"Nothing," Joe muttered. "It isn't mine."

"Yeah, yeah . . ." Liam said as he pushed him into the backseat. Meanwhile up the block, the others had vanished, back through the fence or around the corner. The two men from the Benz had climbed back in, and after watching this unfold in the rearview, had decided to slowly pull away, holding their breath the whole time. As they turned the corner and drove off, free, they began to laugh at the whole crazy incident and lit cigarettes, feeling safe as they put more blocks behind them, and oblivious to Cash, who had smoothly pulled out, following from a distance while Juno tracked them on his iPad.

❖

When Donna came around the corner, she saw Joe getting arrested. She was breathless from dashing around the block, and didn't want to blow the stakeout unless she had to, so she paused when she saw the black Impala parked on the sidewalk, the dashboard flasher throwing red over the dim street, and the other suspects scampering back through the fence or into other buildings. Two white plainclothes cops were rousting Joe and pushing him into the car. Serves him right, whatever he was or wasn't doing. She watched them bounce over the curb and head off the other way. Then, as she turned to go, a black Mercedes that had been parked quietly in the middle of the block suddenly pulled out, turning its lights on as it cruised by. Automatically, she noted the plates as she headed back to the van.

❖

"You okay?" Josh asked Joe, handing him a bottle of water from the front seat while Liam drove them away. Both men were grinning wide.

156

"Yeah, I'm fine," he answered. "The hardest part was letting those mooks hit me and not breaking their arms."

Yelena's voice came over their earpieces. "You away clean?"

"Yes, ma'am," Liam said into his mic. "We are circling back to get you now."

Joe guzzled water, then peeled off his clothes and put on the clean black T-shirt and jeans he'd stashed in the car.

"What about this?" Josh asked, holding up the bundle of dope. He showed it to Liam too, who caught the symbol stamped on each bag, an angel with lifted wings. Liam's eyes flickered darkly.

"I don't care," Joe told him. "Just get rid of it quick. Otherwise Yelena's liable to do a cavity search."

When they stopped for Yelena around the corner, Josh leaned out and tossed the dope in the sewer. No more about it was said. Nor did Joe tell them how, for a second, he'd thought he'd caught a glimpse of FBI Special Agent Donna Zamora, running down the block after them, and then fading into the distance as they sped away from the scene.

❖

As Donna climbed back into the van, Fusco and Parks both turned from the screen.

"Anything?" Fusco asked.

"Maybe so," Donna said, taking her seat. "An unmarked department car just snatched someone up fleeing the scene. Two plainclothes. Can you call in?"

"Sure," Fusco said and got on the radio.

To Parks, she added. "Let's check the footage again. See what we got at least."

Parks nodded and began to rewind the recording, then cursed under his breath as he hit static.

"What's wrong?" Donna asked.

"I don't know." He sped the video back and forth and then with a sigh bent down to examine the equipment. "Goddamn it!" he called out.

"What?" Donna asked, getting frustrated. "Goddamn what?"

"This," Parks said, waving a cable, which he then plugged in. Sheepishly he sat back down. "The cable was loose. Sorry. It was my fault. I forgot to check."

"You mean we weren't recording? For how long?"

"I don't know, five minutes."

"Really?" Donna asked, thinking, *How could anyone be that lucky*, when Fusco also spun back on his stool.

"Nothing," he said with a shrug.

"What do you mean? Nothing at all? Total peace declared in Brooklyn?"

"As close as it gets. Uniforms responding to a domestic. A D&D at a bar. Car thefts. Vandalism. One assault on a bus. But no undercover activity or plainclothes busts anywhere in this sector. At least nothing's been called in. Sorry."

Sorry was the word, all right, Donna thought, her anger cooling and hardening into something more steely.

Fusco sipped from his Diet Coke and belched, loudly, like a roar. "Let's check again in the morning. See what came in." He offered her the bottle.

"No that's okay," Donna told him, calm now. "I have another idea for the morning."

23

"WATCHING YOU GET CHASED around by those kids was feckin' classic," Liam called over his shoulder.

"When you crawled under the car," Josh added. "They had no idea what to do."

As the Impala sped through Brooklyn, Liam and Josh were laughing uproariously, and even Yelena smiled slyly in amusement and relief at how well the trick had worked.

Joe grinned. "My biggest worry was that Yelena would get impatient and start blowing their heads off."

She laughed. "But no, I was very entertained. I can watch you get beat up by children all night."

Juno called in, "Looks like they've gone to ground," and sent an address.

"It's in Brighton Beach," Josh said as he drove. "I can pick up some borscht for Rebbe while we're there."

Joe and Yelena exchanged a look in the backseat.

"Okay guys," Joe said. "Let's not break the champagne out yet. That was amateur hour. Next stop we might be dealing with pros."

❖

Juno and Cash had tracked the black Benz to Zena II, a Russian night-club in Brighton Beach, where the two men had valet parked and gone inside. Josh pulled in behind Cash's car, up the block from the club, so that they could all observe the crowd outside. Shining cars came and went. Couples stood waiting at a velvet rope, men in expensive jeans or suits with women in miniskirts and heels, while a row of double-wide bouncers in black suits stood behind it, like trolls guarding a castle.

"You think that's the main stash?" Liam asked.

"A lot of extra muscle just for a club. Even a Russian one," Cash said.

"I don't know," Joe said. "It kind of makes sense. Thugs can come and go all hours without drawing suspicion."

"And they can keep close control of the entrance," Josh added.

Juno eyed a parade of young women, all hair and curves, who bounced and giggled as the door guy waved them in. He elbowed Cash.

"Yo Joe, you want me and Cash to check it out?" Joe frowned. Juno continued: "I know last time we got grabbed up, but that was because Cash here had to go ordering appetizers and shit."

Cash shoved him. "You the one had to piss so bad. You got snatched up in the bathroom."

"No thanks," Joe said. "That was fun but not tonight. Something's bugging me." To Yelena he said, "Let's take a walk."

Arm in arm, like a couple headed out for the night, they crossed the street to where the crowd was most dense. Multiple languages were shouted through a cloud of smoke and perfume. An old, white-haired man in a custom-made suit shook hands with the door guy who nodded at a bouncer big as the door he blocked. The crowd parted as the entourage came through—three girls whose ages just barely added up to his, plus two bodyguards of his own—the door opened, releasing a blast of ice-cold air-conditioning and throbbing bass, then resealed. The bouncers closed ranks like cyborgs in their wrap-around shades.

Joe muttered, "This could work as a pickup point for re-ups, and for bringing back cash. But where are they bagging the stuff, stepping on it? For an operation this size that must be a team of people. I can't see it all going down in here."

"The basement?" Yelena asked.

"Maybe." He considered the building, a cinder-block box painted black. "If this even has a basement. Looks like a converted warehouse on a concrete slab. Plus you'd need ventilation. Someone to watch the workers. And even then you'd still have your whole crew working right under the nose of the legit employees, with a few hundred people, some of them thieves, dancing right above you. Word would get out." He shook his head as they continued strolling, down the block and around the corner, where the darkness and quiet grew. "It's not safe. I wouldn't do it like that." He turned to her. "What would you do? If you were trying to protect your stash from someone like you?"

"Very difficult," she said with a smile. Then she nodded at a gated-up shop. "I'd hide it someplace like that."

Joe took the place in as they walked by. Grosskoff Caviar & Sturgeon, the sign read. Although the shop was closed, with a gate pulled over the front, the AC was humming. There were no other windows, but he could see dim light glowing in a skylight. There were security cameras at the building's corners. It fit. The shop was essentially a giant climate-controlled vault and no nosy passersby would question the security or the air-conditioner and power going night and day. There was a narrow alley behind it, where a small, refrigerated truck with the shop's logo was parked. Joe called loudly to Yelena in a drunken voice.

"One minute baby!" He veered into the alley, unzipping his fly, and saw that it also ran behind the club, which had a back door, for loading and unloading. Another hulk in a black suit stood guard, and he shouted as he saw Joe coming.

"Hey!"

Joe ignored him, drunkenly leaning against the truck.

"Hey," the guard yelled, coming closer. "This ain't the toilet. Get out of here."

"Sorry, sorry, no trouble . . ." Joe mumbled, waving an arm, and swayed back down the alley. As he passed the truck, the guard turned away to open the club door for someone coming out and Joe dropped, lying on the ground behind it. At first he just saw white sneakers. Then jeans.

Then he saw the tattooed Russian from the Benz, a black satchel over his shoulder, approaching the rear door of the caviar shop. He unlocked it and went in. Joe crept back to Yelena.

"Bingo," he said. "I knew there was a reason I liked you."

She laughed. "I can think of a few." She took his hand as they walked back. "One is that I know how to sneak in and get those fish eggs."

Joe laughed as they passed back by the club, another happy couple. "Just like a good alley cat."

❖

Yelena stepped back into the alley, in a spot where she knew the street-light hit her hair and traced her silhouette. She lit a cigarette, pretending to be hiding from the wind. Immediately, the guard by the door took the bait. One thing about big, dumb, rude men: they were predictable.

"Pssst, pssst," he hissed, and made a kissing sound.

She regarded him, blowing smoke.

"You think you are talking to cat?" she asked, letting her Russian accent thicken.

He began to saunter over. "I know I am talking to good pussy."

She smiled. "Be careful trying to pet. You might get scratched."

He came closer, grinning dumbly. "Don't worry. I can handle this little kitten." And indeed he was twice her size, maybe three times her total mass. He put a big hand out, as if to stroke her hair. In a flash, her left hand was reaching between his legs, grabbing his balls and twisting as hard as she could. As he gasped, her right came up, wielding the cigarette, which she stubbed out into his ear. He howled in pain, lifting his hands to brush the burning coals away, giving her a clear shot, and she punched him, hard, with an uppercut to the nose, which broke with a crunch under her fist. He grunted, as the blood gushed, and reached for her in blind rage, but by then Joe had stepped from the shadows and knocked him out with the crowbar from the pack he wore on his back. The man dropped, and Joe caught him as he fell.

"Pig," Yelena said, and spit on him.

"A heavy pig," Joe grunted, handing her the crowbar and trying to balance. "Let's load him up."

With the crowbar, she popped the rear doors of the truck open and Joe dumped the unconscious guard inside. They rolled him in, removed his gun and phone, then bound his hands behind him with his own shoelaces. As they shut the doors, Joe spoke into his mouthpiece.

"Okay Juno, give us two minutes then knock out the cameras. Liam, get ready."

They strolled past the caviar and sturgeon shop to the building next door, a closed spice shop with a couple of apartments above it. This lock was so flimsy, it was beneath Yelena; Joe simply loided it open with a card himself. They moved quietly to the roof access, which was unlocked, then climbed down onto the roof of the caviar shop. Now they could see the skylight, the alley where the truck was parked, and the busier street out front. The cameras, pointed downward, could not pick them up, but they tread softly so as not to be heard inside.

Meanwhile, Juno and Cash were parked around the corner, and Juno had been hacking into the shop's Wi-Fi, which was on the same network as Zena II, allowing those inside the club to see the security cameras. When Joe said, "Ready," Juno hit a button and crashed the network. To anyone watching, it would appear that their internet service had dropped and needed to be rebooted.

"Cameras out, folks," Juno said.

"Think I'll stretch me legs then," Liam said over his mic.

He had been loitering on the corner, with a brown paper grocery bag in his hand. Josh had parked further up the block as lookout, in a spot that gave him a view of the shop and the cross streets. Now Liam sauntered across the street and along the side of the shop, pausing about six feet from the vent to the AC unit, which was humming away. He pulled a sealed plastic bag from the paper bag: it contained a liquid chemical with another, smaller, sealed bag floating inside it. He threw it hard against the vent, bursting both bags and mixing the fluids, which drenched the vent. Then he ran like hell.

The bag had contained military-grade "Malodor," heavy doses of chemical compounds that when mixed released a noxious, repellent, and intolerable but essentially harmless gas; in other words a stink bomb so foul that the US and Israeli armies considered them weapons. In this case, the fumes were sucked into the vent and pumped into the sealed interior of the shop. Inside, four people were busy bagging dope: One mixed the raw heroin with cornstarch and powdered caffeine on a large tray. Another used a small scoop to weigh doses out on a digital scale. Two more packed these little scoopfuls into the small glassine envelopes, taped them shut, and stamped them with the angel logo. Another guy, the only one armed, watched over them: he was guarding the workers from anyone looking to rip them off and guarding the stash from greedy workers. He also had a rather delicate nose and was the first to react when a powerful scent of human feces began to fill the air.

"Jesus what's that smell?" he called out to the workers gathered around the table. "Was that you Louie?"

Louie, who was in his undershirt and surgical gloves, mixing, looked up. "Not me!" He sniffed and made a face of disgust. "Smells like a sewer pipe burst."

Sonya, who was bagging, stood up, covering her nose. "It's coming from the vent. I think a rat died in there."

Louie stood too. "Or a bum who's been eating rats took a shit in our air-conditioner."

Ronnie, the other bagger, was gagging. "I can't stand it. I have to get some air." She moved toward the back door but the guard waved her back.

"That door's locked from outside for security. Come on." He led them through the inner door, to the front of the shop, which was decorated with displays of caviar tins and vodka bottles. A long refrigeration unit held smoked fish and other treasure, worth slightly less than the heroin in back. Hurrying around the counter, he threw the deadbolt and opened the front door, then unlocked the gate and pushed it open.

"Hurry!" Sonya yelled. "I have to get out of here."

On the roof, Joe and Yelena were waiting. Then they heard Josh laughing over their earpieces. "Here they come," he said. "They look traumatized."

"Thank God none of that shite got on me," Liam said. He was making his way back around to join Josh in the car.

"Yeah, you'd be walking home," Josh answered.

Yelena pulled two gas masks from the pack and handed one to Joe, who fitted it over his face. "Okay," he said. "We're going in."

With the crowbar, he chipped at the paint layered where the window-panes joined, then forced it in the crevice, and using his foot, levered the skylight open. They both stood back, instinctively, to avoid the invisible rush of poisoned air from within. Then, while Joe aimed his gun into the now-empty store, Yelena clamped a winch over the opening. Sitting on the edge of the skylight, she put a foot into the loop at the end of the cord and lowered herself in.

She checked quickly to be sure it was indeed empty, then slid the loop over the leg of the table and signaled to Joe. He slid down.

They were in the back room of the shop. Around them refrigerated cases held tins of caviar and sealed sturgeon as well as cartons of blinis, vodka, and other trimmings. The equipment for the legit front business was on a work bench, while the central table was covered with the bag-ging supplies. A door led to the front of the shop, where, in the daytime, customers were served from behind a counter.

Joe shut that door, keeping it open a crack to watch, while Yelena quickly checked around. One of the fridges held a large black plastic trash bag, which she untied.

"Here's the stash," she said, handing it to Joe, who hefted it.

"Must be at least a dozen keys here." He took hold of the cord and put a foot in the loop. "Let's go," he said, and then, over the mic: "We're coming back out."

Yelena joined him, sliding her foot in on top of his and wrapping her arms around him. Then she yanked the cord to start the winch, and they rose. As they moved past the table, she flipped it over, spilling the rest of the dope onto the floor. Now the plan was simply to go out as they'd come, exit through the neighboring building, and hop into the car with Cash and Juno. When the dope crew summoned the courage to venture back in, they'd find their stash mysteriously vanished. But as soon as Joe and Yelena's heads cleared the window, someone took a shot at them. The bullet ricocheted off of the skylight's metal frame.

They ducked, heads down, and hung there.

"Josh?" Joe asked over the mic. "Any news?"

"Shit, sorry, Joe," he said. "I missed it. They must have a sniper in the building across the street." He was out of his car now and scanning the street. "I'm going to have to move to get a shot."

But now gunfire raked the roof above them, shattering the open skylight. Glass rained down and they swung together on the cord.

"Going down," Joe said, as they yanked it to restart, and it lowered. Yelena jumped off first and ran to the back door, while Joe knelt behind the toppled table.

"It's locked," she yelled. "Give me a minute."

Now the guard came back, hanky around his face, and opened the door, gun drawn. Joe sent a bullet whizzing past his ear and he fled.

"Whenever you're ready," he called back to Yelena.

"Done," she yelled, pushing it open, and he joined her as they went out the back into the alley. This time the door saved them. It was reinforced steel, designed to protect the stash house, and so even fired at close range from a high-powered rifle, the bullet got stuck halfway through its thickness. Joe and Yelena dropped to the ground.

"The truck," he shouted as they crawled around the far side and then climbed in the driver's door, ditching their gas masks. The guard he'd knocked out was just coming around, mumbling and shifting on the floor. In the side-view, Joe saw two men in body armor, heavily armed and set up behind a portable shield, blocking the mouth of the alley.

"Now what?" Yelena asked.

"Let's drive," Joe suggested. He took a folding camp knife from his pocket, busted open the ignition housing with the screwdriver and used the pliers to strip the wires. "This truck is refrigerated. All that metal should stop a bullet."

The engine sputtered to life. Meanwhile, the guard on the floor, stirred by the commotion, was climbing to his feet. But before Yelena could do anything about it, like shoot him, someone else beat her to it. An armor-piercing projectile came through the back of the van, burning through the layers of metal like they were paper and punching a hole right through the guard before exiting out the other side of the truck.

"Next idea?" Yelena asked as she threw herself to the floor, firing back as best as she could through the hole that shot had made.

Joe called over the mic. "We're taking fire back here."

"Damn it," Cash said. "We're on the wrong side of you." He was parked with Juno on the street, waiting to pick them up when they came out next door. Liam and Josh were pinned down by the sniper. "We can try to drive around and ram them," he suggested.

Now the two men in body armor were moving and, to close the trap, the club's alley door opened too, and another armored man stepped out. "Thanks but we got a ride," Joe said, and stomped the accelerator. He ducked his head as the man in the door fired, just one shot, before Joe ran him over, sending him flying and taking the door off its hinges. Joe braked hard, banging into the wall.

"This way," he told Yelena. Crouching low, they abandoned their equipment pack and darted out the driver's side door, into the open, or rather missing, door of the club. They were now in a dim loading area. A dumpster full of trash bags sat to one side, ready to be picked up. Music thumped through the walls. Joe dropped the bag with the stash into the dumpster. Then they tucked away their guns as they pushed through another door into a bustling kitchen and a young busboy, apron around his shirt, stared at them in surprise.

"Excuse me, but where is the dance floor?" Joe asked.

Confused, the busboy pointed toward the kitchen doors, from which the music came roaring every time a waiter hurried through.

"Thanks," Joe said, grabbling Yelena's hand. "Come on, honey, let's dance."

❖

Toomey was getting annoyed. Till now, all his plans had gone off like clockwork. As predicted, these street gangs had been nothing compared to his highly-trained, disciplined, and battle-hardened team. It was thugs versus soldiers and the soldiers had wiped the streets with them, giving them a taste of real urban warfare. Then word had come down that this Brody might be making a move against them. And perhaps, Toomey admitted, he'd been a touch too confident, after the string of easy victories. He'd posted his own man as a sniper in addition to the usual guards, local talent from Brighton Beach. Then, as soon as his point man had spotted Brody's people moving in, he'd sent in the hitters, armed, and armored, to the teeth, while he directed it all on camera. But then the cameras went down. And now he was told that, despite his overwhelming firepower and tactical surprise, Joe and Yelena had fled into the club. He couldn't exactly send storm troopers in to sweep the place with bullets, as much as he'd like to. Like a fly that you missed with the first swat of a magazine, and that zips out of reach, this minor annoyance had become a major hassle.

"Does anyone have eyes on them?" he asked Sergey, the beefy, tattooed Russian who ran this place as well as this end of the operation. That was the division of labor: Sergey peddled the product, handled the stash house and the street crews. Toomey handled security and ran the pipeline, bringing the product in. Victoria was the head case. Every covert network needed one, and Toomey was cool with it: let her chop people's fingers off and electrocute balls, she enjoyed it. Jensen kept Richards's ass well-licked. And Richards and Nikolai played the big shots, overseeing finance, connections, and long-term geopolitical strategy. Or so they thought. Toomey had ideas of his own that would make them look like the spoiled brats they were, playing kiddie games. But for that he needed time, and that was what the large supply of heroin he'd brought in and stockpiled in the caviar shop meant to him: time. Now this Brody had snatched it.

Sergey was on the walkie with his people, the Russian knuckle-heads who threw drunks out of the club and guarded the dope on runs to resupply the dealers. "They are downstairs," he told Toomey. He shrugged. "I think they are dancing."

"Just make sure you seal all the exits. As long we have them trapped, we take our time cornering them. And get back our goddamn dope."

"Right," Sergey said, rushing out to deal with it, which mollified him a little. They'd boxed themselves in, and even if Toomey couldn't kill them right here, they would surely run them down and retrieve the product, maybe even take them prisoner. Endless seconds crawled by while he stared at blank monitors, fists clenched. Then he heard more squawking over the radios and Russian cursing, which he didn't understand, except for one word: *musar*, which in the dictionary means garbage but which everyone on the street, and in this club, knew meant police.

❖

Joe and Yelena were in the cavernous main room of the club. Colored lights streamed and strobed as a mass of bodies gyrated on the large dance floor. The columns that held the warehouse roof up had been lined in mirrors that multiplied the chaos, and tables, chairs, couches, and ban-quets covered in red plush filled in the sides, with a long bar along one wall and more mirrors above, old fashioned ones edged in gilt. A DJ ran the deafening techno and waiters rushed champagne and vodka back and forth. The air was thick with sweat, alcohol, cologne, and perfume. As Joe pulled Yelena into the center of the dance floor, he picked out the guards: more big men in black suits or tight T-shirts, looking grim.

"Two by the front door," he spoke into Yelena's ear. "And one by the kitchen."

"And more by the restrooms," she said, nodding toward the two men who stood glaring at them by the other hallway. A roped-off staircase led to a balcony above, and there was Sneakers, the Russian from the Benz, leaning over the railing, eyes on them, jabbering into a walkie, no doubt directing his troops.

Yelena looked Joe in the eye. "Well Joe, looks like you have no choice. It's a matter of life and death." She put her arm on his waist and began to sway her hips to the music. "You will have to dance with me."

"That sounds like an emergency all right." He pulled out the phone he took off the guard and dialed 911, switching to a frantic voice. "Help! Please!" he shouted into the phone. "I'm at Zena II, the club on Brighton Beach Avenue. The bouncer just pulled out a gun and threatened to kill a customer. He's a big guy in a black suit. Out front! Hurry!" He hung up and then dialed again. "Help! Fire!" he said this time. "I'm at the club Zena II, there's smoke and flames in the kitchen. Oh my God it's spreading please help. The sprinklers don't work." He disconnected the call. "Help's on the way," he told Yelena.

"So is trouble," she said, nodding as she swayed to the rhythm. The guards, having decided not to wait any longer, were converging, making their way through the dense crowd.

"Let's get a drink while we wait," Joe said and took her hand. As the guards drew closer, they pushed toward the edge of the crowd, where the most luxurious banquettes lined the dance floor. The old man they'd seen outside sat in the center of one, with his young female companions on either side, and two personal bodyguards on the ends. Joe reached over and dropped the Russian's phone into one of the girl's cocktails. "Excuse me, I'm so sorry. I slipped."

She stared at him blankly, batting her fake eyelashes. The old man yelled and waved him off. His bodyguards stood up and stepped toward Joe. By now the club guards had made it across the floor and were getting closer.

"You don't mind, do you?" Joe asked the old man, reaching for his expensive bottle of champagne. He pulled it from the ice bucket. "My girlfriend is thirsty." He handed the bottle to Yelena.

"*Za zdorovie*," she said, and took a gulp, just as one of the bodyguards, barking in Russian, pushed Joe. Joe sidestepped him, quickly pivoting like a bullfighter and tripped him, sending him reeling into the club guard, who got knocked to the ground. Angry and embarrassed, the club guard jumped up and punched the bodyguard in the gut.

Meanwhile, another club guard was reaching for Yelena and she spun, stomping his instep and grabbing his arm, then twisted it behind him, kicking his other tendon from behind. He stumbled into the table, dumping champagne and vodka onto the girls' dresses, and then falling into their laps. They screamed in anger and the other bodyguard leaned in to yank him off. He came up swinging blindly, hitting the guard.

The old man bellowed in Russian and the fight grew, as bystanders stepped in to defend him or the women and were confronted by club security, who had rushed over to pacify the bodyguards. Then Yelena noticed two firemen coming in the door, in full gear.

"Our bodyguards are here."

"About time," Joe said as they began to push through the crowd milling like angry bees around the growing brawl. "Fire!" Joe yelled now. "Fire!"

The firemen looked their way.

"I think there's smoke coming from the kitchen," he told them, as more people noticed and began to move toward the exit. Joe pulled his own phone out now and called Juno.

"Hey we're coming out the front now," he said. "How about that lift?"

"Um . . ." Juno said. He and Cash were observing the mayhem from the car. A fire engine was parked out front and cops were scrambling from their cars. "You do realize that there's a whole bunch of city employees out here?"

"Don't worry," Joe told him. "That's our free pass tonight."

They flowed with the evacuating crowd, out the doors and into the street, where firemen ran by three cops who were wrestling the largest bouncer to the ground, his wraparound shades getting crushed underfoot. The door guy was up against the car, getting frisked by other cops. Joe nodded as they walked by. Cash picked them up at the corner.

"Man," Juno said, as they got in. "Are we happy to see you. Uncuffed and bullet-free."

"I feel bad, dudes," Cash said, as he steered them away from the club and into ordinary, backed-up traffic. "I wish there was something I could do to make it up."

"There is, actually," Joe said, sitting back and finally breathing easy as they pulled onto Coney Island Boulevard. "You can pick us up a garbage truck."

24

AFTER DROPPING JUNO AT home, and Joe and Yelena at Gladys's, Cash, Liam, and Josh ditched one car and drove the other into the city, to a depot on the Hudson River where mountains of salt and sand sat, awaiting the roads of winter. It was controlled by a union official who was also a distant relative of Gio's. A call was made and a garbage truck borrowed. Then in the early hours, Cash drove it by the now peacefully closed Club Zena II, which had put out its trash for the night. Liam and Josh rolled the dumpster down the alley and tipped it into the truck, then retrieved the one bag with the dope, and ditched the rest in a construction bin before returning the truck and hiding away the stash. As dawn broke, the three shared breakfast in a Westside diner, then went home to shower and sleep. By then, of course, Joe and Yelena were already tucked in bed, and even Joe was resting peacefully for once, too far under to be stirred by nightmares and wake Yelena, so that, after jetlagged days and dream-scarred nights, they were both finally catching up on their sleep when at 7 A.M. there came a pounding on the door.

Joe stumbled into the living room, towel wrapped around his waist, while Gladys, in her bathrobe, peeked through the peephole. The pounding got louder.

"Open up! Police!" a voice came booming.

Gladys turned to Joe. "It's the cops. And your friend Donna's with them."

"Better open up then, before they bust it down," Joe said.

Gladys put the chain on and opened the door a few inches. "Hi Donna," she said.

"Good morning, Mrs. Brody," she said, strictly business. She was in a suit and she had Janet and Andy with her, as well as Fusco and Parks representing the NYPD. She held up her warrant. "We've got a warrant to search these premises ma'am."

Gladys opened up, stepping back to watch them troop in. "It's kind of early," Gladys told her. "Why don't you come back in a couple of hours for breakfast? I was up late playing cards with your mom."

This got an eyebrow raise from Andy. Fusco wondered if it was some kind of obscure insult. To him, this whole thing was an embarrassment and he was afraid of repercussions from Gio, but he himself had been woken only an hour before and told to mount up. Donna had wanted to let him sleep, considering the suspiciously convenient dropped cable. But Tom had made it clear: this was still an NYPD operation and no way would she be allowed to execute a warrant without them. So here they were, the whole gang, facing Joe, who gave them a shy wave, holding his towel up with his other hand.

"Good morning Agent Zamora," he said. "I hope you'll forgive me for not raising my hands."

"Mr. Brody," she said, with a curt nod. He looked tired, obviously, but otherwise fit, without the pallor and without any signs of drug use, no longer the shambling, wrecked junkie of the night before. Clearly that had just been a ruse. She was both relieved and infuriated, to see him smiling and apparently without rancor now. "You can go get dressed," she told him, "while Agent Newton accompanies you."

"After you, sir," Joe told Andy, and gestured toward the hall. Meanwhile, Gladys settled in to watch the search.

"Any change you find you can keep," she told Fusco as he dug in the cushions of her recliner. Sliding on her glasses, she read aloud from the warrant: ". . . conduct a search of said premises for evidence to wit . . . to wit! What's that mean? To wit heroin and paraphernalia related to the sale and use of heroin. What?" She laughed. "Good luck," she told Donna, who was leading Janet into the kitchen. And to Parks, as he bent to peer under the couch: "You ain't going to find any heroin down there, but see if you can find my missing slipper, Detective. Now that's a real mystery."

"I'll try ma'am," he told her. He wasn't sure what he was even doing here, how this Brody character tied into the investigation. He pulled a remote control out from under the couch and brushed the dust off it. "Have you been looking for this?" he asked Gladys.

"What is that?" she asked. "I have my channel clicker right here." She held up her cable remote. "Then there's this one for the TV, I have to press that red button first."

"This is for the DVD player. See?" He pointed to the logo on the remote, which matched the player.

"Well I'll be," Gladys said, adding it to the pile. "You're gonna be chief one day, young man. That's fine police work."

Parks grinned. "Thank you, ma'am."

"Donna!" Andy's voice rang out from the back bedroom. "I mean, Agent Zamora. You might want to get in here."

Hearing the excitement in Andy's voice, Donna left Janet to check the sugar, flour, and other powdered products in the kitchen and hurried into Joe's room, eager to see what he'd discovered. Dope? A gun? Instead she found a girl, naked, or so it seemed, under a sheet. She was sitting up and smoking a cigarette.

"I asked you not to smoke in here," Joe was saying. He had jeans on now and was pulling on a T-shirt.

The girl shrugged and ashed in a cup on the nightstand. "I am doing by the air conditioner."

"So what?" Joe said. "That blows air in, it doesn't suck smoke out." He turned to Donna. "Maybe you can explain this to her?"

"Miss," Donna said, keeping her voice level. "We are sorry to disturb you. Can I see some ID?"

Yelena leaned over and pulled a passport from her purse, letting the sheet slip off. Donna looked away. Andy stared and smiled. "Here." She held it out.

"Irina Malecovich," Donna read.

"I am dancer at Club Rendezvous," she said, exaggerating her accent.

Joe smiled and shrugged. "Last night was so busy, she was exhausted, poor girl. So I let her sleep here."

"I'm sorry to hear that your job is so tiring, miss," Donna said. "But I'm going to have to ask you to get up and get dressed so that we can search this room. We will avert our eyes of course," she added, glaring at Andy.

Yelena shrugged, dousing her smoke in the cup with a hiss. "You don't have to avert," she said, and stood up.

At this Andy giggled, and Donna, to her horror, felt herself blush. Yelena pulled on her panties and then wriggled into jeans.

"You know how dancers are," Joe told them. "Very in touch with their bodies. I actually think it's a healthy attitude. We have so much shame in our culture."

"Mr. Brody," Donna said. "Please come into the living room while we execute this search."

"Right," Joe said and followed. Now Janet, having finished a fruitless search, was helping Gladys make coffee. Parks, after putting fresh batteries in the remote, was rooting in the hall closet, while Fusco checked Gladys's room.

"Put an extra scoop of coffee and a pinch of cinnamon in the pot, hun," Gladys told Janet. "That's my secret." She elbowed her. "A little sambuca in it doesn't hurt either." Janet laughed

Joe sat on the couch next to Yelena and watched as Fusco reentered. "Bedroom's clean," he said, although he had actually ignored a snubnosed .38 revolver under the mattress. Parks came back with a paper grocery bag from Key Food.

"I found this in the closet," he said, holding it out for Donna to see. "Looks to be about twenty grand."

"That is mine," Yelena said. "My tips from club."

"Twenty thousand dollars? In tips? And you carry it around in a shopping bag?"

"In Russia we don't trust bank."

"Actually Irina needs to get going," Joe said. "She's due at the club."

"In the morning?" Donna asked.

"Staff meeting," Joe said. "Unless your warrant allows you to take her money."

Donna nodded angrily at Parks, who gave the bag to Yelena. She kissed Gladys on both cheeks. "Bye Joe," she said, then nodded at Donna, "Officer." To Andy, who was entering, empty-handed, from Joe's room, she gave a happy wave. "Goodbye Agent Andy!" And she went.

"Aren't you due at this staff meeting?" Donna asked Joe, in a resigned tone, now that she could see this search was going nowhere fast.

"No," Joe said. "I took the day off. For a funeral."

❖

Carol drove Gio to Big Eddie's funeral. His back was still stiff from where they'd dug the glass out, and too much driving, at least the way Gio drove in morning traffic, might pull out the stitches. She'd convinced him to let the kids stay at home. True, they'd known Eddie all their lives, but the manner of his death, shot dead protecting their father, was more than they should have to be exposed to. As it was, visiting Gio in the ER after "the accident" in Brooklyn was supposedly traumatic.

He'd relented, but he wasn't so sure he agreed. God knows, he understood the urge to shield one's kids from the world. What else was his life but a gigantic force field designed to keep them in a different reality than the one he knew so well, the same reality his own father and grandfather had exposed him to deliberately, making sure he knew exactly where the food on the table came from, how the house he slept in was paid for and protected? It was sick, twisted, a form of abuse, Carol said. It was trauma. And he saw her point, he wasn't asking his own son to defrost any severed limbs any time soon, but there was a lot of love there too, even if it was expressed in an odd way. The night his Dad made him watch him kill a man, an informer, was also the night he took him to a high-end brothel to pop his cherry, and then for steak at Peter Luger's. Rebbe was there for the dinner; the hit had been to protect him too. He shook young Gio's hand and said, "Happy Bar Mitzvah, you're a man now," and everyone laughed. Later on, in college, when other guys would freak out about their parents visiting, about grades or asking them for money, he was amused. He knew his family would do anything for him, anything, and so would he for them. That was blood. And when it came time for him to go out into the world on his own, he was ready in a way that those punks never were, even with their degrees. Would his kids be? Wasn't it exactly the "trauma" he'd been subject to that made him strong? Then again, it also got him shot at. So maybe the safest thing for his own kids was to be sure they were nothing at all like their Dad.

The chapel was packed, with heaps of flowers and wreaths from all over the tristate area, even from Philly, Chicago, Boston, and Miami. And along with all the family and friends, and "family" and "friends," the nature of Eddie's death, in that wave of attacks, meant that all the other bosses sent people to show their respect and solidarity. This made Gio a kind of de facto host at the event, and he would need to shake hands with almost every single person there, but he went to the widow first, and hugged her, along with Eddie's kids. Of course he'd been to the house already. He'd explained how Eddie died saving him, a hero, left a fat envelope of cash on the coffee table, and told her not to worry, that he'd make sure her three kids' college got paid for. Still, that depended on them getting into college, and he couldn't make any promises about their elder son, Eddie Jr., known, of course, as Little Eddie, despite standing over six feet tall, and weighing two-fifty, all muscle. He'd barely made it out of high school and already had a criminal record far more impressive than his transcripts. He had inherited his dad's brains. But some of his heart too. What he wanted, he'd made clear, was to come in with Gio, and it might suit him. But could Gio say yes to that while shielding his own kids? Would Little Eddie, like his father, be the shield?

And speaking of shields, as he took his seat next to Carol, who'd found them a spot in the front row, he saw Joe, in a black suit, white shirt, and black tie, standing by the door. Always the bouncer. Though, if he were going to carry the metaphor further, he'd have to describe Joe not as a shield, but a sword. He was the angel of Gio's justice, or vengeance, if there was a difference, slaying those who'd tried to slay Gio, who threatened his life, his family, his town. He nodded his head at Joe in greeting, and Joe returned a quick nod. They'd talk later, after the praying was done.

As it began, with the priest's arrival at the pulpit, Carol squeezed his hand and Gio held it. Their own relationship had shifted since the attack, when she'd rushed into the Emergency Room to find him lying on his stomach, with a doctor tweezing glass shards from his back. She'd said later that even though she knew he was okay—he'd been the one to call her after all—she still had this sudden image of him lying there dead, if not for a few inches and a few seconds, and she'd burst into tears. From that moment on, he knew his marriage would survive. He wasn't saying the problems were over, but rather that their connection, their family bond, would prove stronger than anything else. Her killing Paul—as a realist, Gio knew some of it was sexual jealousy, or possessiveness, or just rage, and that she might just as easily have shot him also, but the real reason, her most primal motive, was to eliminate a threat to their family. Her family. And so, in that way, despite all of her judgment, she was not as different from him and his own clan as she imagined.

As for the "issue," it was on hold, at least until they were ready to discuss it further, and that was fine with Gio. Again, he was a realist, and he knew sometimes, with some problems, just tabling them indefinitely was the best you could hope for. When he got home from the hospital, they had sex, great sex, for the first time since it all happened. It had been awkward, physically—he had to be on the bottom, to avoid pulling a stitch, but also sitting up straight, so as not to rub against his back—but emotionally it had been natural and real, the deep connection between two people who loved each other and who knew nothing, not one night or one kiss more, could be taken for granted in this world. So Gio decided fuck everything else, for now.

Joe watched the service from the back, observing, like an anthropologist, the different social structures interacting as part of this solemn rite. It was, before everything else, a family tragedy, and the tears and moans of Eddie's wife and mother-in-law, the quieter sobs of his children, were the realest, rawest truth. They made him feel ashamed, or perhaps humbled was the better word. Even the bosses in the room, and there were some very powerful and dangerous men here, were humbled by the grief of a wife, or a mother, or a child.

But it was also the funeral of a soldier. Bullshit, of course, in a way: an enterprise like Gio's was about money first and last, money they bled illegally from society and protected with blood if need be. But by choosing to live outside society's laws (if choosing was the right word for someone like Big Eddie, who'd flunked out of junior high and been educated in the streets and juvenile detention centers), they had in effect chosen one another, and over time, developed their own social network, with its own bonds of support or affection, its own code of conduct—to which each one adhered or not, just as straight citizens chose which rules they obeyed: taxes, traffic, adultery—and its own rituals and rites of passage. This was one. Dumb and lazy, Eddie, for all of his faults, had lived closer to the code than most, and had died for it. He was one of them, he'd fallen, and so they came, these unsmiling men in black suits, standing along the walls or sitting in back, with faces that represented every ethnicity, every religion and culture in the city, but all of them marked with a certain hardness, a truth that set them apart from the regular people, the ones sitting in the front pews: they knew it could just as easily be them lying in the coffin, and might very well be, next time. RIP Big Eddie.

That was the thing about Donna. That's how Joe thought of her, still, as someone he knew, Donna, not as Agent Zamora who'd just tossed his crib. His grandmother's bedroom for fuck's sake. He knew that she had violated his privacy, deliberately, that she was making it clear she was onto him, that she was after him, that she was coming for him, and yet he had been strangely elated to see her, to be, even in some sick way, the center of her attention. Like a lovestruck little boy who acts out in class just so his beautiful, brilliant teacher will look at him, yell at him. Angry, yes . . . but at him! He knew, too, that part of what drew her to him, made her come over and nearly kick his door down, was her own feelings for him, the bond that had grown between them, the times they'd saved and spared and covered for each other. Like it or not, they were joined. Their attraction was all the more potent for being unspoken, their complicity all the more binding for being unacknowledged. But it also drove her nearly crazy to know he'd broken the law. She couldn't stand it. Everything in her nature told her to chase him down and catch him, just as he was born and bred to run. She was a cop, a Fed, and when she put on black and stood in a row at a funeral, shoulder to shoulder with her people, it would be for her fallen comrade, not for his. She was law. And he was against the law. So how could they be for each other?

25

THEY BURIED BIG EDDIE in Calvary, the vast cemetery in Queens, a city of the dead within the city, with over three million souls, from Civil War veterans on down to Eddie, fallen on a Brooklyn sidewalk in the line of duty. The endless rows of gravestones created their own landscape, a necropolis mirroring, or perhaps mocking, the Manhattan skyline that blared triumphantly, and vainly, in the background: from ornate mausoleums proclaiming the persistence of ego beyond death, to the family crypts, layered generation over generation, to the crumbling forgotten stones of the poor, their names erased by weather as by history, to the lost traces of the past, sleeping under our feet. Everyone striving, fighting, buying, selling, loving, hating, and feverishly living in those towers across the river that reached for the sun would soon end up here, if there was still room for them. If some even worse fate hadn't already taken us.

After the interment, Carol took the car and went to help Annette get food and drinks ready for the mourners who'd be filling the family house with their sympathy. Gio lingered, to walk and talk with Joe, safe with those secret-keepers, who truly understood the code of silence. Nero waited by the car, finally enjoying a smoke, among those beyond caring about their health, or his.

"How's the back?" Joe asked, as the last mourners got into cars and left.

Gio waved it off. "Fine. Hurts. But I'll live. Unlike some." He looked at Joe. "So it's Anton? That Russian motherfucker double-crossed us."

"Looks that way. Hard to see how anyone could be running that operation in his territory, with Russian talent, without him knowing. And they were ready for us. They had a sniper on point and an ambush waiting. Someone told them we'd be coming sooner or later. Someone from that meeting at Rebbe's. Who else could it be?"

"I knew it. I never liked that prick. First of all, those cigarettes he smokes stink like burning dog shit. And who smokes inside, in a windowless room, with other people? And talk about milking a joke. You ever notice that? Every time I say something that gets a laugh he has to try and top it."

"Sounds like the death penalty to me."

"Petty bullshit I know. But my point is, I never liked him, but I held my tongue, and my temper. Now we have no choice. He hit first. We unite, all of us, and we take him out for good."

"Not yet," Joe said. "You've got to hold it a little longer."

"Why?"

"Even if we are sure Anton is running White Angel, he is not the one behind those attacks. Or the ambush last night. Those police reports Fusco gave you? Nero showed them to me and I read them in the car. The bomb in Alonzo's car was high-tech military stuff. The attack on Maria's crew used high-velocity sniper rounds fired from a distance by a sharpshooter. Last night they fired armor-piercing rounds at us."

"So?"

"That's the shit they shoot at tanks. It cut through the refrigerated truck like butter. I'm pretty sure they had infrared heat detectors on us too. Full body armor . . ."

"I get you," Gio said, nodding now, calmer.

"The guys at the service today? Sure they'd march into battle for you or for Eddie. But I don't care how tough they are. They're still street guys. These were trained soldiers."

"Army? Spies? Who?"

"Mercenaries. Just like the ones we ran across in Afghanistan. The way I figure it, Wildwater and their accomplices are behind the whole Zahir thing, using it as a cover to steal dope, smuggle it, and make money to finance whatever shady shit they're up to, corporate, political . . ."

"CIA?"

Joe shrugged. "Why not? Wouldn't be the first time. And Yelena made a Russian spy at the Wildwater building. Let's say that's the connection to Anton. They bring him in to run their New York distribution, handle the street crews."

"And he's clever about it," Gio adds. "He knows the shit's so good he can expand fast, move in on new territory, but he hires neighborhood people to sling it on the corners, so it doesn't connect back to him."

"Right. These local crews don't even know who they're working for, just a smoking package and muscle if they need it. But the security, the deep security anyway, is Wildwater people. Has to be."

"And with all that money flowing in and all that firepower behind him, Anton figures it was time to step up and move against us."

"Or he knew that with us looking into Zahir, we'd get to him eventually. So he struck first."

"And you hit back hard last night. The street value of that stash once they cut it? You cost him millions. Not a knockout but you hurt him. Why back off now?"

"Not back off, stop to figure the next shot. Like you said, we hurt him, financially. And it is going to be hard to hold all that territory with no product. So what does he care about most right now? The next shipment. That's the key. How are they getting the stuff in? Until we figure that out, we can't cut the head off the monster." Joe shrugged. "Even if we wiped out Anton and his whole gang today, you'd still have that pipeline and that private army loose in the city, just looking for their next front man."

Gio nodded. "Yeah. You're right. It's not a local gang war anymore. It's an invasion. So . . . if we don't whack Anton, what do we do?"

"I wish I knew," Joe said. "I'm thinking about it."

"Think fast, brother. We are both walking on these graves instead of lying in one by luck and a couple of inches."

Joe smiled at him. "But hey no pressure, right?"

Gio laughed and clapped his old friend on the back. "That's right. Fuck it, we're alive today. Let's find Nero and go back to Eddie's house. Annette's aunt made eggplant parm. She can barely tell right from left, and her lips move when she reads, but I'm telling you, that woman is a genius."

26

JUNO WAS IN A fury; that is, a cold, controlled, brain fury. He still
felt responsible, on some level, for the death of Hamid, and now these
same people, these shadows, had outsmarted him and his friends last
night. They'd made it out safe, by luck and by fast thinking, but he'd
come this close to losing Joe and Yelena. For a loner who took a long time
to build friendships, and who trusted only a handful of people outside
his family, this made the matter very personal, especially since Joe had
saved Juno's life at least twice, and come to trust him with his own. And
for the whiz kid side of him, the brainiac gamer, hacker, and hustler, to
be bested like this, first out of town and then in his home court? That
he could not abide.

He went back to work, powered by Red Bull, cold pizza, and even
colder fury. Cash came over too, just as pissed and just as loyal, but while
he was an artist behind the wheel and an ace at video games, he wasn't
much for crunching data and he quickly got bored and fell asleep. But it
kind of soothed Juno to have his pal there, snoring lightly on the couch,
while he ran the numbers like Cash ran the roads. And then, around two
in the morning, he got it. The answer. Or at least a clue to the answer.
He got something. And not by hacking or scamming. He got it by going
full nerd, pulling some deep quant shit, running reports and combing
through the heaps of mostly useless, boring, dust-dry data that Joe had
dumped on him. But all once, staring through his glazed eyeballs, he

saw it: a pattern. And that pattern was an arrow, pointed right at Zahir. Or whoever the hell they were really chasing.

"Yo Cash, Cash," he shook his friend.

"What? What?"

"I got it man, I figured the shit out."

"Awesome," he jumped up, as though there were some place to go, then sat back down, rubbing his eyes. "Call Joe."

"Now? It's two."

"Dude call him. If you really have something, he needs to know."

Juno called, and it went to voice mail. He hung up.

"Voice mail," he told Cash.

"Why didn't you leave a message?"

"For Joe? Does he even check voice mail? I'll call back in the morning. He probably turned his phone off to go to sleep."

In fact, Joe was awake, also thinking about Zahir. He'd silenced his phone for the funeral service and forgotten to turn the ringer back on. Finally, he drifted off, only to be awakened around four by a nightmare. He sat up, breathing hard, bathed in sweat, heart pounding, trying not to wake Yelena, who slept beside him, naked on her back, a loaded handgun under her pillow. Startle her and she might blow his head off. Or if he made too much noise in the living room, his grandmother might think he was a prowler and kill him with that ancient revolver she kept under her bed. As the only unarmed one in the house, he grabbed his phone to see the time as he tiptoed to the kitchen for a glass of water. That's when he realized his phone was off. He flipped it on and saw the missed call from Juno. He called, but by then Juno and Cash had both fallen asleep, halfway through a video game that sat, paused, on the screen.

Donna had a hard time sleeping that night. When the search of Joe's place, of Gladys's place actually, turned up nothing, she was a bit embarrassed and a bit frustrated—okay a lot frustrated—but she took it in stride. She was a law enforcement officer, a federal investigator, and that's what they did, investigate and enforce the damned law. That meant follow the trail of evidence wherever it led, and whatever it turned up. Even if that was nothing. Or a naked girl. Still, she told herself, it felt good to be on track, just doing her job, regardless of her feelings. And she believed that, she really did. At least until she laid down to go to sleep, and those other feelings came out to play, chasing each other around her head.

And what were these "feelings" she had about Joe Brody? She had to admit there was a spark, immediately. And the fact that it struck while she was handcuffing him outside the cheesy strip club where he worked was also the first glaring red flag. That was why, when she got on this case, potentially the biggest of her career, and Joe turned up in the middle of it, again, like a bad penny (or a bad omen or a bad conscience), she'd told herself, screw it, I'm just going to play it straight and do my job. Let the chips fall where they may.

And when the trail went cold in his bedroom, she did what a good investigator does, she went back to the last solid link: the dope operation. She dug out the plate number for that black Benz she saw leaving the scene and ran it. Turns out it was registered to Sergey Popov, who lived in Brighton Beach and worked as a manager at a nightclub, Zena II, that had been linked to the Bratva, the Russian mob. Not only that, when she checked the place out in the NYPD database, there'd been two 911 responses just last night, one a fire alert, which turned out to be false, and one a report of a bouncer with a gun. No arrests, but some of the very confused witnesses did say they heard gunfire nearby. And then there was the girl in Joe's bed: also Russian.

So there it was, a new Russian connection in her case. They decided to place this Sergey under surveillance. Parks and Andy were taking the night shift, and she was supposed to be resting up to take over tomorrow. It was all on track. Until she laid down and tried to shut her eyes. And the feelings came out to play.

❖

Anton was not the worrying type. He'd fought his way to the very top of a mountain made of broken bones and busted skulls largely because of what he lacked: conscience, regret, shame, self-doubt. If he wanted something, he took it. If someone got in his way, he hit them. If they hit back, or if he thought they might, he killed them. That was his philosophy and his business strategy and, though it might be simple, it had worked extremely well so far. He was, in essence, a bully. A thug brutal enough to bully the other thugs and bullies. And in modern Russia, as the lines between businessman, politician, criminal, and spy had all dissolved, bullying was a growth industry. They'd elected one president, the thug-in-chief. And now, here too, in America, they'd chosen a bully to lead, a President Putin of their own. Anton had loved New York since the moment he'd set foot in Brooklyn, but it was only now that he really felt American.

That's why, when Nikolai Koslov had first come to him, the decision had seemed as simple as any other. Nikolai was SVR, a cop and a spy working for the Kremlin, so not to be trusted, but he'd offered a good-faith gift, the identity of his mole in the Russian New York underworld, Yelena Noylaskya. Good, they would skin her alive and stuff her as a trophy, an example to the others. Thank you, Nikolai. Then he'd proposed his real business: some friends from US intelligence and some mercenaries, disguised as jihadi, were stealing Afghani dope, and had a foolproof way of getting it into New York. All they needed was distribution. Through intermediaries, they'd reached out to Little Maria, and it didn't go well, especially not for the dead middlemen. But Anton had his own network, his own people. Maybe he could use an unlimited supply of pure Persian heroin?

Sure. He'd be happy to buy, for his own territory. But he couldn't move that kind of weight without expanding, and stepping on the toes of Little Maria, Alonzo, Uncle Chen . . . half the bosses in the city. Nikolai understood the problem. That's when he introduced Toomey. Ex–Special Forces and now a mercenary, Toomey was the one who stole the dope and shepherded it through. He'd brought a team of his fighters here to New York. They'd clear the territory, then Anton's people would move in. Anton liked this idea: as a bully he understood the difference between a real soldier and a fellow bully, and he knew that few street criminals would be able to put up much of a fight against Toomey and his men. He talked to his top lieutenant, Sergey, who pointed out the problem: a bunch of white boys setting up shop on a Black or Spanish corner would be seen as cops or immediately attract the cops. It was Sergey's idea to recruit the local kids, young delinquents with just enough sense to run a cop spot without caring too much where the package came from, as long as it was on the money. And man was it ever. They called it White Angel because it took you straight up to heaven. The plan worked beautifully and they began to make a fortune overnight. Until Gio and the others began to connect this new dope, White Angel, with the Zahir business. That created new issues. It got Gio's friend Joe involved. Everyone knew he wouldn't do regular hits or enforcement, that was why he was given free reign as sheriff, but now he was on the track of Zahir and that meant he was getting closer to Anton. And if he did unmask him, then Anton would have all the other bosses, the whole town, lined up against him, at once. Not even the other Russians would stick by him, once they knew he was in bed with the SVR.

The one advantage Anton had left was surprise. So he talked to Toomey, and again, there was no hesitation. Like men of action, they acted. Coordinated strikes against their most likely adversaries—Maria, Alonzo, Gio, Chen—and a trap for Joe and Yelena as a bonus. But it hadn't gone the way Toomey promised. And now, suddenly, things were not so simple, and for the first time that he could remember, Anton was worried.

"What are you worrying about?" Toomey asked him. "We've got more firepower than any of them. More than the cops. And no one knows anything yet."

They were on the balcony of his party house, staring at the ocean, with a spread of caviar, coke, and cold vodka in front of him and warm hookers waiting inside, while his wife and kids waited in another, even bigger and better house nearby. The bully life was sweet, as long as you were top bully. But now he had no appetite for any of it, except the vodka and his cigarettes, which he lit end to end.

"It doesn't matter how big a gun you have, Toomey," he answered. "This isn't Chechnya. We can't hold that territory without product." He turned to Nikolai, who was lighting a fat Montecristo, playing the suave European, not concerned. "Do you realize what that bastard cost us, stealing the stash?"

"Of course," Nikolai said, with a shrug. "I can count." He nodded at Toomey. "When does the next shipment come in?"

"Day after tomorrow. We can hold out till then." Toomey smiled reassuringly, and Anton nodded, reassured. Toomey, however, was lying. Joe had thrown a major wrench into his own plans and he was as worried as Anton. But unlike Anton, he was a soldier, a warrior, not a bully or a dumb thug. He was still confident of bringing his mission off with a high likelihood of success, as long as he met that next shipment and kept control of it.

"Good, good," Anton was saying. "And I want Joe dead."

"He can't hurt us," Toomey said, not wanting to get distracted from his own primary objective. Anton slammed a fist onto the table and the caviar scattered, bouncing crushed ice onto the coke, probably a thousand dollars' worth of little fish eggs and white powder ruined. Nikolai cursed as some sour cream got on his pants. He dipped a napkin in water and began blotting.

"He has already," Anton thundered. "I want his head. And Yelena Noylaskya too."

"Fine," Toomey said, magnanimously. Sometimes bullies needed to be appeased. Toomey understood this: Richards, his theoretical boss, was just a smarter, better-connected bully. "We have an operative, a freelance hitter. The best there is. I will put her on Brody and Noylaskya."

"Her? You're sending a woman?" Anton leaned toward Nikolai. "You agree with this?"

"My friend," Nikolai said, tossing the napkin aside. "We are sending the devil."

Anton grinned. "Good." He turned to Sergey who'd been standing at a respectful distance, his stomach growling. He'd had no time to eat and had not been happy to see all the food hit the floor. "Sergey!"

"Yes sir?"

"I'm sending you with Toomey here, to make sure the next shipment comes home with no problems, understand?"

"Yes sir," Sergey said, and nodded at Toomey.

Fuck, Toomey thought, as he smiled and nodded back.

❖

But that wasn't the only new complication to come up that night. Toomey and Nikolai took their limo back to the Wildwater building, pulled into the parking garage, and rode the express elevator to the executive suite, where Richards, his sidekick Jensen, and their new CIA liaison, Powell, were waiting. Powell looked tired and a little freaked out—no wonder if Vicky had been sucking the life force out of him. Nikolai had called her a devil. Fair enough. He would have added succubus if that dumb peasant Anton had understood. Now, however, she'd have a new game to play, and Powell might be tossed aside, like a half-eaten fly.

"So . . . you settled things with our friend in Brooklyn?" Richards asked.

"Yes. No problem," Toomey said.

Nikolai draped himself over a chair. "We told him we'd send Victoria after that Brody."

Richards frowned, brow furrowing as he thought, which always caused him discomfort. He liked having Victoria around because she made him feel tough, like the guy with the vicious Rottweiler on a leash; on the other hand, actually unleashing her made him uneasy, like the guy with the vicious Rottweiler running loose. But, on the third hand, Brody had stolen his dope, not to mention shooting down his chopper and nearly killing him. His pride still stung. "Good idea," he declared, nodding, brow furrows vanishing as he finished thinking and made a command decision. "But now something else has come up. Jensen?"

"Sir." It was the nice, crisp way he said the word that had got him this job. He turned to the others. "Our sources in the FBI and local police have told us that someone new is poking into our operation. They don't know much, but it could become a problem."

Richards pointed at Powell. "It's your ex-wife, Mike."

Powell blanched. "Donna?" he asked. "I mean, Agent Zamora?" Jensen pressed a button and her federal ID photo appeared on the screen. Powell hadn't spoken to her or even seen his daughter since he'd been back. He wanted to, he missed Larissa terribly, but somehow, even though he was home, he still felt too far away.

"What's your assessment?" Richards asked him. "Is she a serious threat?"

"No," Powell said immediately. "I mean, she knows her job, but I can control it, use the bureaucracy to throw them off or even shut it down. We can use national security. Say it's classified."

Richards nodded. "Good. That's smart," he said and gave Powell a firm, friendly slap on the thigh, like a good leader, to let him know he understood. "Thanks for being a team player on this." But still, after Powell left, he pulled Toomey aside, and asked him, "What do you think? Can Powell handle his ex?"

Toomey shrugged and looked at the photo of her. She looked smart. And sexy. Too much of both for Powell maybe. "Who knows?" he told Richards. "He obviously couldn't handle her when they were married. I better keep an eye on her myself."

Yolanda put her reading glasses on and pulled her chair up so that her nose was just inches from the screen. She'd been told by her daughter that this was bad for her eyes, but she felt more comfortable this way, like when she was driving. She was on one of those sites, hunting and pecking among the keys, filling in a dating profile. It had been her friend Gladys Brody's idea; well actually, she had suggested it for Yolanda herself, urging her to get back out there and find herself a new man while she was still young enough. But Yolanda had another, better idea: she was making the profile for Donna.

She knew she'd be annoyed, and refuse if Yolanda asked her, so she didn't ask. She figured she'd just wait till the eligible bachelors started lining up, then show her the choices and let her decide, answer one or delete the whole thing. What was the harm? She added a nice photo she had of her and filled out the questions. Where it asked, *What type of guy are you looking for?*—she wrote: *Handsome. Brave. Honorable. Like law enforcement or fireman.* Actually Donna had never mentioned fire-fighters. That was Yolanda's idea. She'd seen one of those calendars at a friend's house. In some of the pictures they weren't wearing much more than boots and a helmet. Then, after thinking for a second she added: *Ex-military.*

❖

When Joe woke up on the couch the next morning, both Gladys and Yelena were standing over him. He sat up, rubbing his eyes.

"What?" he asked.

Gladys handed him a cup of coffee. Yelena handed him her phone.

"It's Juno. He's been trying to call you."

A couple of hours later, they had once again taken command of the manager's office at Club Rendezvous. As soon as everyone was settled with coffee or sodas and the door was shut, Joe spoke.

"First, before we get into it, Liam, is that stash safe?"

Liam smiled. "It's buried next to some bones that have been there since the seventies. So I expect they'll be all right a few days more."

"Good enough. Now Juno, why don't you tell everyone what you found? You'll explain it more clearly than I can."

"Right." Juno stood up, as though delivering a report to the class. "So basically what I did was set up an algorithm based on the dates we have for when the dope shipments came to town, more or less. I didn't know exact dates of course but within a one-week window. Then I searched the data and captured any events within that window or one week prior. This produced a mapping . . ."

"What difference do the dates make?" Josh asked. "We know they had to send it before it got here?"

"Jesus Christ," Liam added, "you say this is the clear explanation?"

Only Yelena nodded at him encouragingly. "Give him a chance. He'll get there."

Cash tugged Juno's arm and he sat back down onto the couch. "Bro I told you. You've got to translate it into like regular New York English for us. We don't speak brainiac."

"Right, right, sorry. Okay . . ." He took a deep breath. "Point is, I figured out how they're getting the shit in, all right? It's the returns."

"Returns?" Yelena asked.

"It's pretty clever actually," Joe said. "Almost foolproof. Wildwater supplies all kinds of junk to the military overseas. Random, boring shit . . ."

Juno nodded. "Exactly. Like shoelaces, cases for binoculars, tent poles, housings for flashlights . . ."

Joe went on: "It goes through the normal channels, purchase orders, delivery stateside, and then ships overseas. But if something is defective, or the wrong item shows up by mistake, then Wildwater's local office just issues a return authorization and ships it back."

"Get it?" Cash asked, proud of his friend. "Like when Nike sent me the wrong size sneaks, I popped them in the box, printed out the label and sent them back for free."

Juno stood up again, excited. "That's the brilliant part, see? It's coming in as US military property, not as an import, so now customs is nothing. And Wildwater has already accepted the return, so no need for a further military inspection here either. It just flows right through, via air freight, to the terminal for pickup and then back to Wildwater's warehouse."

Cash was grinning now, as the others began to get it. "Except now, those tent poles or flashlights or whatever . . ."

Yelena laughed. "They are full of heroin."

"That's pretty damned good," Liam said. "Just let the government deliver the gear for you."

Josh nodded. "Beautiful. The closest thing to an open pipeline you could have. No customs. No military police. No nothing. Ah, what we could do with that. I better not tell Rebbe. It will break his heart."

"When is the next shipment of returned goods?" Liam asked.

"Two days," Juno said. "Air freight to Newark."

Yelena hugged Juno. "Juno you are a genius."

"Thanks, Yelena," he said, blushing.

"Now how do we stop it?" she asked him.

"Oh . . . that . . ." Juno sat back down and reached for his Coke. "I haven't gotten to that part yet."

Silence descended, and everyone sat back, as though the elation were escaping from the balloon. After a couple of minutes, Joe realized all eyes were now on him.

"Anyone here know any dog trainers?" he asked.

❖

As it happened, the club manager, who'd been conducting business from a seat at the bar while Joe and the others commandeered his office, was a dog trainer himself. Johnny "Santa" Santangelo, who took advantage of his white beard and huge belly to play Santa at the club's Christmas party each year, took in rescued dogs, mainly German Shepherds, Dobermans, and Rottweilers, which he trained as guard dogs, and then sold, or failing that, gave away as housebroken pets. Many of the Caprisi family's warehouses, parking lots, and construction sites were patrolled by Santa's helpers. The dog Joe wanted was of a far more specialized and rare type, but Santa knew a guy who knew a guy and when Nero and Pete went to visit him on Gio's behalf, the trainer reluctantly agreed to fake some paperwork and lend out the talent for a day.

Meanwhile, Cash was busy. He had to obtain two vehicles. One, which he'd be driving, was the crash car. A crash car is what it sounds like, and it could be any make as long as it had some power. Cash chose a Camaro, which he modified with heavy-duty shocks, a reinforced steel front bumper and some additional steel poles welded into the interior. The second vehicle was a specialty item for Joe, which he got from an Armenian guy who owned a salvage yard near Reliable Scrap, the huge auto junkyard Cash ran for Uncle Chen, and which was the center of his car theft business. Cars disappeared and dissolved into parts, then reappeared in new colors and shapes and under new names in that giant labyrinth, itself just a small corner of the junk kingdom that spread over that part of Queens.

Liam and Josh, who'd become familiar with the Newark Airport freight operations through their hijacking, stole a semi, switched the plates to make it pass as legit, and had it repainted. J&L Trucking—"In It For the Long Haul"—was what Liam stenciled on the door, which Josh thought was ridiculous, but sweet.

Yelena handled weapons and costumes.

And Joe tried to explain what he needed to Juno.

"I can get you in easy," Juno said. "But getting out the way you want is impossible."

"Sure, it's difficult maybe, but there must be . . ."

"No man, you don't understand. Am I generally given to hyperbole?"

"Somewhat."

"Okay. But right now I mean literally impossible." He sat forward and explained it slowly to Joe, as though to a large child. "Getting a truck in for a fake delivery is no problem, because it won't be fake. Anybody who wants to can ship some shit somewhere. It's America. I'll just go online with a made-up company name and manifest, say y'all are bringing in a load of whatever to be sent off to Lithuania or some place. You pull up in the truck, show the paperwork, and you're in. But for me to go into their system and find out exactly where they put the can from Wildwater, that's a whole different kettle of fish."

To save on money and logistical hassle, Wildwater, in its capacity as a legit corporation, would consolidate all the items from that general region going stateside and then send an entire truck-sized container, which would be loaded onto a gigantic plane and offloaded in Newark.

Any item in there could, conceivably, contain the dope. And the container could end up anywhere in the depot, since it would be slotted into an open space whenever it came in.

"But why can't you just hack in, even once it lands, and tell me its location? Don't tell me their security is too much for you. It's got to be in their system."

"Ah, but that's precisely what I keep saying, my dude. In *their* system. And their system is closed. It's basically just a local network for moving boxes around their yard. There's no internet access, nothing over phone wires or cell signals. Doesn't matter how good a hacker I am if there ain't shit to hack."

"So who does have access?"

"Folks working there. Shipping clerks at their terminals. And those dudes in the orange vests who drive around in carts, finding your can. They have handhelds, like UPS does, for checking it's the right package. Same idea, but the packages are the size of subway cars."

"So, if you had one of those handheld things?"

"The range isn't much. It wouldn't work outside the yard."

"But if you were in range . . . with one of those devices . . ."

"Then I can find you your Persian. Or at least the can it's in. How you're going to get me in there I don't know. Not to mention back out."

"Don't worry about that. I'll think of something."

Juno sighed. "Oh, I know you will. That's what I'm afraid of."

27

IT WAS BRIGHT AND early. The morning air was still cool and quiet, and you could even hear birds trilling in the wetlands (along with the roar of airplanes) and smell water on the breeze that shifted through the reeds (along with the burn of chemicals), as J&L Trucking's 18-wheeler pulled up to the gate of the high-security air freight depot adjacent to Newark Liberty International Airport, with Liam behind the wheel.

"Good morning," he told the head guard, a forty-something white guy with a flattop buzzed haircut and creases in his uniform pants. The credentials clipped to his ironed shirt read James Barker, Supervisor. Liam handed down the paperwork that Juno had provided. "We've got a drop off."

"Morning." Barker looked it over, while two junior guards circled the truck, checking underneath it with mirrors. "Says here you're hauling fertilizer? What does certified organic, single source mean?"

"Means this is the purest horseshit around, straight from Kentucky, home of the best horseshit in the world," Liam went on. "Now some folks will tell you Virginia, but for my money, the horseshit that you get from a diet of sweet bluegrass . . ."

"Well, we've got to open her up. Give them a hand, Myron."

"Yes, sir. No problem," Liam said, as Josh jumped down from his side. Barker led the way to the rear of the truck, followed by Myron, one of the other two who'd been checking the exterior, a young Black guy with

199

a smooth-shaven head and red eyes behind his glasses. Artie, a plump, fair-skinned redhead and the youngest of the lot, stood around trying to look useful.

"Does it stink bad?" Myron asked Josh.

"Not if you don't break the seals."

Liam, who was watching in the side view, pressed a button and the gate lowered, hitting the asphalt with a clink and making a handy ramp. Then he hopped out and joined them.

"Here it is," Josh said, walking Barker up the ramp. He unlocked the rear and he and Myron rolled the door up, revealing a solid wall of rich, brown fertilizer, sealed into large, plastic-sealed cubes, and marked "Kentucky's Finest—100% Pure Manure."

"How much you hauling?" Barker asked, peering at it.

"Twenty tons."

"Right . . ." He decided he'd seen enough. "All right, looks good." As he turned to descend, Josh slipped on the metal gate for a second and bumped him, then grabbed his arm to keep from knocking him off. Barker stumbled back and knocked into Myron, who dropped his clipboard while fighting for balance. The papers blew around. Artie and Myron chased them.

"Oops, sorry . . ." Josh said.

Liam too reached up to support Barker's back. "Careful!"

Barker regained his balance. "I'm fine," he said, defensively, then shouted at Myron: "Come on, quit fooling around," as he headed back to the front, Artie trotting behind him. Barker told him to lift the entry barrier while Myron reorganized the clipboard.

"Here's your authorization and delivery location," he said, handing Liam back the stack of papers and circling something with a pen. "I marked it on this map."

"Thanks very much." Liam hopped back in the cab while Josh locked up, then climbed back into his seat. Liam lifted the ramp. Meanwhile, the barrier rose and Barker, having regained his authority, stiffly waved them through. Josh pulled two small earpieces from the glove box and handed one to Liam while fitting the other in his ear. He spoke into the tiny mic.

"We're in. You copy?"

"Loud and clear," Juno's voice replied.

While Liam followed the map, Josh removed a small panel that had been cut into the rear of the cab, then reached through and knocked on the wall of the trailer. Juno slid a panel open from the other side, inside the body of the truck.

"Here you go . . ." Josh said and he passed him back the handheld scanner that he'd lifted from the guard.

❖

Inside the trailer, Juno plugged the handheld into his laptop and began to search for the location of the Wildwater canister while Joe and Yelena moved the cubes of fertilizer. They had nowhere near twenty tons. There was just a single layer of large cubes, stacked like bricks, blocking off the rear doors, and now they shifted them aside.

"You find it?" Joe asked Juno.

"Looking, looking . . . Wildwater Corp, one canister, landed at four A.M., from Kabul via Frankfurt. Unloaded at five A.M. Here it is . . ." He spoke into his mic.

"Liam, I found it. I'm sending the location."

"Great," Liam answered. "I'll look for a quiet spot to unload."

The location of the container appeared on the truck's GPS and Josh told Liam to keep going straight, while he stuffed the paperwork from the guardhouse into the glove box. Even with the map they'd been given it was confusing: like a maze built of shipping containers, stacked several stories high and sprawling out for acres, with no one in sight but the occasional worker on a forklift shifting one in or out, or another truck looking to load or unload. Now they followed Juno's digital map, which led them like a red string through the labyrinth. Then Josh spotted a shed that looked like it housed unused forklifts.

"There," he told Liam. "Pull up alongside it."

"Right," Liam said, and backed in, so that the rear of his truck was hidden in the shade of the shed. Stacks of containers shielded the other sides.

"We found a spot," Josh said over his mic. "Get ready." Then he jumped down and came around the back while Liam lowered the gate, keeping an eye out the whole time. In the back, Josh took another quick look around too, then unlocked the door and pushed it up. The fertilizer wall had been cleared, revealing the interior, and Josh waved while backing down the ramp. Slowly, the Jeep rolled out of the truck and down the ramp. Joe was behind the wheel, clean-shaven and in an Army major's uniform, with a standard issue sidearm and his hair neat under the hat. Yelena, also in a uniform, sat beside him, cradling an army issue M-1. A German shepherd in a military harness and leash lay resting on the back seat.

Josh saluted as they drove past.

28

FOR CASH, WAKING UP so damn early was the hardest part of the day, or so he thought. Still he was there, at the salt depot on the West Side when Joe said to be, and at least Joe brought everyone coffee. That's the mark of a true leader. After they got the truck squared away, with the Jeep on board and a little desk set up for Juno, he helped Liam and Josh build the wall of—he was happy to know—hermetically sealed manure and then trailed them to Jersey. When they reached the outlet road for the depot, Liam and Josh got on line behind a row of trucks, pick-ups, and other vehicles waiting for entrance, including a number of ordinary passenger cars, couriers and such, as well as a few military vehicles, green trucks on giant tires, a Humvee. Another line slowly pulled out from the exit. There was a guardhouse with gates, and a chain-link fence enclosing the whole gigantic place, like a super-sized Lego-town built of brightly colored rectangles. Beyond that were the Jersey wetlands, miles of swamp and weeds, with chemical plants firing on the horizon, planes coming and going from the airport.

Cash pulled over. The whole road leading to the entrance was lined with parked trucks and cars, mostly long-haul truckers waiting for something to arrive or be cleared for pickup. Some had been there all night, with the drivers asleep in the cabs. Now a few stretched their legs and smoked. A couple of livery drivers were taking naps between airport runs. Cash slid into a spot that gave him a nice view of the entrance, said "in position" over his mic, and settled in, watching as the truck got through, no problem, and not really expecting much of anything else to happen until it came back out. And for a while nothing did. He sat back and snoozed.

❖

Donna hadn't planned on going to Jersey that morning. She hadn't even planned on leaving Brooklyn. In fact, if Sergey Popov ran true to form, he wouldn't even stir till past noon. But there she was, parked down the block from his apartment building, fighting to stay awake in the car—she'd relieved Andy at six—when his black Benz came rolling out of the parking structure with Popov behind the wheel. She followed him onto the Belt and then through the Brooklyn Battery Tunnel into Manhattan, where he stopped at a corner in Tribeca to pick up a guy she hadn't seen before, an athletic-looking young white dude with a blond ponytail. Still it was nothing to get too worked up about. Maybe they were going to hit some golf balls. But the next thing she knew, they'd crossed the Hudson, if driving through a tunnel beneath it counted as crossing, and were heading to I-9 and the outskirts of Newark Airport. She reported in, as a matter of course, letting her office know she was in New Jersey, but when Popov arrived at the freight terminal and pulled over, as if waiting for someone or something, she decided that this might be more than a trip to see his grandma. So she called Blaze. The deputy federal marshal was just getting into her office in Newark and agreed to drive over and provide backup, if Donna would back her up later by being her wing-woman at a new lesbian bar she'd been meaning to check out that night. Donna agreed to one drink. Then she settled in, eyes on Popov, whose own eyes seemed to be dozing behind his mirror shades.

29

ARTIE WAS ON THE early shift today, pulling a double, covering for his buddy, who was hooking up with some girl he'd met. Artie didn't mind. He needed the money, plus Floyd had given him a little thank you gift for the favor: a fat juicy joint of primo bud that he went off in the reeds and smoked between shifts with his other pal, Myron, who was showing up for gate duty that A.M. The weed definitely made the shift go quicker, but it was stronger than he was used to, a special gift after all, and when this MP, Major Somebody, pulled up in a jeep and started talking about a suspected shipment of illegal substances, it was all Artie could do not to freak out.

"Officer," this MP said as he pulled right up and stopped Artie on his rounds, piloting the three-wheeled cart they gave him to drive. At first he didn't even know who he meant; Artie was just private security and nobody called him officer or anything fancy like that. His plan had been to do a quick tour of the depot then stop at the vending machines and pick up sodas and snacks for him and Myron.

"I'm Major Ardon," the MP said, pointing at a name on his uniform, H. Ardon. He looked serious and tough, like Artie's high school gym coach, and he had a girl, sorry woman, sorry female officer beside him, who was looking straight ahead through her shades, helmet low, and holding a German Shepherd by the leash. "And I need immediate emergency access to this container."

"Um . . . which . . ." Artie fumbled, flustered and already starting to sweat. He knew he was supposed to call this in, but the Major kept banging on the container. Artie checked: it was marked US MILITARY, described as "Returned and/or Defective Misc.," and Wildwater Corp's agents were supposed to pick it up today.

"Open her up, pronto," the major ordered.

"Yes sir . . . I mean . . . don't you need some kind of warrant?"

"Warrant?" the major barked at him. "Is that what you said?" He closed in on him, poking him in the chest with a finger. "First of all, is this item under military authority or your private civilian authority?"

"Um . . . military?" Artie guessed. He had no idea.

"Good answer. Now . . . two . . ." He poked him harder, with two fingers. "We have reason to believe that illegal contraband, to wit heroin, is on that container, officer. But as you see, it is scheduled for pickup today. Is it your intention to deter us in seizing that heroin in time?"

"Um . . . no sir . . ."

"Right again." Now the major poked him with three fingers. "And three. It is for that reason of extreme urgency that I have the corporal here with me, and her highly trained K-9 investigator. This dog is able to sniff out any and all illegal substances, but the longer we spend talking and waiting for warrants the higher the likelihood of a false positive."

"False positive?" He glanced down at the dog with a new respect as it sniffed the wheels of his cart, then his own boots.

"Right. This dog's highly trained senses are so sensitive that if any person or vehicle or even clothing has been exposed to and/or ingested illegal drugs within the last month, the dog will know. Traces remain in the hair and skin cells. They store in fat and become detectable when the subject begins to secrete perspiration. Now, if while we are here chatting, the dog barks at anyone, then I am legally obligated to place said person under court-martial awaiting a full spectrum of blood, urine, and spinal fluid tests."

"Oh . . ." Artie said, sweat pumping from his pores. His armpits burned with fear, and the realization he was secreting panicked him even more.

But how could you hold in sweat? He wondered how red his eyes were and wished he'd worn shades too, like the MPs.

"Now then officer, it is oh nine hundred hours. Are you going to open that container or not?"

"Yes!" Artie shouted. "I mean yes, sir!" And with that he broke the seal and unlocked the can.

"Thank you officer. For doing your patriotic duty," the major said and saluted. "Now step back," he added. "And let the dog work."

"Right, right . . ." Artie said saluting as he gladly ran back to his cart.

The dog's qualifications at least were real, even if Joe and Yelena's were not. The trainer from whom Gio's people borrowed him supplied dogs to government agencies, and this one had just passed its tests with flying colors. The trainer had held up his delivery for a couple days, saying he needed shots from the vet before traveling. However, as far as Joe knew, the only substance he was trained to sniff out was heroin; certainly not people, and of course not for thirty days, but Joe knew a stoner when he saw one, and didn't need the dog's help to know this dude was baked, standing at attention by his cart and trying to hold his breath.

But now it was Joe who was sweating. They were inside the container, packed to the ceiling on both sides, with a narrow path down the center, and Yelena was leading the dog slowly along, while it sniffed at cartons and pallets that, according to their markings, contained all manner of stuff—from fluorescent bulbs and night vision goggles to smoke detectors and shoelaces, but none of it, according to the dog at least, contained a speck of dope.

Yelena looked at him and shrugged. Joe's mind raced. Was it possible to fool the dog? Theoretically yes, but he couldn't see any coffee or other items that might be used to throw off the scent, and it would take all day to search this can by hand. Was it possible there was no dope here after all? Sure. If they had cancelled the shipment for some reason. Then the rest of this crap would just come in through the normal channels, with no one coming by to pull the dope from it.

But before Joe had time to think any further, he received confirmation that someone else did seem to think there was dope on the container. It was Juno, calling him over the earpiece.

"Hey Joe, FYI. I kept the tracking on that Russian's car live, and according to that, he's sitting right outside the gate. So you might want to get a move on . . ."

"Shit," Joe said. He'd hoped, by the time anyone showed, to have the dope and be back inside the truck. "Cash, you there?"

"At your service," Cash responded from his parked car.

"Can you take a look around, see if you can confirm that the Russian goon from last night is there?"

"Hang on . . ."

"Try again," Joe whispered under his breath to Yelena. She gave the commands that the trainer had provided, and the dog diligently sniffed his way up and down the container, then wagged his tail, licked Yelena's hand and lay down for a well-earned rest.

Cash came back on, "Well I've got bad news and totally fucked up news . . ."

"Let's have it," Joe told him. He could see that the guard was starting to get restless, and curious, as the fear faded.

"Bad news is the Russian is definitely here, about thirty yards back."

"And the totally fucked up?"

"That Fed, the female one. Starts with a Z?"

"Agent Zamora?" Joe asked.

"Yeah, that's the one. She's here too."

❖

Meanwhile, Josh and Liam were sitting tight, waiting for word from Joe, while Juno sat even tighter in the back. The plan was that once Joe and Yelena found the dope, they'd return to the truck, and drive back up into the trailer to be escorted out like a backward Trojan Horse. Then the guard from the gate zoomed by in a little cart—the bald guy with the glasses. He paused, reversed, and got out.

"Shit," Josh said.

"What?" Juno answered, hearing him over the mic and squirming with frustration. He was certain he'd been correct in his calculations—the shipment had to be there. Yet they'd come up empty. But the very fact that the Russians and the FBI were both here only proved him right. Or almost right. They were missing something.

"Nothing. Just be cool and don't make any noise in there," Liam said, removing his own earpiece. He waved at the guard and leaned out, grinning big.

"Thank God, you found us," he called to the frowning guard.

"Found you?" he asked, looking up.

"Haven't you been looking for us? We're lost."

Actually, the guard, Myron, was heading to the vending machines behind the shed. He had terrible dry mouth, ever since he smoked that fat joint with his buddy Artie at the start of shift. Then Artie had gone off on his rounds, promising to pick him up a Mountain Dew, and never came back. Now Myron had no choice but to show these two foreigners the way back to the exit.

"Follow me," he said and, with a sigh—the vending machine and its load of cold soda was so close—he got back into his cart and headed off, reluctantly. Liam, also reluctantly, put the truck in gear and followed with Juno fuming in the back. The plan had gone off perfectly, but the results were nil, and now here they were, leaving empty-handed. Josh got back on his headset to call Joe and let him know that he'd need to find another way out.

30

WHEN TOOMEY ARRIVED AT the depot, everything seemed to be under control. He got on line at the entrance, waiting as the trucks and cars rolled up to the gate, showed their paperwork, got checked by security, and admitted. He was driving his own ride, a Jeep Wrangler Willys, the big, tricked-out Unlimited; it drove like the rugged military vehicles he was accustomed to, but with the leather seats, tinted windows, and top-notch sound system he preferred. He rolled slowly forward, sipping his coffee and adjusting the AC, classical music blasting. It was the same routine he had gone through each time since he began handling the shipments and there had never been a hitch. Nor did he expect one this time. He saw Sergey parked on the roadside along with the semis, pickups, and cars that were always there, and nodded as he passed. Toomey's number two, Trey, was beside him, riding along in an uneasy partnership with the Russian, and nodded back. He also noted two of his other men, Dirk and Baxter, sitting in a Hummer, ready to trail and observe from a distance. They were battle-hardened mercs who had accompanied him to New York on this mission. To Dirk this was just another deployment: he was Dutch and had spent a decade fighting wars around the world. To Baxter, an ex-Marine from Atlanta who decided to go into business for himself, operating stateside was a bit of a mind-blower. But he was furious when their ambush at the club went wrong: he was more than ready to prove himself again now.

Toomey reached the gate and showed his papers to the head guard, who remembered him. He was the kind of guy who got all warm and fuzzy around military, and the Special Forces sticker on Toomey's rear window might as well have been a free pass.

"Morning sir," the guard greeted him, standing a little straighter. Toomey gave him a warm smile and a commanding nod.

"Morning, Barker." His papers explained that he'd be loading up an assortment of random, very boring items from the Wildwater Corporation container. Barker gave the Jeep a cursory check then thanked him for his service again and waved him by.

❖

Joe came out of the container fast and called to Artie, who was getting sleepy leaning on his cart in the sun: working a double and getting stoned was catching up to him. He jumped as Joe barked.

"Officer!"

"Um, yes, sir . . ."

"This container has been cleared. Seal it up and then escort us to the exit pronto. We've just had another emergency call. National security."

"Right!"

That intense corporal who didn't talk came out, leading the dog, who sniffed suspiciously in his direction. Artie gave them a wide berth as they got in the Jeep and then shut the door to the container, slapping a sticker on it that said it had been opened and inspected. Then he got back in his cart and began to zoom through the stacks, leading the Jeep to the exit. He still didn't really grasp exactly what all this was about, but if it got these hard-ass MPs and their narc dog out of his life, so be it.

❖

Joe and Yelena sped toward the gate, cruising past the other vehicles waiting to exit as the security guard led them along the edge of the road.

They passed the truck, J & L painted on the door, with Josh and Liam in the cab and, Joe knew, Juno in back. Myron had escorted them this far before going back to his post at the gate, sadly without his soda. Joe shifted his cap casually as he passed, and Liam scratched the side of his nose, letting him know he saw him. Then they reached the front.

"Lift the gate," Artie called out as his cart pulled up, with the jeep idling behind. Myron stepped out of the guardhouse.

"Hey Artie," Myron said. "Where were you? I thought you were bringing me a Mountain Dew?"

"Sorry Myron," Artie said, trying to signal him by nodding subtly at Joe. "Got caught up with this. I'll tell you about it later."

Joe gave the horn a tap. Artie jumped.

"Shoot . . ." He turned back to Joe and saluted at him again, then turned back to Myron. "Listen these MPs got to get out of here. Lift her up."

"MPs?" Myron frowned down at his clipboard. "I didn't know there were any MPs here. Excuse me sir," he stepped up to Joe. "I'm sorry but I didn't see you come in. When did you arrive?"

Joe stared him down from under his hat. "Hours ago, officer," he said. "We were here bright and early. What time do you come on?"

"Nine."

"Then that explains it, doesn't it, officer?"

"Yes sir, but the guard on duty should have logged it here."

"Officer," Joe said, looming over him. "I have an emergency to deal with. A matter of national security. And you're going to hold me up because some incompetent forgot to log something, whoever it was?"

Myron nodded. "That's what's weird sir. The incompetent on duty? It was you, Artie."

Artie looked stunned. Was it possible he'd been so stoned he had forgotten about the MP? Or had he slipped by during one of his very brief naps? That's when Yelena, who'd been briefed on the commands for her highly trained dog, gave the defend command, "Take!" while also pulling back hard on the leash. As a result the dog began barking furiously at the two guards while straining with all his might.

"That's it!" Joe told them. "Hold it right there. I'm going to have to place you both under arrest."

"What?" Myron asked, backing away, looking from the dog to Yelena to Joe with equal fear. Artie groaned.

"You idiot. I told you to let them out."

"At least one of you," Joe said, "has been using illegal drugs or alcohol on duty, which is a violation of the Homeland Security Act, a federal court-martial offense."

"I wasn't on duty yet . . ." Myron said. "I mean . . ."

"Too late for excuses, son," Joe told him. "Now both of you are going to have to give us a bodily fluids sample while the corporal here observes. She's a trained expert interrogator." He turned to Yelena. "Get the specimen jars."

Yelena saluted sharply and directed the dog toward the guards, who backed away. "Let's go, you drugged-out losers. On the double!"

Barker, who'd been busy processing entries on the other side, saw the commotion and rushed over, saluting smartly when he saw Joe and Yelena.

"Good morning Major, what seems to be the trouble?"

"You the CO?" Joe asked, sternly.

"Yes sir . . . I mean I'm the supervisor, Jim Barker."

"Well I'm dealing with a high-threat-type national security crisis here and your men have seen fit to delay us. And now it seems we have a possible drug violation as well."

Barker glared at Myron and Artie, who looked back, wide-eyed with fear, and at least feeling stone-cold sober. The dog growled, and Yelena licked her chops, like they were both ready to rip them apart. Barker spoke in a lower tone to Joe.

"I apologize sir. We try to recruit good men, but it's not like in the Army. We don't have the same training."

"You served?" Joe asked him.

"Reserves. Mostly out of Fort Dix."

Joe nodded in appreciation. "Then you understand."

"Yes, sir, I do."

"Hold it," Joe said holding a hand up and listening to his silent ear-piece. "That alert has just gone code red." He told Myron and Artie: "I'm putting you two in each other's custody till we get back." Then he turned to Barker: "Now for the sake of America, lift that goddamn gate, soldier!"

"Yes, sir, right away. Lift her!" he yelled, and Myron jumped and ran to the guard house.

"Yes, sir!"

Yelena ordered the dog to fall back, and it happily hopped into the Jeep, tail wagging. Joe jumped behind the wheel and saluted as the arm of the gate lifted. Barker saluted and said, "Thanks for your service, Major!" Myron and Artie watched him leave with relief before starting to yell at each other. And as Joe and Yelena cleared the exit and pulled onto the access road, everything seemed to have worked out smoothly, until a bullet shattered the windshield.

31

TREY WAS THERE WITH Sergey to watch out for trouble, so after Toomey, his commander and employer, entered the depot, he put his binoculars on the exit gate and kept them there, waiting for him to return. When the Jeep with the military folks pulled up, he took note, and when he saw they had a dog and the dog barked at the guards, he got curious, but it was only when curiosity made him zoom in tight on their faces that he realized: it was them, the motherfucker who killed Tony back in the helicopter and the girl who rode the motorbike like a BMX champ. The same two who'd hit the stash and walked away untouched. This, he decided, qualified as trouble and he called Toomey, who told him to take them out. Immediately.

"Yes, sir. It's done," he said with satisfaction. He got on the phone to his back up, Dirk and Baxter, who had the sniper rifle. "Team Two come in."

"I'm here Team One."

"Dirk, we've got a target. The Jeep about to come out. Driver and passenger both. This one's for Tony."

"Negative," Dirk said. "We don't have a clear shot."

"Understood," Trey said, secretly pleased. "I will engage. Take the shot if you get it." He drew his machine pistol. "Pull out," he told Sergey, as he racked the slide, "we're taking these two down."

Sergey, however, did not take orders from Trey. Nor did he take orders from Toomey. He worked for Anton, a demanding and unforgiving boss, and Anton had ordered him to protect the shipment, nothing else.

"I'm not going without the dope," he said.

"We have to move."

"We're not moving."

"But Toomey's orders . . ."

"Fuck Toomey," Sergey said. "We wait."

Now the Jeep was moving, coming through the gate. "Fuck Toomey?" Trey asked. "Fuck you." And he leaned out and took a shot, shattering the Jeep's windshield. From that angle, with the target moving, he missed, but he left Sergey no choice: now they were going to move.

❖

Donna did not see that coming. She'd sunk into a torpor really, as the sun began to climb, toasting her face through the window, and the minutes clicked by, watching the slow traffic, like a lazy two-way river flowing in and out of the depot. Then, before she even registered what was happening, the guy in the car with Sergey, Unknown Subject with Ponytail, who'd been watching the same boring show through binoculars, swapped them for a gun and took a shot at a vehicle as it passed, shattering the windshield. A Jeep, with what looked like military personnel aboard. Actually, looking closer, as she drew her own weapon and pushed her door open to take a protected stance, it was a man, a woman and a dog, which was even weirder. And then, as if to twist her mind completely, she thought—or maybe she was just going crazy—that as the Jeep accelerated, swerving past her, that she saw Joe driving, no longer looking like a desperate shuffling junkie, but now in crisp fatigues with a cap and shades.

❖

"Get the dog down!"

When the windshield shattered, Joe hit the gas, and began to swerve deliberately, slaloming along the road to make it harder for the shooter to aim. Meanwhile, Yelena pushed the dog onto the floor, petting him swiftly and commanding him to lie down and stay, then raised her weapon and hunted for the shooter. But with two lanes of traffic, much of it big trucks, and two more rows of vehicles parked along the shoulder, it was hard to see exactly what was happening, and there wasn't anywhere to hide. So Joe floored it, and as the Jeep picked up speed, he saw Donna, out of her car, gun drawn, also searching for the source of the bullet.

That became clear when the black Benz, which Joe recognized, pulled out, drawing honks as it screeched through a U-turn and came after them, with a Hummer looming behind it. A few seconds later, Donna was back in her car and chasing them.

"You back there, Cash?" Joe asked over the mic.

"Yup. Right on your tail. Which keeps getting longer, by the way. What's with this Hummer?"

"I don't know but if you can help give us some breathing room, I'd appreciate it."

"Say no more."

Cash gunned his engine, which roared with power as he slipped onto the shoulder, passing the Fed in her Fedmobile—a black Impala, perfectly respectable but no match for what he had—then checking out the Hummer as he passed that—two guys, one white, one Black, clean-cut army types. Despite its power, neither the Hummer nor its driver were anywhere near as nimble as Cash, and he slid into the gap, nearly moving horizontally, like an expert parallel parker snatching somebody's spot. Then he braked. The Hummer driver hit his brake and his horn, both too hard, rocking forward and barely kissing Cash's bumper, and his ass, as Cash threw his car into higher gear and stomped the gas, slipping away. The big beast fishtailed as it tried to do the same, but the Fed, who Cash had to admit was not bad, swerved around it and took next place in the race, behind the Camaro. She hit her flashers and siren, trying to tell him to clear the way. He waved and hit his turn signal, as if he was going to, but then kept swerving in front of her, slowing as did, like a dipshit driver who was panicking and had no idea what to do.

❖

Behind the wheel, Donna was on the radio now. "Calling all law enforcement. This is a federal agent, calling for assistance. In pursuit of . . . two or three suspect vehicles."

Newark police and the NJ State Troopers both responded and Donna identified herself and described the vehicles. Then Blaze came on.

"Zamora is that you?"

"Affirmative Deputy Logan."

"I was just on my way to meet you."

"Change of plans. Want to help me catch a couple suspects?"

"That's what I do. I'm joining up with the posse now at the highway junction. We'll cut them off at the pass."

"Thanks."

Now she had this black Camaro in her way though. It was a brand-new muscle car, jacked up and gleaming, but the dude inside it—and it was always a dude—had no idea how to drive. Typical. He had his blinkers on, first the left, then the right, then the hazards, and was slowing down, but couldn't seem to get out of the way. She got on the squawk box:

"Pull over to your right . . . Right!" she ordered as he swerved right, then started to skid on the gravel at the shoulder and swerved back left, cutting across her and dangerously close to the traffic coming the other way.

Jesus, she thought, how did this guy get a license? Then she heard automatic gunfire from up ahead. And a moment later, more gunfire, from her left, as the guy in the Hummer shot out her tires.

32

ONCE THE DOG WAS safely on the floor, and Joe was on the open road, Yelena crept into the rear seat and, aiming carefully out the back, opened fire on the Russian and his gunman in the Benz. She knocked out the windshield and both headlights before the driver took evasive action and peeled off, dropping to the rear of the pack, leaving Cash right behind them and then Donna in her car behind him. Cash smiled at Yelena, as he held Donna back, and the Jeep moved further away. Then Yelena saw the Hummer pulling up alongside Donna, roaring along the shoulder, full speed, with a gunner now upright through the opening in the roof, aiming an AR-15. He carefully took out Donna's tires, sending her skidding off the road. The Hummer's driver muscled in on Cash in the Camaro, threatening to push him into oncoming traffic, while the gunner took a shot at Cash through the roof.

"Shit, that was close," Cash called over the mic. "He's trying to get through me to you. I'll try to hold him back a little longer."

It didn't matter though. Riding high above the Camaro, the gunner was able to fire over Cash's car and into the Jeep. Yelena hit the floor, hugging the dog, as bullets tore into the back seat and the rear panel.

"You okay?" Joe asked, still speeding forward.

"So far," Yelena told him. "He hit the extra gas tank." The plastic container of extra fuel strapped to the rear of the Jeep was now leaking dangerously.

"Better ditch it then," Joe said, and reached under the passenger seat for the emergency kit. He pulled the flare gun out and handed it to her. "Give them this as well."

"Right."

The Hummer bucked against the Camaro, trying to brush Cash aside.

"Let them through, Cash," Joe said over the mic. "And watch out. Yelena's going to light them up."

"Cool. I'm out," Cash said, and swerved away, letting the Hummer pass. As it closed in on the Jeep, pulling in right behind them, Yelena rose up and threw the leaking gas canister. It thumped onto the windshield, gasoline spilling from the bullet holes. Immediately, she fired the flare, blasting it into the fuel can. It blew.

Like napalm, the gas caught, first the fumes from the ruptured container, then the liquid fuel splashing on the roof, and then, a split second later, the whole can. Instantly the hood of the Hummer was covered, as flames danced over the liquid, licking everywhere it spilled like tongues of blue and orange. The terrified gunner ducked back inside as the driver swerved, his windshield blind with flames. In a panic, he veered wildly, drove onto the shoulder, and banged into a tree, as they both bailed out of the truck.

Now it was just the Benz still trailing behind Yelena and Joe, and they had a decent lead. But there was trouble ahead. Juno had been monitoring the law's frequencies from the rear of the truck and he warned Joe about a roadblock a mile ahead, at the last exit before they joined the main highway.

"Are you clear back there?" Joe asked.

"Yeah we're like a quarter mile behind you," Liam put in. "Normal traffic now. No cops."

"Then we'll come to you," Joe said and made a hard left. Leaning on his horn, as on-coming cars honked and swayed around him, he cut the wheel, and skidded into a U-turn, then straightened out, and rejoined the flow, going the opposite way. The Russian stayed with him, repeating the move, as terrified drivers veered away, honking frantically. Joe stayed in the left lane, pushing as hard as he could, until he saw the truck on his left, coming toward them. Liam gave a quick wave. Then Joe did it again.

Cranking the wheel left, he cut across the double yellow, and swung into the traffic, which braked and honked and yelled, then gunned it and re-joined the flow, now a few dozen yards behind the truck. This time the Russian took a beat longer, but soon he was there again, behind them.

"Okay," Joe said over the mic. "Same getaway plan as before but with a slight change. We're going to have to keep moving."

Liam kept the truck rolling steady while Josh, watching in his side mirror, waited for Joe to work his way up, passing other cars, and finally falling into place right behind them. "Ready," Joe said, keeping about one car length back. Then Josh lowered the gate. The metal ramp came down on its hydraulics, and when the lip began to scrape along the asphalt, Juno flung the door up from inside. Joe slowly increased his speed, nosing the Jeep's front wheels onto the ramp. The Russian, seeing what was happening, sped up too, bumping them from behind. Yelena fired a couple shots, brushing him back, while Joe gave it some gas, racing the motor, and drove up into the truck.

"Lift it!" he yelled over the mic, and Josh hit the power, bullets ringing off the metal gate as it came up, shielding them inside. The Russian was right behind them now.

"Need a gun?" Juno asked, as Joe and Yelena jumped out of the Jeep.

"Nope," Joe said, "I got it," and pulled his folding camp knife from his pocket. He began to slash at the plastic-wrapped bales of manure stacked along one side of the truck. "Help me lift it," he said, and Juno and Yelena came to his aid. "Time to unload this shit."

Together they hoisted the bale over the gate and it dumped onto the hood of the Russian's Benz, where it burst open, spilling an avalanche of manure over the hood and through the blown-out windshield. The driver and passenger tried to brush it away, but another bale followed, burying them. Unable to see, and with fertilizer blowing around them like a small brown hurricane, the driver pulled onto the shoulder and stopped. His passenger, the guy in the ponytail, leapt from the car and tried to take a shot, but the truck was gone in the flow of traffic.

Juno and Joe lowered the door. A few minutes later, the truck had slowed to a crawl, as they reached the roadblock, were waved on by bored state troopers, and made their way to the Lincoln Tunnel.

❖

Meanwhile Toomey, who had proceeded to the Wildwater container with no problems, selected the items on his pickup list, loaded them into his own Jeep, and left. By the time he reached the exit, the excitement was all over, and he proceeded on his way without impediment. He was a little annoyed at all the backed-up traffic; after all, he had a schedule to keep.

PART IV

33

JOE WAS TRYING TO think. They were in Old Shenanigan's Ale House, the sprawling, packed Irish pub in the West 30s, (or Irish-ish—it had green tablecloths and Guinness on tap but bore little resemblance to anything Liam remembered from home) that once belonged to Patty White and that Liam and his brothers now controlled. They were in a barren upstairs room, half-finished and in a permanent state of construction, off limits to employees and unknown to the tourists and local office workers who packed the street-level saloon. It was safe—swept regularly for bugs, windowless, and stripped to the beams. There was even a secret sub-basement where, decades ago, Pat had buried a rival, and where Liam had now hidden the stolen stash. All in all, Pat had been smart to use it for meetings; except, that is, for the night he came to meet Liam here and found Gio, who shot him.

Now the crew were on folding chairs with their drinks on a bridge table, mostly beers, with a Coke for Juno and a black coffee for Joe. But he hadn't touched it. He was pacing around, hearing the faint hum of the bass from the bar below, and trying to think while the others watched and waited. Finally Juno broke the silence.

"How come with this job I feel like we're always one step behind, you know?"

Yelena nodded. "Yes, right from the start in Afghanistan."

Cash put in: "A little more bad luck today and we would have been the ones eating shit instead of that Russian."

Juno grimaced in anger, waving his tablet: "That's what burns me most. I mean, at first I thought, okay, I got it all wrong about the delivery. But then why were all those cops and crooks there, if there was no damned dope?"

Joe, who had been standing outside the circle, staring into space, turned to Juno, as though he'd been woken from a nap. "You're right," he said, brightly. "Something went wrong."

Juno nodded. "I know, man, no need to rub it in."

Joe went on, as if talking to himself. "I mean with them. Look, you're right, all of you, we've been a step behind this whole time. Why? Because they knew more than us. But they must have thought there was going to be dope in that container also. And with no more product they're going to be feeling the pressure. So we keep turning the screw."

Liam nodded. "Now you're talking. How?"

"Maybe it's time for me to talk to the boss, directly."

Cash frowned. "You mean Anton?"

"I mean the little man in the glass tower who pulls the strings."

"Oz?" Juno asked.

Josh, who had been texting, turned to Joe. "Sorry to interrupt, Joe. But I have an urgent message."

"What is it?"

"It's not the kind of thing you text. It's waiting outside."

❖

Donna was trying to think. Andy, Blaze, Fusco, and Parks were all crammed into her little office, Fusco of course filling the armchair, Andy on a smaller straight-back chair, Blaze and Parks leaning on her desk, and Donna behind it. She was explaining what went down that day.

"Look, the way I see it, I had no choice. I played my hand. The suspect led me to Jersey. I called you, I called the office, and I called a friend who was local for backup. Then it all went sideways before anyone got there. What could I do?"

"You could have caught somebody," Fusco offered. "Or found some dope. Or learned something. Or not lost track of our suspect. Any one of those would have worked."

Blaze gave him a dirty look, Andy and Parks groaned, but Donna laughed.

"I'm starting to like you, Fusco."

He grinned. "You too, Zamora."

"But you're only half right. Or three quarters. I did learn something. We know how the dope is getting in. What else were they all there for, armed to the teeth at a freight depot? Andy . . ." She turned to him. "Can you find out who had international pickups scheduled this morning? Let's see if anyone jumps out at us."

Andy nodded and opened his laptop.

"As for our lost Russian." She turned back to Fusco. "Who does he work for?"

"Anton Solonik," Fusco said. "I got it from OC Task Force."

"Right. Our files say the same thing. So now we know: the Russian mob is behind White Angel, they're using hired muscle to take more territory to sell it, and they're bringing it in via air freight from somebody in that depot."

"Well I can make a pretty good guess about that somebody," Andy said. With his FBI clearance he had logged into the listing of shipments. "There was a whole pile of pickups this morning, it's a busy place. But when I narrow the field, only one pops out."

He showed them the screen. Fusco squinted at it. "I can't read shit without my glasses."

Parks leaned in. "It says, defective merchandise. Shipped from West Germany."

"Amazing," Fusco said. "Thank God for the high-tech FBI."

"Even we have to scroll down," Andy said. "That's just where it was consolidated. The goods originate at offices in . . . Frankfurt, Rome,

Istanbul, Saudi Arabia, Tel Aviv, Iraq, and . . . hold your applause: Fucking A. F. Ghanistan."

"That's got to be it," Donna said, leaning in. "What's the company?"

Andy read: "Wildwater Corporation. Headquarters are right here in town."

"What do you say, detective?" Donna asked Fusco. "Is that a lead or what?"

He grinned. "Not bad for a f . . ." he began, but Blaze cut him off.

"You better not say for a female, or I will shoot you dead right now."

"I was going to say for a feeb," he said and winked at her.

Blaze laughed. "Sorry. I shouldn't presume you're an asshole. It's not fair."

"Oh, it's fair," Parks said. "He is for sure an asshole."

Andy added, "You just can't presume what kind."

Even Fusco cracked up at that, and Donna was leaning back in her chair laughing, when her computer screen flashed a flagged message alert at the same that her phone vibrated. She leaned in, still smiling and clicked to see what was so urgent. Zahir had sent her an email.

❖

Joe and Josh walked out of the pub. A black town car was idling in front. When he saw Joe, the driver, a young, bearded man in a black, wide brim hat, with a gun bulging the side of his black suit, hopped out and opened the rear door, then waited, bumming a cigarette from Josh, while Joe got inside.

"Good afternoon, Rebbe, how are you? We going to the deli again?"

Rebbe laughed and squeezed Joe's hand in both of his, kissing him on the cheek. His beard tickled. "I wish! Better than the dry corned beef Patty used to serve here, *olav ha-shalom*. But I'm going to the cardiologist after this. Never eat pastrami before you get your cholesterol checked." He sat back. "I'm afraid this is a business call. Unpleasant business."

"Tell me."

"I wanted to warn you, personally, since I know you're friends, that there's a contract out on the *rushish meydl*. The shiksa."

"Yelena?"

He nodded.

"Who put it out?"

"Anton . . . a curse on his name, he should crap blood and piss pus. Black sorrow is all that his mother should see of him . . . but . . ." He held up a finger. "The situation right now is complicated. We know he attacked us, but we can't prove it enough to get all the other New York bosses on our side yet, or convince the Russians to give him up. And he hurt our friends too bad for us fight him on our own, with his mercenaries." Rebbe shrugged. "On the other hand, he can't admit that the stash you took was his and that he is behind White Angel either. And he can't come after you, because you are with Gio and this . . ." He tapped Joe's chest, high on the right side, where the brand was. ". . . marks you as untouchable."

"You say that," Joe pointed out, "but the number of people who want to kill me keeps going up overall."

Rebbe shrugged. "What are you gonna do? But with Yelena it's different. No offense, but the word is out she was a snitch, informing for SVR in Moscow."

"She had no choice but to agree," Joe said. "But she told them nothing once she was here."

"I know, I know, boychick, but this way Anton has a legitimate reason no one will dispute, and she has no powerful friends to back her up."

"She has me," Joe said.

Rebbe smiled like a grandpa and patted Joe's knee. "Then we understand each other perfectly."

❖

When Joe got back upstairs, the others were waiting.

"We checked," Liam said. "And if you really want to see Richards, he will be hosting an event at his office tomorrow."

"What kind of event?"

"You know, a big 9/11 thing, full of important patriots."

"Can you get me in?" he asked Juno.

"Of course. But Joe, there will be a hundred witnesses."

"Don't worry, I'm just going to have a quiet word with the man. And what about the tracker on the Russian's Benz, is it still active?"

Juno shrugged. "Yeah but it's at a repair shop, no doubt getting the shit scrubbed off it."

Joe turned to Cash. "Keep on it, will you? I want you to see if he takes you to Anton." He glanced over at Yelena. "Looks like we are going to have to pay him a visit too."

❖

"Americans claim they remember 9/11 but they remember nothing of the terror they cause. This year we will remind them. I am bringing a gift to Ground Zero. The mountains of dead and the smoking wreckage I leave will be the true memorial."

Immediately after reading Zahir's message, Donna ended the meeting in her office and went to her boss, Tom's. She was told he was busy but when she explained she had just received a serious threat, she was called in anyway, where she found him in an important, classified meeting . . . with her ex-husband.

"Shut the door," Tom said, as she froze on the threshold. She shut it and stepped in. "Donna, you know Agent Powell here of course."

"Mike," she said, managing a polite smile. "When did you get back into the country?"

"Just now," he said. "I wanted to brief Tom on 9/11-related intel we gathered overseas."

"And when he mentioned Zahir, I figured we better bring you into the conversation," Tom said.

"You've been investigating Zahir?" Donna asked him, sitting down now.

"We pick up chatter, though it sounds like you might know more than us at this point," Mike said.

"You say there's a new threat?" Tom asked.

"Yes, sir." Donna opened her folder. "This message came in addressed to me." She read the whole thing out, facing Tom, but when she glanced over at Mike, his eyes were wide and his mouth hung slightly ajar. "Are you okay?" she asked.

"What?" He sat up and regained his composure. "Of course. I mean . . . it's an alarming development."

"Yes, it's bad news," Tom said, leaning back in his chair. "But we get a lot of threats. What makes this one credible?"

"It's from Zahir," Donna said. "We have reason to believe he is here, sir. Or his agents are."

Again, Mike seemed to jerk in his chair, like someone had yanked his chain. Then he turned back into the condescending, whining Mike she knew so well. "Are you sure of this Donna? I mean, where's your evidence? As far as we know, Zahir operates overseas."

"Then I guess there's a lot you don't know," she answered calmly. "What a surprise."

Tom stood. "That's exactly why I brought you in, Donna, since you and your team have been working this. Now look . . ." He pointed at both of them. "I know there's some personal feeling here, some anger and past resentment . . ."

Mike and Donna both looked at the floor in embarrassment as Tom went on: "But it's time to put that behind us. To drain the bad blood and bury the hatchet. And that's why I'm asking. Do you, Agent Zamora, think you can work with this man . . . even though he's CIA?"

"Sir?" Donna cleared her throat. "I mean, yes, of course, sir."

Tom waved a hand. "I know, it's tough on me too. But there's a bigger picture here. Don't you agree Agent Powell?"

"Ah, yes, sir," Mike said, sitting up straight. "I agree completely."

"There's one thing we all want: this Zahir's balls on a hook. Let's keep our eye on those balls. What difference does it make who does the actual chopping and who holds him down? And who wears them on a necklace?"

"Absolutely sir," Donna said. "That's why I came to work this morning."

"Exactly. Good. Excellent. So in that spirit, why don't you update us now on where your investigation is at present."

"Well . . ." Donna hesitated. She glanced at Mike, who was listening attentively. She still didn't trust him for shit, whatever the boss said. "Actually sir, I was just about to meet with my team when this threat came through. Perhaps I should prepare a report and submit it to you later . . ."

"Just give us the gist, Donna." Tom sat down and leaned back, ready to hear a tale. "Do you have a lead in this case or not?"

"Yes, sir, we do." Donna sighed. "We have reason to suspect that a corporation, or some of its employees, is involved, possibly cooperating with Zahir in the heroin smuggling or else being used by them."

"What corporation?"

Now Donna glanced sideways at Mike, while still addressing Tom. "It's called Wildwater, sir. They have an office here in Manhattan."

"Wildwater," Tom repeated. "Never heard of it. Ring any bells Powell?"

Mike shrugged. "Nope. But I will check it out and get back to you."

"Okay, then," Tom said and leaned over to shake his hand, signaling the meeting was done. "Back to work."

"I will keep you posted, sir," Donna said.

"Right," Tom said. "Do that. After tomorrow."

"Sir?"

"In case you forgot to look at the calendar today, or the paper, or the goddamn internet, it's September 10th. Tomorrow you will be on the ground with everyone else, working security."

"But you just said yourself we've got to hunt this Zahir down and chop his nuts off. Don't you think . . ."

"I think the place to be sniffing around for those nuts tomorrow will be down among the sweaty crowds of tourists at Ground Zero, Zamora. And that's where you'll be."

"Yes, sir."

As they walked into the hall, Mike touched Donna's arm, but she instinctively drew back.

"Sorry if that was weird," he said. "I had no idea you were working the case . . ."

"It's fine," Donna said. "But when were you going to tell your daughter you're back? Or were you?"

Mike looked genuinely stricken, and she felt a twinge of regret. "I was, I just . . . you know what it's like in the field for me. Just please, tell her Daddy will see her soon. I promise."

"Okay," Donna said. "I will." And for the first time that day, she believed him.

❖

Mike Powell was trying to think. As soon as he heard that message, purportedly from Zahir, he knew he had to get ahold of Richards and Toomey. What the hell were they thinking? Any hope he had of burying the FBI investigation and stonewalling Donna went out the window when they issued a domestic threat, in New York, the day before 9/11. Unless it wasn't them. Was it possible someone else was now posing as Zahir? And how to get in touch, now that he knew they might be under surveillance? He couldn't walk into the building. He couldn't use his cell. Even going to his own office and calling from a secure line suddenly made him paranoid. So he did it the old fashioned way: after much searching, he found an actual working payphone near the men's room in a hotel, called Richards, and told him to call the payphone from a safe line. But Richards was no help at all: Toomey had left early that morning to pickup the latest delivery, and somewhere along the way, he had shaken off the Russians and never returned. They knew nothing about the Zahir message or who had sent it. Richards started going on about Donna, and how much of a threat did she pose, and could Powell still handle it? Powell lied and said yes; to his own surprise, he found himself worried about her now, about what it might mean if Richards decided to "handle" it another way. He was also worried by the edge of panic he now heard in Richards's voice. The shadow they had created had come to life.

34

AFTER WORK THAT NIGHT, Donna met Blaze at the bar as promised, though she hadn't promised to be a fun date, brooding in the beer Blaze bought her about work and the sudden return of her ex-husband.

"What a shit show," Donna muttered. "The most epic shit show in a long-running hit series."

Blaze shrugged. "You got to learn to let it go. Shit goes sideways sometimes. So be it."

"Yeah but the thing of it is, this was my first time really running with the ball, you know? My idea to begin with, my lead to Jersey, practically my team. Then it all blew up in my face."

Blaze shrugged again. "Not really. I mean, yeah, it kind of did, but you learned something, right? Wildwater. That's the next step. You keep going. And sooner or later you catch up. Like on a manhunt." While she talked her eyes wandered. A pale young woman with long red hair was alone at the bar, sipping a mixed drink and sneaking looks at their table.

"Or a womanhunt," Donna said.

"What?" Blaze asked, returning her own gaze to Donna.

"Nothing. Anyway, you're right. Got to persevere."

"Exactly."

"As long as we survive tomorrow's foreign invasion. And I mean tourists, not terrorists." Donna talked on, though now Blaze was back to smiling at the redhead. "Am I boring you?"

"A little," Blaze said, with a grin, then laughed. "No, sorry, of course not. Just tired."

"Yeah, me too," Donna said, and stood. "I'm going to go home and practice smiling for tomorrow. I'll let you stay here and . . . rest." She laughed and bent over to kiss Blaze on the cheek. "Thanks for the beer, buddy," she added and went.

"See you, special agent," Blaze called after her, then returned her gaze to the redhead. She stood and sauntered over, like marshals in saloons have been doing for over a century.

"Good evening," she said to the redhead. "Sorry if this is too forward, but my friend left, and there's an empty seat at my table, and I thought you might be tired of standing."

The redhead beamed. "How thoughtful," she said in an English accent, which was an added attraction for Blaze. "Not too forward at all. I'd love to join you."

"Great," Blaze smiled back and held out a hand. "My name's Blaze."

"Lovely to meet you, Blaze," she said, placing her soft, childish hand in Blaze's, the black nail polish chipped. "My name is Victoria. But my friends call me Vick."

❖

"So . . . I have a confession to make. Don't be mad."

"Um . . . okay." Donna had just walked into the house and found her mom there waiting, with her laptop in her lap. She put her bag down and stowed away her gun, then kissed her on the cheek. "Do I need to read you your rights?"

"No, but you have to promise not to be mad and not to just say I'm crazy."

"How can I?"

"Promise."

"Okay I'll do my best."

"Honey . . ." She opened the laptop. "I made you a profile."

"A what?"

236

"A profile."

"Like for a serial killer?"

"For dating!" She showed her the screen, which showed a dating website profile, complete with a photo of Donna.

"Oh, my God, you're crazy."

"I'm sorry but I had too."

"What do you mean had to? Of course you didn't have to."

"I felt so sad. Seeing you still so young and beautiful and so lonely. So I made a nice profile for you, and yes, most of the messages are from serial killers . . ."

"Great. I will forward them to the bureau."

"But tonight one came that I think you will really like. Mija, he's perfect! Just your type."

"My type? I don't even have a type."

"Look, he's a veteran. Special Forces. Got a whole bunch of medals. Purple heart. Now he does consulting. He's handsome. Strong jaw. Blue eyes. He's in town for 9/11."

Reluctantly, Donna glanced down at the profile her mom clicked on. She was right, he was handsome. And his service was impressive.

"He walks with a cane," Yolanda added. "Bad leg from a gunshot. But I think that's kind of sexy, you know, wounded warrior. Manly. I mean as long as what's between his legs wasn't shot off."

"Mom, please. You're going to give me nightmares."

"Anyway, I didn't want to lose him," Yolanda rattled on. "So I wrote back for you!"

"What? How could you? Jesus."

"And he wants to meet tomorrow! At the ceremony."

"Well I hope you two have a nice time," Donna said. "Because I will be busy working."

"Mija, please, you have to answer him at least. He's a war hero. You can't ghost him."

"Ghost? How do you even know about all this?" Donna sighed as she looked through the email exchange. He was literate at least, with correct spelling and punctuation. And polite. And patriotic. A squared-away soldier boy. And she had to admit, to herself if never to her mother, he was her type. "God, I'm so sorry I ever taught you to use the internet."

She wrote back to him, just apologizing for her Mom's meddling and explaining that she'd actually be working tomorrow.

I understand completely, he answered. *My niece talked me into making my profile. Well, I will be down at Ground Zero anyway, paying my respects—I've lost a lot of friends since 9/11 and I've never seen the memorial. But it's hard to get around on this leg. Maybe you'll have time for a drink after?*

Donna smiled. He was a good guy at least. Her mom had decent instincts, after all, and she meant well. *I can't promise about the drink, but why don't you call me in the morning when you get downtown? I think the least I can do is arrange VIP access.* She sent her work number. *Ask for Agent Zamora. Donna.*

Really? He wrote back. *That would be outstanding. My full name is Rick Toomey. And thank you!*

Thank you, Rick. For your service.

❖

Blaze didn't realize her badge was gone till she woke up. She had a few drinks with that English chick (or British? She got them mixed up), then they started making out, then dancing, then dancing and making out, and then, just as she was about to suggest taking the party elsewhere, the damn girl went to the bathroom and vanished. Gone, just like that, a fugitive in the night. Cold feet, Blaze figured, and a wicked case of blue balls for her. Probably a pillow princess anyway, a soft pale redhead like that, with that stuck-up accent. But by then a couple of Blaze's pals had turned up and they bought her tequila shots to commiserate. By the time she made it back out to Jersey City, the room was spinning and she barely got her shoes off before hitting the bed.

The way Blaze figured it, there were a lot of places her badge could be: on her own floor somewhere, under the couch or table, on the floor of her friend's car from when they drove her home, or on the floor of the bar, which she'd call as soon as they opened. And if she did think about the redhead, Vick (cute name), holding her close when they danced, grinding against her, she didn't think about how her nimble hand might have slid into her pocket. And as she washed her Advil down with Diet Coke followed by black coffee, she definitely didn't feel lucky to be alive. But she was.

❖

Vicky felt a bit sad leaving the bar. It would have been fun to go home with that tough, sexy marshal and play with her some more, in private. But, business before pleasure: she couldn't kill everyone cute she met, unfortunately. A dead federal agent, the night before 9/11, would kick up a lot more fuss than a drunk one who got her ID stolen. So Vicky, who still had a hard time finding her way around New York the second she left the Manhattan grid, got in a cab on Bleecker Street and took it all the way out to Brighton Beach. She suspected the cabbie took the scenic route, but who cared, it wasn't her money. She was on expense. She just relaxed and enjoyed the ride out to the address that Nikolai had gotten from his Russian connections. It looked nothing like the real Brighton of course. But it was a bit cooler than downtown had been. And she did smell the ocean on the breeze.

❖

The old man was suspicious at first—some girl he'd never seen before, and English too—but when she dropped Anton's name he could hardly refuse. So he let her in, offered her tea, which she accepted, took her picture, and then left her sipping on the couch while he altered the federal marshal's ID she gave him. He didn't ask any questions. He couldn't, since he barely spoke English and her Russian was rudimentary.

When he emerged with the finished product, she praised his work and then, reaching into her bag for the money, tasered him instead. He woke up chained to his balcony, dangling over the side, with the sound of the ocean in his ears and wind twisting all around him. Fear crashed in like the waves. His legs kicked helplessly like he was drowning.

"It's lovely out here," Vicky told him. She was smoking one of his Russian cigarettes. "Though you can feel autumn in the air, can't you? Makes me a bit sad. A poetic feeling really."

"Help . . ." he managed to croak in English. "Help. I give you money."

"Not money." She leaned closer. "Information."

He nodded. She leaned even closer, blowing smoke into his face. "Yelena Noylaskya. Where is she?"

He shook his head. "Don't know."

She took another drag and coughed. "Bit harsh this," she commented, and ground it out on his hand. He howled and yanked away, losing his grip on the railing and putting his full weight on the cuffs, which cut into his wrists. He grabbed the bar again.

"I'll stick to my own if you don't mind," Vicky said now and lit another, English cigarette. "Yelena?" she asked, holding it over him. "What name is she living under?"

He shook his head. "Don't understand English. Sorry."

She burned him again. He screamed again but held on. Then she asked him again in Russian. This time he looked her right in the eye and whispered something back that she couldn't translate but didn't need a dictionary to understand. It was a curse.

She tried a few more times, just to be thorough, but all he did was continue to mutter in Russian, curses and, she thought, prayers. She'd played him wrong, she realized: He'd made the connection between Anton and the SVR and Moscow powers, and probably hated them worse than death itself. He was a stubborn, tough old bastard and he wasn't going to budge. So instead of torturing him with it, she put the last smoke in his mouth and he sucked it eagerly, even gratefully, she thought, and then she unhooked him and let him go.

Joe and Yelena watched TV with Gladys, a *Parks & Recreation* marathon, the idea being to take their minds off of the day ahead, but Joe couldn't focus and went into the bedroom and read instead. Finally, when Gladys drained her last drink and went to bed, Yelena did the same.

"Still the poetry?" she asked, lying beside him. "You know, I didn't go to school, but in Russia we honor our great poets." She shrugged. "At least until we execute them." She shut her eyes. "Read me some?"

He read her the first of the *Duino Elegies*, and then told her the little he knew about their creation, how Rilke, in the midst of a severe psychological crisis, was invited by the Princess Marie von Thurn und Taxis to stay in Duino Castle, overlooking the Adriatic Sea, where walking on the cliffs, he heard the wind whisper the opening line in his ear: "Who, if I cried out, would hear me among the angel's hierarchies?" It was ten more years of struggle before he completed the poems.

Yelena liked that. She reached for the book: "Whom can we turn to in our need? Not angels, not humans," she read, approvingly. "And it says this, too, about lovers . . ." She ran a finger along the text: "They keep on using each other to hide their fate."

Joe smiled. "Oh yeah? That strikes a chord for you, does it?"

Yelena shrugged and tossed the book onto his stomach. "Anyway he reminds me of you." She laughed, as she stood and peeled off her T-shirt and jeans. "I bet you would go live in a castle alone and walk the cliffs." Leaving her clothes in a pile, she switched off the light and slipped into bed beside him. She pressed her mouth to his ear. "Then I'd be the angel that comes and whispers in your ear," she added, and stuck her tongue in his ear.

"Ha!" He squirmed and turned to face her, though his eyes could not yet make hers out in the dark. "You know what part reminds me of you?" he whispered back.

"Tell me."

He moved closer, his lips brushing her ear now. "Beauty is nothing but the beginning of terror."

35

Donna's day was going pretty well, if you didn't mind suffocating crowds, boring speeches, and a wide variety of New York smells, including hot dog, spilled beer, and overflowing toilets. Then her walkie squawked. It was NYPD.

"Agent Zamora, you on? Over?"

"Zamora here. What's up?"

"We've got a vehicle out here at the perimeter. Driver said you gave him clearance to enter. Name of Toomey. Rick. You know him?"

Donna scowled at her walkie. "I know him but I didn't clear him. Vehicle you say?"

"Yeah, he's a disabled vet. Trying to get into the memorial."

"Okay hold him there. I'm on my way."

"Roger that."

"Can you cover me?" Donna asked Andy. "My date's here."

"Date?" he asked, eyes automatically sweeping the crowd behind his shades while he spoke. "Are you joking?"

"I don't even know," she admitted. She moved through the crowd, forcing her way gently and showing her badge, until she finally got to the perimeter, where the cops had their barricades, the National Guard stood around in fatigues and rifles, and Homeland Security, slightly more discreet, moved around in Kevlar vests and sunglasses. Most discreet of all were her own kind, FBI and Secret Service, many of whom were dressed as tourists, or vendors, or hidden in sniper positions around the area. She showed her badge and kept walking to the closest corner where a vehicle was allowed. She approached an NYPD sergeant, a dark-skinned woman with her braids up under her cap.

"Excuse me Sarge, I'm Zamora, FBI. Someone called for me?"

"Right." They shook hands. "I'm Cole. Hoping you can handle this for us. The guy's a vet, even got a Special Forces decal on his truck, but there's no way we can let him drive any closer. You understand. No disrespect."

"No, of course not. I've got it. And thanks."

The sergeant touched her brim and pointed, and Donna went around the corner, where she saw a Jeep Wagoneer, one of the big ones, double parked, with a big white guy leaning against it. He held a cane. He was handsome, she had to admit. And parked illegally.

"Mr. Toomey?" she called out as she drew closer. "I'm Agent Zamora."

"Hey . . ." he gave her a wide, craggy smile. Dimples even. "I thought we were Rick and Donna. Have I been downgraded?"

She laughed. "Not at all, just in work mode, sorry." She held out a hand and he shook, firmly but gently, and gave it just a second of extra pressure. "Now what seems to be the problem?"

"Didn't know there was one. Just another disabled vet trying to get in. I don't know where to park though. Thought you'd have some kind of VIP access for special needs parking."

"I'm afraid there's no way we could clear every car. Not to mention no place to park them. You'll have to use a lot or find the closest legal spot. But the upside is alternate side of the street rules are suspended. And if walking is a problem, I can get you a ride with the police." She smiled. "So don't worry, you'll still be getting the VIP treatment."

He laughed. "That kind of special attention I don't need. The walk will do me good."

Donna smiled. "Sounds like a plan," she said and got on her radio. "Sergeant Cole? This is Agent Zamora. You on? Over."

Her radio squawked. "I'm here. What can I do for you?"

"Mr. Rick Toomey is going to park his vehicle legally and return. Can you send him my way?"

"No problem."

"There you go," Donna told him with smile.

❖

Toomey kept his cool. As always. The parking problem had thrown a wrench into his plans but of course he had a backup. As always. So he reparked his truck and took a cab back down to the memorial, or as close as it would get him, fiddling with his cane in the back. Now that he'd ditched the vehicle, the whole disabled vet thing was a bit of a nuisance, and he considered "forgetting" his cane in the taxi, but no, he had to keep the limp. He was visiting a secular holy site, not Lourdes, and a little extra pity never hurt, he found, especially with women. Extra especially with women like Zamora—Donna—who clearly had a need to rescue and protect.

He paid his taxi, got out, leaning on the cane of course, then found that African-American sergeant, the one who had given him shit before, smiled, and called her ma'am and was waved on through, pushing his way through the crowd, his VFW hat and his cane helping, people more or less clearing a path, but still, a mongrel crowd, every kind of person mixed up together, like a garbage dump. Half the people selling food or drinks or goddamn 9/11 T-shirts and flags even looked like Islamics. Now what kind of mixed-up world was that?

He wouldn't be sorry when he had to leave New York.

❖

"Hey, Richards, I've got a question? How's your heroin import business going?"

Still with his gracious host's smile stuck to his face, Richards turned to Joe.

He was in his adventure gear: multi-pocket hunting vest over white dress shirt and khakis, though most of the men around him—and they were pretty much all men except for some of the caterers and a couple of sleek female PR operatives—wore suits and ties or formal military uniforms with rows of medals. Joe had noted the military vehicles in the parking lot when he'd come in—a few Humvees, limos with military plates, as well as expensive private cars with USMC or Army emblems on the windows and bumpers. Even a Jeep Wagoneer with De Oppresso Liber, the Special Forces motto, on a sticker on the back. He'd ditched yesterday's uniform himself, passing unnoticed now in a jacket and tie as he followed the crowd into the elevator and up to the mezzanine, pausing in front of the table where guests were checking in. Then his turn came:

"Good evening ma'am, I'm Yurami, first name Ken," he said with a slight country twang.

The woman smiled and searched the list.

"Here you are, Mister Kenneth Yurami," she said, writing his name on a tag.

"Mister Yurami? Only my mother calls me that," Joe said, with smile. "Just make it Ken please." He stuck the name to his chest and went through, getting a seltzer from the bar, then mingling with the crowd that circulated around Richards like a giant organism, or one of those huge trash islands that form in the ocean currents. Finally, he floated close enough to ask his question. That got Richards's attention.

"Excuse me? I'm afraid I don't know what you're talking about."

"Don't be modest. It doesn't suit you, Bob," Joe laughed. "I'm talking about your new product White Angel. You should be proud of it. It's killing more junkies than anything else on the street."

Now the men in suits and the men in medals were frowning and looking uncomfortable. Richards forced a smile, while his eyes searched for security. Jensen, seeing his master's discomfort, moved closer to Joe.

"I think our friend here has had too much to drink," Richards said. "I think he needs some air." He gestured toward a side door, which Jensen held open. "If you gentlemen will excuse us a moment?"

"Yeah why not?" Joe said. "Back in a moment, gentlemen. And waiter . . ." He handed his empty glass to a general. "Get me a refill meantime will you?"

He sauntered through the door after Richards and into the hall, where a security guard was waiting. Jensen shut the door and put a hand on Joe's left shoulder, while the guard grabbed his right. Richards turned to him with a snarl, hand clenched around his martini glass.

"I don't know who you are or what you think you know but look, Mister . . ." He narrowed his eyes at the name tag. "Ken Yurami?"

"Drop your pants and I'll consider it," Joe said.

The security guard snickered. Richards glared. Jensen pointed at the tag. "That's not a real name!"

"I'm Ken Yurami to you," Joe said. "Remember it. Because what I think I know is all about you and Zahir, about the dope coming in through the Wildwater returns, about your deal with the Russians . . ."

Richards laughed. "I have no idea what you're babbling about. Even if these things happened, they have nothing to do with me. There isn't a shred of evidence. Threaten me in front of witnesses, and you'll be the one to get arrested, Joe." He grinned. "That's right. I know just who you are. And those men in there? Generals, diplomats, millionaires. If I snap my fingers they will be happy to lock you up. If I don't have these boys right here snap your neck first. You think I broke the law? Son, as far as you're concerned, I am the law."

Joe smiled back at him. "You're right. But you've crossed into my world now, where the law can't protect you. Your money can't protect you. Not your powerful friends. Or your hired goons. I saw your speech the other day, about leaving war to the professionals. It's the same with crime. You should have taken your own advice. If you know my name, then you should know it would take less than ten seconds for me to cut your throat with that glass right now."

Richards laughed louder, and the two other men joined in, gripping Joe tighter. "Now that I'd like to see." He raised his glass to Joe in salute, then downed his martini.

"As you wish," Joe said, and dislocated Jensen's right arm. Jensen had made the mistake of grabbing Joe up on his shoulder, and though his grip was strong from working out, like a knuckle-buster handshake, his positioning had left him vulnerable. Joe was able to jump back and twist his left arm around Jensen's extended right, eluding the guard's looser grip. As Jensen stumbled forward, Joe forced the right arm up between the shoulder blades, till it left the socket with an audible pop. Jensen groaned. In a panic, the guard tried to grab at Joe while also reaching for his shoulder holster, but Jensen was stumbling between them and, with both hands busy, the guard had no defense when Joe hit him, hard and fast in the throat. He gasped for air, clutching his throat, and Joe quickly dipped into the holster and slid out his gun, then hammered him on the forehead with it. He dropped to his knees. Now Jensen was reaching for his own gun, awkwardly, with his left hand, and Joe grabbed that arm and bent it back the same way. "Sorry, but no guns. Someone could get hurt." Another pop. Jensen screamed.

Richards, who had been watching in shock, flinched as Joe moved toward him with the gun, swinging hard. He shut his eyes. The gun barrel cracked the glass in his hand, breaking it off at the stem, which Joe snatched in his left. Then he pushed Richards up against the elevators, with the edge of broken glass against his jugular.

"How did I do?" Joe asked. "Was that ten?" The guard was on his knees, still trying to breathe. Jensen seemed to be in shock, regarding his two arms, which dangled helplessly. Richards stared at him, frozen in stark terror. Joe could feel him tremble, like a rabbit in the jaws of the wolf. He pressed the elevator call button.

"I'm going to let you get back to your friends. But just remember. You're living in my world now. Not theirs. And there's no going back."

The elevator doors opened. Two uniformed waiters stood there with a serving cart. "Going down?" Joe asked.

They nodded. Joe dropped the broken glass and got on.

❖

Liam and Josh, who were dressed in waiters' uniforms they'd taken from Old Shenanigan's, waited for the elevator doors to shut before grinning at Joe.

"That seems to have gone well," Liam said.

Joe glanced up at the camera. Josh nodded. "We took care of it."

"It went just like we planned," Joe said, relaxing. "What about you and Yelena?"

"Ask her yourself," Josh said and tapped on the cart. The tablecloth parted and Yelena, who'd been curled beneath it, hopped out.

"How'd it go?" Joe asked, helping her to her feet.

"Fine," she said, brushing out her hair. "He'll never know I was there." She was wearing leggings and a sleeveless T-shirt. Now she pulled a clingy dress from her bag. Kicking off her sneakers, she stepped into the dress and pulled it up, then grabbed black heels from her bag and slid them on while Liam and Josh put her sneakers in the bag and stowed it back under the cart. As the doors opened on the lobby, she took Joe's arm and they walked out while Liam and Josh continued down to the basement.

Joe and Yelena smiled and laughed as they crossed the lobby, nodding at others who came and went. The PR woman was by the door, with a couple of guards.

"Goodbye," Joe said as he passed her.

"Goodbye, Mr. Yurami . . . I mean Ken . . ." she laughed. "And happy September 11th . . . I mean . . ." she looked disconcerted.

"I know what you mean," Joe told her. "God bless America."

Yelena waved happily and they went through the revolving door onto the street. Cash and Juno were waiting in a black limo with tinted windows. As soon as they shut the door, Cash pulled out, rolling half a block to where Liam and Josh had emerged from the parking garage. They'd abandoned the cart in the elevator, and now Josh had Yelena's bag over his shoulder. They hopped in and, as Cash drove away, Joe leaned to Juno. "Cameras?"

"I'm on it, Boss," he said, tapping away at his laptop. "I'm erasing the last hour to be on the safe side. Since before you all entered the building."

"Perfect," Joe said. "Now that Russian, Sergey. Tell me where his car is."

"Yeah," Juno said. "I've been checking like you asked. It was at the repair shop and detailing place all day. But now it's rolling again. Guess not even a Russian gangster can throw out a brand-new Benz just 'cause it gets a little shit on it."

"A lot of shit bro." Cash chuckled from behind the wheel.

"True that," Juno agreed. "Ol' Sergey had a real shit day."

Everyone laughed except for Joe, who glanced at Yelena.

"But not his worst," he said.

❖

Richards didn't move a muscle till the elevator doors closed. Then he rushed over to the others. The guard was curled in a ball, taking deep, measured breaths. Jensen was standing there stunned, arms hanging limp like a rag doll.

"Call for help," Richards ordered him, out of habit.

"I can't," Jensen said, staring down at his useless appendages. "My arms won't move. My walkie is in my pocket."

"Jesus Christ," Richards muttered, frowning in distaste as he reached into his underling's pants. He pressed a button. "This is Bob Richards. We need security in the South Hall on the mezzanine floor."

❖

Ten minutes later, he was back up in his penthouse office with Nikolai and the team of mercenaries. Trey, who'd had medic training, was seeing to Jensen. The other injured guard had been quietly taken to another room to recover.

"I'm going to have to pop his shoulders back in," Trey said to Richards. And to Jensen: "It's going to hurt. A lot."

Nikolai spoke: "Take him in the other room. All of you. We need to think."

"Yes, sir," Trey said, leading a reluctant-looking Jensen out, as Baxter and Dirk followed. As soon as the door shut, Nikolai asked, "Any news from Victoria?"

"She says she is on it," Richards told him. "And you know what that means."

"Good." Nikolai nodded. A blood-curdling scream came from beyond the wall.

"That's the first arm," he observed. He put a cigar in his lips and lit it. "And now," he said, "I take these soldiers of yours to Anton, and let them handle this Brody and his crew."

"And that girl, Noylaskya. She's your problem."

"In a sense, perhaps," Nikolai reflected. "After all, I created her." He waved his cigar. "And I will destroy her. She's just a tool after all. If she fails you, throw her out."

Another wrenching scream came from the other room.

"Speaking of which," he added. "Sounds like your tool is just about repaired."

Richards nodded, then glanced at his watch. "And I better get back to that party. Keep me posted." But he hesitated before leaving, suddenly feeling a wave of insecurity, remembering the pressure of the jagged glass against his throat, the totally dead, flat look in Brody's eyes. Until Brody was dead, was he safe anywhere, even here? As if to reassure himself, he looked around his office. Everything appeared to be in order.

36

DONNA SAW TOOMEY—RICK—MAKING HIS way toward her in the crowd. She smiled. She wasn't sure what to make of him. In some ways of course her mom was right, he was her type of man—but seeing him here in his VFW hat, and the whole thing with the parking—it all reeked of a certain kind of arrogance and entitlement that she got more than enough of on the job, where dick-swinging was a major pastime, and the egos behind it were as fragile and volatile as an angry toddler's. Then again, at least he'd earned the right to swing his a little if he wanted.

"Hey, Rick," she said, smiling. "Glad you made it back. Sorry if walking in the crowd is a pain."

He shrugged and looked down at his cane as if he was surprised to see it. "You know, on a day like today, I carry this bullet fragment with more pride than any medal, because I got it defending America, and avenging 9/11."

"That's true," she said. "We all owe you a debt of gratitude."

"Not necessary," he said, with a shrug. "But a little respect would be nice." He sidled up closer. "You understand what I'm talking about, don't you? You've chosen a life of service too. You wear that badge. Live by a code. Whether or not others honor it."

"I like to think so."

"Donna, let me ask you, one warrior to another. Is there something in your life you love so much you'd do anything to save it, no matter the sacrifice?"

"Sure . . ." Donna said. "My daughter."

He smiled. "Of course. Your mother mentioned her." He took his hat off, looked around, and then put it back on. "Well that's exactly how I feel about America. Like a protective parent."

"Huh . . ." Donna said. "Well I guess everyone here feels that way."

"Do they? I don't think so. I think a lot of them need a reminder. A wake-up call. Before it's too late."

Too late for what? she was about to ask, definitely getting a bad vibe now, but also, as always, another part of her was working, eyes and ears scanning, and she heard a voice, a cop, saying, "Go right ahead, Deputy Marshal Logan," and she thought, *Oh, Blaze is here*, and turned and saw, coming through the crowd, a curvy blonde with a Yankees cap and dark glasses and a blue blazer, white shirt, and khakis who looked sort of familiar, and kind of like a Fed, but was certainly not Blaze Logan, despite holding up a Federal ID and walking with her other hand lightly on her side-holstered gun.

And just as it was clicking in Donna's head and she was remembering, *That's the redhead from last night*, she also saw her draw the gun, and extend her arm, like in slow motion, and point it right at, of all people, Rick Toomey.

"Gun!" she yelled as, instinctively, she threw herself on him and knocked him to the ground, and something seared across her back, like a burning ember, and the sound of a gunshot echoed in her ears. And then she didn't have time to think because total chaos broke out.

❖

Vicky was annoyed. With herself mostly but also with that Fed, Zamora, who she knew was Powell's ex and who was definitely on her to-do list now, though not yet at the top.

In the seconds after the shot went off, and she missed, her bullet nicking Zamora and then flattening into the ground, panic broke out around Vicky, with people yelling and pushing in every direction. She joined right in, pushing her way through the crowd, waving her badge, yelling "Federal Marshal!" and even holding the gun in the air, which scared the punters shitless. And witless. They turned and fled or ducked, as cops and Feds ran toward her and she waved them on, pointing toward the vortex of the disturbance. But the crowd was so big and so loud that within a few minutes she had crossed into another area where people had no idea anything was wrong, and she pocketed her weapon as she found a line of women waiting for a bathroom.

"Security check, step aside," she announced, brandishing the badge and brushing past the line. Quite useful really, these things, she thought, as she entered the first open stall, where she stuffed her hat and wig in the toilet, then removed her shirt and blazer, revealing a very tight T-shirt that said "Never Forget" on the front, with an image of the towers, and on the back, over a US flag, read "These colors don't run." Lastly she slid down her pants, stepping out of them to reveal a pair of cutoff shorts that barely covered her bum.

"That one's clogged," she said to the next woman in line as she opened the door to the stall, then stuffed her bundled clothing, along with the gun and badge, into the trash.

"I feel dizzy," she giggled in a high, Southern accent, weaving through the crowd, bumping off of men, who didn't mind, and then stumbling into a cop. "Oops! Sorry officer! I just feel so ditzy. I mean dizzy!"

He smiled and put a hand on her back. "No problem miss, let's get you some air," he said, and led her out to freedom.

37

"SURE YOU DON'T WANT us to come in with you?" Josh asked. He was turned around, talking to Joe and Yelena in back, while Liam drove. They were downtown, near Wall Street, but the quiet, dark block, a narrow gorge cut into the towering buildings of old stone that seemed to almost touch above them, was a world away from the noise and crowds that were fading as things wound down at the 9/11 memorial, right across the narrow island. They pulled up behind Cash and Juno, who had been tracking Sergey's black Benz, which was parked down the block.

"That's okay," Joe said. "It looks less suspicious if we just go in together. You wait out here and catch any rats who try to flee." To Yelena he said, "Ready?"

"Of course." She held up a bikini.

"Brilliant," Liam said, and to Joe. "Where's yours?"

He frowned at Yelena who was stuffing hers back into her tote bag. "I thought they gave you something. You didn't tell me . . ."

She shrugged and opened the door. "You better hope. Otherwise you will be fighting one handed."

He got out after her and shut the door, and they walked down the street, pausing by Cash and Juno as they passed.

"Sergey went in about an hour ago. And it's been a cast reunion since then."

"Anton?" Joe asked.

"Yup and the soldier boys we met in Jersey. I'm sure they'll be happy to see y'all." He frowned. "Though I know I'd feel safer if you two had guns."

"No place to hide it," Joe said. "Everybody has to strip in the locker rooms. We'd never get through to the baths." Both had also left their phones, wallets, and keys in the car.

Cash leaned across from behind the wheel. "This *banya* place. Is it like the massage joints Uncle Chen runs? A rub and tug?"

"Only if your idea of a happy ending is a big Russian dude beating you with birch branches and cracking your neck."

Cash shrugged. "To each his own."

"It's a *shvitz*," Yelena told him. "More like the Korean spa in Queens."

"Gotcha," Cash said. "Well maybe I will try it sometime. If it's still standing after tonight."

❖

"You do the talking," Joe whispered to Yelena as they walked down the steps. A young woman, blondly plump and rosy-cheeked, looked up from her phone. Yelena greeted her in Russian, and Joe paid cash for two. After a bit more back and forth, she handed over a brand-new pair of men's swim trunks, large, baggy, and decorated with a beach scene in tropical colors—sand, sea, palm, birds. Joe paid another twenty for it and she cut off the tags. Then they were given keys and sent to separate locker rooms. They changed quickly and met in the hall, Yelena emerging in her stylish black bikini and holding two rolled white towels, one of which she handed to Joe. He was in his new trunks.

"You look great," he told her.

"Beauty and terror?" She smiled and gave a little spin, then gestured for him to turn as well. He raised his hands as if under arrest and turned.

"Straight to terror?" he asked.

She laughed. "No, I like these for you. The parrot makes your ass look good."

"Thanks," Joe said, and opened the inner door for her.

They were in the banya, the Russian bathhouse, one of the oldest in the city. The signs on the wall were in Russian, Hebrew, Yiddish, and misspelled English. An underground warren, its hallways connected a series of chambers, including a restaurant, saunas, a steam room, a cold plunge, massage rooms, and, down a floor below, a large swimming pool and Jacuzzi. The overall decor was fake Roman grotto—white painted columns, patterned tiles, plaster statues of naked cherubs and demure maidens, and murals depicting pastoral antiquity—hills, sea, ruins—not a bad job on the landscapes, but the people looked like they'd been done by kids. Everything was warm, wet, dank—moisture clung to every surface and water dripped like you were in a cave. You *were* in a cave—deep in the bowels of the city, the old saunas built into the foundation of the building.

Yelena led Joe through the restaurant where wet customers wrapped in towels ate blintzes and drank borscht. A few ogled her as they passed, but no one seemed concerned, and she turned down the hall toward the Russian-style sauna. Two big, hairy men sat on a bench outside, one in baggy trunks and a heavy gold cross, the other with a wet towel around his shoulders and another around his waist. Yelena set their rolled towels on the bench and Joe reached for the door.

"*Sozhaleyu. Zakryto,*" the one with the gold chain said, standing to block Joe's way. "Broken," he added in English, though steam was visible through the small window in the door. Meanwhile the sitting man winked appreciatively at Yelena, who smiled back.

Joe nodded, humbly, and turned to go, then, spinning back for momentum, slammed his right fist into gold-chain's solar plexus, knocking the wind out of him. He gasped, leaning forward, and Joe stepped aside, grabbing his arm and tripping him in one motion. The big man slid smoothly on the wet tile and went down, knocking his head hard on the bench. Yelena, meanwhile, had moved fast, yanking the wet towel from around the sitting, leering man's neck and whipping it across his eyes. He cursed and reached for her blindly. She eluded him easily, kicking his ankle out from under him and, as he stumbled to his knees, she looped the wet towel around his throat, pulling it tight. Grunting, he struggled, but she had her foot on his back now and gripped hard. After a few seconds, he passed out, and she let him drop. She grabbed her rolled towel and handed Joe his. He opened the door to the sauna.

The room was like the inside of a brick pizza oven, or a deep inner VIP chamber of Hades. Raw bedrock, granite blackened with age formed one whole wall, the others were stone and brick. Staggered rows of wooden benches ran along three sides, and, in the corner, an iron furnace wheezed and growled, radiating waves of stunning heat, a red heart flaming behind the window in the furnace door. A wooden bucket with a ladle sat under a dripping faucet. Anton was laid out like a lox in a smokehouse, face-down on the top bench, close to the ceiling, while a minion scrubbed him down with soapy water. Sergey sprawled on the other top bench, and man-spread across the lower shelves, legs wide, arms out, were the three mercs, Trey, Dirk, and Baxter, slicked in sweat.

The intense heat seemed to slow everything down, vision blurred, time melted, and it took a second for the men to react to the two new bodies in the room. First they all looked at Yelena, grinning like wolves. Then Trey looked at Joe.

"Hey." He opened his eyes wider. "You killed Tony!"

Joe frowned, trying to remember. He looked to Yelena. "Who's Tony?"

She shrugged, then, before anyone else could move, she kicked Dirk in the chin, as Joe snatched up the wooden bucket and whacked it across Baxter's head. Now everyone moved. Trey leapt up in a rage and came at Joe, swinging, while Sergey, thinking a bit further ahead, reached into a robe that was hanging on the wall and drew a switchblade, which he clicked open. Dirk bounced back up and dove for Yelena's legs while the big boy who'd been sluicing down Anton turned and swung his bucket at her head.

As Joe turned to block Sergey's knife with his towel, Trey landed a hard right to his head, knocking him off center, then came up with a roundhouse that caught his jaw. As he spun, Joe kicked back, catching Trey behind the ankle, and elbowing him hard in the chest so that he slid on the wet floor, landing with a hard thud. He stopped Sergey's blade with his towel, which was slashed and, stepping back, drew a combat knife, a long, evil blade that had been rolled inside the towel. He faced both men, winding the towel around his arm for defense.

Yelena, meanwhile, having deflected the bucket, was twisting free of Dirk's grip while striking him hard across the ear with a cupped palm, rupturing his eardrum. By now, however, the big masseur was on her, leaping down from the upper bench. She pivoted into his body as he landed on her and both went flying back against the stone wall. Then, abruptly, he stopped, his broad body pressed against hers, gasping as his eyes went wide in surprise and pain. She stared right back into them, now holding him tight, as though in a dance she was leading. She let go and he slid away, torso covered in blood. Blood dripped from the combat knife she'd had sheathed in her own towel. He dropped to the floor and the red ran into the wooden slats and away.

By then, however, Dirk was back on his feet and Anton was in motion. Cursing in Russian, Anton lifted the squeeze bottle of soap and squirted it in Yelena's eyes. Blinded, she tried to slash out at Dirk but he slammed her hard and she skidded back, hissing like a scalded cat when her shoulder fell against the furnace door.

Joe saw this, but was too penned in to help, fending off Sergey's blade with his towel-wrapped arm and slashing and kicking at Trey, who was closing in. Then Baxter, who'd been stunned on the floor, reached under a bench and drew a .32, a flat automatic that he aimed up at Joe. Joe jumped. The bullet went under him and ricocheted off the stone wall, echoing in the small chamber. As he leapt over Baxter, who was crouching, Joe's left foot connected with Trey's chin, knocking him off balance on the soapy floor. He fell back. Sergey was lifting his arm high for a downward stab with his blade, and as Joe passed, he slashed deep across Sergey's wrist, severing the arteries and tendon. The switchblade clattered to the floor.

Gritting her teeth, Yelena caught the handle of the furnace and kept from falling as the door swung back, then shoved her towel into the open mouth. It caught immediately. As Dirk came at her, she flung the burning towel onto his face and he stumbled back, panicked by the flames. Anton, seizing the moment, ran from the sauna, leaving the door open, yelling in Russian for help.

Now Joe, landing on the upper bench, spun around, kicking Baxter in the back of head, sending him sprawling, and stuffed the bucket down on Trey's head just as he regained his feet. He hurled his blade, which arced through the humid air and struck deep into Sergey's chest. Launching himself, Joe jumped onto Trey and knocked him forward, into the open door of the sauna. Sergey lay fallen against the furnace now, his eyes blank, his body steaming against the hot iron, but he felt nothing. He would never feel anything again. Joe pulled his knife free and grabbed Yelena, giving Baxter another hard kick in the kidneys.

"Come on." They pushed into the hall as Trey rolled under their feet. The two goons were gone, fleeing or maybe fetching weapons. There was no sign of Anton. "How's the burn?" Joe asked as they hurried down the hall. Now he heard yelling from upstairs.

"Hot," Yelena admitted.

"Maybe this will help," Joe said, and they jumped into the cold plunge. A small, chest-high pool full of frigid water, it was meant to shock the system after the hot rooms and it worked, dulling Yelena's burn slightly. Then, as the two goons returned and Trey came down the hall, they ducked low in the water, up against the wall of the pool where they hoped the extended concrete rim would hide them from view.

"You see where they went?" Trey asked the goons. Baxter and Dirk were following behind him from the sauna. The goons shook their heads. One now had a gun, the other a bat.

"Okay," Trey said. "Let's check everything. Spread out."

Joe and Yelena remained motionless, careful not to splash, heads still under the rim of the pool, breathing slow with their bodies still submerged in the water. It was very cold. Joe could feel his fingers and toes going numb. Finally, the men moved.

"Now," Yelena whispered, and they crawled up onto the floor. They ducked into the closest door, the steam room. Joe's towel was shredded from Sergey's blade and soaked from the cold water. He tore it into strips and tied them around Yelena's arm while she kept an eye on the glass door. They were in a tiled box with benches and vents on the floor for steam. Joe climbed to the thermostat and stuffed the remains of his wet, ragged towel around it. The cold water triggered the mechanism and the room began to fill with thick clouds of hissing steam. Soon he could barely see his own hand in front of his face. Yelena was invisible beside him. Then the door opened.

❖

When Anton made it out onto the street, he couldn't believe his luck. He'd fled crazily through the banya, sending his men back to fight, and huffing up the stairs. He even had time to grab his robe, which contained his wallet and keys. He pulled it on now as he hit the sidewalk, tasting the fresh (or at least city-scented) air, seeing the night sky (or at least the city's lamplit ceiling), feeling the flow of normal life around him, and he realized, putting a hand in a pocket, even his cigarettes were there. He was alive and dying for a smoke. That's when a car door opened, blocking his path.

"Hey there, Anton, you need a ride?" It was Liam, one of the Madigan brothers, the pretty one with the smart mouth. "You'll get in trouble walking the streets in your dressing gown."

Now the other door was opening, and it was Josh, the Israeli, a tough-looking Sephardic who worked for Rebbe Stone. He was holding a gun. "You look tired," he said. "Puffing like you're going to have a heart attack. Better ride with us."

Anton stopped. Liam came up beside him. "It's the smoking," he told Josh. "I'm telling you. It's a killer, right Anton?"

Anton held his arms up. "Money," he said. "Lots of it. And the dope business too. I can tell you all about it."

"Excellent," Liam said. "We can't wait to hear. But we have to talk on the way. We're late."

"Late?" Anton asked, feeling the hope drain from his body.

"It's a surprise party," Josh told him. "And you're the guest of honor. All your friends are waiting."

❖

Joe and Yelena remained completely still, holding their breath. The fogged-over glass door to the steam room opened and enough light streamed in from behind for them to see it was the two goons from the hall, armed with a pistol and a bat. Then the door swung shut and the steam swallowed them. The men looked around, peering into the thick fog, failing to see the ghosts just in front of them.

"Let's go," one said. "I'm dying in here." They turned to go. Simultaneously, Joe and Yelena moved. They crept silently forward, emerging from the clouds. As the thug with the bat glanced right, he saw Yelena's blade, appearing as if from nowhere, slice across his friend's throat, releasing a ribbon of blood. He started, but it was too late. Joe's arm was snaking out around his own neck and Joe's blade found his throat too, cutting the jugular. He staggered forward, blood spraying, and fell. Then a bullet shattered the glass door.

Joe jumped back as the bullet cut through the clouds of steam and cracked the tile wall. Yelena dropped to the floor and felt for the goon's fallen gun. As the gunman approached, stepping into the doorframe, Joe saw it was Baxter and tossed the bat. That distracted him long enough for Yelena to raise the gun and fire, chasing him back. Yelena went into the hall after him, firing again as he took cover around a corner. A statue of Cupid had been shattered; now headless, it looked more like a real ruin than the cheap plaster copy it was.

"This way," she called back at Joe, who came after her, crossing the glass that now covered the steam room floor from the broken door. He felt it cutting into his feet, but there was no time for that now. Crouching low, he followed Yelena, who fired another shot to keep Baxter back and led Joe down the hall into the next room.

These were the massage booths. A long, low-ceilinged room, dimly lit and divided by curtains hung on crisscrossing cords, with a massage table in each nook. Yelena and Joe moved through quickly and quietly, brushing the curtains aside, she with the gun poised in one hand and the knife in the other, he with his knife hand cocked back and ready. Then, in a corner, there he was: Nikolai, laid out on a table, his back red and scored, while a big bald Russian in a tiny speedo worked over him with a leafy birch branch. He paused when he saw them, holding the branch aloft.

"You—back," Yelena said. He raised his hands and stepped back. Nikolai rolled over, squinting his eyes. "And you, pig," she told him, "wake up. I want you to see the bullet coming."

Nikolai blinked at her. "Ah," he said. "Yelena. I was hoping we'd meet."

Just then, from the corner of his eye, Joe saw the shape of Baxter's gun pushing against the curtain to his left. He grabbed the muzzle, forcing it aside as it fired, the bullet tearing through the curtain, whizzing past, and tearing the curtain beyond, leaving two smoking burn holes in the fabric. During that moment's distraction, the big Russian tossed the branch at Yelena and snatched up a knife. As he raised his arm to throw it, Yelena fired: the first bullet went through his knife hand, and the next two went through his heart. Then her gun clicked. Empty. She turned to the empty table and the rustling curtains. Nikolai was gone.

"Go," Joe said as he wrestled Baxter through the curtain, keeping him wrapped tight. His pistol went off twice more, burning more holes in the curtain. Then he heard Baxter's gun also hit an empty chamber. Holding Baxter in a hug, Joe reached high and brought his knife down in a sweeping arc, stabbing through the curtain. He felt him slump, as blood began to seep through the fabric, and let him drop.

Joe went after Yelena, out through the back of the room to the hallway, but stopped when he saw Dirk and Trey go by, calling to each other, "She went down here." He waited for them to pass and then followed, down the stone steps. He could see that he was leaving bloody footprints, but it didn't matter: he was the pursuer now, not the pursued. He didn't need to hide.

Yelena entered the pool room. This was a large space, farther underground, and it felt cool and quiet, as if further from the city. A swimming pool filled its center like a blue window, sending reflected ripples across the ceiling, also painted blue. Beside it was a big Jacuzzi, a tiled circle in which the water churned and foamed. There was a bar, a mural along the long wall depicting a waterfall tumbling from forested cliffs into an ocean where a ship sailed to an island with a castle, where a poorly painted king and queen stood on a tower waving, their faces and hands pink smudges. There were tables and chairs and lounges, all empty.

From behind the bar came Nikolai, hefting a machete. He was wearing trunks and a gold cross but had no tattoos; he was not a criminal. He smiled as she came around the pool to face him, holding her blade.

"Do your American friends know what your tattoos mean, Lenochka? Or do these dumb hipsters just think it's cool? A fashion trend like theirs? You don't have to even hide them here in New York."

"I never hide them," she answered, moving closer.

"And what about your boy, Joe? Does he know that they mark you as trash? A whore and a thief? Scum born to scum in a sewer? The child of a junkie whore and God knows who? Some drunk who couldn't afford better."

Yelena smiled. "He knows. That's why he likes me." She waved the blade point at him. "But you don't need any tattoos do you? The mark of the pig is right there on your face for all to see. Now I'm going to carve it into your hide."

Nikolai laughed. "I'm sure you'd love to try." He shrugged. "But are you good enough? Remember, I taught you everything you know."

Now Yelena laughed. "You taught me to dress and fix my hair. To be polite. To eat caviar and to lie in five languages. But to fight? I was born into that, like you said. I inherit it from my whore mother. And now I'm going to kill you in her name. Whatever it was."

And she charged toward him.

❖

When Joe came into the pool room, he saw Trey and Dirk, backs turned, in silence. Dirk's skull was buzzed close; Trey's long ponytail hung down. They were watching Yelena and Nikolai, across the pool, dueling. Well matched, they thrust and parried, dodged and darted, as tightly-focused and oblivious to their audience as any pair of champion dancers. Joe came up fast and kicked Trey, sending him into the Jacuzzi. Then, before Dirk could react, he drove his knife between his shoulder blades. Trey was fast, though, and strong, and he came up quick, grabbing Joe by the ankle. Joe lost his balance and fell into the whirlpool with Trey, his knife still in Dirk's back as he too plunged into the churning water, dyeing it red as he bled out.

When Joe felt his chin hit the bottom of the shallow pool, banging it hard, he pushed out with his arms, trying to propel himself back up. But he was too far under, and as Trey locked his grip on his legs, standing over him and forcing his head beneath the water, he had no choice but to struggle like a snake, arching his back, fighting to get his head up and breathe. He broke the surface just long enough to glimpse Yelena and Nikolai, clutched together now, each holding the other's knife arm, each raising a blade, topple together into the pool. Then he was under again, with the whirlpool swirling around him and the massage jet pummeling his face. Trey had the leverage, his own legs planted so that he was standing in the water, clenching Joe's legs with all his considerable upper body strength. Joe struggled and kicked, his head remained below the surface, and he knew it was only a matter of time. A couple minutes. The length of a breath.

Instead of fighting to rise up, toward the air, Joe went down, thrusting himself deeper into the water. Trey kept his grip, his clench was tight around Joe's ankles, but Joe managed to reach Dirk's body, to grasp his dead hand and pull it closer. As his vision clouded and he felt himself about to pass out, or just as bad, breathe in a lungful of water, Joe drew the knife from Dirk's back and then curled lower, swimming between Trey's legs. He sawed across both his ankles, severing the tendons.

Trey let go. As his legs gave out, he dropped Joe and Joe somersaulted away. His feet touched bottom and he stood, gasping for air. Trey collapsed, sitting in the water as his useless legs folded, and Joe grabbed his right hand and cut the cord in his wrist too, squirting more blood into the already crimson whirlpool, which now seemed to boil like a cauldron. Limping on his bloody feet and still catching his breath, Joe hobbled up the steps and felt Trey grab him. His one good hand, his left, still with some strength in it, was holding Joe's ankle. Joe looked down to see Trey, grunting with effort, trying to come after him. A look of confusion came over him as he realized his body would no longer obey. Joe had cut his strings, severing the tendons in both feet and one hand. He sprawled back onto the lip of the Jacuzzi like a broken marionette, staring up at Joe. He nodded. Joe nodded back. Then he shut his eyes, in surrender, as Joe leaned over and sank the blade into his heart.

That was when Joe realized: Yelena was nowhere in sight. She and Nikolai were both gone. He stood and saw that the pool was rippling, stirred from below, and that a cloud of red was blooming across the blue skin. He held his breath. Then the surface broke and a body floated up. It was Nikolai with a knife in his back. A second later, Yelena emerged, rising from the water like a siren, or a nightmare, one of those avenging furies who haunt men's dreams. She came up the steps, back straight, head up, eyes forward, a newborn goddess, blood spreading in her wake.

PART V

38

"HOLY SHIT," JUNO SAID, when he saw Yelena and Joe come limping out of the bathhouse. Cash put the car in gear, honking once lightly to let them know he was there. Joe was in ridiculous clown-like bath trunks, like something a retired Jimmy Buffet fan would wear, and had what looked like bloody rags tied around his feet. Yelena was wrapped in a robe, and so seemed slightly less conspicuous, until she was close enough for Juno to realize she was more or less covered in blood.

Cash braked in front of them and Juno rushed to open the back door. "Damn, Yelena . . ." he said.

"Don't worry, Juno. It's not my blood."

"Hospital," Joe said. "Make a left on the next street."

Cash looked in the rearview as he hit the gas. "What's wrong? Who's hurt?"

"She is," Joe said. "A burn. She needs first aid fast."

"So do you," she said. "Your feet."

"She's got a point," Juno said. "You look like you been in Valley Forge with George Washington. I mean from the knees down. Knees up you look cool."

"I've got glass in my feet. It hurts like hell, but it can wait. And I can pick it out myself. That burn is for real and needs professional attention. Quickly."

Yelena sighed and rolled her eyes. "Okay Dr. Joe. If you say so."

"Thank you," Joe said, and smiled. Yelena smiled too. In the rearview, Cash noticed that she laid her hand over his.

"ER's coming up on the right," he said he drove down the narrow street. "You planning to escort her in or what?"

Joe looked down at his outfit. Juno was right, he looked like a mess. They'd throw a net on him. "Hey what size shoes do you guys wear?"

❖

It was tough but Joe managed not to limp. He was in his shorts, Cash's clean white T-shirt, and Juno's very expensive new sneakers, with his hair smoothed back. He didn't look much worse than a lot of the tourists who'd wandered into the ER. With one arm around Yelena, he went up to the counter and called to a woman in scrubs.

"Excuse me, please, you've got to help her."

Distracted, the woman regarded them over her glasses as she looked up from her desk. "Now calm down sir, I . . . oh my God." She goggled at Yelena, then reached and pressed a button. "Assistance! Now," she called into an intercom. Her eyes ranged over Yelena. "Miss, where is the bleeding coming from?"

"I think that stopped," Joe said. "But she's been burned." He pulled down the robe and revealed the raw and suppurating burn on her shoulder. He squeezed Yelena, who responded by beginning to wail loudly. "She's hysterical," he added. "It's the pain."

Two medics rushed over and took gentle hold of Yelena. The nurse turned to Joe, hand on keyboard. "What's her name sir? Is she your wife? Girlfriend?"

"No. I don't know her. I don't even think she speaks English. There was an accident at the spa. So I just brought her in."

"At the spa?"

Meanwhile the medics eased Yelena into a wheelchair, talking to her the whole time. She cried and yelled at them in Russian.

"Calm down, we're here to help you. What's your name?"

"Do you have ID? Do you have insurance?"

The nurse who was talking to Joe persisted, as Yelena was wheeled away. "I'm still going to need some info from you sir, for the file."

"Sure," Joe said, rubbing his forehead. "But can I get some water first? I feel a little faint myself. This was really scary."

"Right away," the nurse said, anxious not to have another intake. "Why don't you have a seat?"

She fetched a paper cup of water and came back, searching the seating area, but he was gone.

❖

When Victoria got to the banya and saw a young woman fleeing, followed by some other customers, a few still in their bathing suits, she realized she was late to the dance. And when she spotted first one and then two cars, each with two men in it, sitting and watching, she decided to stay and watch herself, moving to a discreet spot at the corner. And when Anton, the Russian mob boss, came running out, looking like he'd just seen a ghost, and the two men in the front car grabbed him up, she grinned. It looked like someone else besides her was on cleanup duty for a change. She was not surprised to see that it was Joe and Yelena who came out shortly after and got in the other car, looking ragged and bloody. And when no one else chased after them, she knew what that meant too: everyone else was dead.

Impressed, she watched as the car passed by, then followed after it. It was a tight space down here, at the bottom of the island, and the crowded ER was just a few short blocks away. So she waited for Joe and Yelena to enter, and the others to drive off, and then wandered in, picked up a discarded newspaper, and sat down with everyone else to wait. She wanted to see what happened next.

❖

By the time Donna could ask where Toomey was, he was gone. In the first minutes after the gunshot, while chaos reigned, they had tried to lock down the area, but the crowd was too big and the perimeter too wide, to search everything and everyone for one suspect. Plus, the description of the suspect—white, blonde, twenties—and the fact that she had fired just one shot at a tourist visiting the site, made it feel like some personal drama or random insanity, not a serious, organized terror attack. They put out an APB and had all the cops at all the checkpoints watching, but the rest of the event was allowed to go on. While a medic bandaged her wound—it was a mere grazing—Donna called Blaze, who was mortified and pissed but alive and well except for a brutal hangover. She went on the hunt for the shooter herself, walking the perimeter, searching the crowd, squatting in the van with the facial recognition boys. Nothing. Then Tom found her and made her sit still while she was extensively debriefed, and re-debriefed, and filled out a report. She said she wanted to question Toomey, and Tom told her that he'd given a statement and gone home.

Well, all she had to do was get on the laptop and dig a little for that statement of his to start melting away: Yes, Toomey was a vet, like he said, and he was in the Special Forces. But he was never wounded, as far as she could see. And his last known employment was indeed as a "consultant." For Wildwater. She bolted down a dinner of takeout beans and rice and plantains and café con leche from the Cuban place that was about to close—she hadn't eaten all day—and then she called Fusco.

"Hey," he said. "Where the hell you been? You're missing everything."

"I've been getting shot at and saving America, asshole," she said, realizing that she was actually happy to hear his voice. "What about you?"

"Shot at?" Fusco asked, sounding genuinely concerned. "By who?"

"By a Wildwater employee as it happens. What do you think of that?"

"I think you better get your ass down here to the bathhouse. The one by the Stock Exchange."

"Why?"

"Because almost everybody else who works for Wildwater is floating around here dead. We're still fishing them out."

So she walked over. Tom had ordered her to get her wound looked at. It was nothing, but he wanted everything covered, so she said she'd go to the ER, then put an FBI windbreaker on over her torn shirt and walked to the bathhouse address, which was practically on the way. It wasn't hard to find: NYPD was out in force, with the block taped off and the whole circus set up. She waved her badge and a tech handed her booties and a zip up suit. Then on the way downstairs, she saw Parks, who was wearing a suit too, plus a hairnet and rubber boots.

"What is there—kryptonite down there?" Donna asked him.

"You're gonna need it, believe me," he said. "One stiff's ponytail got caught in a drain and the whole place backed up with bloody water. It's like a horror movie."

Donna put on the gear and followed him, then whistled when she saw the bodies laid out on tarps. The steam and heat were turned off and everything was lit, but there was still blood everywhere, on the floors and walls. "Yeah, we're up to seven dead."

"Eight," Fusco said as he came up from the pool room. He looked like a cartoon character, big and round in his baby blue hazmat suit, with his red, round face in the hairnet. It was hard not to smile. "We drained the pool and, guess what, found a Russian spy."

"A spy?"

"An intelligence officer. Nikolai something. Attaché for business affairs or whatever. But apparently he's with their CIA."

"I see," she said, thinking about Mike's impromptu visit yesterday.

"But most of the Russians are more familiar. Remember Sergey, who you lost at the airport?"

"Rings a bell," Donna said, through gritted teeth.

"Well the good news is you can stop looking. Someone stabbed him to death in the sauna."

"Mostly all knife wounds," Parks said. "I guess this is a tough place to sneak in a gun."

"And extra clips," Donna added. "I mean if you're taking on an army."

"And speaking of army, here's the other good news. The three dead guys who aren't Russian? They're all mercenaries."

"Mercenaries? Why is that good news?"

Parks grinned at her. "Because all three were contractors, supposedly overseas, working for the Wildwater Corporation."

"Really?" Donna couldn't help but smile big now too. "So I was right."

"It makes sense," Fusco said. "They landed here and tried to take over the dope trade."

"And now they got hit back," Donna said. "Hard."

Fusco nodded. "They should have learned their lesson in Afghanistan."

"But hit by who?" Parks wondered aloud. "And how many? I mean it had to be like an assault team right? And with knives. I mean who the hell knows how to cause all this mayhem with just a knife?"

He looked from Fusco to Donna, but now they both just looked at the floor, and shrugged.

❖

Donna called Tom to check in and let him know about the new developments, ask about getting some more FBI down there, maybe Janet to help with forensics.

"What bathhouse? I thought you were at the hospital."

"I was on my way, sir, but this is an important piece of the case . . ."

"I understand, but if you get an infection and they amputate your arms or something, it's going to fuck up my whole week, so get your ass to the ER and then report on this tomorrow."

"Yes, sir," she said, and told Fusco.

He shrugged. "Take your time. This party is going to go all night."

She walked down to the ER, which was madness like always, a hundred other dramas playing out, less bizarre than hers maybe but just as important to those caught up in them. She showed her badge to the woman behind the counter, hoping to get bumped ahead in line.

274

"You here for the Russian girl?" she asked.

"Russian girl?" Donna asked, feeling a tingle go up her spine. "What Russian girl?"

"I don't know her name, she doesn't speak English so I hope you speak Russian. I mean I guess it's Russian. But she came in with a bad burn and all covered in somebody else's blood. So we called the police, but they never came so I figured you're them. Except, like I said when I called it in, you got to speak Russian."

"What room is she in?"

The nurse gave her the number and pointed and Donna went down the hall, but when she pushed the door open and entered there was no Russian girl and no patient in the bed at all. The only person there, sitting in a chair in a nice gray suit, was Gio Caprisi.

❖

When Victoria saw Donna her first impulse was to kill her. After all, she'd ruined her play, so beautifully planned and staged, and caused her a fair bit of trouble. It was extremely annoying, and as with anything annoying, a bug let's say, your first impulse is to crush it. But then again, she reasoned, this Donna was only doing her job, and doing it bloody well actually, better than most of these clods, and she felt she should really be more supportive of a fellow woman excelling in such a male-dominated field. It really was a boy's club still, and what with the Russian, Noylaskya, this was turning into a real female empowerment kind of moment. So, good for her. Besides, Victoria knew that impulse control was one of her issues, and that part of what made her a professional was focus—in this case, focus on her primary targets. Who were still out there. So when Agent Donna spoke to the nurse and then rushed off down the hall, no doubt looking for Yelena, whom she was not going to find, Victoria silently wished them both well. And she left.

39

"GOOD EVENING AGENT ZAMORA," Gio said, with a big smile, standing politely. "Lovely to see you again."

"Mr. Caprisi," Donna said, taken aback. "What brings you here? Visiting a sick Russian friend maybe? Or business associate?"

Gio shook his head, still smiling. "I don't think I have any Russian associates."

"Not anymore maybe. There's a bunch of dead ones floating around in the bathhouse."

Gio shrugged it off. "My family business is ices and gelato, as you know. Actually, we had three trucks out here today. All spotless. Not even a dead fly floating in a melted sundae, I promise."

"I'm impressed you didn't get a spot on your suit either," Donna noted.

"Well I mostly supervise these days."

"Then why are you here? Trouble in the ice cream world? A tummy ache? Brain freeze?"

"What do you think? I'm looking for you. It's urgent. I called your office line and they referred me to another agent, Newton I believe. And he sent me here. I have a tip."

"About?"

"A guy named Robert Richards. Maybe you've heard of him. He's the CEO of a company called Wildwater."

Donna breathed in sharply, but she kept her poker face. "I've heard of him. What's he got to do with you?"

"Me?" Gio shrugged lightly. "Nothing. As far I know, they don't sell ice cream. But I've been told, by reliable sources, that if you search his office, particularly the safe, you will find the evidence you need to prove he's been selling heroin and using it to fund a terror cell. I believe that's your business, Agent Zamora?"

She stood and leaned over him. "Who told you this?"

"Sorry. I don't remember."

She raised her hand and was about to put a finger in his face, something that even an FBI agent would be wise to think twice about, then thought twice and lowered her hand. "Enough games," she said, calmly. "I can take you in as a material witness."

He shook his head, sighing heavily. "Agent Zamora, don't you even read your own website? I did, when I checked for your phone number. You know what it said? Anonymous tip line. No questions asked." Noticing the mirror on the wall, he shot his cuffs and buttoned his jacket. "I'm going to go now. I had a long day. And I suggest you get some rest too. You have a big worm to catch. Get there early."

Then, with a smile and nod, he left. Donna kept the frown on her face until he was out of sight, then pumped her fist once and broke into a grin as she called Andy. "Get started on a warrant. We're going into Wildwater tomorrow. Early. Bob Richards's office. Right. I'll see you back at the office. And I'll bring the coffee. Thanks, bro." Then she called Fusco and Parks. Then she called her mom and told her she was pulling an all-nighter.

"But what about the date, mija?" her mom wanted to know. "Did Toomey come? Was he nice? How did it go?"

"It went so-so," Donna told her.

❖

Gio kept his face blank until he left the hospital, but as he got into Nero's car, he was grinning. He was riding shotgun. Pete and Little Eddie were in the back.

"Liam called, Boss," Nero told him as he pulled out. "They're all ready for us."

Gio looked in the rearview at Little Eddie, who looked like he was sitting in a dentist's waiting room or the principal's office. "You ready for this?" he asked. "It's Okay if you're not."

Eddie nodded, a little too quickly. "I'm ready Uncle Gio . . ." Then he blushed. "I mean Boss."

Gio laughed. "Uncle Gio is fine. I held you when you were a baby. Now you could put me on your lap." He turned around, making a serious face. "But you better not fucking try it."

"I would never . . ." Eddie blurted and everyone laughed. Pete patted his arm.

"Relax, kid. You're among friends. And I know your Dad is looking down now too, and he's proud."

❖

Old Shenanigan's Public House was packed with a raucous, roaring crowd, but they entered through a rear alley, where one of the Madigan crew was waiting to lead them directly into the basement storeroom and then to a long-forgotten sub-basement, the stairs to which were normally hidden behind a painted-over metal door concealed by storage cabinets. They filed down the narrow stairs—Little Eddie had to go sideways—and found Liam and Josh waiting by the light of a battery-powered lamp. It was a low, damp, dusty space with a dirt floor. Now a couple of yards of that floor had been dug up, and Anton was sitting in the hole among the soil, broken concrete, and rock, still in his bathrobe. On closer inspection, you could see that some of the debris in the hole with him were actually fragments of old skull and bone.

"Gio!" Anton said when he saw him, and started to get up. "Thank God you're here . . ."

"Relax, Anton," Gio said. "Have a seat." Josh kicked him in the chest and he sat back down. "You must be tired. But it's over now. Your crew are dead. Your dope operation is shut down."

"That wasn't me. It was Sergey." Anton put a cigarette in his lips with shaky fingers and searched for his lighter.

"Sergey didn't take a leak without your order, we all know that," Josh said.

"You were White Angel," Liam said. "That crap almost killed me brother."

"Now I'm responsible for addiction?" Anton asked. "It's a disease. They'll find some other poison."

"Never too late to quit though," Liam said and snatched his cigarette. "Hey!"

"Sorry, New York State law. Smoke free environment."

"Gio, these kids are crazy," Anton went on. "They can't just kill a boss. You have to listen to me. We're friends for fuck's sake."

"You're right." Gio nodded. "Old friends."

"Yes!" Anton agreed.

"I saw another old pal of yours today," Gio added. "Alonzo."

"How is he?" Anton asked.

"Better. Talking, eating, you know. It's a slow recovery but boy did he smile when I told him I'd be seeing you tonight. Really cheered him up."

"Oh . . ." Anton wasn't sure how to respond.

"And another friend of yours, Maria, she sent a message too. What was it again? You know her funny way of putting things, right?" He chuckled and the others grinned.

"She's a pisser," Nero said.

"She sure is," Gio said. "Oh, now I remember. She said, when you chop him up, save his balls and I'll feed them to my new puppy."

Everyone laughed except Anton.

"Funny, right?" Gio said. "I guess she thinks they'll help the puppy grow up stronger. Me, I'm not so sure." He looked at Anton critically. "I think we'll just feed you to the rats and worms."

Anton snarled. "You'd know all about licking balls and sucking dick, wouldn't you? Faggot."

"Hey!" Liam kicked him in the head. "Show some respect. Me and Josh are the faggots here."

Still smiling, Gio raised his gun. "Suck on this," he said, and fired. The first bullet entered his gut and he sat back, grunting and holding the wound. Gio handed his gun to Nero, who aimed carefully as Anton shook his head.

"This is for Eddie," Nero said and fired. He passed the gun to Pete.

"For Eddie," he said, and shot him again.

Now Anton was on his back, bleeding into the dirt, eyes rolling, and gasping like a fish on dry land. Pete put the gun into Little Eddie's hand and Nero whispered to him, "Just aim right in the center of his chest. Take a breath. And then squeeze the trigger, don't pull."

Little Eddie nodded. "This is for my father," he said, and then carefully squeezed.

❖

Afterward, Gio took Nero, Pete, and Little Eddie for a steak at Peter Luger's, then they drove out to the island and Nero dropped Gio at home. The kids were in their rooms for the night and Carol was in bed reading, wearing his old Mets T-shirt. When Gio walked in, she looked up from her book and took off her glasses.

"There you are, I was getting worried."

He made a face. "Why? I called. Only danger I was in was from a massive red-meat coronary."

"I know. It's just. You know. Ever since what happened."

He sat on the bed and took his shoes off. He was supposed to take them off downstairs but forgot about half the time. Then you still had to remember to carry them up and put them in the closet, or you got scolded for leaving them in the hall. It wasn't really a good system.

"Listen," he said, squeezing her foot under the blanket. "I don't want you to worry anymore. As of tonight, that problem is taken care of."

She sat up and put a hand on his shoulder. "You worked it all out? You found a solution?"

"Yeah. A permanent one."

"Oh . . ." A chill went through her as she realized people had died tonight. But she didn't remove her hand. She squeezed his shoulder.

"Wow your shoulders are tight," she said. "You need to relax."

"What's that mean?" he asked, lying down with his head across her legs. "I forgot."

She kept kneading his shoulders. "Maybe we should have a barbeque, you know, before the weather turns. Invite your sister and Jimmy and your mom. My family. The kids can ask their friends to use the pool. And you can invite Joe, and some of your friends, like . . ." She hesitated, wondering who that might be. "Nero. And Pete."

"Sounds great," he said into the blanket. He knew he had to get up and brush his teeth, but he was already half asleep.

❖

Joe entered quietly, because that was his habit and training. His grandmother was so used to his coming and going at odd hours that she rarely woke up. He moved through the dark apartment and into the bathroom, silently shutting the door before he hit the light. Sitting on the toilet cover, he ran the cold water in the tub, unwrapped his feet, and washed away the dried blood. Then, with a tweezers and a bottle of hydrogen peroxide, he began to pull the little slivers of glass from his feet and drop them into the wastebasket one by one.

40

THEY SERVED THE WARRANT at six. Donna was first through the door, Fusco stepping aside and gesturing for her to precede him, which she acknowledged with a nod. It was her tip, but it was also a tip of the hat, and she took it as such. Then came Parks, Andy, and a swarm of others, plenty of work for everybody sorting through this large, sprawling office, collecting the evidence—papers, computers, files, phones—that would take many hours to process. Donna, however, led her party straight to Richards's office, while he was being woken up and fetched from his private apartment. It was like some duke's den—polished wood and burnished brass, old carpets and oil paintings, even a fireplace—all transported, through the magic of money, to a glass lookout floating in space, far above Manhattan. Andy went by, leading the executive assistant, Jensen, with one hand and carrying a laptop in a plastic evidence bag with the other. Then came Fusco, half-guiding half-dragging Richards by the elbow, while Parks had his camera out, taping everything. He grinned at Donna, who kept a straight face for the camera. Richards was dressed in rumpled khakis and an untucked dress shirt, but his feet were bare and his sparse hair floated around his head. Minus his toupee, he already looked defeated, like he'd been scalped. As luck would have it, Donna was sitting in his luxurious desk chair, behind his grand mahogany showpiece when he came in, going through his drawers.

"What the hell are you doing?" he roared.

"Executing a search warrant sir," Donna said and stood up, holding his day-planner in her gloved hand. "Can you direct us to the location of your safe please?"

"Safe? What safe?"

"Janet," Donna called to the forensics specialist who was busy directing two men as they loaded a filing cabinet onto a dolly. "Can you get some guys with tools in here to start tearing out the walls?"

"Gladly."

"Wait," Richards said, looking at his gorgeously polished and grained woodwork. "It's behind that painting."

"The one of the hunting dogs, sir?" Donna asked.

"Hounds, yes."

"Grab the hounds, will you?" she asked Janet, who carefully removed the painting. There it was, a built-in safe with a digital keypad. Parks moved in closer for a shot. Fusco dragged Richards over.

"Now then sir," Donna continued, speaking loud for the camera. "Will you confirm that this is your safe?"

"Yes, obviously, but it has nothing to do with the business. It just has purely personal items in there and I haven't even opened it in weeks. I almost forgot about it."

"Does anyone besides you have the combination?"

"No. No one."

"Then, for the record, will you state that no one but you has access to this safe or has used it, to the best of your knowledge? And all items within are your personal property?"

"That's what I said," he barked, losing his temper. "You're wasting your time. There's nothing but my personal private property in there."

"Did you get that?" Donna asked Parks.

He gave her a thumbs-up.

"Sir, please open the safe." She stepped back and Richards, after a push from Fusco, stepped forward, grumbling. He punched in a code and reached for the handle.

"Sir, step back now please," Donna said, and Fusco pulled him back. Parks stepped up, focusing in, as Donna pulled open the door. Along with some files and manila envelopes, she found a large black plastic garbage bag. "Can you tell me what this is, sir?"

Richards stared. His mouth was open.

"Sir?"

He shook his head. "I don't understand. I've never seen that before."

She lifted it out, it had some heft to it, and put it on the desk, Parks panning along with her. Carefully she opened the bag and revealed the nice neat bricks of Persian heroin, vacuum sealed and taped. She spoke to the camera. "This bag contains what seems to be fifteen kilos of a powdered substance. Mr. Richards, for the record, do you know what this substance is sir?"

She kept her face totally blank, like a pro, but she could see, behind the camera, Parks, Fusco, Janet, and, from the doorway, Andy, too, all smiling at her. But it was the look on Richards's face that really struck her. Stark terror, which makes sense for someone about to go down for heroin smuggling and murder conspiracy, but also total confusion. He looked like he was having a nightmare.

❖

Looking as though he had aged ten years in ten seconds, Richards sat silently on the couch while the evidence against him was exhaustively photographed, measured, packed, and transported. It wasn't until Donna and Fusco headed over to get him on his feet and out to the car that he spoke.

He addressed her. "Agent, I have some important information I want to share."

"You'll have a chance to make a statement when we get to the office, sir."

"There's no time," he said. "I want to inform you right now that I have firsthand information about a possible terrorist attack. Here in New York."

Donna looked at him. Then she looked at Fusco, who was also staring in surprise. "When?" she asked him.

Richards shrugged. "Any second."

❖

Richards went dumb again after that. Donna demanded to know the details, when, where, who, and Fusco was this close to turning the camera off and beating it out of him, but when he refused absolutely to talk any further without a deal, Donna decided not to waste time arguing and got on the phone to Tom, who was already on the way, having heard about the big dope score. He told her he'd call for a US Assistant District Attorney to meet them there. So when the elevator doors opened, she expected a few extra suits, but she didn't expect Mike, though she supposed she should have. This was, no doubt, why he'd been nosing around all along.

"What do you know about this?" she muttered as they all trooped into the Wildwater conference room, which had been searched and cleared.

"Right now probably less than you," he said, and while she had given up trying to guess when he was lying—the answer, she'd found, was pretty much always—he did look genuinely freaked out. So did they all, except for Richards, who had recovered a little of his cockiness, now that he was back in the driver's seat.

They all took seats as the ADA put out a recorder and turned it on. "I am here with the full authority of my office to offer you consideration on the charges of drug possession with intent to sell and smuggling of a prohibited substance in exchange for all information regarding terrorist activities."

"I want full immunity," Richards said. "From all charges, including murder and conspiracy to commit murder, stemming from all federal and local investigations into Zahir and Wildwater."

"Bullshit . . ." Fusco muttered under his breath.

The ADA shot him a look. "Agreed," he said.

"And . . ." Richards began.

Fusco erupted. "There's more, you scumbag?"

"Sit down and shut up!" Tom yelled at him and Fusco snarled. Parks put a hand on his arm and he sat.

Richards waited for quiet. "And," he went on, "I want a new identity and permission to leave the country freely. No offense . . ." he looked around, eyes lingering on Powell, "but with what I know, US agencies are the last people I'm going to trust."

The ADA huddled with Tom and Powell for a moment, then faced Richards. "My colleagues from the FBI and CIA assure me this can be done. You'll be placed under my supervision with Secret Service protection."

Richards nodded. "Deal," he said.

Now Tom, who'd barely moved, leaned over and spoke. "Start talking."

Richards sat back. "The name of the man you are hunting is Rick Toomey."

"Shit . . ." Now it was Donna who muttered under her breath.

"Where is he?" Tom asked.

"I have no goddamn idea."

"What is your relationship to this man?"

"He is, or was, my employee. He led my security forces overseas . . ."

"Mercenaries," the ADA put in.

"Whatever. Soldiers. All perfectly legal."

"And illegally? What else did he do for you?"

"He seized heroin shipments from suppliers. Smugglers and warlords. He also handled transporting it to the US and delivering it to our partners here."

"He was the one who attacked the other dope operations?" Fusco asked. "Here in the city?"

"Yes. He and his men."

"Where are his men now?" Fusco asked.

"You'd know that better than me, detective," Richards said. "I assume they are dead."

Tom interrupted: "Tell us about the terrorist connection."

Richards cleared his throat. "Part of our strategy, politically, was to use this money to seed small terror strikes overseas . . ." He held a hand up and raised his voice. "Only overseas! In order to keep elected officials and the American people focused on what we thought was the real threat to our way of life."

"And what threat is that?" Tom asked.

"Islam, of course."

Parks, who'd been the calmest one there, finally leaned in. His voice was bitter. "And that also kept government funds flowing into your bank accounts, and paid for all this, did it not?"

Richards nodded.

"What happened?" Fusco asked. "What could have possibly gone wrong with this brilliant plan?"

Richards clenched his jaw. "It was Toomey. He's a fanatic. He went off on his own."

"When did you become aware of this?" the ADA prompted.

"When the last shipment never arrived. You were there," he nodded at Donna, "at first we thought you grabbed it and him. But then he disappeared, and we realized you hadn't gotten anything either. So the product was never there, even though Toomey told everyone he'd sent it like always and was going to pick it up. That's when I checked with our people in Afghanistan and found out that Toomey had been making secret purchases on his own with our dope money. And that he sent his own shipment through instead."

"What was in his shipment, Mr. Richards?"

"Uranium. We estimate about sixty kilos."

"Jesus . . ." That was Mike, saying the first thing he'd said. Audible sighs went around the room.

"How could that just come through in a normal container?" The ADA asked.

Richards shrugged. "It's benign until it's weaponized. More or less. The same radiation as kitty litter."

The ADA spoke carefully, controlling his rage. "And what did you do when you realized that your colleague had perhaps smuggled material into the area suitable for building a nuclear weapon?" Everyone stared at Richards, like a jury about to order execution. But now Richards stood up, defiantly.

"What did I do? I tried to stop him. I sent our best operative to take him out, and she would have too, she was this goddamn close." He pointed at Donna who stared back, stunned. "And then you saved him." He sat back down, waving an arm, dismissively. "And the rest of you let him go. Congratulations."

❖

By the time they got Richards cuffed and shod and downstairs, there was quite a crowd. The caravan of law enforcement vehicles stretched down the block and someone had tipped off the media, so reporters were buzzing, and that drew an outer ring of onlookers, many of whom had no idea what they were waiting to see. They probably would have been disappointed when it turned out to be a disheveled old man being escorted into a black Tahoe by a bunch of exhausted government workers in suits. But that's not how it turned out. As they were leaving the building and crossing the courtyard to the waiting cars, with Parks leading the way, parting the crowd, and Fusco and Donna holding Richards by the arms, with Tom, Mike, and the ADA bringing up the rear, suddenly Parks clutched his chest as if he were having a heart attack and fell. Donna knew it was not a heart attack though, because she saw the exit wound erupt, like a red blossom opening in his coat. The bullet flattened itself on the sidewalk.

"Shooter," she yelled, drawing her own gun, but with no idea where to even look. Then the top of Richards's head came off, and she knew, as he collapsed into a heap, that there was a sniper somewhere in one of the gigantic buildings across the street. But before she could even think about taking cover, she was knocked off her feet by someone grabbing her by the shoulders and yelling, "Lookout!" As she fell, she realized it was Mike on top of her. By then the pileup had begun, with bodies covering each other everywhere and people pushing to get away and everyone yelling, so it wasn't until a few seconds later, when she tried to move that she felt the wet spot on his back and realized that he too had been shot. "Agent down!" she yelled as she rose up on one knee. Across the street, in a window, she saw a muzzle flash, and another shot entered Mike's chest. She fired at the window, glimpsing a female silhouette with long hair and, she could have sworn, a quick wave. Then she was gone.

Donna leaned over Mike now as she heard the ambulance sirens coming. He smiled up at her and whispered something. She leaned in.

"Tell Larissa I love her," he said.

"Tell her yourself," she answered and he smiled. And then he was dead.

Vicky hadn't planned to kill the cop. But then again, until the night before, she hadn't planned on killing Richards. But once the hit on Toomey had—she hated the word but it was unavoidable—failed, she was told that it was time to cut their losses, to tie up loose ends and go. The call came from a familiar voice, one of those who had sent her to work for Richards in the first place. Now he'd become a liability and she had a new primary target. The cop was just in the way. As she watched through the scope, from the window of an office that wouldn't open till 9:30, she saw that the only way to get a clear shot at Richards before they reached the car was to clear the path. So she shot the cop. Then she took out Richards, who'd always rubbed her the wrong way. She was going to put one more in him, just to be safe—no more unfortunate accidents—when that cute CIA boy Mike Powell stepped in front of it. Heroic or suicidal? No one would ever know. But it was just as well; he was a sweet playmate but one more loose end who needed to be tied off. As for the FBI agent, his ex, Donna Zamora—good luck to her. Vicky bore her no ill will and rather hoped she caught Toomey, since he was part of the mess Vicky had been sent to clean up. And those other two, Joe and Yelena: she was sorry not to be playing with them any further, after seeing what they were capable of. They were her kind of fun, especially the girl. But for now, she was walking away. In five minutes she was back on the street, mixing with office workers who had no idea something awful had happened a block away. In an hour she'd be on a train to Boston. And then on a plane back to London, for a well-deserved rest. But before leaving, she did bend over the rifle and press her mouth to the stock, leaving a lipstick print, just as a kind of farewell kiss.

41

JOE WAS STILL IN bed. He'd slept deeply, physically exhausted, but also with the clear mind of someone whose labors were at an end. He had no nightmares and woke up feeling good. Even his feet were okay, now that he'd cleaned and bandaged them; the cuts were minor and staying off them for a day or two sounded fine to him. By the time he got up, Gladys had the coffee brewed. She brought him a cup and was suggesting scrambled eggs and toast for breakfast when the door buzzed.

Gladys went to the hall and opened the door but kept it on the chain. It was Donna. "Sorry, hun, but if you're going to keep doing this I'm going to have to call Mrs. Padera in 3B. Her son's a lawyer."

"I'm sorry about last time Gladys. I was wrong. I apologize. But this is serious, really serious. People will die. And I need Joe's help."

Gladys didn't ask any questions. She undid the chain and stepped back. "Have a seat. Coffee's fresh if you want some," she said. "I'm about to make scrambled eggs."

"Nothing for me, thank you." Donna said, walking into the living room. Joe, who'd heard them, was dressed now, in jeans and a clean black T-shirt. He held a cup of coffee.

"Don't worry about Mrs. Padera's son," he said. "I think he just does housing law."

❖

Joe took Donna into his room and offered her the chair.

"Thanks for seeing me," she said. "But first I owe you something."

"An apology for tossing the place? I heard it."

"No, that was for your grandmother," she said, "this is for you," and slapped him hard across the face.

"Ow," he said and then sat on the edge of the bed. She took the chair.

"Do you want to know what that's for?"

Joe rubbed his cheek. "I'm not sure it matters now."

"It does to me," Donna said. "It's for violating my professional integrity. For using me to further your goals, and in so doing, leading me to compromise my core values of honesty, fairness, and justice. I don't care if you're a criminal. But making me one." She shook her head. "I can't forgive that."

"Remind me. When did I do this?"

"The tip? About the safe in Richards's office?"

Joe shrugged.

"I know, I know, you sent your buddy Gio Caprisi, another patriot, and he fed me the info about the safe."

"And?"

"It was full of heroin, as you well know, heroin that I'm sure will connect to the dope being brought in by Zahir and to White Angel. Case closed."

"So? What's the problem? Congratulations."

"The problem is that I could tell from the expression on Richards's face when we popped the safe, he had no fucking idea how that dope got there. And why would he? Hide dope in his own safe? Confirm the contents were all his? He was set up by someone very clever."

"Is that what he said?" Joe shrugged again. "I'm not Mrs. Padera's son or anything, but that sounds like a pretty weak defense. He won't make that work in court."

She shook her head. "It doesn't matter now. He's dead."

"What?" Now she could see Joe was genuinely surprised. Thrown.

"And that's why I'm here," she went on. "Ready to grovel and ask for help, even from you. Because lots of people are going to die, innocent people. Some already have. And it's all my fault."

Then she told him the whole story as best she knew. Joe listened in silence, except for when she got to the part about there being uranium in the container, when he said "Of course . . ."

"What?"

He shook his head. "Nothing, go on," but he was thinking of the strange assortment of items on the shipping manifest Juno had dug up, all objects that emitted a small, harmless amount of radiation, nothing that would throw up a red flag with anyone. Certainly nothing that would alarm a dog trained only to sniff for drugs.

"So," he said, "when he tried to get you to arrange disabled parking . . ."

"His truck was wired the whole time. He wanted to set it off at Ground Zero. A goddamn truck bomb, right there, and I let him drive it away."

"At least you didn't let him in. You followed protocol. That saved hundreds, maybe thousands. You did your job."

"And then I saved his fucking life."

"That's also part of your job," Joe said. "Just like trying to save Richards." He started to put on his sneakers. "But fortunately it's not part of mine. I'll call you."

"Where are you going?" she asked, as he tied the laces, wincing just a little and leaving them a bit loose. "What are you going to do?"

"Something that violates your core values. But don't worry." He put his phone and keys in his pocket and then headed for the door. "You won't be involved. I'm used to government officials needing my help, but not wanting to know anything about it."

"Joe, wait . . ."

He turned back. She stood and came closer. "I'm thinking about, just in case it goes bad, having my mom take Larissa out of town, just to the beach or something. Your grandmother can go too. They can go to AC. They won't need to know the truth."

Joe smiled. "Thanks, Donna, but if anyone can spot a bluff, it's Gladys. That's why I just don't say anything." On the way out he grabbed a piece of toast. "Sorry, I've got to run. But Donna is staying for breakfast."

42

WHEN JOE TOLD DONNA that she didn't want to know where he was going, it was partly because his feelings were hurt, but it was also because he actually didn't know himself. He called Gio, keeping the details vague, just to be sure he and his family were all out on Long Island, then began walking aimlessly. He just needed to move, to feel like he was doing something, if only wandering through the streets of his own neighborhood. As always, in Jackson Heights, the world was on display. Women in saris shopped at the Mexican-run fruit stand. Dominican and Ecuadorian kids rode their bikes to the Yemeni candy shop. Taiwanese businessmen from Elmhurst walked into the bank, crossing paths with the delivery guy from the Thai place. The colors, sounds, voices, tastes, and smells of the whole globe mingled and merged around him. He'd been told, back in PS 69, that over a hundred languages were spoken just in his school. No doubt that figure had only grown. But to him this was normal. It was only when he grew up and ventured into the big world that he realized how special his little corner was, a unique and wondrous ecosystem. But to someone like Toomey, it was more like a petri dish, which he'd be happy to wipe out with a nuclear blast, to cleanse with radiation.

His feet started to hurt; he needed to sit, but felt like he had to keep moving, so he climbed to the train and rode into the city, descending into the darkness under the river. He surfaced finally in Columbus Circle, walking uptown now, lost in thought, drifting up Broadway, until, thinking he should be heading somewhere at least, and that it might be good to try talking to someone other than himself, he called Frank. He didn't sound happy to hear from him.

"Oh hey kid what's up?"

"I'm in your neighborhood, well almost, and I wanted to see what you thought about something. Can I come by?"

"I'm kind of in the middle of something. Is it urgent?"

"You could definitely say that."

"Okay. Give me like half an hour to finish this up and I'll make coffee. Do me a favor and pick up some milk?"

So Joe walked the rest of the way to 125th Street, the main drag in Harlem, where Frank had kept his studio for more than thirty years. It was a large space, half a high floor of a building that had once been offices, then illegal dwellings, and now luxury apartments above and cool offices below with trendy retail—an organic market, a silly clothing shop, a fusion restaurant, a chain café—on the ground floor. Joe got on the elevator with a blond family, a bearded dad and slim mom both in expensive jeans, with one kid in a stroller and the other holding mom's hand and gazing up at Joe.

"You're sweaty," the little girl said.

"Shhh . . . that's rude," the mom said, and smiled at Joe. "Sorry."

"Not at all," he said and smiled at the kid. "You're right. I am. Stinky too I bet."

She giggled.

The dad noticed that he'd pressed ten and said, "You're going to see Frank Jones?"

Joe nodded.

"I want to see Frank!" the little girl yelled. "Let's visit Frank!" The baby seemed to agree, gurgling and shaking his rattle.

"Frank's busy honey," the mom said. "He's uh . . . got a friend visiting." The elevator stopped at their floor and she smiled apologetically as they got out, the husband still looking back curiously.

"Yeah the kids like me, because I'm always covered in paint," Frank said when Joe told him this, "but the parents hate me. They paid millions for their lofts and I still pay less than it costs them to park their cars. Plus I'm always covered in paint." He was wearing house slippers, worn cotton pants that had frayed at the cuffs, and a T-shirt so old it was disintegrating, revealing gray chest hair through the holes, with a blue Cuban-style guayabera shirt over that, leaning on his cane. Everything was indeed covered in paint.

"Fuck them. You were here first," Joe said, following Frank down the hall to the big open raw space, which commanded a view of 125th Street and the city beyond. There was an easel with a half-finished nude, larger than life–size, an iron-framed daybed—pictured in the painting—an armchair with the stuffing falling out of the cracked leather, a straight-back chair, and a bunch of tables, shelves, and stools, all covered in heaps of brushes, tubes, rags, books, papers, magazines, cans, cups, art supplies, and other random debris.

"It's not just money though," Frank went on. "It's guilt. Harlem is like an Indian reservation. First the white folks said, you better stay up here. Now, a century later, they're saying, actually we need that space. Deep down they know it and feel bad. Which they resent me for. I'm hanging around, haunting them like the ghost of Harlem past."

"Coffee's ready." A woman came out from the curtain that separated the living quarters from the larger work space. She was a voluptuous white woman in her early thirties, with red hair loose to her waist, barefoot and wrapped in a kimono that slid from one bare shoulder as she carried out a tray that held a French press full of steaming coffee and three mismatched, chipped cups.

"Eva," Frank said, "meet Joe."

"Nice to meet you Joe." She set the tray down on top of some old newspapers.

"Hello Eva," Joe said. He set a quart of milk on the tray. "Thanks for the coffee. Here's some milk." He realized that Eva was the nude in the painting. "Sorry if I'm interrupting."

"You're not," Eva said, pouring the coffee and adding milk to hers. "I'm about to take a shower. Then Frank is taking me to an opening at a museum."

Frank groaned. Eva laughed and waved as she wandered back behind the curtain with her cup. Frank shook his head. "Goddamn openings. Too crowded to see anything. Too noisy to hear anything. And a bunch of people you don't want to see or hear anyway." He lifted both cups and handed Joe his. Neither took milk.

"Sounds like she still wants to go," Joe said.

"She has to. She's the director of the museum." He sipped his coffee. "Makes better coffee than I do too. Have a seat."

As always, Joe took the straight-back chair and Frank sprawled in his armchair.

"So . . ." Joe cleared his throat. "Well . . . when I told you that I worked as a bouncer at a strip club for a living, that was only party true."

"I suspected as much."

"I mean I really do work there."

"I believe you."

"But sometimes I get asked to . . . help out in other ways."

"Right. A man of your talents."

"Yeah. So to speak. But right now I'm afraid those talents aren't cutting it . . . I need help . . . it's kind of a bad situation . . ."

Frank waved his cane. "For fuck's sake kid, spit it out already." So he did. More or less. He told him about Toomey, the uranium, the truck bomb, and the 9/11 memorial.

"Jesus fuck," Frank said when he was done. "You weren't kidding. That really is a bad situation. You better catch this guy. What the hell are you doing wasting time here?"

"I need your help."

"Mine? True, I've seen some shitbag officers like him. And back in the day I would have fragged this bastard no problem. But I'm an old man with a bum knee. I can't do shit about shit."

"I need your brain. I've got no leads, nowhere to look. The FBI accidentally let him go, the asshole who he worked for got taken out, and everyone else who worked for him or knew him . . ." Joe shrugged guiltily. "I might have already killed."

"Damn Joe. No wonder you get bad dreams."

"No shit. But what I need now is someone who can help me think like he thinks. Figure his next move."

"How the hell do I know? I just hope he doesn't decide to blow up a museum opening. Okay, okay . . ." Frank leaned back and rubbed his eyes. "No chance he's just gonna say fuck it and go home? Retire and coach Little League?"

"No way. He's a fanatic."

"You know him?"

"I know the type. So do you. Gung-ho and juiced up on all that warrior code bullshit. He's just full of rage and looking for a reason to destroy. Thinks he's serving a cause, but really it's just an excuse."

Frank cocked an eyebrow. "That does remind me of someone a little."

Joe looked at him in confusion. Frank leaned forward on the cane. "Look. He's hard core, right? Special Forces badass, right?"

"Yeah."

"So. You're the only other Special Forces badass sitting here. What would you do? Let's say you're dropped behind lines, on a mission, search and destroy, and it goes to shit. You can't reach the primary target. Would *you* just pack it in and go home?"

Joe narrowed his eyes. "I'd proceed to the secondary."

"Right."

"So when Donna—I mean the FBI agent—chased him away from Ground Zero and he was driving that truck bomb . . ."

"That was his primary, sure."

"He told her he'd park it and come back."

"He fell back and got in position for his secondary target. So where did he go?"

"Someplace he could park and not get towed or messed with. A parking lot? A vacant? No, he needs another high-value target. Someplace busy, with people." Joe stood and pulled out his phone. "A building with underground parking." He dialed. "I'm going to call the FBI. Tell them to start checking."

"You do that." Frank stood, too. "I'm going to get changed and go to an opening. And pray you take this motherfucker out." He clapped Joe on the shoulder as he limped by. "De Oppresso Liber, brother."

43

DONNA HAD THE SAME idea, more or less. After trying and failing to convince Gladys to take a trip out of town—"I live here so might as well die here too, hon"—and insuring that her mom was taking Larissa to an amusement park in New Jersey (she said it was because of a measles outbreak that had been kept out of the news), she had headed back toward her office. Thinking about the time interval from when Toomey tried to get what she now knew was a truck bomb into the memorial, and when he returned on foot—was it an hour? A bit more?—she called and suggested to Tom that they begin searching soft targets where a truck could be parked without suspicion, like indoor parking structures or busy streets that had legal parking that day. Tom assured her that they were on it, then ordered her to go home. She'd been wounded yesterday and had her ex-husband killed in her arms today; officially she was off-duty until she could be de-briefed and cleared by a shrink. She'd even had to turn in her gun after it was fired.

"You've done good work, Donna," Tom said, using her first name for the first time she could recall. "Excellent work. But we'll take it from here. And who knows? If Toomey's got half a brain he is long gone by now. He knows we're onto him."

Fusco, who never agreed with the bosses about anything, sort of agreed: "We're on it. The whole force is out, for Parks. Working with the

300

FBI and even the goddamn CIA with no bullshit for once. We've got hundreds of people to go door to door if we have to."

Finally, she headed home and was on the subway when Joe called her, but she was in a tunnel and the signal was too weak. So she got off, and checked her voice mail in the station. He'd left a message, more or less suggesting the same plan. She thought about getting back on another A uptown, but what would she do then? Sit in her now-empty apartment and wait by the window for a mushroom cloud? Watch CNN? Go to the local church and pray? Not her style. She needed to be doing something, to work—though she might throw a few prayers in there too along the way.

So, okay, back to basics: when you lose the trail, what do you do? Go back to the last clear spot, the last solid link in the chain and find a fresh clue. It worked before in this case, when she checked a license plate and it led to Sergey. What the hell, she was just a short walk from the Wildwater building, anyway, so she left the station and walked over.

❖

Joe was on the train heading downtown. He was not sure why. He'd already called Donna to suggest she look into large buildings with underground parking, and he doubted the cops were going to let him help with the search, but his instincts drove him to move toward the center of the crisis. Standing still was unbearable and walking away felt like . . . walking away. He knew it was in large part his conditioning, his training, and he knew that in some ways it was a dubious, even bedeviling, impulse: a strength that became a weakness in the wrong hands. That's how you ended up like Toomey, perhaps. Because the people who sent people like Joe and Frank and yes, even Toomey, into the shit, turned out to be people like Richards. That's why Joe knew that, despite the scars on his body and the still-unhealed wounds in his mind, he was one of the lucky ones; he had kept his soul. De Oppresso Liber indeed. Free the oppressed. And start with yourself.

That's when Joe froze, right in front of the train doors as they opened, so that the person behind him bumped right into him, and had to divert, muttering, "Damn tourist."

"Motherfucker," Joe said aloud, more in amazement than anger. The guy who'd bumped him looked back, insulted, but by then Joe had started running, pushing through the mass of people who were waiting to board the train.

"Fucking asshole!" the guy shouted as Joe sprinted up the stairs to the street. Joe pulled out his phone, dialing 911 as he began to run down the street. He knew where Toomey had parked the truck.

Richards's office was still taped off and there was a young cop standing guard, but he respectfully lifted the tape when Donna showed her ID. The place seemed more than just physically empty. Even its opulence, its preening and power, seemed hollow now, a pointless charade. A bunch of big shots, trying to run the world as they saw fit, and taking it to the edge of ruin. What else was new? It would be a joke, this extra-toxic brand of vanity if it weren't so deadly to so many. Mike's face flashed in her mind. Why did he take a bullet? Was it for her? For Richards? How could he be that man and also the one who'd tormented her? How did love and hate, insecurity and honor, fear and rage get so hopelessly tangled? What the fuck was wrong with men?

Then, as if on cue, her phone rang again. Speaking of fucked-up men, it was Joe. She sighed and answered.

"Where are you?" he asked, out of breath.

"Back at Wildwater . . ."

"Meet me in the basement. I know where the truck is."

"Where?" she asked, but just then the uniform ran in.

"Ma'am!" he yelled.

"Hold on," she told Joe. "Yeah?"

"We've got to evacuate. A bomb threat."

She nodded and spoke into the phone. "Never mind. I'm on my way down."

"Good. I'm a block away," he huffed and she realized he was running. To the bomb not from it.

"Joe?" she asked, louder into the phone.

"Yeah?"

"Are you sure about this?"

"No," he said and hung up.

❖

The irony was not lost on Toomey, although his patience was wearing thin. For as long as the Wildwater building was a crime scene, swarming with cops and feds, surrounded by reporters and gawkers, he couldn't gain access and actually commit his intended crime. So for most of the day he wandered the surrounding streets, imagining what it would all look like destroyed, once the device he had in his truck turned the Wildwater tower into a flaming torch, a column of smoke rising into the sky, visible for miles and miles, like a beacon of destruction, sending out shock waves that would flatten all these blocks, shattering the stores, apartments, restaurants around him, the schools and offices, blasting them into bricks and stones and girders, blowing them into dust, sending the trucks and buses and cars flying like toys, like specks of dirt through space, tossing them like a tornado, along with trees and streetlamps and benches. And the people, the people who walked around him now, talking, laughing, cursing, eating, drinking, minding their own business or butting into someone else's, each busy with his own thoughts, her own problems or desires or joys or fears, dressed in every kind of clothes, from suits and dresses to shorts and rags, every kind of person, every race, religion, class, gender, type, and taste, strangers gathered by chance in this one place on this one day—they would all die together. Most before they knew what happened, vaporized instantly or melting into air. The less lucky slowly and painfully, from fire or wreckage. And then, last of all, the lingering deaths of the radiated.

That would wake them up. Perhaps there would be a statue of Toomey in this place one day. A monument to victory this time and not a remembrance of defeat, like down in Ground Zero. For this, his strike, would be the opening blow in a final battle for the soul of America and the future of the world. It would be a battle cry, leading the forces of civilization, white Christian civilization, to final victory, and to a glorious future. And the rabble who died today? Expendable. Ready to be flushed out and erased, plowed into the earth from which the new world would rise.

Feeling good, Toomey ate a couple of hot dogs and a soda from a stand and then felt not so good—the goddamn foreigner who sold him this crap probably hadn't washed his brown hands—and then he had to pay for a coffee at a diner just so the bitchy tattooed waitress would let him use the john—probably a freak with those piercings, or a lesbian. Then, finally, feeling better, he walked back over and found the building open again. Thank God, he could finish up his mission and go. He'd had a bellyful of New York.

So he went through the revolving door and took an elevator down to the parking levels in the basement. The bomb in his truck was remote-activated, and he had the control, but no cell or radio signal would reach it underground unless he was close—another inconvenience caused by the loss of his primary target, and his own relatively basic bomb-making skills. He was a fighter, not an engineer. His plan now was to set the timer and then walk away, leaving plenty of time for him to get on a subway and be out of the blast area and deep underground by the time it went off. If he rode the train under the river, he could even pop out in safety and watch the smoke rise from the other side.

44

DONNA WAS ON THE elevator going down to the basement, while the cop went floor to floor on the stairs, herding people out. But too many people were now trying to desperately jam onto the elevator, which was completely full but still stopping on every floor, like a local train at rush hour. So she got off and ran down the stairs to the underground garage instead, then began searching among the cars, looking for Toomey's Jeep, working her way down the levels, trying to call Joe, though there was no signal on her phone. Then, on the bottom floor, she saw him, standing in front of the truck. He'd broken a side window, the one with the Special Forces sticker on it, and opened up the back. And now he was just standing there, staring, holding an unfolded camping knife in one hand. Then she got close and saw why.

"Hey," she said, softly now, catching her breath.

"Hey," he answered.

They were both looking at a very large explosive device—cakes of uranium, stacked in metal canisters, wired to dynamite that was taped in bands around it, with a detonator on top.

"Do you know how to disarm one of these things?" Donna asked.

"Not really," Joe said. "Do you?"

"Sort of. I mean, I took a class. Twice. But I failed it both times."

Joe handed her his pocket-knife. "Better luck this time."

"Thanks."

"Is it activated?" he asked, as she leaned in closer, looking at the mechanism, still not touching anything.

"Not yet," a voice behind them said. It was Toomey. He stepped out from where he'd been watching, between two parked cars, holding a remote in one hand, and a Glock in the other. "Easy now." He pointed the gun as them as they spun around.

"Toomey," Donna said.

"Nice to see you again Donna," he said. "Sorry our date didn't work out."

"Date?" Joe asked.

She shook her head. "Wasn't a real date."

"And you are Joe Brody. I feel like our date has been coming a long time."

Now Donna glanced quizzically at Joe, who shrugged.

Toomey went on. "I guess I should thank you too, Donna, for saving my life."

"Why not return the favor then?" she asked.

He smiled. "Actually, I mean to. You see, once again you two have fucked up my plan. I was going to set this timer and go. Be long gone before it blew. But now, with the alarm out, it's all a big rush. Even if I kill you both, the techs will be here to defuse it in what, ten minutes? So here's my proposal. I set the timer for half an hour, you cancel the emergency call, say it was a false alarm, and we all walk away alive together. Or I set it for three minutes, and we just see what happens." He looked at Donna. "What do you think?"

"I think this is definitely our last date."

He laughed. "Full disclosure," he said, "there is a trip wire on the bomb," and then he pressed the button on the timer. "Go."

Donna turned to the device, silently praying under her breath.

"You got this," Joe said softly.

"Joe . . ." she said, grabbing his arm as he turned. "I . . . what I said before . . ."

"It was all true," he said, squeezing her hand back, then: "See you in a few minutes." Hands raised, he walked across the garage toward Toomey.

❖

"I'm impressed with you both," Toomey said, when they were about twenty feet apart. "But not surprised. You're warriors. Too bad we can't all be on the same side, the right side, together. But the next best thing to dying with a brother-in-arms is at the hands of a worthy adversary. Don't you think?"

"I can think of a few I like better," Joe said. "Like getting really old and dying of boredom on a beach in Florida."

Toomey smiled and shook his head. "You're kidding yourself. That's not going to happen to you. Family? Marriage? Retirement? Not for our kind. The most we can hope for is an honorable death." He set the gun and the control down on the pavement in front of him and stepped back. "Red button stops the bomb," he said, and then, like he was running into the arms of a lover or a best friend, he ran at Joe.

❖

In the split seconds that he had, as he ran toward Toomey, Joe thought of the many ways he knew to kill a person. Most of course required weapons, however simple—a piece of glass, a pencil, a straw. But he had none of that here. Then he thought of the ways he could kill with bare hands—shattering the larynx, breaking the neck, choking the carotid—but these depended to some extent on surprise and an opponent who did not share the exact same knowledge. Toomey was right about one thing: they were evenly matched, and in an even match, even if he won, he'd lose, when the seconds of his life, of many lives, ran out.

So he did the one thing that would surprise Toomey, the thing a true warrior would never do—he retreated. As Toomey gained speed and momentum, crouching to lower his center of gravity and ducking his head for protection, hiding the vulnerable organs and swinging a fist at Joe, Joe, who was running full speed toward Toomey, jumped instead—he jumped as high as he could, clear over Toomey, and landed on the hood of a parked car behind him.

Toomey stumbled forward, hitting his knees, then jumped up and whirled around to face Joe as Joe hopped up onto the car's roof. Joe saw Donna look up at him for a moment, her face a mask of fear and despair. Just for an instant, their eyes connected, as Toomey closed in.

"Fine," he said. "You want to play games. It's your last wish. Let's play." He jumped up onto the hood of the car, taking a karate stance, but Joe immediately leapt to another car. Toomey came after him, but Joe simply hopped back to the first one, bouncing off the roof, and jumped higher to the roof of a minivan that was parked next to the wall.

"Fuck this shit, Brody," Toomey said, leaping to the ground and trapping Joe by getting between him and the next vehicle. He was cornered. Toomey reached into the back of his waistband and drew a knife, short, curved, and vicious.

"I thought you were playing fair," Joe called to him.

"And I thought you were the real deal, Special Forces. Bullshit! You're just a coward." He moved in swiping the knife, as Joe backed into the wall. "You fight like a fool. And now you'll die like a fool, after I cut those strings."

He came at Joe, lashing out with the razor-sharp blade, and Joe jumped, like he was jumping rope, knowing that if the blade caught him, it would do what he'd done to Trey, sever his tendons and drop him like a ragdoll. He jumped high as Toomey sliced the air, closer and closer, knowing one false move, one slow jump, would end him. He could feel the cuts on his feet opening again. The knife flashed, catching his pants, slicing the skin. Toomey smiled at the blood. Joe jumped.

Then a shot rang out, shattering the side window of the van and echoing in the basement.

"No more fools are going to die today, Toomey. Except you maybe."

Toomey swung around and looked. Donna was holding his own gun on him with her right hand. In her left she held the control, which was stopped at 0:09. She shrugged. "There's no way I was going to disarm that thing in time. I've got to retake that class."

Toomey roared. A howl of rage came up in him, clenching every muscle, every tendon, distorting his face, and his arm came up, to throw the blade. Donna shot and killed him.

45

THE TWO MILLION DOLLAR bounty was paid. After expenses, for everything from the flights to Afghanistan to the fake military uniforms and the weapons and vehicles, the payment, split seven ways, came to $264,285 each for Joe, Yelena, Cash, Juno, Liam, Josh, and the family of Hamid. They met in the basement of the building behind Club Rendezvous where once before they had come together and branded Joe with their mark. Once again, Joe stood before the gathered bosses with Gio at his side.

It was Little Maria who presented the cash. She'd lost the foot—infection set in and it had to be amputated. She was on crutches now, with one leg in a cast and the other still in a stocking and red high heel shoe; rumor was that her prosthetic would be shaped to fit into stiletto heels. Her new boyfriend, a beautiful young man with a goatee, black T-shirt, and heavy gold cross, carried the bag of money and led a pit bull pup on a leash. Everyone stood up when she entered. First she kissed Gio on the cheek. *"Hola guapo,"* she said. Then, leaning on her crutches, she hugged Joe and kissed him on the lips.

"Gracias amigo, con todo mi corazón."

Joe nodded in acknowledgment, a smear of bright red lipstick on his mouth. Alonzo was home but still not ready to travel; Reggie was there to represent him. He shook Gio's hand, earnestly thanking him, then said to Joe, "My brother said to give you this," and gave him a big hug. Jack Madigan was there, in a navy suit, white shirt, and red tie, with Liam at his side.

Jack shook Gio's hand respectfully, then pumped Joe's hand hard. Liam clapped his back.

"How's your brother?" Gio asked them.

"Fine, Gio, thanks for asking," Jack said.

Liam shrugged. "Anyway he's better. The fucking eejit."

Rebbe, escorted by Josh, kissed both Joe's cheeks. "You did it, boy-chick. Just like I knew you would," he said, eyes twinkling, a sweet and kind old man with ice water in his veins. "Though I don't think I'll be going to that shvitz anytime soon."

Uncle Chen chuckled at this, and patted Joe on the back. Then he told Gio, "We know you made your father proud."

"Thank you Uncle," Gio said. "That means the most coming from you, who know."

Anton's name went unmentioned. In his place at the table, representing the Russian gangs, sat Yelena, regarding Joe with a sly, ironic smile. She looked different: she wore a tightly tailored black suit skirt and jacket, with a sleeveless silk blouse beneath it, and her hair was up. She barely spoke, but shook hands elegantly with the others, and gracefully accepted kisses from Rebbe and Little Maria.

No one questioned her presence or authority. In the days since Joe stopped Toomey, Gio's men, along with the other crews, had mopped up the last of the White Angel gang, brutally reasserting their domains. Bodies were still turning up in alleys and dumpsters all around town, but overall, things were returning to normal. A couple of Anton's men were rumored to have fled back to Russia; others turned up dead in Miami or LA. And one was hauled out of the water near Brighton Beach, at least whatever had been left by the fish.

Afterward, the group left separately, and Joe walked Yelena to her car, a sleek black Mercedes. She had taken her jacket off in the stuffy base-ment, and now, as she leaned back against the hood and lit a cigarette,

Joe could see the scabbed over scar from her burn—like an arrow—where the corner edge of the furnace had seared her.

"It's healing well," he said. "But you'll have a mark."

She shrugged. "We all have marks. That's life." She laughed. "But this one doesn't suit you." She wet a finger and scrubbed away Maria's lipstick.

"Speaking of new marks," Joe said. "You've been busy." Yelena had several new tattoos to join the ones that had already decorated her body: Now an eagle soared above the church cupola on her back, beneath which, Joe knew, a Madonna and child indicated that she was born in prison. A dollar sign and a skull rode on each hip, indicating a safe-cracker and a killer, and a dagger ran down her left thigh, entwined with roses and a snake, whose raised head signaled "I began in stealing and robbing." Another dagger, piercing a heart, ran down her right, and Joe could guess what the several newly added drops of blood meant. A new devil's face had been inked on her arm, next to her burn mark.

"What's that?"

"Enemy of the authorities. For taking out the SVR man."

"Right," Joe said. "And these?" he asked, brushing the row of stars on the top of each shoulder. He squeezed her right ring finger, which now bore a small crown. "And this?" He touched her chest, where between her breasts and under her clavicle, an eight-pointed star now shone.

"As you think," she said, looking him back in the eye.

Joe smiled. "Congratulations. You're a boss now. Is that what you want?"

Yelena laughed. "Want? It's like your grandma taught you. We play the cards we are dealt. And we win."

"Do we?" Joe asked her.

She leaned up and kissed him, very gently, on the lips. Then she knocked on the roof of the limo. Immediately, a huge man in a black suit jumped out of the passenger side and opened the back door, waiting with a respectful nod. The driver started the engine.

"I have to go to Moscow," Yelena said. "To settle a few matters."

Joe nodded. "Fly safely."

"You too Joe," she said, smiling, and got in the car. The bodyguard shut the door and nodded to Joe as he got in front. Joe stepped back and watched them drive away. He looked down at Yelena's cigarette, still smoldering on the ground, and stamped it out.

"Hey," Gio called to him. He was leaning from the window of his car. Joe wasn't sure how long he'd been there, listening. "Need a ride?"

46

"SO YOU'LL COME TO the cookout?" Gio asked. They had been driving several minutes in silence. "Next Sunday?"

"Sure," Joe said.

"Bring Gladys."

"Right."

"I'd say bring Yelena too, but I get the feeling she is going to be busy for a while."

Joe smiled and nodded. "Off to Moscow. On business."

"They won't know what hit them," Gio said. Then he shrugged. "Just as well maybe. The sight of her in a bikini might blow my kids' minds. But then you'd know."

"Well, when I saw her, there was a lot more blood than I expect will be in your pool."

"Right." He snuck a look at Joe then put his eyes back on the road. "Might be just as well for you too."

"Probably so."

Gio had been thinking; they had gathered today to reward Joe and his crew for saving their city, as well as delivering justice for themselves. That's what Joe had been recruited for and what he'd agreed to do. Nevertheless, this whole thing had ended up working out pretty well for Gio. His enemies had been vanquished and replaced with friends who owed their own positions partly to him and to Joe. His allies were grateful, and his own strength was reinforced. He had never been so rich, so powerful, and, now that accounts had been settled, so secure. Much of this was due to his own cunning. Gio was very smart and very careful. But there was more: he had a gift for playing the game of power, a Machiavellian prince's instinct for turning crisis to profit, even when he didn't realize he was doing it. It was in his guts, the legacy he'd inherited from his father and grandfather. But he also had Joe. And that was why he turned to his friend now, as they cruised through the old neighborhood, and said, "I was thinking."

"Yeah?" Joe turned back from staring out the window, catching the tone in his voice.

"Now that you've got this fat nest egg, maybe you want to do something more with it than hide it under Gladys's bed."

"I do. I hide most of it in your safe."

"That's what I wanted to ask about. What if I helped you do something else with it?"

"Like what? You going to open me up an IRA?"

Gio shrugged. "It's not a bad idea. But I was thinking more along the lines of a house, for starters."

"A house? Where?"

"Out on the island. Near me. We could hang out, take the boat out or whatever. Don't worry, I won't let Carol bug you too much. This cookout is just a special thing. You won't be expected to come over every weekend unless you want to. Really it would be for Gladys. She might like a little bit of luxury, you know, some space, a yard, a pool even."

"I didn't realize houses on the shore in Long Island were going for two fifty these days. With a pool."

Gio laughed, then looked shyly out the windshield as they turned down Joe's block. "I could help out. You know, with the deposit. And with the paperwork to get you a mortgage or whatever. We can run it through the club. Or make you head of security for one of the other companies." He stopped in front of Joe's building and put the car in park, then turned to Joe. "I'd be happy to do it, brother."

Joe nodded. "Thank you, brother. That means a lot." Then he grinned at him. "But you know Gladys, she'd never move anywhere in a million years. She'll never change."

"Right," Gio said, smiling. "Gladys will never change."

Joe tucked a large chunk of cash into his own pocket and left the rest in the shopping bag on the seat. "Pop that in the safe for now, will you?" he asked, and opened the door. "And thanks for the ride."

Gio called after him: "You back to work at the club tomorrow? Or you too rich now?"

"I'll be there," Joe said and shut the door. Gio drove away.

❖

Liam and Josh went to see Sean at detox. They decided on the way not to mention the money Liam had just received, since it would just tempt his brother to hit him up for a loan. Nor, it went without saying, did they bring booze. They brought a deck of cards and a box of brownies instead.

"Hey!" Sean shouted when he saw Liam. He still looked a bit shaky, but his eyes were clear and wide open, the pupils a normal size. "What's in the box? A file I hope? I'm ready to bust out of here."

"Brownies," Liam said. "They got any coffee in this joint or is that off limits too?"

"They've got it. But you're a harder man than me if you can drink it."

"You remember Josh," Liam said. Josh nodded to him. Sean peered back.

"You the Jew poofter?" he asked.

Liam spoke: "He's the poof who saved your worthless fecking life. You'd be in a box right now if it had just been me there that night. Serve you right too."

Sean stared at Josh thoughtfully. "Then I've just one question."

"Go ahead," Josh said.

"Isn't it a sin for you to suck my brother's cock? Tain't kosher!"

Josh smiled. "I say a special Hebrew prayer."

"And I sprinkle some holy water on his prick before it goes up me bum," Liam added.

"Well all right then," Sean said. "That's all I wanted to check. Now hand over those fucking brownies, and let's play some cards."

❖

The medals were presented at 4 P.M., so Yolanda was able to pick Larissa up from school before coming to the ceremony. Donna had mixed feelings. Of course she was very proud to have her daughter see the mayor, the chief of police, and her local city council member present her with a plaque expressing the city's gratitude, and the assistant director of the FBI hang a medal on her. On the other hand, she had hidden the fact that she had been wounded and shot at, not to mention the bomb. And then there was Mike. But in the end it was decided that his name would go unmentioned in the public ceremony, and Donna alone would represent the family at Langley, CIA headquarters, when they added another star to the wall that represented those who died in the field, secret and nameless. As for the gory details, the PR people assured Donna that none of the politicians would say anything that a child couldn't easily digest. No one wanted to needlessly upset the public.

So she stood on the stage, beside Fusco, who was there to accept on Parks's behalf. It was the sight of Parks's two young boys, sitting as if stunned in their suits and ties, on either side of their weeping mother, that broke Donna's heart. The tears that ran down her face when the medal was placed around her neck, and the assembled officers saluted, were for them.

Fusco's eyes were dry. When he looked down at the plaque and the little velvet box that contained the medal in his hands, he was only thinking of Victoria. "I'll feel better when I bring them that bitch's head. They can mount it next to these on the wall."

"She's long gone," Donna answered. "And all we've got is a description and a lip print."

Fusco nodded. "Well, we ain't the only ones hunting." He knew that for Gio and the other bosses, she was unfinished business.

"And you're okay with that?" Donna asked him. "With them?"

"Okay?" Fusco laughed. "They scare me shitless. But I will say one thing, for better or worse. No matter how long it takes, they never let a debt go unpaid."

47

DONNA'S MOTHER THREW A party on the roof. The view was fantastic, the river and the bridge and the city. They strung up lights and set out heaps of food—Yolanda and her friends cooked for days. (Gary sent lovely flowers, which were displayed on the table, and asked about another dinner date, but when she texted thanks, Donna didn't mention it; God only knew what kind of fantasy he'd want to act out now.) Andy and Janet and an assortment of other cops and Feds came and mingled with her relatives and neighbors. Fusco and Blaze huddled in a corner, laughing darkly and sharing a flask that either of them might have produced. And Gladys came. Tom stopped by too and, at one point, Donna's heart skipped a beat when she saw him talking to Joe's grandma, but the old grifter charmed him, going on and on about what a wonderful girl Donna was. He assumed she was an old family friend, and maybe, at this point, that's what she was, though Donna sighed when she saw a card game shaping up. But then they cranked up the music and the dancing started and she didn't think about it anymore until after midnight, when Gladys came over and kissed her goodnight.

"How are you getting home?" Donna asked. "Let me call you a car."

"I'll call Joe. He said he'd pick me up."

"Really?" Donna hadn't heard or said his name since they last saw each other in the basement. Moments after Toomey fell, he was gone, blending into the crowd that was still fleeing the building. Seconds later a tac team and bomb squad showed up, Donna still standing over Toomey, gun in her hand. She smiled now at Gladys, keeping her tone light. Casual. "Tell him to come say hi," she said. "Have a beer. Or a soda."

"Joe up here?" Gladys rolled her eyes at the law enforcement officers dancing and drinking. "Like inviting a cat to the dog pound."

"Or a fox to the hen house," Donna said.

Gladys laughed. "Tell you what. I'll ask him to meet me at your apartment. I'll tell him I need to use the john. But don't rat me out."

Donna smiled. "I promise."

❖

Joe knocked. Donna answered the door.

"Hey," she said. "Caught you."

"Hey! It's the national hero."

She laughed. "I wouldn't say national. New York City and Puerto Rico for sure."

Joe shrugged. "Where else matters? You're the princess of the city."

"Exactly. I'm getting free Yankees tickets, if you want to come."

"I'm a Mets fan," Joe said. "Queens boy. Another tragic history keeping us apart."

"Of course," she said. "You'd pick the losing the side."

He laughed. "Someone has to."

"Really though, Joe," she said, lifting off the medal that she'd been wearing all night, suddenly embarrassed by it. "You should have one of these too. Shit you should have a collection. Wear them all like a rapper. Here." She tried, playfully, to put it on him, but he pressed it back into her hands.

"Not my style," he told her. They were close now, and he was still holding her hands, with neither one letting go. "It looks much better on you."

"That's right, I forgot," she said, looking up at him, their faces close now. "You already have a star, don't you? Right here." She touched the spot on his chest. "Can I see?"

"It's nothing. It's just a burn."

"Please?" she asked. Her hand was on his heart now, her eyes on his. "Show me? Share that with me at least?"

He took a breath, about to say something, then changed his mind. He pulled off his T-shirt and raised his arm. He put her hand on his star.

"Here it is. You see. Just a scar. I've got plenty of others. It's nothing. Yours is better."

"No," she said, shaking her head, and tracing lightly with her fingertips. "Yours means much more. The people who gave it to you—they don't make speeches and they don't do PR." She looked him in the eye now, both of her hands on his chest, his hands on her shoulders. "And you can't ever take it off, can you? Not even for one night?"

He shook his head, as he slid her medal back over her head, and then wrapped her in his arms, holding her close, his mouth just a whisper from hers. "No. But we can both shut our eyes and pretend. For a minute," he said, shutting his. She shut hers too, and clung to him tightly, as she felt his mouth on hers.

❖

Neither of them spoke after that. Not when they clung to each other, arms and legs entwined, swaying together as their devouring mouths joined. Not when they found themselves, blindly, in her room, leaving their clothes in a trail. He spoke her name once in the dark, *Donna*, as she lay naked on top of him, pressing her skin against his. She laughed, feeling the medal knock against him, and tossed it on the floor. She gasped his name once, as he slid inside her, and moaned it once later, as he looked into her eyes, holding her face, and then whispered *Donna* again into her ear. After, they rested in silence, and slept for a little, and then made love again. Finally they lay still, her head on his chest, and she saw that the moon had set. It was very late. She glanced down at her phone: The party was over, Larissa was asleep at her mom's, Gladys had been driven home by Fusco. But still she said nothing, just curled back up, and he held her close in silence, as if they both understood that the moment they spoke, it would break the spell and reality would come crashing back in. Time passed. Then, as the first flush of dawn began to glow outside her window, she saw a cat, her neighbor's, a black tuxedo with a white shirtfront on his chest and socks like spats on his paws. He meowed and they both laughed which scared him and he darted away up the fire escape, but that was enough. Their night was over. She turned to Joe then, looked at him frankly, pale and rumpled in the dawn.

"Now what happens?" she asked.

"Now?" Joe repeated, returning her gaze. "Now our troubles really begin."

ACKNOWLEDGMENTS

As always, I want to thank Doug Stewart, the world's greatest agent, for his invaluable foresight and friendship, without which I'd be lost, as well as everyone at Sterling Lord Literistic, especially Szilvia Molnar, who has helped my books find their way around the world. Thank you also to Danielle Bukowski and Maria Bell for all their help. I am immensely grateful to Otto Penzler, my editor, whose idea it was to embark on this serial adventure, and who has guided me every step of the way. I am also thankful to everyone at The Mysterious Press and at the Mysterious Bookshop. Thank you to Matilde Huseby and William Fitch for reading the early drafts, and a very special thanks to Nesa Azimi, Antonio Chinea, Nivia Hernandez and Anastasia Lobanova for their generous assistance with the various languages spoken in this book. Lastly, I want, once again, to thank my family for their infinite love and support. I could never have done it without them.

ABOUT THE AUTHOR

DAVID GORDON holds an MA in English and Comparative Literature and an MFA in Writing from Columbia University. He is the author of *The Serialist*, which won the VCU/Cabell First Novel Award and was a finalist for an Edgar Award. His work has appeared in the *Paris Review*, the *New York Times* and the *Los Angeles Review of Books*. He was born and lives in New York City.